ACCLAI

"Beautifully written, ... e tale, involving hostage taki ... ... omance, guilt, and suspense all ... ... Corban Addison is a truly gifted story-teller, and *The Tears of Dark Water* will stay with you long after you've read the last page. *The Tears of Dark Water* is pure gold!"

—LIS WIEHL, Fox News Legal Analyst
and *New York Times* bestselling author

"This is great storytelling. A riveting story of modern day piracy, a clash of cultures [and] people's lives torn apart." —Booksellers New Zealand

"Read [*The Tears of Dark Water*] for entertainment, and you will find yourself pondering the machinations of the world's largest democracy, and who really wields the power." —*Cape Times*, South Africa

ACCLAIM FOR *A WALK ACROSS THE SUN*

"Since my first novel was released over 20 years ago, I have been presented with many opportunities to endorse the works of other authors hoping to find a publisher. I have always declined. But now, Corban Addison has written a novel that is beautiful in its story and also important in its message. *A Walk Across the Sun* deserves a wide audience. And I strongly suspect that Mr. Addison will be heard from again and again."

—JOHN GRISHAM

"In his debut novel, lawyer Addison uncovers the labyrinthine underside of human trafficking in this dazzling transcontinental story about the power of conviction, the bonds of family, and the tenacity of love. . . . The novel successfully explicates the magnitude of the human trafficking business, the complexities of international legalities, and the impact of the Internet's role in this horrifying underworld." —*Publishers Weekly*

"A compelling read. Corban Addison deals with challenging issues but in a way that keeps readers gripped to every page—a remarkable literary feat."
—DR. SAMANTHA NUTT, author of *Damned Nations*

"This chilling, suspenseful, and powerful debut weaves fictional characters into the reality of contemporary slavery. . . . The story is compelling, but the message is greater and will leave an impact on every person who picks up the book. Readers will mourn the injustices depicted and celebrate the triumphs long after the last page is turned."   —*Library Journal*

"An insightful take on the all-too-real problems of international human trafficking."   —*Booklist*

"A pulse-revving novel with a serious message."
—*O, The Oprah Magazine*
(16 Books to Watch for in January 2012)

ACCLAIM FOR *THE GARDEN OF BURNING SAND*

"A compelling novel with a conscience and a heart, gripping in its drama and unique in its insights into a hidden and dangerous world. Resonant with authenticity, *The Garden of Burning Sand* rewards the reader on every level."
—RICHARD NORTH PATTERSON,
New York Times bestselling author

"Corban Addison is a rare find in the world of thriller writers. Timely, topical, and impeccably researched, his novels embrace the full sweep of the human experience. Depravity. Destruction. Heroism. Love. If you like stories of good people struggling to do right in the world's forgotten places, there is no one better suited to take you on the ride of your life."
—JOHN HART, *New York Times* bestselling author

"Addison's second novel is both an affecting tale of a tragically abused girl and a convincing plea for humanitarian support in Africa."
—*Kirkus Reviews*

THE TEARS OF DARK WATER

THE TEARS OF

DARK

WATER

A NOVEL

C O R B A N   A D D I S O N

HarperCollins*Publishers*Ltd

The Tears of Dark Water
Copyright © 2015 by Regulus Books, LLC.
All rights reserved.

Published by HarperCollins Publishers Ltd

First published in Canada by HarperCollins Publishers Ltd
in an original trade paperback edition: 2015
This mass market paperback: 2017

HarperCollins books may be purchased for educational, business,
or sales promotional use through our Special Markets Department.

HarperCollins Publishers Ltd
2 Bloor Street East, 20th Floor
Toronto, Ontario, Canada
M4W IA8

www.harpercollins.ca

Library and Archives Canada Cataloguing in Publication
information is available upon request.

ISBN 978-1-44345-183-3

Printed and bound in the United States of America
QUAD 9 8 7 6 5 4 3 2 1

For the jewel of the Indian Ocean, may you rise again.

And for all those who bear your scars as their own.

I am in the sea and a sea is within me.
—Ahmad-e Jami

The devil flows in mankind as blood flows.
—Muhammad

*Whatever things may appear, the
meaning is always deeper.*
—Gaarriye

I

THE WAY OF THE GUN

In those days there was no
king. Everyone did what was
right in his own eyes.
—THE BOOK OF JUDGES

DANIEL

Daniel Parker woke with a start, a line of perspiration on his brow. He looked around the darkened cabin of the sailboat, searching for her face, but she was gone. He shook his head, as if the sudden motion could shake off the anguish of the dream, but the chains of the past bound him to her, as did the vague whisper of a prayer that she was wrong. Her words were stuck in his mind, like a prophecy playing in an endless loop, the truth of half a life spoken as if from the beginning.

It won't last.

The declaration had escaped her lips without effort, but not uncharitably. She had smiled at him when she spoke, her green eyes dancing above the dimples in her cheeks, her candlelight dress and red-brown Bissolotti violin luminous in the concert hall.

Nothing does. Why would you expect us to be different?

He looked out the porthole at the lights of Victoria Harbour, sparkling in the twilight before the dawn. The sky was the color of ash, but the stars were beginning to retreat on the coattails of the night. He listened to the main halyard knocking against the mast and the gurgling sounds of cavitation as the *Renaissance* bobbed on the occasional swell. *At least we'll have a decent wind*, he thought, throwing back the thin sheet and scooting out of his rack.

He placed his feet on the polished mahogany floorboards and took a slow breath, relishing the smoothness of the wood on his skin. He had loved the feeling of going barefoot on deck since he was a boy handling lines and trimming sails on his father's Valiant 40. But he had paid a price for it. The soles of his feet were a patchwork of scars.

He opened the door to the saloon and slipped stealthily into the living quarters. Dim light from the harbor filtered in through the curtains covering the windows, but the saloon and galley were still shrouded in darkness. He stepped around the weak spots in the floor and took care not to wake his son, Quentin, who was sleeping on the settee berth across from the dining table.

He flipped on the accent lights in the galley. The LEDs glowed softly under the cabinet rails, illuminating the gas stove and granite countertops. He heated a pot of water and filled his French press, waiting precisely four minutes before pouring the steaming coffee into his Naval Academy mug. His father had given him the mug at the rechristening ceremony of the *Renaissance*, along with a hearty laugh and a slap on the back. It was as much a gag as a gift, for Daniel had gone to Boston College instead.

He opened the main hatch and inhaled the moist island

air. Across the water sat the city of Victoria, tucked like a jeweled blanket between mountains of granite and the hem of the sea. He rummaged in the locker by the stairs and retrieved his writing chest—a genuine gift from his father, an antique from Zanzibar, in honor of their voyage. He collected the mug and went topside.

On an ordinary morning the sight of sailboats at anchor crowned by winking stars would have brought a smile to Daniel's face. But this morning he scarcely noticed them, troubled as he was by the portents of the dream. He sat down in the cockpit and put the mug on the bench beside him, opening the carved wooden chest and laying out paper and pen on the life raft container, which he used as a writing surface. He lit a battery-powered lantern and took a sip of coffee, struggling to suppress the dread her words had inspired. They were wrong. They had to be. The smile, the dress, the violin, the concert hall—all were exactly as he remembered. But her words had carried a different meaning. They had been ironic, not tragic; a welcome, not a farewell.

His mind raced on the current of memory. New York City. April 1993. Daffodils blooming in Central Park, buds on the dogwoods and azaleas, a blaze of sunlight chasing away the early-spring chill. He had seen the handbills posted all over Columbia University—the Juilliard Orchestra performing at Carnegie Hall. He wouldn't have given the concert a passing thought, if not for the photograph of the soloist. Her name was Vanessa Stone, and she was a student at Columbia, not Juilliard—a double major in biology and music. She was pretty but not remarkably so in New York

City's hall of mirrors. It was her expression that made him pause—then halt—his mad rush to a law school seminar to which he was already late. He took down one of the flyers and studied her more carefully. She held her violin tenderly, her bow just touching the strings, and looked at the camera almost curiously. The question in her eyes was as frank as it was astonishing: *Why are you staring at me?*

Two days later, Daniel walked into the grand lobby of Carnegie Hall clutching the handbill and the face he couldn't forget. His seat was on the parquet level of the Stern Auditorium and close to the stage. He settled into his chair and listened to the musicians tune their instruments, annoyed at the butterflies crowding his stomach. At last, she appeared with the conductor at her side. She was dressed in a diaphanous gown that complemented her auburn hair. She nodded to the audience and then placed her violin beneath her chin, waiting for her cue.

His eyes never left hers from the beginning of the performance to the end. The music was Beethoven, his first and only violin concerto, and she played it immaculately, even the most virtuosic passages in the Kreisler cadenza. At the close of the third movement, the audience gave her a rousing ovation. She received it with an almost perfunctory bow and exited the stage with a swiftness that confirmed Daniel's suspicion. She had come to be heard, not to be seen. The magic was in the violin.

The receiving line outside the auditorium was long, and Daniel took his place at the end. While he waited, he tried on phrases like costumes until he felt more confused than confident. When the moment came and she offered her hand, thanking him for coming, he spoke purely by instinct.

"You play like your name," he said.

"I beg your pardon?" she asked, taking back her hand.

"Vanessa in the old Greek. It means 'butterfly.'" Something changed in her eyes, but she didn't reply, so he forged ahead. "It's like you're somewhere else—in the air, dancing with the sun."

She stared at him for long seconds before her lips spread into a smile. "It doesn't last," she said, surprising him with her candor. "It fades like everything else."

"But it's why you play, isn't it? Even when it makes you uncomfortable."

He saw it then: the inquisitive look she wore in the flyer in his pocket. She tilted her head and her eyes glittered in the light. "Do I know you?"

He shook his head. "I'm Daniel."

"Are you a student?" she asked, trying to place him anyway.

"Columbia Law," he affirmed.

"Law. I would have guessed poetry." Suddenly, she caught the eye of the conductor as he bid farewell to his last guest. "I'm sorry. I have to go. It's nice to meet you."

She said it almost regretfully, and he took courage. "When will you play again?"

He saw it a second time, her instinctive curiosity. "I'm graduating in May."

He nodded. "So am I."

She glanced at the conductor again. "I really have to go.

There's an after party."

"Right," he replied, feeling the moment slipping away.

Then she said the words that changed his life. "I practice at Schapiro Hall. Maybe I'll see you there sometime."

Daniel picked up his pen in the waning dark and began to write her a letter. "Dearest V: Is love like the body? Does it begin to die the day it is born? Is it like the breath of transcendence you feel when the Bissolotti is in your hands—evanescent, a chasing after the wind?" The words flowed onto the page like spilled ink as the sky brightened and the dawn came. The first light caught him by surprise and pierced his eyes when he looked toward the east. He took another sip of his now lukewarm coffee and watched the sun rise above the distant masts of a large ship. The advent of day transformed him, lifting his spirits. He looked down at the unfinished sentence before him and thought, *She doesn't need this.*

He folded up the pages he had written and placed them in the chest. He took out fresh paper and began again, telling his wife about Quentin, about climbing boulders with him on the island of La Digue, about the transformation he had seen since they set sail so many months ago. He signed his name and wrote out the address on an envelope. It would take three weeks to reach her. By then he and Quentin would be in South Africa—her last chance to join them before the long passage to Brazil.

"Morning, Dad," Quentin said, appearing in the companionway dressed in board shorts and a T-shirt, his wavy brown hair past his shoulders now. He had been growing it long since he met Ariadne in the South Pacific. The Australian girl had transformed everything about him—well, the girl and the sea. Every day, he seemed surer of himself, less afraid. He was even calling himself Quentin again, after years of going by "Quent." The eighteen-year-old boy was slowly becoming a man.

"I checked the Passage Weather report," Quentin said, taking a seat in the cockpit. "Steady winds out of the north at eight to ten knots, seas less than a meter, and no tropical activity in the forecast. We should make decent time with the gennaker up."

"Ten days if it holds," Daniel replied. "More if it doesn't."

Quentin pointed at the letter. "Do you think she's going to come?"

"She might," Daniel said, giving voice to a hope he didn't feel.

Quentin placed a postcard beside the envelope. "I wrote her something, too."

"Good man," Daniel said. "I'll get the harbormaster to mail them."

"Hey, did you hear about the Navy ship?" Quentin asked. "It put in yesterday with a bunch of Somali pirates. They're going to be tried here."

Daniel was intrigued. "An American ship?"

Quentin nodded. "The *Gettysburg*. François says it's a cruiser."

Daniel looked toward the sunrise and focused on the silhouette of the ship just visible above the port. He saw details he had missed earlier: the gray paint; the twin super-structures, bristling with masts and antennae; the raked bow and athletic lines. "Did François say anything else?"

Quentin nodded. "He said the Navy caught them off the coast of Oman after they tried to hijack an oil tanker. They've been in the brig until now."

"François seems to know everything that happens in this place," Daniel said.

Quentin smirked. "The guy's got more friends than marbles in his head."

Daniel laughed out loud, thinking of the garrulous and absentminded captain of the catamaran *La Boussole* anchored nearby. Inside, however, he felt a vague disquiet. The num-ber of pirate attacks had dropped off substantially in the past year, thanks to patrols by international naval forces and armed security teams on merchant ships. But the pirates were still a threat from Egypt to India to Madagascar, a vast area of ocean that included the Seychelles. Since August, he had been monitoring reports from maritime organiza-tions in London and Dubai to see whether the end of the Southwest Monsoon—a period of high winds and heavy seas around the Horn of Africa—would trigger a fresh wave of hijacks, as it had in years past. But for two months, the pirates had been largely quiet, their attacks infrequent and distant. Looking at the *Gettysburg*, Daniel felt the weight of his responsibility. Quentin's life was in his hands. No matter what it took, he would bring his son home.

"Something wrong, Dad?" his son asked, examining him carefully.

"It's nothing," Daniel demurred. "Are we set for supplies?"

Quentin nodded. "I went through it all yesterday."

"How about a system check?"

"I did a full workup. Engine, generator, instruments, radio, everything's good to go."

"And our course?"

"I plotted it twice. Outside the harbor, we take the channel south, avoiding the shoals near Isle Anonyme and the Isle of Rats. After the airport, we turn south and follow the coast of Mahé to Point du Sud. Once we're clear of land, we sail almost due south for a thousand miles to Réunion."

Daniel smiled. "Well done, Captain Jack. There's just one thing you forgot."

"What?" Quentin looked puzzled.

"Breakfast. It's your turn. I'd like an omelet and some fresh-squeezed papaya juice when I get back from the harbormaster."

"I was actually thinking of Spam," Quentin dead-panned, "and some of that Vegemite Ariadne's mom left with us. I remember how much you loved it." He laughed when his father threw his pen at him, and then disappeared into the cabin below.

"Make it quick," Daniel called after him, taking the letter and postcard in hand. "Anchors aweigh at eight."

✳

It's called crossing the bar, when a ship leaves the harbor and puts out to sea. For Daniel, the feeling it evoked was the same in all latitudes—an epinephrine shot of intoxication and danger. The blue horizon beckoned like the sea stories his father had read to him when he was a boy. Voyaging under sail was an adventure unlike any other, the ultimate test of courage and will. The risks were enormous, but the rewards were greater still.

He stood in the cockpit of the *Renaissance*, feet wide apart, one hand on the helm, as the forty-six-foot yacht glided effortlessly through the cobalt waves, bow pointed just south of east, toward the open sea. The custom-built sailboat was lithe and graceful in the water, with the high mast and spare rigging of a sloop and the bulb keel of a racing craft. Manufactured in Sweden to the exacting specifications of her original owner—a surgeon from Maine—she was the most pleasant boat Daniel had ever sailed. She had also proven herself to be exceedingly durable, surviving two knock-downs in a Force 10 storm off the coast of New Zealand with only minor leaks and a few tears in the mainsail, and shrugging off a lightning strike in the Strait of Malacca that might have split the mast of a lesser boat.

Daniel watched as Quentin worked the main sheets and let the boom out to port, allowing the mainsail and gennaker—a headsail much larger than a jib—to drive the *Renaissance* forward on a leisurely four-knot run. The winds off Mahé were as fair as predicted, which surprised Daniel.

In the Seychelles, November was a month of transition between the dominant monsoons, which meant that anything was possible, including a perfect calm. Two days ago, Daniel had topped off the fuel tanks, expecting to motor-sail all the way to Réunion. Now, however, he powered down the engine and enjoyed the gentle swish of the wake dovetailing behind him.

"Motor's off," he called to Quentin as his son spider-walked to the foredeck, the strains of Bob Marley's "Get Up, Stand Up" wafting out of the cabin below.

Quentin gave him a thumbs-up sign and sat down beside the bow rail, his long hair flowing out behind him. Seeing his son so at peace with the world brought Daniel a joy he could scarcely describe. It was as if Quentin had been sent back into the womb and reborn. After three quarters of a year at sea and twenty countries sprinkled like fairy dust around the equatorial belt of the earth, the years of parental anguish he and Vanessa had suffered almost seemed like someone else's history.

Quentin had been a challenge from birth. As a newborn, he had squalled while other children cooed. As a child, he had made impossible demands and thrown tantrums when they weren't met. In adolescence, his moodiness had grown into low-grade misanthropy. He was extremely bright—his IQ was in the genius range—but he had treated people like irritants. After years of struggling, Daniel and Vanessa had sought professional help, but the therapy and medication had only confused him further. He was highly sensitive and emotionally immature, the psychologists said, but he was too functional to be autistic, too socially capable to have Asperger's, and too stable to be bipolar. His agitation wasn't mania, just intense frustration with a world that never met his expectations. He was, in short, undiagnosable, which left everyone around him floundering.

There were only two things in Quentin's life that brought him consistent happiness: sailing and music. He was a gifted pianist. When his fingers were on the keys, he entered a state that seemed almost dream-like—especially if Vanessa was accompanying him on the violin. And on the water, with the deck of a sailboat beneath his feet, he came alive. Sailing was pure, Quentin had said at the age of fourteen. So were Mozart and Mendelssohn, Vivaldi and Dvořák. The world, on the other hand, was a wretched place, full of injustice and suffering. People were the problem. They were petty and vain and desecrated the beauty around them. Those were his exact words, and they had given Daniel a rare insight into his son's heart. Quentin carried on his shoulders a burden greater than a person could bear. Like Atlas of old, he felt the weight of the world.

Then came the train wreck that was his junior year of high school: the Harvard-bound dancer who paid no attention to him, the senior computer whiz and wannabe anarchist who hooked him on first-person shooter games, and the drug deal that landed him a suspension and—but for his grandfather's intervention—might have put him behind bars. It was in that place of abject humiliation that Daniel had conceived of the circumnavigation. It was a second chance, a radical departure, and the fulfillment of a dream Quentin had first voiced when he was six years old. Many had called Daniel crazy to leave his law practice and sail around the world with a troubled teenager. But the doubters had been wrong. *If only they could see him now*, he thought. *If only Vanessa could see him.*

They rounded the Isle of Rats at half past nine and turned south on the course Quentin had charted. The deep blue of the ocean stretched out before them, as did the rest of their lives. His son was not the only one who had changed in twenty-one thousand miles. Daniel felt like a different man, the man he could have become two decades ago if only he had taken the risk and followed his dream. He sensed them again—the rays of optimism breaking through the storm clouds of the past. The future was open. Anything was possible. Even with Vanessa.

He glanced at the GPS unit in front of him, checking depth and drift, and helped Quentin tighten up the sheets, bringing both sails closer to the yacht's centerline and perpendicular to the wind. They were on a beam reach, making four and a half knots along the east coast of Mahé. At moments, Daniel was tempted to turn on the engine again and supplement the wind. But each time he let the thought go. They were on a timetable of sorts. They had to return to Annapolis by May so Quentin could prepare for college. But that didn't mean they were in a hurry. If Mother Nature had seen fit to give them a decent wind, they would sail at her pace.

"Dad!" Quentin cried suddenly, pointing toward the bow. "Dolphins!"

Daniel put the helm on autopilot and followed his son to the foredeck. He saw the pod right away. They were swimming alongside the sailboat, their gray bodies glistening in the clear water. They took turns in the lead, one jumping, then another. Occasionally, they would dive below the surface, only to reappear seconds later. The dolphins stayed with them for almost a mile, never straying more than twenty yards from the hull. When at last they broke away, they swam in a lazy circle, fins in the air.

"Look at that!" Quentin exclaimed. "They're waving farewell!"

"It's a good omen," Daniel said, putting his hand on his son's shoulder.

Together, they waved back.

PAUL

The party was too formal for Paul Derrick's taste, the people too self-absorbed to really be interesting. He sipped the wine—an excellent red from Stellenbosch—and listened to conversations around him, noting the timbre of laughter that was genuine and that which was feigned. He stood by a window that overlooked the terrace and the lights of Clifton Beach and minded his own business, except when his sister, Megan, saw fit to introduce him to someone. He wasn't antisocial—far from it. By profession he was a student of human beings, a kind of behavioral scientist, a connoisseur of the mannerisms that reveal hidden feeling—the place where truth resides.

He watched a woman in her late twenties chatting with a large man in a pinstripe suit. He was a film producer and a windbag, a bloviator accustomed to having an audience. She was a pretty girl, in the fresh-faced, Drew Barrymore sort of way, but she had dressed like a vamp in a red shift as slinky as lingerie. By the way she touched the man's arm and laughed at his jokes, it was obvious what she was offering. But she was also self-conscious, tucking her brown hair over her ear, fingering her necklace, shifting her weight between heels, and straightening her dress. She was playing the seduction card to the hilt, but it was a false note in her personality. Paul felt sorry for her. The man he held in contempt.

He turned toward a large group clustered around Simon Lewis, a celebrated British-born photographer and Megan's husband. He had always liked Simon. He was a person who wore his success lightly and had an accurate estimation of his own worth, which is to say he understood the world would go on with barely a hiccup if he suddenly stopped breathing. He was witty, ironic, and self-deprecating, and his photos were actually quite good. But Paul's admiration didn't rise to the level of respect. For all his sangfroid, Simon was a hedonist who refused to be domesticated, even after tying the knot. His womanizing was something Megan had come to accept, or so she claimed. But Paul knew otherwise. The wound in her heart was real. Simon would never be hers alone.

"Paul! There you are," Megan said, approaching him through the crowd, a young woman in tow. "I want you to meet Anna Kuijers. Anna, this is my brother. He plays the shy part, but he's actually quite charming."

"Afrikaans?" Paul asked Anna, giving his sister a look only she could interpret.

"How did you know?" Anna asked dryly. She was tall—nearly six feet—with a friendly face, blonde hair, and blue eyes a shade lighter than her sapphire dress. "Pleasure."

"All mine," Paul replied.

"Enjoy your conversation," Megan said cheerily. "I just saw someone I need to greet." In seconds, she was across the room again.

"She throws the best parties in Cape Town," Anna said. "To our national shame."

"I'm sure it has nothing to do with her famous husband."

"No, I mean it. She's the most hospitable person I know. She's always going out of her way for people. But I suppose you know that."

Paul was intrigued. "That's the most unpretentious thing I've heard all evening."

Anna smiled wryly. "It's the curse of the artistic crowd. We like to talk about ourselves." She paused. "You're twins. I thought you'd look more alike."

"We played with a wishbone in the womb. She came out with the bigger half."

Anna laughed. "I imagine you've heard that before."

"A few times."

She looked out at the night. "I'd love some fresh air. Care to join me?"

"By all means," he said and followed her onto the terrace. "Is the sky always so clear here?" he asked, leaning against a stone railing that overlooked the sweep of the sea. "The stars are so bright."

"Not in the winter. You came at the right time."

"Too bad I'm only here for a week."

Anna's eyes widened. "That's not much of a holiday."

Paul nodded. "It's an occupational hazard. I don't get

away very often."

"Megan told me you're with the FBI."

His expression turned coy. "Do I look like a special agent?"

Anna examined him thoughtfully, taking in his charcoal suit, white shirt, green tie, and blond surfer's hair. "Not really."

"Then Megan did a good job. We spent all afternoon at the mall."

Anna laughed. "You work in Washington?"

"I work in a lot of places. But I have an office near DC."

"You're a hostage negotiator," she said. "I'm fascinated."

"You make it sound sexy. Most of the time I don't even carry a gun."

Anna shook her head. "I disagree. There are too many guns in the world."

He gave her a frank look. "Now you have my attention. What do you do?"

"I'm a publicist. I work with authors."

"Which means you make them look better than they actually are."

Anna smiled. "Like your sister did?"

"Touché," he said with a laugh. He studied her in the dim light. She was an attractive woman—intelligent, insightful, and comfortable in her own skin. But it didn't matter; he wasn't interested. He hadn't been in a relationship in a decade, ever since his divorce. Love was a game that women played and men lost. And sex without love was complicated and disappointing. His job was his mistress. What the Bureau demanded he could give without reservation, unlike Kelly, who had left enough poison in his heart to paralyze someone less acquainted with pain.

"This is good wine," he said, redirecting the conversation toward something less personal.

"I know the winemaker," she replied. "I'll tell him you said that."

"You publicists get around."

"We have a lot of occasions to drink." She looked him in the eye. "The winery isn't far away. They have an excellent lunch menu."

And there it was: the proposition. He had to play this carefully. He didn't want to offend her. "Sounds tempting. I'll mention it to Megan. We're taking the Garden Route this weekend."

"I can take you if you like," Anna replied, bringing her intentions fully into the light.

"That's nice of you," he said, delivering the blow softly. "If only I had more time."

Anna stepped back gracefully. "Of course. Well, if you're ever bored, Megan has my number."

"I'll keep that in mind." He held up his wineglass. "Cheers."

"Nice chatting," she replied and left him with a smile.

When she was gone, Paul turned toward the sea and listened to the distant sound of the surf. A gentle wind blew off the water and stirred the trees around the villa. The property was owned by one of Simon's many friends—a fund manager in London. He allowed Simon to use it as a base for his photographic excursions in Africa, and Megan joined him when her trial calendar permitted. She had invited Paul on a whim the last time she had visited his apartment in DC.

"What kind of life is this?" she had asked, running her fingers over the top of his outsized plasma television and holding up a year's worth of dust. "This place is a dump. The only things that are worth anything are your entertainment system and your piano."

As if on cue, he sat down at his Yamaha baby grand and banged out a jazzy rendition of "What a Wonderful World" sans vocals—he'd never been able to sing.

"You just proved my point, Ray Charles." She put her hands on his shoulders. "Look, I believe in what you're doing as much as you do. But you need something permanent to come back to. You can't be living here in twenty years."

He had accepted her offer of a getaway, both because he loved her more than anyone else and because the Bureau owed him more vacation days than he could count. But Cape Town, for all its splendor, had done nothing to assuage his restlessness. It was like a drug, the adrenaline he had been living on since September 11, 2001. As a special agent with the FBI's New York–based extraterritorial squad, he had worked the 1998 embassy bombings in Kenya and Tanzania and developed an interest in Islamic radicalism. Over the next two years, he had turned that interest into an expertise, taking courses on Middle East studies at the City College of New York. With the help of his SSA—supervisory special agent—he had also cross-trained as a negotiator, attending the two-week course at the FBI Academy taught by the

Crisis Negotiation Unit, or CNU, the most respected team of high-stakes negotiators in the world. After distinguishing himself in the training, he had come to the attention of the CNU's director during an exercise in which he played the role of lead negotiator.

Then al-Qaeda attacked the homeland and America went to war in Afghanistan and Iraq. No one quite expected that the wars would trigger a new wave of international kidnappings. But they did. As Western contractors flooded into the conflict zones, the insurgents saw opportunity and began to stage abductions, extort ransoms, and conduct brutal public killings. In June of 2004, soon after the jihadist cleric Abu Musab al-Zarqawi beheaded Nick Berg, an American businessman, the director of the CNU had brought Paul on board as a full-time negotiator. Two weeks later, he had been deployed to Baghdad as an advisor to US and coalition troops.

For the past seven years, he had been a human pinball, bouncing from one hostage crisis to the next and racking up over a million airline miles. In his downtime, he taught negotiation skills to police agencies around the world and did research on hostage scenarios. He had a gift, his bosses said. He could see through people—especially people in distress. They made him the number one international hostage negotiator in the Bureau. It was the job he had coveted since watching the Waco tragedy unfold in college. But it came with a steep price. He had no life outside of it.

"Hey, good looking," Megan said, appearing beside him. "I'm disappointed. I was sure you and Anna would hit it off."

"We did," he replied, smiling at her. She was an elegant woman with raven-dark hair, hazel eyes, and a face that smiled easily. In the right light, she looked like Vera Farmiga. "You know me well."

"But you're not interested." She said it simply, without judgment.

"My job isn't conducive to a relationship."

She shrugged. "Neither is mine, but Simon and I make it work."

You work while Simon takes his photography students to bed, he thought but didn't say. At the age of forty, Megan Derrick was one of the most respected criminal defense attorneys in Washington. After graduating second in her class from Virginia Law School, she had clerked on the US Supreme Court before joining a boutique litigation practice run by a former Solicitor General that specialized in high-profile criminal cases and constitutional appeals.

"I'd be interested in you, if you weren't already spoken for," he said, giving her a sly look.

She laughed in a deep, authentic way. "Do you remember when we were kids? We used to joke about marrying each other. We'd had a nine-month courtship in utero and were best friends. What better foundation for a relationship?"

"Now we live in the same city and go months without seeing each other."

She smiled. "I don't need to see you to know what you're thinking."

"A telepathic lawyer," he said with mirth in his eyes.

"That's about as terrifying as a clairvoyant car salesman." He paused. "So what am I thinking?"

She eyed him seriously. "You really want to know?"

"I know already." It was a game they had played many times, but they never tired of it.

"Okay." She stared out at the night sea. "You're still thinking about Anna. Maybe not actively, but in the back of your mind some part of you wishes you were free enough to enjoy her." She looked into his eyes. "You are, you know? I've driven the Garden Route before."

As usual, she was spot on, but Paul pretended otherwise. He shook his head. "I was thinking about my last assignment."

"Nonsense," she retorted. "I know it's hard to believe, but not every woman is like Kelly."

The name of his ex-wife landed like a spear in his gut. He covered his emotions with jest. "It's decided then. You should leave Simon and we should elope."

"I mean it. Your music and your film collection will never warm your bed."

He let out a slow breath. "I've missed you, Meg. You're the only person in the world who understands me."

She gave him a hug. "I'll always be here for you. But the Bureau shouldn't have your soul."

"I'll think about it," he said and held her tight.

ISMAIL

THE INDIAN OCEAN
09°04′45″S, 56°52′34″E
November 8, 2011

The cargo ship was a gray ghost on the western horizon, a smudge of coal against the backdrop of the predawn sky. Ismail looked across the tropical sea draped with the shadows of twilight and clutched the stock of his AK-47. The wood was clammy in his hands, the metal barrel sweating in the warm, salt-laden air, but he had no doubt that it would work. The Soviet-era carbine—a throwback to the days of Siad Barre and the Somali National Army—was as trusty as an old camel.

He sat in the bow of the second skiff as it raced across the dark water. His ears were full of sound—the roar of the large outboard engine, the bone-jarring percussion of the bow as it leapt the waves, the wind moaning like a herd of cattle disturbed from sleep. They were eight miles from the ship and closing fast, their speed just under twenty-seven knots. The Omani *dooni*, or dhow, they had lived on for the past three weeks was miles behind them, its painted hull no longer visible.

He felt the twist of nerves in his gut along with the gnawing void of hunger. For two days he had eaten only bread and rice. The goat meat they had brought from the village—a gift from the clan elders, most of whom had a financial stake in the mission—had run out. There were nineteen men aboard the dhow: fourteen Somalis and five Omani fishermen who were both hostages and indentured servants—essentially a charter crew acting under duress. They would be released as soon as their "passengers" caught a ship, but not before.

Ismail looked into the faces of his companions, gauging their commitment, their willingness to risk life and limb in service of the mission. He was one of twelve attackers—six in each skiff. All were armed with vintage Kalashnikovs and motivated by a singular desire: to take something valuable from a world that had given them nothing. Their commander went by the nickname Gedef, or "mask" in Somali. His story was famous among the crew. He was a veteran of the Central Regional Coast Guard, formed in 2003 by the world's most notorious pirate kingpin, Mohamed Abdi Hassan, or "Afweyne." On Gedef's first mission in command, he had brought back an extraordinary prize—a Saudi oil tanker carrying over $100 million in light sweet crude. Yet of the $3.3 million ransom paid by the ship's owners, he had received only $46,000 and a Land Cruiser. He had left Afweyne in contempt and formed his own gang, obtaining financing from his father and other relatives in Somalia and the diaspora. Since then, he had hijacked two more vessels, one of which—a Singaporean freighter—had netted a $2.3 million ransom. The second—a Malaysian container ship—was currently at anchor near Ceel Huur while the negotiators in Hobyo and London haggled over the price.

Ismail caught Gedef's eye across the twenty-foot gap between the skiffs. The commander's expression was as fierce as it was emotionless, like a bird of prey. Physically, he and Ismail looked nothing alike. Gedef was relatively short and muscular with a countenance as arid as the desert of Galmudug where he was born. Ismail, meanwhile, was tall and athletic with a face that combined his father's penetrating gaze with his mother's clear skin and symmetrical beauty. Psychologically, however, they might have been brothers. Though separated in age by over a decade—Gedef was thirty-one; Ismail twenty—both had fought in the Somali civil war and turned to piracy as a way out. They were thinkers and men of action, desiring peace but wielding the sword to achieve it on their own terms.

Ismail was Gedef's second-in-command, trusted for his fearlessness and valued for his command of spoken English. He had been the first attacker to board the Malaysian cargo ship, the first to commandeer the bridge and subdue the terrified Chinese crew while calming their nerves with fluent reassurances. Gedef called him "Afyareh," or "agile mouth." It was Gedef's intention—expressed the night before they left Hobyo—to give Ismail command of his crew. If the current mission went well, Gedef intended to retire from the piracy business, build a sturdy house near the sea, chew *qat*—a leafy narcotic shrub—and have many wives and children.

Ismail watched the sky brighten in the east. The sun would rise in ten minutes, about the same time the two skiffs would appear on the cargo ship's radar. They had been trailing the vessel all night on AIS—the radio-powered identification system that ships use in international waters—and they had timed the attack precisely. They would ride in on the scythe of light, and if they were lucky, they would be aboard the ship and in control of the crew within half an hour. After that, it would take them about two and a half days to deliver their prey to the Somali coast. They were deep in the Indian Ocean, on the far side of the Seychelles—an unconventional hunting ground, but safer than the navy-patrolled Gulf of Aden or the Arabian Sea in cyclone season.

Closing his eyes, Ismail mouthed two lines from the *Fatiha*, the opening sura of the Quran, in Arabic. It was the first prayer his father had taught him when he was a child, before the advent of madness and murder, before the Shabaab—the militant Arab–Somali Islamist group turned cult of blood—had stolen his life and much of his soul. Notwithstanding the gun in his hands and the nature of his mission, he didn't speak the words ironically. Instead, he turned them into a prayer of preemptive repentance.

"*Bismallah-ir-Rahman ar-Raheem* . . . In the name of God, Most Gracious, Most Merciful. You alone do we worship, and you alone do we ask for help. I take refuge in Allah. I seek forgiveness from Allah. Glorified is my Lord, the Highest. Amen."

The sun appeared suddenly, as it does close to the equator, turning night into day and lighting up the cargo ship like a torch. It was a mammoth vessel, with a towering white superstructure and a hull the color of red clay weighed down by hundreds of containers, stacked six and seven high from stem to stern. Ismail picked up his binoculars and surveyed the fantail. The ship was the MV *Jade Dolphin*, from Mumbai, India. The Indians were notorious among the Somali gangs for their hatred of piracy, but their dollars were as green as those of any other nation. They would surrender, and they would pay. The law of the sea was the law of war—he who has the gun is king.

Ismail watched for the inevitable turn that would signal the ship's crew had spotted them. As the seconds passed, he grew puzzled. The skiffs were only three minutes out—about one and a half nautical miles—yet the *Jade Dolphin* had yet to conduct any evasive maneuvers. Its speed and course were constant. No water hoses had been turned on, no alarm triggered. There were two explanations: either the ship had a prehistoric radar system that couldn't detect the skiffs against the clutter of the sea, or the watch officers weren't paying attention. Ismail smiled thinly. *They're making it easy for us.*

He glanced across the water as Gedef's skiff broke away. Their strategy was simple. They would approach the ship like the pincers of a scorpion. Gedef's team would fire warning shots at the bridge, and Ismail's team would board the ship just forward of the stern. Ismail and two other attackers would make for the bridge while the rest of his men located the crew. For being the first to board, Ismail would receive triple the *sami*, or ransom share, of the other attackers, except for Gedef, who would take half of the gross to cover expenses and pay himself and his investors.

When the skiffs were less than a mile out, the *Jade Dolphin* finally sounded the alarm. In seconds, the ship accelerated and made a hard turn to starboard, then back to port, churning its wake into waves. This attempt at evasion came far too late. The skiffs fanned out to avoid the chop and zeroed in on the *Jade Dolphin*'s stern, racing across the sea like bull sharks moving in for the kill.

The Somalis drew their guns and aimed them at the tower. Through the binoculars, Ismail saw movement on the bridge—black shadows of men scurrying and gesticulating. Adrenaline surged through his body as he readied himself for the attack. He pictured his sister then, as she was in the world before—the delicate oval of her face, framed by an embroidered hijab, or headscarf, her small nose and lips, and wide eyes that glowed when she smiled. Yasmin, innocent as a flower. She was his pole star, his secret reservoir of courage. Gedef knew nothing of her existence, nothing of Ismail's true motivation, or the lengths to which he would go to set her free.

Suddenly, gunfire erupted from Gedef's skiff—the signature *rat-tat-tat* of the AK-47 known in war zones the world over. One burst, then two and three, all directed at the bridge. As Ismail watched, the *Jade Dolphin*'s crew dropped out of sight. Then something happened that took him completely by surprise: he heard the high-pitched crack of a rifle. Then another.

He jerked the binoculars toward Gedef's skiff, and

terror seized him. One of the attackers was slumped over the gunwale, his arm dragging in the water; another was holding his bloody chest. Gedef was shouting at his cowering crew as he fired back at the tower. Then he, too, took a bullet in the thigh. His leg collapsed beneath him, and his gun fell overboard, disappearing into the sea.

At that instant, Ismail knew what he had to do. He dropped the binoculars and took the tiller from the terrified helmsman. His men were screaming at him to break off the attack, their dark faces tortured with fear, but he had no interest in their cowardice. He had heard only one rifle, which meant there was a single shooter. He was good, but he couldn't be everywhere at once. If Ismail could get aboard, he could flush him out. He had done it before on the streets of Mogadishu.

He opened the throttle to the max and pointed the skiff at the fantail of the *Jade Dolphin*. The huge ship loomed above them like a castle of hardened steel. Ismail focused on the open windows in the vertical stern. They were at main deck level, thirty feet off the water, but they were accessible. The hook ladder his crew carried had been engineered precisely for this purpose.

He heard more rifle shots and glanced toward Gedef's skiff, one hundred yards away. His eyes widened as his brain registered the spectacle. Gedef was crouched in the center of the boat, balancing a rocket-propelled grenade launcher on his shoulder. It was the most powerful weapon in their arsenal, but it was meant only to cement the threat, not to be used against a ship. Ismail waved his arm wildly, trying to catch Gedef's attention before he turned an act of piracy into an attempted murder.

What happened next shook Ismail to the core. Gedef raised the RPG launcher toward the *Jade Dolphin* and pulled the trigger. As the shell launched, its back-blast ignited the skiff's engine and the engine became a bomb. The explosion was so violent that it sent flames high into the sky and flipped the skiff like it was a toy. The waves quickly encircled the broken hull and dragged it under. It sank in less than a minute, leaving behind a scatter of bodies and an oil slick that continued to burn.

In the wake of the blast, Ismail sat paralyzed while his skiff drifted to a stop, bobbing idly in the *Jade Dolphin*'s wake. He didn't process the shouts of the men around him. He didn't notice the container ship slipping away. He was in Mogadishu again, crouched behind an overturned jeep on Maka al Mukarama Road, Yusuf huddled beside him, crying. Bullets were flying around, some ricocheting off the jeep, others burying themselves in the house behind them. Men were shrieking in Somali, some injured, some dying, as the government tanks made their advance. Then came the explosion and the black void of unconsciousness. His eyes blinked and he saw the blood again, felt its viscous stickiness on his skin. He heard the shriek escape from his lips—

—and returned to the present just as suddenly. His men were yelling his name.

"Afyareh! Afyareh! What are we going to do?"

They were staring at him, terrified. Guray, aged twenty-four, an illiterate goatherd from the interior whose only talent was wielding a gun; Dhuuban, aged nineteen, the runt of his seven siblings, scarecrow-thin, and desperate to prove himself to his father; Osman, aged twenty-five, headstrong and juvenile, a fisherman with a sixth-grade education; Liban, aged twenty, the trustworthy son of a camel broker, and Ismail's right-hand man; and finally, Sondare, an introspective boy of seventeen whose mother sold *qat* to feed his five brothers while his father wasted her earnings on his new wife. Without Gedef, they were like orphaned children. They needed someone to lead them.

"We'll search for the living," Ismail said, speaking with a voice of authority. It was the only gift the Shabaab had given him—he knew how to command.

He took the tiller in hand and piloted the skiff to the site of the wreck. His men plugged their noses against the stench of burning oil and pointed out the bodies. They found three of them quickly, floating facedown on the water. All were dead, riddled with shrapnel. The fourth they found in a haze of pink some distance away. He was missing half a leg. The sight was so grotesque that Sondare turned away and Dhuuban retched over the side. The rest shouted Gedef's name and that of his cousin, Mas, into the vastness of sky and sea, but no reply came.

"They're dead," Liban said in a voice tinged with shock. "We have to find the dhow."

"No," Osman replied fiercely. "We can't leave them."

Ismail forced himself to be patient. Osman was Mas's best friend. "We'll keep searching," he said and turned the skiff around again.

He watched the *Jade Dolphin* recede into the distance while his men looked for survivors. The RPG shell had missed. Perhaps Gedef had only meant to scare them. Ismail would likely never know. The attack had degenerated into a fiasco. But the mission itself could be salvaged. The dhow had enough food and fuel for another week at sea. Other pirate bands had hijacked ships with one skiff. It was hazardous, but preferable to the alternative. They couldn't return to Somalia without a prize. Gedef's investors would have their heads.

"Look!" Osman shouted, staring toward the east and the sun. "It's Mas!"

The young man was floating on a piece of wreckage in water turned molten by the sunrise. He was half drowned, but he turned his head in their direction. Ismail brought the skiff alongside him, and Osman and Guray pulled him into the boat. He curled up in the fetal position, spit drooling out of his mouth. Apart from shock and exposure, he appeared to be uninjured, except for a two-inch-long laceration on his right cheek. *Just my luck that he would survive and not Gedef,* Ismail thought.

Mas was a twenty-two-year-old hothead, jealous and contentious. The only son of Gedef's uncle, he had worshiped at Gedef's feet and questioned Ismail's place in the band. "Afyareh is *fakash*—from a rival clan," he had said many times. "He fought for al-Shabaab. He can't be trusted." Gedef had ignored him. The pirate bands were largely meritocratic. Skill mattered more than clan, daring more than creed. Gedef elevated Ismail because he was gifted at hijacking ships; he didn't care that Ismail's father was Sa'ad, not Suleiman like the rest of them. With Gedef dead, though, Mas could be dangerous. Ismail would have to watch him carefully.

He fetched the handheld radio from the waterproof bag behind his seat and switched it on, pressing the "talk" button. "Abdullah, Abdullah," he began, "come in." He listened to the static but heard nothing. "Abdullah, Abdullah, this is Afyareh. Can you hear me?"

He frowned and looked toward the sun. The radio had an effective range of eight miles on the water. *The dooni should be close enough*, he thought. *Why is Abdullah not answering?* His men were staring at him, all but Osman, who was tending to Mas.

"Don't worry," he said confidently.

He took control of the tiller and massaged the throttle, driving the skiff through the low waves. He pointed the bow east and watched the horizon for a shadow, a discontinuity, anything that might be a glimpse of the dhow. Every few minutes, he let go of the throttle and tried to raise Abdullah on the radio. Each time, he heard only static.

After half an hour, he began to grow worried. His men were watching him anxiously, Osman included. Mas was still semiconscious, but he had begun to babble. He would soon come to his senses, and when he did, he was sure to provoke a fight.

"Abdullah, Abdullah," Ismail said for what felt like the hundredth time. "This is Afyareh. If you can hear me, please respond." A minute later, he decided to lie: "Abdullah, this is Afyareh. Gedef is with me, but his radio is dead. What is your position?"

Liban was the first to ask what Ismail feared. "Do you think they left us?"

"No, no," Ismail said forcefully. "They are just out of range."

As more time passed, however, Liban's question began to fester. Guray and Osman started to complain about Abdullah and Shirma, the guards they had left on the dhow to manage the Omani fishermen. Dhuuban perched himself in the bow and held his skinny knees to his chest, staring at Mas as if he had brought a hex upon them. Liban fingered his Kalashnikov as if it were a talisman. Only Sondare kept the faith, sitting beside Ismail and hanging on his every word, as if at any moment Abdullah's voice might break through the static and provide a rational excuse for his silence.

But Ismail's assurance was feigned. Inside, he was profoundly troubled. Abdullah was an experienced pirate and fiercely loyal to Gedef. He wouldn't abandon them without cause. But with cause . . . Ismail's mind raced with the possibilities. What if he heard the explosion and saw the flames? The *Jade Dolphin* had surely alerted the authorities about the attack. What if Abdullah heard chatter on the radio about a disabled skiff and a Seychellois coast guard vessel en route to the scene? Or what if the Omanis had mutinied? There were five of them. They might have overpowered Abdullah and Shirma in a moment of distraction and turned the dhow toward home.

He searched the horizon again, squinting against the

glare. He checked his handheld GPS unit for the coordinates. After nearly an hour of cruising, they were close to the spot where they had left the dhow. The day was clear; visibility was excellent. But the dhow was nowhere to be seen.

"They're gone," Liban declared, looking Ismail in the eye.

Osman gripped the stock of his gun. "If I ever get my hands on Abdullah, I'm going to put a bullet in his head."

"What are we going to do?" Dhuuban moaned from the bow.

At once, a shouting match broke out among the men. Ismail allowed them to vent their frustration while he pondered their situation. He knew exactly what they had to do, but he dreaded it at the same time. It would drive him farther away from Yasmin—much farther. But any distance was better than death.

He lifted his Kalashnikov and fired a burst into the air. *"Shut up!"* he said harshly.

Silence descended on the skiff. Osman and Guray took turns glaring at him, but no one disputed his authority. He looked at the six faces around him, shining with sweat and fear, and told them the truth as clearly as he could articulate it.

"We have no food. We have water for two days at most and three quarters of a tank of fuel. Does anyone know how far that will take us?"

He asked the question to put them in their place. He was the only one among them who had committed the engine specifications to memory.

"Two hundred and fifty nautical miles," he answered for them. "Maybe two hundred and seventy-five, if the seas are calm."

No one spoke. He had their complete attention. He held up his GPS unit. "The closest land is Coëtivy Island in the Seychelles. That's one hundred and twenty nautical miles from here. Mahé is two hundred and seventy nautical miles away. Both islands are in the same direction. I don't want to be a refugee, but neither do I want to die. If we ditch our weapons in the sea, we can claim asylum."

"We are Somali," Liban objected. "They would say we are pirates."

"They would have no evidence," Ismail replied. "We would pretend to be fishermen." He gestured at Osman. "He can teach us everything we need to know."

Osman shook his head. "We don't have nets or bait. And there are too many of us."

"It doesn't matter," Ismail countered. "If we tell the same story, they will have to accept it. Maybe they will send us back to Somalia. Maybe they will let us stay. Either way, we don't die."

It was then that Mas spoke, as if from the grave. "I think we should find another ship."

Ismail didn't allow his distaste to show. "And how do we do that without radar or AIS?"

Mas clenched his teeth. "I want the Land Cruiser Gedef promised me."

"And I want a big house by the sea and four wives," Ismail replied, playing the part of the pirate boss without really meaning it. "We don't get there if we're dead."

Mas didn't reply, but his eyes smoldered.

"We could do both," Liban suggested, and heads began to nod all around. "Maybe we'll find another ship closer to Mahé."

Ismail watched the consensus grow until even Mas seemed placated. It was the plan he had envisioned all along. He had no interest in giving up until he absolutely had to. But he needed their consent to save their lives, and his own.

"It's a good idea," he said. "We'll head toward Mahé. But if we run across a ship"—he looked each of them in the eye—"then, *inshallah*, we will take it."

VANESSA

Dr. Vanessa Parker put down her pen and stared at her hands, cursing the moisture in her eyes. It was late in the day; her last patient—a young woman with a bladder infection—had just left; and she was filling out her report for the file. It was a simple task, nothing more than a few scribbled notes and a signature, but she couldn't manage to write a coherent sentence. Her usually tidy thoughts were a jumbled mess. She felt the burning in her cheeks, the flush of emotions she couldn't control. *It's done*, she thought. *You can't change it now.* But that wasn't entirely true. Time wasn't the issue. It was desire.

She sat back in her chair and stared at the photograph beside her computer. She had taken it a year and a half ago at their summer house—a cottage on Lake Winnipesaukee that had been in Daniel's family for generations. Daniel and Quentin were sitting on the dock, the forest behind them bronzed by the late-afternoon sun. Daniel's arm was draped over his son's shoulder and they were smiling. Their power-boat, a four-hundred horsepower Nautique, was off to the side, tethered to the pylons. *The quiet before the storm*, she thought. *How did we miss the warning signs?*

The door to her office was open, and she heard a knock. She blinked away her tears, hoping it was Aster, her longtime colleague and best friend. She turned around and tensed. Chad Forrester was the last person she wanted to see.

"I'm sorry, Vanessa," he said, looking at her awkwardly. "I'll come back later."

"It's okay," she replied. "I'm about to leave."

He examined her intently. "Are you all right?"

"Of course," she said too curtly. "What can I do for you?"

Forrester narrowed his eyes but decided to leave it alone. At thirty-five, he was the youngest of her three part-ners and the darling among patients and staff. A graduate of Duke University and Duke Medical School, he had the approachable demeanor of a favorite cousin. As a physician, his personality was a gold mine. For Vanessa, however, it had become a minefield.

"I'm having some people over on Friday night," he explained. "Nothing formal, just a friendly autumn party. If you don't have plans, I'd love for you to come."

"Thanks," she said, "but Aster and I are going to St. Michael's."

Forrester's smile returned. "A girlfriend getaway?"

She nodded once and didn't elaborate.

"Good for you. I can't remember the last time you got

out of town."

"My thoughts exactly." She left her patient report undone and put on her coat, which Forrester correctly interpreted as his cue to wrap up the conversation.

"We'll miss you on Friday," he said. "Enjoy your evening."

When he was gone, she put her computer to sleep and went to the ladies' room. She grimaced when she saw her reflection in the mirror. Her porcelain skin was pink and blotchy, and her mascara had smudged, leaving dark circles under her eyes. *No wonder Chad looked at me strangely*, she thought. She wiped away the residue and composed herself. She didn't know why she was in such a rush to get home. With her husband and son on the other side of the world, only Skipper, their golden retriever, was waiting for her there. Still, she felt it, the compulsion to move, to do something—anything—to silence the guilt raging inside of her. *You need to choose*, her conscience said. *You can't make him wait forever.*

She took a deep breath and left the restroom, feeling like a fraud. The practice was quieting down after a busy Monday. The physician assistants and lab techs were already gone, and the office staff were tidying up their workspaces. She waved to the receptionist and escaped through the back door.

It was only five thirty, but night had already fallen. She glanced around the parking lot and walked quickly to her Audi SUV. Her practice was located in an office park in Silver Spring, a suburb of Washington, DC. The neighborhood was safe, but she had been mugged once—in

Manhattan when she was a college student—and she had no intention of letting it happen again.

Suddenly, she heard her name. "Vanessa, wait!"

She turned around and saw Aster Robel striding toward her, her handsome ebony face and white coat colored amber by a nearby streetlamp. Aster was Eritrean by birth, but her family had fled Asmara in 1981 during the endless war with Ethiopia. She and Vanessa had met in their first year of medical school and had bonded like sisters. Though they hailed from different worlds, they were both refugees from childhood. Their suffering had hardened them and turned them into overachievers, obsessed with transcending their roots. When they saw this in each other, they had never looked back.

"I talked to Chad," Aster said, a residual trace of Africa in her English. She examined Vanessa's face and saw her doubt. "Daniel sent another letter, didn't he?"

Vanessa nodded, holding back her tears.

"Are they still in the Seychelles?"

"According to the schedule, they left yesterday."

Aster touched her arm. "I know it was a hard decision."

"I didn't decide," said Vanessa, shaking her head. "I just kept putting it off."

Aster pondered this. "What did the letter say?"

Vanessa brushed a stray hair out of her face. "He asked me to remember."

"And?" Aster asked softly.

"I tried. I can't be selective about it."

Aster didn't have to respond. The look in her eyes was

enough to convey her understanding. All at once, Vanessa began to cry. Aster wrapped her arms around her and held her, expressing without words the truth Vanessa had struggled all her life to believe: *I'm here for you. You're not in this alone.*

"Thanks," Vanessa said after a while, drying her eyes on her coat.

"I bet you could use some company," Aster said. "Abram can take care of the kids."

Against her instinct, Vanessa shook her head. Aster's husband was a trauma surgeon at Johns Hopkins in Baltimore, and his free evenings were rare.

"Suit yourself," Aster said. "Call if you need me."

"I will," Vanessa replied and gave her friend a hug good-bye.

She drove out of the lot in a daze and braced herself for a long commute. The Capitol Beltway and US-50 East were bumper-to-bumper. She listened to Vivaldi's entire *Four Seasons* concerto before she emerged from the congestion. In time, she left the highway and drove through Annapolis toward the Wardour neighborhood, an upscale enclave of wooded lots and waterfront estates near the Naval Academy. Her home was at the end of Norwood Road on the banks of the Severn River.

When she pulled into the cobblestone driveway, she found the two-story Cape Cod ablaze with light, courtesy of the home automation system Daniel had installed before the voyage. She sat for a moment and stared at the house. She loved it as she had never loved another place in her life. But she had never quite thought of it as hers. Daniel's parents had bought it for them before Quentin was born.

She gathered her purse and walked through the grape arbor to the front door. Skipper barked once and greeted her in the foyer. The house had been the pet project of a retired architect, and it looked the part, with vaulted ceilings, a sprawling floor plan, and windows everywhere. Vanessa had filled the walls with paintings and mirrors and the rooms with classic furniture. Daniel's contributions were few, but they dominated the great room—a six-foot brass search-light, an outsized map of ancient Rome, and a hand-built Bösendorfer grand piano for Quentin.

Vanessa went to the kitchen to open a bottle of wine, and Skipper followed in her wake, his feet clicking on the wide planks of the reclaimed wood floor. She poured the wine into a decanter and then took Skipper for a walk down to the boat dock.

As he always did, the dog bounded ahead of her into the trees beyond the swimming pool. Vanessa walked at her own pace, following the lighted path between the forest and the lawn. The stars were bright overhead, as was the Naval Academy Bridge in the distance. She inhaled the crisp air and listened to the gentle sounds of the river lapping against the shore. Her yard was a magical place, the kind of Arcadia she had dreamed of as a young girl, as her mother, Trish, dragged her from the cabarets of New York to the casinos of Las Vegas to the Hollywood rock scene, trying men on like wedding dresses until she lucked upon Ted, Vanessa's stepfather. No matter how insane married life had driven

Vanessa—negotiating Daniel's compulsive productivity, Quentin's emotional instability, and her own relentless perfectionism—the river had always brought her peace.

She met Skipper at the end of the path and followed him across the sundeck—another of Daniel's innovations—to the stairs that led down to the dock. In the summer, she might have taken the dog out on the bay to watch the sunset, but it was late autumn and she didn't like navigating the channel after dark. Instead, she strolled past the Nautique and the *Relativity*—Daniel's trusty old Passport 40 yacht—and stopped at the railing at the end. The wind blowing off the water turned her eyes moist and her hair wild. She scratched Skipper's head and allowed the solitude to envelop her.

She thought of her husband and son on the other side of the night. She had no idea what it felt like to sleep on a sailboat beneath the stars. The thought of it terrified her about as much as it thrilled Daniel and Quentin. In a few hours, the sun would rise over the Indian Ocean and they would sail on into another tropical day. What would they do for all those hours surrounded by sea and sky? Daniel had tried to explain it in one of his letters—the notion of ocean time; the observation of winds and weather; the repairs necessary to keep the *Renaissance* shipshape; the plotting and logging of course and drift; the conversations with Quentin about his correspondence courses; the reading and journaling and thinking and dozing. He was certain that the sea had changed him. But Vanessa wasn't so sure. It was easy to say half a world away. The proof would come when he returned home—when his clients started calling and Quentin went off to college and they were alone again. Would he be different then?

In time, she returned to the house and her bottle of wine. She poured herself a glass, switched on the fireplace, and sank into the plush cushion of her favorite chair—a Belgian wingback. Skipper followed her into the living room and curled up on the Oriental rug beside the fire. She took a few sips of the wine and placed the glass on the table beside her. Her heart lurched when she saw the letter there. She thought she remembered putting it with the others in Daniel's office, but she must have forgotten. She stared at it for a long time, struggling with the voices inside her head. At last, she picked it up and read it again. He had written it on October 11, a month ago.

Dearest V:

We're in Sri Lanka, about to depart for the Maldives. We made decent time crossing the Bay of Bengal. The winds were intermittent, but the weather held and we made the passage without any sign of a tropical depression. We were fortunate. The harbor-master in Phuket insisted we wait until January. I told him we had survived fifty-five-knot winds and thirty foot breaking waves in the Tasman Sea. He said we were crazy, but I don't agree. We just decided not to be afraid.

I've been thinking a lot about fear in the past two weeks. I feel like I've spent the last twenty years managing my own insecurities. You said it during our courtship—that I grew up in the shadow of my father and never quite stepped into the sun. I avoided the Naval Academy because my mother intervened. But Dad didn't change his strategy. He told me in a thousand not-so-subtle ways that my passions for thinking and writing were a waste of time. "Philosophers don't make history," he said. "It's the inventors, the entrepreneurs, the engineers, the businesspeople who take their ideas and shape the world."

It's ironic, but he was right in a way. Boldness is what I lacked—boldness to break out of the straitjacket he had fitted for me. Instead, I went to law school, like he did. I packed away my feelings in my mental attic and reduced my life to a pragmatic equation. It pains me now to think about it, but I understand why I did it. I was scared of failure, of being the laughingstock of my more successful peers. I accepted his theory that pragmatism is the keystone of progress, that idealists drive themselves insane or die at the Bastille. But the pragmatic path, I have found, also requires a sacrifice—a sacrifice of the soul.

Of course, I don't completely regret the choice I made. If I hadn't gone to Columbia, I never would have met you or known Quentin. Approaching you at Carnegie Hall was the boldest thing I'd ever done. I've been reflecting on that moment a lot—what I was thinking and what we said to each other. Do you remember? The butterfly metaphor came out of nowhere. It was like an epiphany, as was your reply.

Your honesty gave me courage to take the next step. And you met me there. You took a risk and invited me into your world.

I'll never forget that spring. Every word you spoke, every song you played for me, every hour we spent in Central Park, every time we made love, it was as if I was living someone else's life, someone with far better luck than my own. I've felt that only one other time—out here on the ocean with Quentin. Beauty is all around us; the world is bursting with it; and nothing else really matters.

I wish I could share it with you. I'm still holding out hope that you will meet us in the Seychelles. People say that La Digue is the most beautiful island in the world. Please come, Vanessa. Like I came to Schapiro Hall. We could find that joy again.

Do you remember?

—D

When Vanessa finished the letter, she let the pages fall onto her lap and stared into the distance, her eyes unfocused, her body still. An idea had taken shape in her heart as she read her husband's words. It was a litmus test of sorts, a challenge that, if met, might resolve her indecision. She had never believed in fate, in the mystical alignment of stars and planets—even, if she were frank, in the notion of Providence. That was the stuff of fairy tales, one of many myths her childhood had debunked. Life was what you made of it; God helped those who helped themselves. But there was a contradiction in her worldview, a wild strand of feeling that refused to be confined by rationalism: her music.

She stood up from her chair and walked slowly toward the piano, its black case glistening beneath halogen bulbs. Skipper raised his head and watched her go, intuiting her destination. Beside the piano was her violin. Handcrafted by Francesco Bissolotti in Cremona, Italy, the hometown of Antonio Stradivari, it had been a gift from Ted at her high school graduation. The insurers appraised it at $22,000 and her bow, a Bernard Millant from Paris, at $4,000—valuable but not exceptional in the rarefied world of violin making. To Vanessa, however, they were priceless.

She lifted the Bissolotti off its stand and assumed the starting position, her chin on the chinrest, her bow just above the strings. She closed her eyes and felt a twinge of apprehension. She hadn't played the Beethoven in years, and never without an orchestra behind her. The solo parts weren't meant to be played alone. But therein lay the test. If she could play the third movement from memory—including the eminently difficult final cadenza—perhaps she could take a step as bold as Daniel had taken.

Her bow began to move almost without bidding. The fiddle-like opening notes flowed out of her with an exuberance that surprised her. She paused at the right moment, hearing in her head the orchestra's entry, reprising the rondo theme. Then she came in again and hit the high notes with perfect pitch. Her fingers danced on the fingerboard, her body rocking back and forth with the rhythm of the music. Minutes passed like this as she alternated between the solo and orchestra parts, the latter playing only in her mind. She imagined herself in Carnegie Hall again, a twenty-two-year-old girl who had no idea what the future held but who was determined to make something of it. She remembered the thrill of those moments—and the fear. Then came the Kreisler cadenza. She nearly tripped on the double stops in the long run of sixteenth notes, but somehow her bow found the strings. At last, the rondo theme returned, sweet and delicate at first, then passionate and powerful as it built to the climax. The voice of the Bissolotti rang in her ears like the song of an angel—pristine and perfect.

When she finished, she let out the breath she was holding. The muscles in her arm were on fire, and her neck was stiff as it always was after she played an extended piece. But her heart was feather-light. She returned the violin to its stand and took her glass of wine to the dining room table where her MacBook was charging. She opened Safari and searched for flights to South Africa before Christmas. That was Daniel's plan—to sail into Table Bay on December 21 and spend the holidays in Cape Town. She felt the doubt again, like an echo in her heart, but she made the choice to set it aside. She wanted to be there on the wharf when her husband and son arrived. The music had made her remember.

She wanted to see if the change Daniel spoke of was real.

DANIEL

The squall came upon them just before noon. Quentin was the first to see the thunderclouds on the horizon, moving toward them like the vanguard of an army. He shouted a warning to Daniel, who was at the navigation station in the cabin updating the logbook. Daniel looked out a porthole and saw the dark haze of rain in the distance. The storm was still miles away, but they didn't have much time.

He stowed the logbook and secured the lockers and the galley. When the swells hit, everything that wasn't attached to something or contained in a compartment would be tossed about. He turned off the audio system, stopping Billy Ocean's "Caribbean Queen" in midbeat, and listened to Quentin operating the winches. After many squalls at sea, they knew the drill. They would sheet in the headsail and put two reefs in the main, leaving just enough canvas to give them steerageway in the storm.

As soon as the cabin was battened down, Daniel removed a panel in the floor and closed the seacocks—the holes in the hull through which sink water and sewage emptied into the ocean. Then he checked the bilge pump and the seals on the hatches. He glanced at the barometer. Only minutes ago, the pressure had been 1005 millibars. It was now 990. In the gale off New Zealand, the mercury had dropped to 962 millibars and stayed that way for over fifteen hours. Daniel doubted this storm would take the pressure below 975. Squalls in the tropics could be fierce, but they were short-lived. He made a note in the logbook and went topside to help Quentin tie off the sheets and secure the dinghy.

"We're ready," Quentin said after a time, stowing the winch handle in one of the cockpit lockers and clipping his safety harness into the port-side jack line.

Daniel gave his son a careful look. "Are you sure you want to ride this out on deck?"

"I'll go below if you do," Quentin said.

Adolescent bravado, Daniel thought, but he couldn't blame his son. There was nothing quite like the thrill of a storm at sea.

They saw the first gust of wind before they felt it. It stirred up whitecaps on the water and changed its color from cobalt blue to resin gray. "Here comes a blow!" Daniel exclaimed, gripping the helm with one hand and the deck with the other.

The gust struck the *Renaissance* like an invisible hand, and the sailboat heeled over hard. Daniel held on tight, his legs bent and feet wide apart, and watched as Quentin did the same. The wind gauge peaked at twenty-six knots before dropping back to seventeen.

The waves came next. In a matter of minutes, they built from three feet to ten, hitting the *Renaissance* on her aft quarter and setting her rolling like a pendulum. Daniel fought to keep her on a southerly course, but there was only so much he could do.

The clouds trundled in, effacing the sun, and the wind gusted harder, driving the anemometer above thirty-four knots before stabilizing at twenty-five. Daniel watched as the rain approached, blotting out the sky. The drops were huge and struck at an angle, pelting the sailboat and their bodies like rubber bullets. The waves were now fifteen feet and climbing, and the winds were holding at thirty knots. Daniel gripped the helm tightly as the *Renaissance* bobbed like a cork in the tempestuous sea.

Over the roar of the storm, he heard Quentin whoop with frenzied joy. The heavens answered with a crackle of lightning and a crash of thunder. The skies darkened and the winds blew ferociously, driving the rain sideways. The waves grew to eighteen feet, then twenty, heaping up like walls of water, their crests strewn with spindrift. When the wind gusts passed forty knots, Daniel decided to run off before the storm. He brought the *Renaissance* about and headed southeast with the swells.

"Do you want the drogue?" Quentin yelled, his voice muted by the torrential rain.

For a split second Daniel considered it. The drogue was a cone-like sea anchor that deployed from the stern, protecting a sailboat against its greatest nemesis—a large breaking wave. He glanced at the anemometer and saw that the winds had topped out at forty-two knots. The storm was a fresh gale, a Force 8 on the Beaufort scale. It was nasty weather, to be sure, but not deadly. He shook his head, and Quentin nodded in understanding.

The next fifteen minutes confirmed Daniel's instinct. It was the decrease in sound that first alerted him to the passing of the storm. The relentless roar of the raindrops slackened to a growl, and the winds began to abate, falling to thirty knots, then twenty, then ten. The waves tossed and frothed for a while, but soon they dropped off, too, bringing an end to the roller-coaster ride. Suddenly, the clouds opened up and the sun bathed their sodden skin with light.

Daniel wiped his face and slapped Quentin on the shoulder. "That's lucky number thirteen," he said with a smile. "Not too much worse than the last."

Quentin patted the bulkhead beside him. "She hardly seemed to notice."

Daniel turned the helm and pointed the *Renaissance* south again. "Let's get the sails up. I'll check our position. I don't think we lost too much ground."

While Quentin hoisted the mainsail and let out the boom, Daniel went below and assessed the damage. Apart from a few pillows and chart books on the floor, the cabin looked as he had left it. He went through the cabinets and storage lockers and found a cracked water glass and a bookshelf in disarray. After straightening up, he opened the seacocks again and checked the bilge. The water level was higher than normal, but the pump was doing its job. He turned on the audio system and selected a playlist on his iPhone, listening as the ethereal opening bars of Sting's "Desert Rose" filled the cabin. *Sailing requires a soundtrack*, his father had always said. His words were nowhere truer than on the open ocean. Without music, a sailor could drown in the silence.

Daniel went to the nav station next and fixed their position with GPS. The storm had driven them five miles to the east. It would take them an hour to make up the distance. He felt his stomach rumble and checked his watch. It was 12:32 p.m., almost time for lunch. He updated the logbook and then removed his laptop from the chart table drawer. He checked his e-mail by satellite and saw the bulletin from the UK Maritime Trade Organization. The subject line made his skin crawl: WARNING: PIRATE ATTACK SOUTHEAST OF SEYCHELLES. His sense of foreboding grew as he read the text.

To the Master of the SV *Renaissance*:

At 06:44 Local time (02:44 GMT) today, Somali pirates attacked the container ship MV *Jade Dolphin* approximately 280 nm southeast of Victoria, Seychelles. They approached the vessel in two skiffs, carrying heavy weapons. The vessel returned fire and destroyed one skiff. The second skiff was last sighted at 09°04′45″S, 056°52′34″E. Its current whereabouts are unknown.

Please be advised that sailing vessels are

extremely vulnerable to pirate attack. We strongly
recommend that you return to Victoria. If you proceed
through the High Risk Area, please take precautions to
avoid attack and keep this office regularly informed of
your course and position.

Daniel felt a burning sensation in his gut. He read the
warning a second time and plotted the site of the attack
on GPS. They were 150 nautical miles away, but their current course would bring them within fifty miles of the last
known position of the second pirate skiff. Mahé Island was
140 nautical miles to their north. They could reach Victoria
by sunrise at top speed. But where would the pirates go in the
same period? They were hunting for a ship in the Seychelles.
What was more perilous: sailing closer to the inner-island
group, with its high density of shipping, or farther out to sea?

He stood up and paced the length of the cabin, racked
by frustration and guilt. He saw Quentin lounging in the
cockpit, typing away on his iPhone—likely sending Ariadne
an e-mail about the storm. By some miracle, the girl had
turned him into a conversationalist. *Damn it all to hell!* he
thought, remembering Vanessa's words and the vow he had
made when she agreed to the circumnavigation.

"I'm not concerned about you," she had said, standing on
the terrace beside the swimming pool, her arms crossed to
ward off the cold. *"Whether or not you come back is your decision. But if you put my son in danger and he gets hurt, I'll never
be able to forgive you."*

"You have my word," he had promised. *"I'll keep him safe."*

At once, Daniel returned to the nav station with an idea. He used the laptop and GPS to collect some information and ran a few calculations. The nearest landmass was the island of Coëtivy, home to a shrimp-processing plant and 250 residents—exactly the kind of place the pirates would avoid in their search for a valuable target. He went topside and took the helm.

"Change in plans," he told Quentin, starting the engine and turning the yacht to the west. "Somali pirates attacked a container ship a hundred and fifty miles to the southeast. They're still out there."

Quentin blanched, his mouth agape. "Shit," he said, then, "Sorry."

"You're not kidding." Daniel pushed the throttle to the stops, and the rumble of the engine drowned out the sounds of the sea. "We need to get the sails down. They're too visible."

He took the main sheet in hand and brought in the boom. After a pause, Quentin followed his lead, retracting the headsail and lowering the main. When they finished, Quentin took a seat again.

"Where are we going?" he asked, his tone nervous and uncertain.

"Coëtivy Island. We're going to find an anchorage and figure out what to do."

Quentin was still for a long moment. Then his expression transformed, his jaw clenching and his blue eyes darkening. He brought his knees to his chest and hugged them tightly. It was a posture Daniel had seen countless times but never since they had sailed out of Annapolis harbor. It was a protective mechanism, a shell Quentin deployed whenever the world spun out of control.

Daniel felt a spark of anger. The confidence his son had gained in their months at sea was genuine. Yet it was also fragile, like sea turtles hatching beneath the predatory gaze of gulls. He made a promise then to Quentin and to himself: *You're a new person. You're not going back. I'm not going to let you.*

They reached Coëtivy just before sunset. The wind had died down to a whisper, and the water around the island was as tranquil as glass. Daniel made the approach from the west, keeping his eyes on the depth gauge and aiming the bow toward a beach lined with palm trees. They didn't have a chart for these waters, only cryptic comments in a nautical book. He saw waves breaking on a reef to the southeast, but here they were breaking on the sand.

When they reached a depth of thirty feet, he put the throttle into neutral and nudged his son. "Are you going to help me?"

Quentin snapped out of his trance faster than Daniel expected. "Sure," he said, scampering toward the bow and dropping the anchor.

Daniel put the engine in reverse and let out a long length of chain. When the plumes bit into the bottom, he tested the hold and then shut off the engine. The *Renaissance* swung slowly around until it faced toward the west and the sun. They were alone in the anchorage, the beach fifty yards behind. Daniel saw movement on the shore—a man combing the sand. He waved, and the man waved back.

Before long, Quentin returned from the foredeck. Daniel examined his face and saw that it had changed. There was a light in his eyes again. Daniel started to speak, but his son preempted him.

"I've thought about it, and I want to go on," Quentin said. "Anything else means we give up."

Daniel felt the pride down deep, but he knew the difference between courage and carelessness. He met his son's eyes. "Going back to Mahé isn't the same as going home."

Quentin was skeptical. "I don't follow you."

"It's simple. We'll hire a deliveryman, somebody like François, who won't mind a little hazard pay. We'll meet up with him in Réunion and make the passage to South Africa on schedule."

Quentin frowned. "You mean we'll fly to Réunion."

Daniel heard the hesitation in his son's voice. "Just this leg. After that, we'll go on as planned."

Quentin's displeasure deepened. "And how do you know we won't get hijacked between here and Mahé? If they're looking for another ship, isn't that where they'll go?"

Daniel shrugged. "We'll get the Seychelles coast guard to escort us."

"How are you going to do that?" Suddenly, Quentin grimaced. "Don't tell me you're going to get Grandpa to pull strings."

Daniel took a breath and let it out. "Do you have a better plan?"

Quentin nodded. "It's called finishing what we started. We chose this route with full knowledge of the pirate problem. We change it now and we *are* giving up."

There was truth in what he said. They had agonized over the passage from Thailand to South Africa, weighing the danger of venturing into the High Risk Area against the reward of visiting the Maldives and Seychelles. They had agreed to avoid Zanzibar, much to Daniel's chagrin—the waters off Africa's east coast were still treacherous. But the ocean route from Sri Lanka to Réunion by way of Male Atoll and Mahé Island was different. The ocean was vast, the chance of an attack in such remote waters negligible. They had decided to take the risk.

"You're right," Daniel replied, softening his tone. "And I admire you greatly for saying it. But things have changed. I made a promise to your mother."

Quentin clenched his fists. "This isn't about Mom. This is about *me*." His voice broke with sudden emotion. "You have no idea . . . You have no idea how humiliating it was when they caught me with the drugs. I was just doing Hans a favor. I wasn't a dealer. I wasn't even a user."

Daniel felt every ounce of his son's misery. "I know."

Quentin's eyes shined with tears. "You *don't* know. I thought my life was over. Getting suspended was bad enough, but the police treated me like a criminal. They told me I'd go to prison if I didn't help them out."

At this point, Quentin made a confession that cleaved

Daniel's heart in two. "Do you know how close I came to ending it all? I was going to do it that morning I took the *Relativity* down the bay. I even wrote a note. But you caught up to me. You said you'd work it all out. I didn't believe you. I kept the note. Then you told me about this crazy idea you had . . ."

Quentin struggled to hold himself together. "This trip saved my life, Dad. Literally. I didn't expect it to change anything, but I gave it a chance. When I met Ariadne, she saw past all of it. She just wanted to be with me. I promised her . . . I promised *myself* that we'd finish the trip."

Daniel sat down heavily. He felt as if he had been put through a meat grinder. He spoke his question gingerly: "And if I don't agree?"

Quentin shook his head. "If you go back, I'm not going with you."

Daniel turned away and watched the sun dip its golden toe into the sea. He replayed Quentin's words in his head and thought of all the miles they had covered, all the days and nights they had spent together on the deep, all the laughter and conversations and unforgettable experiences they had put between them and the past. It seemed almost sacrilegious to step foot on an airplane when they had come so far. Yet the threat remained, as did his vow. *To hell with it*, he thought. *You only live once.*

"Okay," Daniel exhaled, hope and dread entwined in his heart.

Quentin pumped his fist in jubilation. "Sweet!"

"But there's only one way to do it. We go tonight under power with sails stowed and lights and AIS off. We stand two-hour watches. By the time the sun rises, we'll be past the attack site. By sunset tomorrow, we'll be across the tenth parallel and out of the High Risk Area."

Quentin gave Daniel the look of intrigue and curiosity he had inherited from Vanessa. "You keep surprising me," he said. "I never used to think of you as brave."

Tears welled in Daniel's eyes. The compliment filled a void that was as old as he was. How many times he had longed for his father to affirm him in this way. But Curtis had only pointed out his flaws.

Daniel put a hand on his son's shoulder. "You know what? Neither did I."

ISMAIL

THE INDIAN OCEAN
08°25′25″S, 56°23′24″E
November 8, 2011

Ismail sat in back of the skiff, one hand on the tiller, watching the sun sink into the sea. His men were huddled around him, their eyes glazed, their forms motionless. The ocean was calm, like a giant lake without beginning or end. At just under six knots, the skiff plowed across the surface with barely a bump, creating a headwind as languid as human breath.

When the sun disappeared and the sky began to darken, Ismail searched the heavens for the first stars of the night. He saw *al-Nasr* high in the west, then *Dhanab* and *al-Waqi* to the north. The moon hung round and full in the east. He felt no fear of the coming night. Dark was nothing more than the absence of day. His equanimity was the result of experience—the numberless nights he had spent in the Shabaab camps stretched out on the hard ground beside Yusuf; the weeks he had spent at sea, sleeping beneath the wheeling constellations, many of which his father had taught him to name.

His companions, however, were terrified of night. The same waves they scoffed at under the sun, they treated like monsters in the dark. Ismail prepared himself. Tonight would be worse than other nights. All of them were weary and hungry and conscious of their massive misfortune. Along with losing the *Jade Dolphin* and Gedef and the Omani dhow, they had lost one of their water jugs in an afternoon squall. The storm had blown with the malevolence of a djinn, coming within a hairsbreadth of capsizing the skiff and leaving them battered, waterlogged, and foul-tempered.

According to Ismail's GPS unit, they had covered a distance of fifty-two miles in nine hours. At this rate, Mahé was still two days away, but already his men were showing signs of strain. Osman and Guray had been grumbling about their empty stomachs, and Mas had fanned the flames with a false alarm about another cargo ship. Looking at the shape through the binoculars, Ismail had declared it to be a cloud left over from the storm. But Mas had waved his gun around and forced them to chase the phantom. In a way, Ismail was grateful for the mistake—it had reduced Mas's standing among the men. But he had been careful not to gloat. He had to keep them together to maintain command.

When the light began to fade from the horizon, Ismail cut off the motor, and the skiff slowed to a stop. He found a flashlight in the bottom of the boat and turned it on, spreading his fingers across the lens to diffuse the glow.

"I know you're hungry," he said. "I am, too. We should

pray the *Maghrib* like we were home. We need Allah's help to stay alive."

Sondare, the most pious of the group, agreed first. The others soon followed. Their religious commitment was dubious—especially that of Osman and Guray, whose pastimes on land were drinking liquor, chewing *qat*, and fornicating. But all of them had been raised Muslim, and they knew the prayers.

"Who will lead us?" Mas inquired, speaking the question as a challenge.

Ismail opened his hands in invitation. "How about you? You know the *takbir*."

Mas's eyes reflected his surprise, along with a hint of fear.

"No, no," Liban said. "You should lead us. You know the entire Quran."

"Liban is right," Guray chimed in. "Allah will listen to Afyareh more than any of us."

Ismail waited until the vote was unanimous. Then he pointed north. "Mecca is that way. There is not enough room to stand or kneel, but we can bow our heads."

As the skiff rocked on the gentle swells, he closed his eyes and pictured his father, Adan, as he was in the world before—the handsome, angular face, accentuated by a traditional mustache and beard; the intense brown eyes veiled by rimless spectacles; the smiles that came so unexpectedly and disappeared so suddenly that you missed them if you weren't paying attention. He heard the echo of his father's voice, the way Adan had taught them the suras. Ismail remembered the smell of frankincense burning in the dining room, the way his mother, Khadija, had created a haven of peace in a city torn apart by violence. It was there in that small house overlooking the Mogadishu airport and the sea that Adan had first permitted Ismail to lead the prayers. He was fifteen—in his father's estimation "a man becoming." Ismail had been ready then, as he was now.

He began to recite the *takbir* in a low, even tone. "*Allah-hu-akbar* . . . God is great. I bear witness that there is no god but God. I bear witness that Muhammad is the messenger of God."

His men recited the words with him, their voices blending together in a harmony of half whispers. When they reached the *sadja* where they would normally prostrate themselves, they bent at the waist and lowered their foreheads as far as they were able.

"Glorified is my Lord, the Highest," they said, repeating the refrain twice more and then sitting straight again. "I ask Allah, my Lord, to cover up my sins, and unto him I turn repentant."

In time, Ismail spoke the peace and brought the *Maghrib* to a close. He opened his eyes and saw the effect the prayers had on the group. The men's bodies were relaxed, their faces serene. It was the result Ismail had hoped for. Unity, his father had taught him, was fostered by brotherhood, and no brotherhood was more durable than the community of faith.

"We've made good progress today," Ismail said, taking advantage of the moment. "But we still have forty hours of travel time left. We need to keep moving."

The men began to murmur their discontent. They would never admit they were afraid, but Ismail could see the anxiety written in the shadow lines around their eyes. It wasn't just the sea that scared them; it was the prospect of navigating by the GPS unit none of them knew how to use. Ismail used their fear to his advantage.

"I'll stand the night watch," he said. "But I need one of you to keep me awake."

"I'll do it," Liban volunteered. "We can talk."

"Good," Ismail replied. "The rest of you get some sleep. But have your guns ready. With the moon so bright, we might see a ship."

The hours of darkness crept by on the quiet ocean. The stars in the west set and the moon rose behind them, silvering the water and painting the skiff and its sleeping bodies with a ghostly light. Ismail and Liban talked until they grew tired of their own voices. Then they lapsed into silence and listened to the steady drone of the engine as it converted petrol into miles.

Just before midnight, the skiff glided across a patch of bioluminescence. For minutes, the sea sparked and glowed a mesmerizing green. Ismail let off the throttle and dipped his hand in the brilliant water. Liban watched him carefully—his superstition plain—until he saw that Ismail's hand was still whole. Then he joined Ismail on the transom and stirred the phosphorescent water with his toes.

"This is amazing," Liban said in wonderment.

"It's beautiful," Ismail replied.

After a while, they set off again. Ismail turned on the GPS unit and fixed their position. Then he found the constellation Cassiopeia and aimed the skiff just west of the brightest star. A verse came to him from the Quran: *He makes the stars as lights for you, that you may guide yourselves through the dark spaces of land and sea.* He took some comfort in the words, but not much. His throat was parched, and he felt the ache of exhaustion in every muscle. He wanted nothing more than to lie down and dream of Yasmin and the day he would take her back from the hands that stole her.

He grabbed the water jug and touched it to his lips. The feeling of refreshment was exquisite but fleeting, and it wasn't long before he began to drift. He blinked his eyes and looked at Liban, hoping to start another conversation, but his friend had fallen asleep.

To keep himself awake, Ismail began to work mathematics equations in his head—first multiplication, then division. His exertions only delayed the inevitable. Weariness encircled him and laid its siege, waiting until at last his eyelids fell and his internal defenses crumbled before overtaking him and drawing him into sleep.

It was awhile before he woke again. He was on the bench beside Liban, his head resting on a piece of tarpaulin. The motor was off and the skiff adrift, its bow pointed north.

He didn't recall pushing the kill switch or lying down, but he must have done it. He stood up and took a deep breath to clear away the cobwebs in his mind. His companions were still slumbering—most were curled up on the bottom of the boat. The moon was well past its zenith, the air cooler and still clear.

Ismail powered on the GPS unit. The clock on the display informed him that it was just after 01:20, local time. He fixed their position and found that the current had driven them two and a half miles to the west and two tenths of a mile closer to Mahé. His back was sore and his mouth sticky with thirst. He took a swig from the water jug. Then he picked up the binoculars and swept the horizon. The GPS unit, which he'd bought secondhand in Galkayo, offered almost no detail about the ocean. There could be shoals or even an island nearby, and the display wouldn't show it.

It took his brain a moment to register the anomaly. The sea to the west was a patchwork of reflected moonlight. There were dark lines between the glistening waves, but there was something else—a void of some kind. He examined it carefully and saw it resolve into a shape. His heartbeat quickened. The shape was actually a silhouette with a pole on top. *Is that a sailboat?* he wondered. *But where are the sails?* His thoughts went into overdrive when he saw the boom extending from the base of the mast. *They're under power and running without lights. They're trying not to be seen.*

He watched the sailboat motor across the silver sea. It was a small craft with a single mast—not a valuable prize, but a prize nonetheless. In the midst of his elation, he felt a pang of shame. He knew that what he was about to do was *haram*, forbidden by God. He remembered the lessons his father had taught him about divine justice and the wronging of the soul. Allah was merciful, but men by their evil acts delivered themselves to ruin.

For a brief moment, Ismail considered letting the boat go. Better to suffer the agonies of death, Adan had said, than to become a companion of the eternal fire. But his father was gone, cut down by the men whose teachings he had decried. His mother was gone, too, and probably dead. Of their family only Yasmin remained, and she had been taken by the devil himself. In the nightmare of the present, the rules of conscience no longer apply. There was only one way forward—the way of the gun.

"*Astagfirullah*," he said quietly, begging Allah's forgiveness. Then he shook Liban's shoulder. "Get up! I see a ship."

Liban grunted and squinted at him through sleep-laden eyes. "What? Where?"

"There!" Ismail replied, pointing west.

Liban took the binoculars and stared into the distance. "It's a sailboat," he said, tensing visibly.

"Help me wake the others," Ismail said, prodding Osman and Dhuuban.

The men struggled into sitting positions, shaking their heads as if casting off the cords of sleep. They passed the binoculars around, and their eyes grew wide when they sighted the boat. They began to whisper excitedly among themselves.

"A ship!" they exulted. "We're saved!"

"Quiet!" Ismail hissed. "Get your weapons ready. But do not shoot unless I give the order. No one is going to die tonight—neither you nor the sailors on that boat. Is that clear?"

He saw nods all around. They were with him, even Mas. He was their leader, the sailboat his prize. He spoke unequivocally: "This is our chance. There won't be another."

Then he turned and started the motor.

DANIEL

A strange vibrato sound interrupted Daniel's dream. He was climbing a cliff surrounded by snowcapped mountains. He didn't know why he was there, but he didn't question it. Vanessa was calling to him from above, her face obscured by clouds. Quentin was below him, playing out the rope. A breeze was blowing, but it was muted somehow, a murmur in the preternatural scene. The buzzing noise stood out, then faded as quickly as it came. Daniel's unconscious mind tried gamely to find a place for it, but the disturbance was enough to disrupt the flow of the dream.

He rolled onto his side and opened his eyes halfway. The cabin was dark as pitch. He touched the bulkhead beside him and remembered where he was—the aft berth of the *Renaissance*. He heard the rumble of the engine through the soundproofing he had installed in the retrofit. The glowing hands of his dive watch told him that he had twenty minutes to sleep before he had to spell Quentin. He listened for a few seconds and heard nothing amiss. Then he closed his eyes again and dozed off quickly.

The next sound, when it came, tore apart the night.

He sat up straight, his nerves ablaze, as the clamor of automatic gunfire pierced his ears. There were multiple guns, and they were close.

He heard the shouts next, in high-pitched English: "Captain, don't be afraid! We don't want to hurt you! We just want the ship!"

He moved without thought, his reflexes driving him out of the cabin and into the nav station. He switched on AIS, sending out a signal with their course and speed. Then he pressed the unmarked red button. It was a safeguard of last resort, something he never imagined he would have to use. It felt inconsequential beneath his fingertips, but it was the only thing that could save them now.

His next instinct was to rescue Quentin. He launched himself up the companionway and found his son standing in the cockpit with his hands in the air. Daniel saw the skiff closing in from astern, dark faces and gun barrels glinting in the moonlight. He spoke to Quentin with a firmness that belied his terror.

"Don't move. Do whatever they say."

The hijacking was a disorderly affair. The pirates swarmed over the gunwales of the sailboat as if they were scaling the ramparts of a fort, shouting lustily and pointing their guns in every direction. They were dressed in Western-style T-shirts, shorts, and flip-flops in various stages of wear. A large-boned Somali lashed a towline from the skiff to a cleat on the *Renaissance*. A second pirate—tall and clever-looking—trained his gun on the Parkers. The other Somalis took flashlights from their pockets and went below to ransack the saloon.

In the melee, only one pirate seemed composed. He was young and handsome, with high cheekbones and eyes that burned with transparent intelligence. He was wearing a red Nike T-shirt, khaki cargo shorts, and Velcro sandals. He slung his weapon over his shoulder and sat down on one of the benches, gesturing for Daniel and Quentin to join him. Daniel swallowed the lump in his throat and nodded, moving slowly to avoid provoking the guard. Quentin sat beside him.

"I am Afyareh," the pirate said in English. "I am sorry for this." He waved his hand toward the galley where his companions were raiding the refrigerator. "They are hungry. I will make sure they leave your belongings alone." He looked at Daniel with understanding. "I know this is difficult for you. But you have nothing to fear from us. We are not killers. We are here for money, nothing more."

You're bandits and thieves, Daniel thought angrily, the adrenaline still surging through his veins. But he kept his expression passive. "What are you going to do with us?"

"We will take you to Somalia," Afyareh replied. "And then we will talk to your family and see about a price. If they are reasonable, it will be over soon. If not . . ." He allowed the threat to hang in the air, then shrugged. "But America is the land of *caano*—milk. I'm sure they will comply."

How does he . . . ? Daniel thought in confusion. Then he remembered the flag on the mast. The stars and stripes were a dead giveaway. He felt nausea swirling in his stomach.

"The US government will never let you get away with this," he said, injecting steel into his voice. "They'll treat you like terrorists. It would be much better if you let us go."

The pirate raised an eyebrow. "Your government is not omnipotent. If they were, they would have captured General Aideed in 1993 and ended the war that made all of us beggars."

Daniel was taken aback. Everything he had read about Somali pirates suggested they were illiterate peasants, trigger-happy and perpetually high on *qat*. Their masters were the educated ones, not the grunts in the boats. "Where are you from?" he asked, hoping to buy more time. Every second that passed took them farther away from Somalia.

The pirate tilted his head. "I am from many places. But enough talk. Now we go."

He stood and moved to the helm, studying the throttle and controls. He took a device out of his pocket and stared at the glowing screen. *GPS*, Daniel thought. *He's deciding on a heading.* Seconds later, the pirate pushed a button and nodded as the rudder turned five degrees to starboard. He pushed the button repeatedly and the *Renaissance* came about, passing through the eye of the wind. When the boat was pointing just west of north, he shoved the throttle to the stops.

"It handles well," he said to Daniel. "And you have plenty of fuel. That makes everything easier. Now çome. Let's save your boat from my men."

They went below—Afyareh first, then Daniel and Quentin, and finally their guard. Daniel switched on the lights and was shocked by what he saw. The galley was a disaster. The cabinets and refrigerator had been tossed. Milk cartons were upended in the sink. Food was strewn across the countertops. A pirate was scooping peanut butter out of the container with his hand. Another was chugging water straight from the bottle.

To his surprise, Afyareh seemed just as angry. He began to shout in Somali, waving his arm around and pointing at the mess. Most of the pirates looked ashamed, but one of them—a young man with ermine-like eyes and a cut on his cheek—yelled back. Afyareh fixed the pirate with a wintry stare and spoke a few words in a low tone. It must have been a question, because all of the pirates nodded except the man with the cut. The man looked around in disgust and barked what sounded like a curse.

Silence descended on the saloon. Afyareh picked up a wedge of cheese and broke it into chunks, passing one to each of the pirates. He examined the refrigerator and took out a package of deli meat and a loaf of bread. He handed out slices of bread and meat to his companions, then took the bottle of water and wiped the mouth on his T-shirt before taking a long drink.

He looked at Daniel. "From now on, my men will behave." He pointed at the dining booth. "You will sit there. Liban and Sondare will sit with you." He gestured at the tall man who had guarded them in the cockpit and a gangly kid with eager eyes. "They will not disturb you when you sleep. If you need to use the bathroom, they will accompany you. In the morning, you can cook breakfast. I have questions about the boat, but they can wait until tomorrow."

With that, Afyareh turned to address his men again. Daniel slid into the back of the booth while Quentin took a seat on one of the wings. Daniel examined his son carefully. He was clearly scared, but his eyes were still bright. He hadn't withdrawn like the afternoon before. Daniel felt the pride again, along with something more elemental—love.

"It's going to be okay," he said quietly. "They're not here to hurt us."

Quentin looked suddenly guilty. "I fell asleep on watch. I'm sorry."

Daniel shook his head. "It was better that way. You didn't resist." He saw Liban moving toward them and lowered his voice. "I got a message out."

Quentin's eyes widened. "SSAS?"

Daniel nodded almost imperceptibly.

"No talk, Captain," Liban said in heavily accented English, taking a seat on the starboard bench a few feet away, his AK-47 stretched across his lap. "Sleep."

Daniel complied without a word, lying down and

bending at the waist to conform to the shape of the booth. Quentin followed his lead on the opposite side. There was just enough room for them to rest in relative comfort. Daniel closed his eyes and imagined Vanessa and his parents on the other side of the world, oblivious to the peril that had befallen them, but not for much longer. Afyareh and his band of brigands had no idea of the storm they had unleashed or the power of the people who would move heaven and earth to contain it.

II

PROOF OF LIFE

We know what dark persuasions
dwell in the soul of man;
for we are closer to him
than his jugular vein.
—THE QURAN, SURA 50

VANESSA

Vanessa's iPhone vibrated on her nightstand just after midnight. She was in the bathroom brushing her teeth and paid little attention to it. Chad Forrester was the doctor on call, which meant that she was off-limits to after-hours inquiries. It was a boundary she had established early in her practice after getting one too many nonemergent "emergency" calls from parents of young children worried that some run-of-the-mill event—a fever spike, a bout of diarrhea—might turn catastrophic.

She put her toothbrush back in the stand and went to the kitchen to get a glass of water, Skipper trailing dutifully in her wake. She was bone-tired after a long day at the office, but in her heart she felt invigorated. All day she had replayed the Beethoven in her head, feeling the Bissolotti vibrating in her hands, the bow dancing in Kreisler's run of sixteenths. The music had reawakened something in her—a sense of possibility. She'd printed out her airline ticket and placed it on her desk at the office beside the photo of Daniel and Quentin. There was something about seeing her name and destination in ink that confirmed that what had happened inside of her was real.

She checked the security system to ensure the house was locked and then returned to her bedroom, water glass in hand. The noise machine was her next stop. She had spent her early years in big cities and couldn't fall asleep in silence. The unit sat atop an antique rolltop desk that Daniel had inherited from his grandfather. After powering it on, she gave Skipper a pat and turned off all the lights in the house by way of a master switch. She climbed into bed and pulled the comforter up to her chin, imagining Daniel at the helm of the *Renaissance*, surrounded by the sea and the dawn—

Suddenly, her iPhone vibrated again.

You have to be kidding, she thought. She almost ignored it, but curiosity got the best of her. She picked up the phone and frowned. The caller was Curtis Parker—Daniel's father. It was his third attempt. He'd also sent her a text message: Vanessa, call me as soon as you get this.

She felt a twinge of concern. She sat up in bed and called him back. "Curtis? What's going on?"

"Vanessa." As soon as he said her name, she knew something was wrong. There was a slight tremor in his voice—an incongruity she had never heard before. "It's Daniel and Quentin."

Her heart fell like a stone into a well. "What happened?"

Curtis took a pensive breath. "There's no easy way to say this, so I'll just say it. They were hijacked by pirates. I just talked to my friend Frank Overstreet, the assistant secretary of defense. The Navy confirms it. The sailboat is on a course for Somalia."

A wave of dizziness swept over her, and she almost had to put down the phone. "How did this happen?" she demanded at last, trying to make sense of the nonsensical.

"I don't know."

She felt the sudden urge to move. She stood from the bed and walked down the hallway to the darkened living room, stopping just short of the windows. Skipper followed her and lay down at her feet. "How did you find out?" she asked eventually, staring out at the night.

Curtis spoke with quiet gravity. "I got an e-mail from the *Renaissance* late in the day. It said they'd been hijacked. I called Frank right away, and he said the naval authorities in Bahrain received the same message. The Seychelles sent a plane just after dawn. The sails were down, and the yacht was under power. They were towing a skiff with an outboard motor. The pilot tried to hail them on the radio but got no response. I waited to call you until I heard about the overflight. There's no question now."

Vanessa shook her head in complete confusion. "How did he have time to e-mail you?"

Curtis hesitated. "It was an automatic message. Daniel installed a warning system before he left. All he had to do was press a button."

Vanessa's bewilderment transmuted into betrayal. "He never told me that."

"He thought it would only worry you," Curtis said, his

tone defensive. "The risk was purely theoretical. Neither of us expected it to materialize."

In an instant, Vanessa felt all the old resentments again. *Of course he kept it from me. He always treated me like a child, making decisions for me, trying to preempt my anxiety.* She felt a pain in her chest. It began at the center and radiated outward to her limbs. She took a seat on the couch and forced herself to breathe. The pain was an alarm bell, an indication she was about to slip into panic. Skipper padded over and put his nose on her hand. She scratched his head and waited for her heartbeat to stabilize.

"Okay," she said at last. "Tell me what to do."

Curtis sighed with relief. "Everything I'm about to say is confidential. I got it from Frank on the condition that we would tell no one. That means Aster, too."

She felt the world shrinking around her. "All right."

"This is what I know. The Navy had a cruiser making a port call in the Seychelles. It's already been dispatched. It should arrive at their position in a few hours. There's a group at the White House called MOTR—the Maritime Operational Threat Response Center. They've had two meetings already. This is a top priority. They're going to do everything they can to get them back."

Vanessa was overwhelmed. "What does that mean exactly?"

"There's a limit to what they can tell us. A lot of this is classified. But Frank mentioned the SEALs and the FBI."

The SEALs, Vanessa thought. *The FBI.* She could just see it—men in black swarming the sailboat, guns blazing, and Daniel and Quentin in the center of it all. She felt sick.

"What about a ransom?" she asked. "Don't they just want money?"

"I asked Frank the same thing. He said a ransom is not the government's objective."

Vanessa felt a spurt of anger. "What the hell is *that* supposed to mean? The only thing I care about is getting my son back." Tears sprang to her eyes. "Tell me what *we're* supposed to be doing right now, what *I'm* supposed to do."

Curtis exhaled. "As soon as I hang up, I'm going to make a few calls. There are people in private security who have experience with these matters. They can offer us independent advice." He paused. "Also, I think it would be best if you had some company."

Aster would know how to support me, Vanessa thought. "What do you have in mind?"

Curtis's voice softened. "Yvonne already packed a bag. I don't know how long this is going to last, but we're going to need each other."

It was the most vulnerable thing he had ever said, and Vanessa saw the wisdom in it. As much as she hated Curtis's paternalism, he was a man of exceptional skill and experience who knew everyone in the DC power machine. He was exactly the kind of advocate Daniel and Quentin needed. And Vanessa adored her mother-in-law. Yvonne was a strong woman who had made the best of fifty years of marriage to an egotistical husband and forty-three years of motherhood to an egocentric son, both of whom gave her little in return. It would be good to have her around.

"I'll get the guest wing ready," she said, grateful she didn't have to bear the burden alone.

PAUL

"Cheers," Paul Derrick said, taking the cappuccino from his sister's outstretched hand. It was half past six in the morning, and he was sitting on the terrace watching the seaside hamlet of Clifton come alive in the spotless dawn. He had no plans for the day, but that was the point, or so Megan kept insisting. As it happened, he felt indolent, but he knew it was an illusion—a by-product of adrenaline withdrawal. *Humans are meant to relax*, he repeated to himself. *You're a human. Ergo . . .*

"Every time I come here, I wonder why I go back," Megan said, sitting across from him at a café table and taking a sip of her frothy mocha. They had always been early risers. Her husband, Simon, on the other hand, loved to sleep in.

He looked at her closely and grinned. "No, you don't."

She laughed and rolled her eyes. "Talking to you is like talking to my conscience. It's much easier to get things past

Simon."

He shrugged. "You're the one who invited me."

"And I'm so glad you came." She spoke the words with feeling. "You're right, I don't know what I'd do with myself on a permanent holiday."

"A purgatory in paradise," Paul teased. "But the coffee would be good."

It was one of the many ways he and Megan were facsimiles of one another. They were John Derrick's children: passionate, driven, and restless—some, like Simon, would say pathologically so. Their father had been as compulsive as he was brilliant, a homicide detective whose deductive powers had been legendary in the Washington Metropolitan Police Department. He had also been a human steamroller, running over his emotionally sensitive wife and oldest son with devil-may-care cruelty and provoking a tragedy that had shocked their community. Their genetic inheritance was a ghost in their psyche. They hadn't spoken of their father in many years. They had buried their memories along with him.

"Are you happy, Paul?" Megan asked, turning the tables on him.

"Sure. It's hard to beat the view."

"That's not what I mean."

He looked at her thoughtfully. "If I'm honest, I'm not sure what happy is. Satisfied, yes. I do something that matters. So do you. Isn't that enough?"

She nodded. "It's what gets me up in the morning."

"Speaking of morning, what are we going to do today?"

Her hazel eyes sparkled. "You're already tired of sitting still?"

Just then, he heard the ringtone on his FBI-issued BlackBerry. He glanced at Megan and saw the dejection in her eyes. *Don't answer it*, he could hear her saying. *They can wait.* But he had to answer it. It was who he was. He picked up the phone and saw that the caller ID had been blocked. There was only one person at the Bureau who had the audacity to interrupt his vacation.

"Hey, Boss," he said, connecting the line, "you're up late."

"Dammit, Paul," replied Brent Frazier, the director of the Crisis Negotiation Unit and Paul's closest friend. "How do you always know it's me?"

"I think it's the smell," Paul joked, putting his hand over the phone and whispering, "I'm sorry," to his sister. She accepted the apology with a resigned smile and went inside.

"I was really hoping I wouldn't have to bother you over there," Frazier began.

"That's little consolation when you're doing it," Paul said, enjoying the chance to rib his friend. In truth, he felt relieved. That Frazier had called meant something bad had happened, which, in Paul's world of crisis management, meant something good.

"We have a situation in the Indian Ocean. Two sailors from Annapolis—father and son—were hijacked by Somali pirates. They're VIPs. Have you heard of Parker and Jones?"

"The law firm," Paul replied. "They're heavyweights."

"Exactly. Curtis Parker is the quintessential Washington

insider. He was first in his class at the Naval Academy and served as a flag aide on the Joint Staff before going to Columbia Law School and joining the firm his father founded. He took it over a decade ago and built it into the premier regulatory compliance firm in DC. His son, Daniel, and his grandson, Quentin, are on the boat."

Paul took this in. "When did it happen?"

"A few hours ago. Apparently, they sent an SOS to the right people. MOTR has the ball. The president has been briefed. DOD is in charge. The Navy has ships en route. There's a cruiser—the *Gettysburg*—nearby that's going to take the lead. They have an aircraft carrier and another cruiser coming from the Gulf of Aden. They want a negotiator on the *Gettysburg* to assist."

"A negotiator," Paul said. "As in one."

Frazier grunted. "That was DOD's idea. They're sending a SEAL team from Virginia. A couple of the SEALs have negotiation training. They want FBI support."

DEVGRU, Paul thought. It was an acronym for the Naval Special Warfare Development Group, or SEAL Team Six. "I'm surprised they're asking for us."

"They're not asking for us. They're asking for you."

Paul pursed his lips. "And you said?"

"I told them you don't work alone and you don't play second fiddle. The minimum team we send into the field is a primary and a coach."

"And the guys from DOD bought that?"

"No," Frazier admitted. "The State Department pushed them on it and the White House agreed. Everybody knows you're the best we've got. If you're not there and this thing goes south, the president will be left with questions he can't answer."

Paul was intrigued. "Who recommended me at State?"

"Amanda Wolff in the Bureau of Political-Military Affairs. She knows this issue better than anyone else in the government."

Paul filed the name away in his brain, thinking, *I'll have to send her a thank-you note.* "So here's the team," he said. "Rodriguez comes with me, along with the best Somali linguist we have. I assume New York Field will send somebody from ERT."

ERT was short for Evidence Response Team, a collection of agents specially trained to manage crime scenes. The agent would come from New York because that was the field division that handled crimes against Americans in Africa and the Indian Ocean.

"Yeah," Frazier confirmed. "They're also sending a couple of guys with interrogation experience and an SSA to coordinate the investigation." An SSA was a supervisory special agent. "But you don't have to worry about them. You answer to me."

"Tell me more about the Parker family. I want assets on all the key players."

"By my count there are three: Vanessa Parker, the wife and mother of the hostages, and Curtis and Yvonne Parker. They all live in Annapolis. Vanessa's stepfather is in New York. Her mother died a few years ago. We don't know who her father is."

"Send Mary to Annapolis," Paul said. "Vanessa will trust her. Let's leave her stepfather alone unless she brings him into the loop."

"I was thinking the same thing," Frazier affirmed.

Paul walked into the villa and set his coffee cup in the sink. Megan was reading on the couch. He met her gaze, and she shook her head, laughter in her eyes.

"How quickly can you get me out there?" he asked Frazier, heading for the stairs.

"We booked you a commercial ticket to the Seychelles via Johannesburg. Your flight leaves in two hours. A Navy helicopter will shuttle you to the *Gettysburg*. You should arrive by 21:00. We'll send your team by military transport. They should be on the ship by midmorning tomorrow."

In his guest room, Paul went to the closet and took out his duffel bag, which he had never unpacked. At home he kept a jump bag in the trunk of his car, ready to go at a moment's notice. On vacation he simulated the jump bag by living out of his duffel. *I really need to learn how to take a vacation*, he thought, changing out of his polo and shorts and putting on his field attire—Royal Robbins 5.11 Tactical pants, a loose-fitting white shirt, and Merrell trail shoes.

"I need detailed profiles on all the people in the command structure," he said to Frazier. "The captain of the *Gettysburg*, the commander of the SEAL team, and anybody who'll be calling the shots back home. I also need dossiers on Daniel and Quentin Parker and a memo about Somali piracy."

"We're already working on the memo," Frazier replied.

"The ship's captain and the hostages will be easy. The Spec Ops guys will be harder."

"Talk to the White House. If they want me there, they'll get me the information."

Frazier took a breath. "I'll see what I can do. As it happens, I'm heading down to Dam Neck in the morning. I'll be in the command center for the duration."

Paul whistled. "DEVGRU's crib. Have fun babysitting."

Frazier laughed. "I'd rather be on the ship with you."

Paul felt the familiar rush of action. "When this is over, I'm taking a month off, and I'm going to leave my BlackBerry in your office."

"Roger that," Frazier replied and hung up.

Paul stuffed the dress clothes Megan had brought him in the duffel and zipped it closed. Then he collected his backpack from beside the bed and carried everything downstairs. He found Megan waiting for him in the foyer, keys in hand.

"How long do you have?" she asked, leading him down the walk to her black Porsche Boxster S convertible—her rental of choice in Cape Town. Like her brother, she had always had a fascination with speed. Unlike Paul, she could afford it.

"Not long," he replied, climbing into the low-slung sports car.

"Perfect," she said and gunned the engine.

The dossiers arrived by encrypted e-mail just before Paul boarded the South African flight to Johannesburg. Frazier promised to send the piracy memo during the layover at OR Tambo. Paul saved the profiles on his laptop and walked down the Jetway to the plane. His seat was in the last row, but he had the cluster all to himself, which meant no one would bother him.

The plane took off on time and climbed into the cerulean sky. Paul put a pair of noise-canceling headphones over his ears, turned on Mendelssohn's *Songs without Words*, and opened the dossier of Captain Gabriel Masters, the commander of the USS *Gettysburg*.

Masters had been in command of the guided-missile cruiser for eighteen months. It was his first sea tour after being promoted to the rank of captain. Paul skimmed his résumé and focused on the nuances that revealed the man behind the uniform. Masters was a scholar as well as a surface warfare officer, holding a bachelor's degree in history from the Naval Academy and a master's in strategic studies from the Naval War College. He had also published a book called *The Weinberger Doctrine: Military Strategy and Democratic Consensus*. After perusing the introduction, which Frazier had included, Paul inferred that Masters was a warrior with a conscience, a man who saw force as a counterbalance to the plethora of threats in the post–Cold War environment but who understood the perils of favoring military solutions over diplomacy. Paul liked him already.

He opened the second dossier—that of Captain Frank Redman, the SEAL team commander—and regarded it in annoyance. It was under a page in length, a highly redacted summary of Redman's pedigree. *I have the clearances*, Paul thought. *They just didn't want to give it to me.* He read the document carefully, searching for clues. An ROTC candidate at VMI, Redman had entered the Navy and gone straight to SEAL training. After a sniper tour with SEAL Team Four, he completed the Green Course and joined DEVGRU, working his way up the ranks until he took command of Red Squadron. It was clear to Paul that Redman was a superlative soldier. But his personality remained a mystery. What kind of heartbeat animated this man-turned-lethal-weapon? How did he think about his adversaries? What perspective did he have of his role in the wider world?

The third dossier was for Rear Admiral Jonathan Prince. It was even leaner than Redman's, setting forth only his education, a few career highlights, a carefully packaged sound bite about his history in the teams, and his current commission as commander of DEVGRU. Paul shook his head, feeling like Dorothy on the yellow brick road. Redman might command the boots on the ground, but Prince was the Wizard of Oz. Unfortunately, the dossier revealed nothing about the man behind the magic, and that was a problem. *Appearances are like used car deals,* John Derrick had taught his son, holding up an article about John Anthony Walker, the Navy warrant officer turned Soviet spy. *The only way to test a man's character is to get under the hood.* It was one of the few truths Paul regarded as gospel. He had learned it from Dr. Jekyll himself.

As the plane flew over the arid expanse of the Karoo, Paul turned his attention to Daniel and Quentin Parker. Ordinarily, kidnapping victims were prisoners of the hostage bubble with little say in their fate. Occasionally, however, they played a larger role, improving their chances by connecting with their captors or endangering themselves by being cavalier. Everything in Daniel Parker's background suggested that he would play it safe. As a young man, he had followed the trail his father and grandfather had blazed with only a single deviation—his decision to study philosophy at Boston College. But there was a discontinuity in his profile: the brute fact of the circumnavigation. Sailing around the world was hardly an adventure for the risk-averse.

The *Capital Gazette*, a local Annapolis paper, had done a feature on the Parkers before they set sail. It was short on insight and long on romanticisms, but Paul read between the lines and saw things the reporter missed. Chief among them was the timing of the voyage. According to the story, Quentin had attended Annapolis public schools since kindergarten. Why then had his parents suddenly removed him from the system in the middle of high school? If he wanted to sail around the world, he could have taken a gap year after graduation. In Paul's experience, abrupt changes in long-standing patterns weren't compelled by deliberation. They were compelled by crisis.

Also, what did it say about the state of Daniel Parker's marriage that he had left on a seventeen-month voyage without his wife? According to the story, Vanessa wasn't a fan of offshore sailing and had a busy medical practice—both sensible excuses, but illuminating for what they omitted. Wouldn't a wife and mother saddened by the prospect of such a long separation have planned to meet up with her husband and son at least once in a year and a half? Yet she mentioned no such plans to the reporter. Her only quote in the story was remarkably detached: "Of course I'll miss them, but Daniel and Quentin are exceptional sailors. I have no doubt they'll make it home again."

Paul looked out the window at the desert far below and imagined Daniel Parker aboard the *Renaissance*, the shock of the hijacking giving way to the vacuum of captivity, the unknowns of the future as haunting as ships' bells in the fog of submerged fear. *You've been running from something*, Paul surmised, *something big enough that it inspired you to leave your cloister and live on the edge. But you've also been running toward something—the inevitable homecoming. Who's waiting for you there? Is Vanessa keeping the candle burning? Or is it your father and your firm? How far will you go to get back to them?*

These were the questions Daniel had to answer to keep his hope—and his son—alive.

ISMAIL

Ismail stood in the cockpit of the *Renaissance*, scanning the horizon with his binoculars. The equatorial sun was high in the sky, and its rays were sizzling his skin. The sea stretched before him into the trackless distance, the line drawn by the planet's curve unbroken by the shadow of a ship. But a ship was coming. About this he had no doubt.

It was almost noon, nearly five hours after the coast guard plane from the Seychelles had appeared overhead and attempted radio contact. The overflight had terrified his men and thrown Ismail into a silent rage. His oversight was inexcusable. In his exhaustion after the hijacking, he had allowed himself the luxury of sleep before checking the sailboat's instruments. If he had turned off the AIS beacon earlier, the pilot probably wouldn't have found them. But he had no idea that the Captain had gotten a warning out or that the authorities would mobilize so quickly.

He had held it together well enough to deceive his companions. With emphasis from his gun, he'd forced the Captain to confess to sending out the secret message and then added an embellishment to the translation. His men thought the *message* had led the plane to the sailboat, not AIS, and had thus poured out their invective on the Captain. Ismail had stepped in to restrain them, winning points with the Captain and his son—Guray had nicknamed him "Timaha" because of his long hair. But it didn't change the fact that they had been discovered.

They were 850 nautical miles from Somalia and cruising at a speed of six knots with the skiff under tow. Even if the weather held and the seas remained manageable, they wouldn't reach the coast for six days. The ocean was vast, but navy ships traveled fast. It was only a matter of time before one arrived. And when it did, the game would change dramatically. If the Captain and Timaha had been European, the situation would be different. The EU ships almost never intervened. But America was like a leopard in the bush. Their snipers would kill them if they got the chance.

Suddenly, he heard shouts coming from below. He dropped the binoculars and slid down the companionway. He saw the Captain and Timaha huddling in the booth with their hands in the air while Mas glowered at them from behind his gun. The air in the saloon smelled faintly of human waste.

"Daanyeer foosha xun!" Mas was cursing at the Captain. "Ugly monkey!"

"Put your gun down!" Ismail barked in Somali.

"He poisoned our food!" Mas exclaimed.

"I didn't do anything!" the Captain said in English, his voice an octave higher than normal.

Ismail placed his hand on the barrel of Mas's Kalashnikov and forced him to lower it. "Calm down," he ordered in Somali. "What are you talking about?"

He heard a groan and saw that the door to the head was open. He peered in and saw Osman straddling the toilet, facing the wrong direction. "What's wrong with him?"

"That's what I mean!" Mas yelled. "The Captain poisoned our food!"

Ignoring Mas, Ismail asked Liban, "What happened?"

His friend pointed at a box of peanut butter sandwich crackers on the dining table. "Osman said he was hungry, and the Captain gave him those."

Ismail picked up one of the plastic-wrapped packages and waved it at Mas. "Haven't you ever seen these before? They're made in a factory."

Mas's anger turned into confusion. "Then what's wrong with Osman?"

"He must be allergic to peanuts," Ismail replied. It was astonishing how little his crew knew about the world. He turned to the Captain. "I'm sorry for the misunderstanding," he said in English.

"Your men are animals," the Captain hissed. "If you don't control them, you'll never get what you want."

Ismail put on his best disarming smile. "Don't worry about that. They listen to me." He wrinkled his nose at the stench coming from the head. "Do the windows open?"

The Captain shook his head. "The hatches do."

"Good. Please open them. Then you can make us lunch."

After the altercation, Ismail cleared out the saloon and sent everyone but Liban topside to keep watch. When Osman finally emerged from the head, Ismail gave him a lecture about how to use a toilet and ordered him to clean up his mess. Then he sent him on deck with the others. Once the hatches were open, a fresh breeze swept in and cleansed the fetid air. Ismail reclined at the table and watched the Captain and Timaha move around the galley, fixing the midday meal.

"You are making spaghetti?" he asked when he saw the Captain put noodles in a pot.

The Captain nodded. "Isn't that what Somalis eat?"

Ismail was fascinated. "You know our culture?"

"I read it in a book somewhere."

Soon Ismail grew bored of sitting and decided to survey the cabin. It was the first time he had been on a sailboat, and he was astonished by the craftsmanship. Almost all of the surfaces outside the galley were finished with brown wood that gleamed beneath the recessed lights in the coachroof. The portholes were fitted with curtains that diffused the sunlight. The head was outfitted with a sink and a shower as well as a toilet. And the bulkheads were studded with bookshelves filled with tomes ranging from Jules Verne's *Ten Thousand Leagues under the Sea* to Thomas Merton's *Seven Story Mountain*.

Ismail felt a faint echo of grief. His father had been an avid book collector, spending all his spare earnings from the University of Nairobi on rare books. When he moved the family back to Somalia, he had left the bulk of his collection with a cousin. But he had taken his best titles with him to start a library at the secondary school he founded in Mogadishu. It was Adan's conceit and connections that had convinced him he could shield the school and his family from the strife afflicting the city. The warlords had played along for a fee. But then the Shabaab came, and everything changed.

Ismail turned away from the books and opened the door to the front berth. It was stuffed with supplies and gear—bins of toilet paper and paper towels, stores of clothing, packages of dried fruit and pasta, stacks of spare canvas, and sailbags marked with tags that read "Spinnaker" and "Spare Mainsail." The walls of the berth were lined with charts in protective sheaths, and the floor was covered with boxes of fresh vegetables and tropical fruit. Ismail removed three papayas from a mesh bag and returned to the galley, placing them on the countertop.

"The men will enjoy these," he said to the Captain.

The Captain gave him an exasperated look. "Any other requests?"

Ismail shook his head. "That's all."

"Can we play some music?" the Captain said, pointing at speakers embedded in the coachroof. "We usually have it on when we're sailing."

The request took Ismail aback. He hadn't listened to Western music since the attack. The Shabaab had banned it and taken a bullwhip to anyone who defied the prohibition. The beatings were more draconian among the recruits. The Amniyat—Shabaab intelligence—had spies everywhere in the ranks, and Ismail had seen a soldier lashed until he could barely stand for allowing a girl to keep a cell phone with a Western ringtone. In the towns and pirate camps of Galmudug, he had occasionally heard Western songs piped out of ancient boom boxes or computer speakers, but they had still carried the taint of the forbidden. For some reason, he felt differently now.

"Do you have U2?" he asked, and the Captain's face softened.

"Of course," the Captain said, nodding to his son.

Ismail watched in amazement as Timaha took a smartphone from his pocket, tapped the screen, and brought the cabin to life with a pulsing guitar riff. "How did you—" he started to ask, but Bono cut him off, saying, "I will follow." Seconds later, the band came in and the rock star began to sing.

Ismail took a seat in the nav station and listened to the song all the way through. He allowed the music to wash over him and rinse away a layer of filth in his soul, exposing, for a moment at least, the young man he had been before the horror—the devoted son, the doting brother, the university-bound student. He felt the sailboat rocking beneath him, saw the Captain slicing papaya, but for a few precious minutes he was back in Mogadishu, in the bedroom he shared with his brother, listening to songs he had downloaded on his hand-me-down laptop. Yusuf was there beside him, a sloppy grin on his face. Yasmin was on the bed, running fingers through her hair. Their mother, Khadija, was in the kitchen preparing goat stew, and Adan was on the couch, sipping tea.

When the song ended and another began, Ismail found himself smiling. He gestured at the phone in Timaha's hands and spoke the question again: "How did you do that?"

"It's connected by Bluetooth," Timaha said. "There are speakers everywhere, even on deck."

Out of curiosity, Ismail climbed the steps to the cockpit and heard the music over the churn of the engine. Guray, Osman, and Mas were dozing on the benches in the sun, their Kalashnikovs splayed about. Dhuuban and Sondare were resting on the coachroof beneath the boom. He went below again and felt the hunger growling in his belly. He looked around for a diversion and saw that the door to the aft cabin was open. He decided to take a look.

"I thought you were going to leave our belongings alone," the Captain said.

Ismail put up his hands. "Don't worry. I'm just curious."

He stepped through the door and examined the berth. It was shaped like a wedge, with storage lockers near the door and a mattress that tapered down and slid underneath a bulkhead with portholes that looked into the cockpit. The space was confined but not cluttered. The Captain was a meticulous man. His sleeping bag and pillow were carefully arranged on the bed. His reading materials—two books and a magazine—sat neatly on a shelf beside a small lamp, secured by rigid bookends.

On the bulkhead was a digital display. Ismail pressed a button and saw the boat's speed appear on the screen. Another button press and the wind velocity and direction appeared. A third press and he saw the depth under the hull. *This is a fine boat*, Ismail thought. *Not large but well outfitted.* It was a propitious sign. If the Captain had means, then Gedef's negotiator could demand a higher price.

Ismail took one of the books off the shelf. It was called *Sailing Alone around the World* by Joshua Slocum. He read the description and shook his head in fascination. The man had been the first to complete a solo circumnavigation. He put the book back and selected another one. It was a heavy volume with no words on the spine or cover. When he opened it, he realized it was a photo album. He sat on the edge of the bed and flipped through the pages.

He saw the Captain as a young man in a park full of trees. His hair was longer, and he was with a woman with wavy red hair. Then time seemed to pass and their faces aged. Suddenly, they were with other people: a couple with graying hair, a baby who became a toddler and then a boy—Timaha. The settings, too, were different. They were at a lake surrounded by forest; at the helm of a sailboat; on an island with white sand and palm trees; in a concert hall dressed in tuxedos and gowns; skiing on a mountain; swimming in a pool beside an elegant house. *The American dream*, Ismail thought. *A world out of reach for the rest of us.* He looked closely at the red-haired woman—the Captain's wife. When she dressed up, she wore emeralds that complemented her eyes. The older woman had diamonds. The older man wore tailored suits and a gold watch. *They will pay well*, Ismail concluded.

It was then that a thought occurred to him. With Gedef dead, would the investors honor his claim to the commander's share? He knew the answer immediately. *No, they will claim it for themselves, and they will find someone from their clan to replace Gedef.* Ismail felt the bitterness again, along with the doubt he had long repressed. His parents had lived righteously, giving to the needy, being patient in adversity out of their love for God. But God had left them to the dogs. *I will not be wronged like my father was*, Ismail decided, putting the photo album back on the shelf. *Gedef's share is mine. If I have to take it, I will take it. And then I will be finished with this godforsaken business.*

Then I will go and find my sister.

VANESSA

Vanessa Parker rose with the dawn. She had been awake for most of the night, tossing in her bed, but she didn't start the day until the sun's rays peeked through her window curtains, casting gauzy light on the floor. She went to the bathroom and disrobed, leaving her nightclothes on the hook beside the tub. She stepped into the shower and allowed herself five minutes in the stream, as she always did. She was tempted to stay longer, to turn the water hotter and let the fear bleed out of her in pain. But there was an order to her day, even a day like this. And that order she would keep.

For as long as she could remember, she had been a creature of routine. As a child, her rituals had been signposts in a dislocated world, a way of coping with her mother's free-spirited recklessness. Over the years, the rituals had grown into an architecture of life, stabilizing her in the throes of motherhood and giving her direction as her marriage deteriorated. She had often wished she were more adaptable—the sort of person who takes the world as it comes. But her internal compass had been broken long ago. It worked now only in motion, within the arc of a predictable day.

After the shower, she went to her closet and dressed in a blue sweater and white jeans. She wasn't going into the office today—she'd sent Aster an e-mail the night before. She went to the kitchen and found a note from Curtis on the island: *Walking at Greenbury Point. Back soon. Keep the faith.* Skipper trotted to the patio door and she let him out after giving him a good scratch. She turned on the espresso machine Daniel had given her for her birthday and fixed a single shot, which she downed straight. She was relieved to have a quiet moment alone before the security consultant arrived. She needed a little time to find her bearings and prepare for the ordeal ahead.

Her musical workout came next. Much like a trip to the gym, she played exercise pieces in the morning and evocative pieces in the evening—her reward after work. She picked up the Bissolotti and checked its tune, preparing to play Paganini's fourth caprice. But the telephone rang before she could begin. She put the violin down and walked to the office nook in the hallway. The caller ID on the handset read "Blocked." Her heart skipped a beat. It had to be someone official.

She answered the phone, trying to sound normal. "Hello?"

"Mrs. Parker," said a woman in a voice as soothing as a late-night radio DJ. "My name is Mary Patterson, and I'm with the FBI's Crisis Negotiation Unit. I'm sorry to call you at such an early hour, but I wanted to reach you as soon as possible. Do you have a minute?"

Vanessa's heart rate increased. "Of course."

"I understand you've been informed about the situation."

"I have," Vanessa said, struggling to banish the image that had been haunting her since the call came from Curtis—Quentin staring down the barrel of a gun.

"Then you know that we're absolutely committed to bringing your husband and son home."

Vanessa choked up. "Yes."

"Good," Mary said. "The Navy is taking the lead, but my unit is essential to the effort. We've dispatched two negotiators to the scene. My job is to offer you support. We can't predict how this is going to go. But we have a lot of experience. And Paul Derrick, the lead negotiator, is the best there is."

Vanessa felt her head beginning to spin. "What kind of support?"

Mary waited a beat before answering. "If I were in your shoes, I'd feel very much alone right now. Maybe you're stronger than I am, but in a crisis everyone can use a friend. I'm calling in case you'd like a friend in the government. A lot of things are going to happen before this is over, and it can be overwhelming. I'd like to help you make sense of it."

Vanessa took a deep breath and let it out. "We have a security consultant coming over in an hour—Duke Strong from the Sagittarius Group. Will that present a problem?"

"I know Duke," Mary replied without breaking stride. "He was with the Bureau a long time."

Vanessa considered the offer. She had never been one to give her trust away easily, but somehow Mary Patterson had managed to charm her over the telephone. She was obviously a professional, and she had access to the people at the center of the action, which meant she could keep the information flowing. "Are you in the area?" Vanessa asked, telegraphing her consent.

Mary spoke frankly. "I'll be at your house in fifteen minutes."

Vanessa heard the car pull into the drive and opened the door for Mary. She was surprised by what she saw. Instead of a DC power suit, as Vanessa had expected, the FBI agent was wearing jeans, a collared shirt, a hacking jacket, and leather boots. She had a pleasant face, chestnut hair, and expressive hazel eyes that crinkled when she smiled. She met Vanessa in the foyer and offered her a hug, as if they were old friends. From any other stranger, the gesture would have seemed awkward, but Mary did it so naturally that Vanessa accepted it without resistance.

"I'm glad to meet you," Mary said, stepping back. "I'm sorry it's under these circumstances." She glanced at Skipper. "Who do we have here?" she asked, letting the dog lick her hand.

"That's Skipper," Vanessa replied and showed Mary to the couch in the living room. "Would you like some coffee? Espresso, cappuccino, latte—whatever you prefer."

Mary took a seat. "I'd love a cappuccino. I never turn down caffeine."

Vanessa served the drink in a ceramic mug, then sat in her favorite chair. "Daniel's parents are staying in the guest wing. They should be back any minute. Should we wait?"

Mary shrugged. "That's up to you. But I don't mind repeating myself."

Vanessa's nerves made her decision for her. "Go ahead."

Mary smiled compassionately. "I should get one thing out of the way at the start. While my team is a part of the government, we leave matters of foreign policy to the White House and the State Department. Our goal is to negotiate the release of your husband and son. We want nothing more than to bring them back to you as soon as possible."

Vanessa tried to keep her feelings in check, but she felt her eyes moisten. "I'm sorry," she said, embarrassed. "I never imagined this would happen."

Mary shook her head. "That's something else you should know. You never have to apologize. A lot of what we're going to be doing is waiting. It'll get under your skin. It always does. If you find at any point that you need to scream or curse or cry, go right ahead. No emotion is invalid."

Vanessa laughed through her tears. "You sound like a therapist."

Mary's eyes twinkled. "I take that as a compliment. Here's another ground rule. I will never lie to you, and I will never conceal critical information. I'm your advocate for as long as this lasts. If I can't do something you want me to do, I'll tell you why. If there are things Duke Strong can do that

I can't, I'll defer to him. If you ever feel that I'm representing the interests of the government over the interests of your family, I want you to show me the door. Is that fair?"

Vanessa was astonished by Mary's candor. She nodded, her mind abuzz with questions. "Are the SEALs going to try to rescue them? I remember a story from a couple of years ago. I don't recall the captain's name, but they got him out."

"Every case is unique," Mary answered. "With Richard Phillips, there were four pirates and one hostage in a lifeboat. The pirates agreed to put the lifeboat under tow, and the Navy reeled it in until the snipers were in position to take a simultaneous shot. We don't know how many pirates are on the *Renaissance*. A tactical operation might be too risky. That's for the Navy to decide."

Vanessa felt the pressure inside her rising. She remembered her first emergency room rotation as an intern at Georgetown—the intensity of the atmosphere, the litany of need. The panic she felt had almost derailed her medical career. But she had discovered a way out of the badlands. She had to focus on the problem in front of her, nothing else.

She went to the window and looked out at the forest robed in crimson and gold. "If the Navy doesn't rescue them, we'll need to come up with a ransom payment, is that right?"

Mary angled her head thoughtfully. "A lot of overseas kidnappings are resolved by ransom. If it comes to that, Duke Strong can help you more than I can."

Vanessa gave her a quizzical look, and Mary explained herself.

"The government has a bright-line policy when it comes

to hostage scenarios. We will negotiate, but we won't make substantial concessions. If a ransom is the safest way to end a standoff, we won't stand in the way of the family, but we won't touch the bag."

The bag, Vanessa thought. *Yet another debt we'll owe to Curtis and Yvonne.* "Wouldn't it be better if we just paid? That way we can guarantee their safety."

Mary joined her at the window. "Unfortunately, we can't guarantee anything. The pirates are in it for the money, but they're unpredictable. This has to be handled delicately."

Vanessa took a sharp breath. "What you're telling me is that I have to trust people I've never met to decide how to save my son's life?"

Mary met her eyes. "Isn't that what an oncologist would do if I went to him with cancer?"

Vanessa allowed her silence to convey her answer.

"When I said Paul Derrick is the best there is, I didn't just say it to make you feel better. He trained me. I've worked with him for years, and I've seen him do things no one else can do."

Vanessa saw the passion in Mary's eyes. "You're saying I should trust him."

Mary nodded. "If it were my family out there, I'd want them in Derrick's hands."

PAUL

The Airbus A340 landed on the island of Mahé at half past seven in the evening local time. Paul collected his duffel from the overhead compartment, threw his backpack over his shoulder, and left the plane for the warm embrace of the tropical night. A consular officer in a khaki suit met him on the tarmac beneath the glare of floodlights and checked his identification.

"I'm Roy Hartman," he said. "Welcome to paradise. Maybe next time you can enjoy it."

Hartman led him away from the terminal to a gray helicopter waiting in the shadows at the edge of the airfield. Paul guessed it was a Seahawk, the Navy variant of the vaunted Blackhawk. The helicopter's door stood open and its rotors were already spinning. An aircrewman approached Paul through the downdraft and took his duffel, tossing it into the cargo bay. Then he handed Paul a safety harness and helmet with a headset and goggles and watched as Paul put them on.

"I'm Petty Officer Bass," he shouted over the roar of the blades. "It's a hundred and twenty miles to the ship. Flight time is forty-five minutes."

Paul nodded and turned to shake Hartman's hand, reading the consular officer's lips as he yelled, "Best of luck!" Then he followed Bass into the helicopter.

The inside of the Seahawk was like a sardine can— boxy, metallic, and crammed with supports and gear. Paul strapped himself into a seat behind the cockpit and watched as Bass secured the door. He heard the concussive waves of sound increase and saw the pilot and copilot pressing buttons on the control panel between their seats. Suddenly, the pilot took the stick and lifted the helicopter off the ground. They hovered for a moment, and Paul felt the tug of weightlessness. Then gravity returned as they banked to the east and climbed into the night.

The flight to the *Gettysburg* was a singular thing, like a capsule suspended in time. They left the lights of Mahé behind and flew out over the dark expanse of the Indian Ocean. The sea was a pale shadow, the stars above dimmed by the full moon. The noise of the rotors was deafening. Paul imagined the Parkers sailing off into the void. *Madness and magic*, he thought. *Like spacewalking or climbing Everest.* He scanned the horizon for a sign of the cruiser, but the sea was empty. *There's nothing out there for a thousand miles, nothing but a sailboat, a warship, and us.* The scene was so bizarre Paul almost smiled.

At last he caught sight of the *Gettysburg*'s wake, and

then the ship itself, slicing through the water like an arrowhead at the tip of a silver shaft. The Seahawk circled the cruiser once and then descended toward the helipad. The airframe shuddered as the rotor wash ricocheted off the ship, roiling the air around them. Then the wheels touched down, and the helicopter settled onto the deck. Bass wrenched open the door and jumped out, grabbing Paul's duffel and beckoning him to follow.

Paul threw his backpack over his shoulder and trailed Bass to the edge of the helipad and forward to the rosy glow of an open hatch. Beyond the hatch was a hangar bay illumined by red night-lights and housing a second helicopter. A middle-aged man and a young woman, both in dark coveralls, stepped out of the shadows. The man shook Paul's hand while the woman took his duffel.

"Agent Derrick," the man said, raising his voice over the din, "I'm Lieutenant Commander Cardwell, the executive officer. This is Ensign O'Brien." He gestured at the young woman. "She'll be your liaison for as long as you're with us. Captain Masters is waiting for you on the bridge."

Paul nodded and followed them to a hatch that opened onto a passageway lit by crimson bulbs. As soon as Ensign O'Brien sealed the hatch behind them, the noise fell to a whisper. Inside, the cruiser had the feel of a subterranean bunker. Pipes and cables snaked across the ceiling, doors and equipment panels lined the walls, and there were no portholes anywhere. Apart from the muted hum of the engine, the only sound Paul heard was the squeak of their shoes on the floor.

Ensign O'Brien opened one of the doors and turned on a light. The stateroom beyond was outfitted with four racks, a quartet of metal closets, and a compact vanity and sink.

"This is your berthing," said Cardwell as O'Brien deposited Paul's duffel on one of the racks. "Your team will stay with you. The head is down the passageway."

After O'Brien secured the cabin, Cardwell led them forward into the darkened ship. They followed the passageway through a seemingly endless series of hatches—some standing open, some closed—past the officers' wardroom and the admiral's cabin, and around a number of blind corners to a steep, red-lit stairwell with handrails that led upward to the next level. Beside the stairwell was a plaque with three numbers separated by dashes.

"That's the bull's-eye," Cardwell explained. "It tells you where you are on the ship. The first coordinate is the deck; the second is the compartment; the third is your position relative to the centerline. Don't worry about learning it. If you get lost, just ask." He pointed toward the overhang above the stairwell. "Watch your head. The bump can be nasty."

Paul had always prided himself on his fitness, but the ascent to the top deck left him winded. On each level he checked the bull's-eye and saw that the first coordinate had increased from 01 to 02 to 03, and so on. At the summit was a sealed door. Cardwell opened it and ushered them onto the bridge.

Paul was immediately struck by the near-complete absence of light. He blinked until his eyes adjusted to the gloom. There was a navigation station to port with a nautical chart illumined by a red bulb and surrounded by seamen. To starboard were the helm and throttle controls, manned by female sailors staring at a dim display. More seamen stood in the forward part of the bridge, some huddled around faint computer screens, others standing by and watching the gray-black sea.

A tall man approached them. "Agent Derrick. Gabe Masters. Welcome aboard the *Gettysburg*."

"Thanks," Paul said, studying Masters in the shadows. He was handsome in a neighborly sort of way, with close-cropped hair and a carefully trimmed mustache. "So where do we stand?"

"Let me show you." Masters led him to a computer screen on a pedestal in the center of the bridge. He touched the screen and it brightened a bit, revealing an interactive map of the ocean with an array of symbols and notations. "This is us," he said, indicating a green arrow, or vector. "This is the *Renaissance*." He pointed at a red vector. "They don't know we're here yet. We've been on station for seven hours, but we've stayed over the horizon. We put a bird up to get a radar fix. Thankfully, the seas have been calm, and we've been able to track them without difficulty."

Masters zoomed out and drew a line on the screen between the sailboat and the Somali coast. A box appeared with two numbers: 798 and 5.54. "They're on a course for Hobyo in central Somalia. They're making about six knots under power with the pirate skiff in tow. Those numbers in the box are the distance to the coast in nautical miles and ETA in days, assuming nothing changes."

Paul remembered Hobyo from the brief Brent Frazier had sent him. Until a few years ago, it had been a nondescript coastal village three hundred miles north of Mogadishu, its desert climate hospitable only to livestock herding, artisanal fishing, and lobstering. Then came the piracy boom in Puntland farther to the north—young Somalis taking to the high seas in skiffs, hijacking commercial ships, and earning soaring ransoms. In a land as vast and minimally governed as Somalia, it was only a matter of time before a criminal entrepreneur turned hostage taking into a business. This opportunist was Mohamed Abdi Hassan, or Afweyne—"Big Mouth." Trading on his clan network, Afweyne had invited wealthy investors into the piracy fold and pioneered the use of motherships—usually hijacked fishing dhows—to escort the skiffs deep into the ocean. Under his patronage, the rump region of Galmudug had eclipsed Puntland as the capital of the pirate empire, and Hobyo had become its principal lair. That the *Renaissance* pirates were headed there meant they were likely Afweyne's heirs.

"What are your orders at this stage?" Paul inquired, facing Masters again.

"We're to keep our distance until tomorrow when your team and the SEALs arrive. At that point, Captain Redman will take command. I'm sure he'll have ideas about how to handle this."

Paul heard a trace of resentment in Masters's words. It was an innovation of the special-operations age that the SEAL captain would supplant the ship's captain as the on-scene commander, answering not to Navy Central Command in

Bahrain but to the Joint Special Operations Command back home. The streamlined chain of command made operational sense but had ruffled feathers among surface commanders, who felt overshadowed by their sexier counterparts in Spec Ops.

"Do we have any intel on the pirates?" Paul inquired.

Masters zoomed in again on the GPS display. "Sixteen hours before the hijacking, the cargo ship *Jade Dolphin* was attacked by two skiffs carrying six men each. That happened here." He pointed to the first of two "X" symbols on the screen. "One of the skiffs exploded after shooting off an RPG shell. I'm guessing the backblast ignited the engine. The crew of the *Jade Dolphin* saw the second skiff searching the blast area, but they didn't stick around to see who survived." Masters moved his finger to the second "X." "The *Renaissance* was hijacked eighty-four nautical miles northwest. If it's the same gang, there are at least six and as many as a dozen pirates on the sailboat."

Paul digested this. In a hostage crisis, there was an inverse relationship between the number of armed kidnappers and the likelihood that a tactical response would succeed without injury to the hostages. The more bad guys, the more crucial the negotiator became to the ultimate resolution. *The SEALs might not be in the driver's seat after all*, he thought. "Anything else?"

Masters shook his head. "Not until we talk to them."

"I understand there are other ships en route."

Masters zoomed out until they could see the northern Arabian Sea. He pointed to two blue vectors bearing south.

"The *Truman* and the *San Jacinto* will offer support. The SEALs are bringing their own RHIBs. They'll be based on the carrier." RHIB was short for a rigid-hull inflatable boat. "But we're the quarterback. All decision making and communications with the *Renaissance* will happen here."

"I need to see the comms systems in the morning," Paul said. "Everything we say from beginning to end will be recorded. And my team will need a workspace on the bridge."

"We'll put you at the chart table," Masters responded, pointing at a table a few feet away piled high with books and binders. "It'll be cramped, but we'll make room."

Paul walked to the window and stared out at the night sea. He could feel the vibrations of the *Gettysburg* beneath his feet, like the purr of a sleeping tiger. In conventional warfare, the cruiser had no equal, but this would be a contest of wits, not might. All the Star Wars weaponry in the world couldn't save Daniel and Quentin Parker from a pirate's bullet.

"Here," Masters said, handing him a pair of binoculars. "These have night vision."

Paul put the binoculars to his eyes and saw the ocean glowing in a hundred shades of green. He looked toward the horizon and imagined father and son trying to sleep in the midst of a ragtag army of gun-toting mercenaries. The thought turned his stomach.

"I feel terrible for them," Masters said quietly, as if reading Paul's mind. "You plan for everything out here, but you never think something like this is going to happen."

It was then that Paul learned something about Masters,

something that might prove indispensable in the end. This mission had a personal dimension for him. These weren't just any Americans at risk; they were mariners. And mariners were family. Military, civilian, American, Indian, Russian, Chinese, the rules established on land were superseded at sea by a code of honor known to every sailor—that humanity was the highest dignity, and that transcended all.

The first stanza of the old Navy hymn came back to Paul then. He'd memorized the poem at his grandfather's house in Northern Virginia where he and Megan lived after the killings. Grandpa Chuck had left the service early for a lucrative career in defense contracting, but his blood had flowed Navy blue until the day he died.

> *Eternal Father, strong to save,*
> *Whose arm hath bound the restless wave,*
> *Who bidd'st the mighty ocean deep*
> *Its own appointed limits keep;*
> *Oh, hear us when we cry to thee,*
> *for those in peril on the sea!*

DANIEL

Daniel had never been fond of praying. He was a Parker and Parkers were Catholic. But attending mass on Sundays was as far as his devotion had taken him. The rituals of public worship and penitence had a certain resonance—he had always appreciated the gravitas of ceremony and tradition—but the more mystical aspects of faith made as much sense to him as sitting on Santa's lap at the shopping mall and asking for a gift. Life at sea hadn't altered his habits much. Even sudden storms didn't inspire him to pray, only to batten the hatches and trust his sailing instincts and the workmanship of the hardy Swedes who built the *Renaissance* to stay upright and afloat on the heaving sea.

After thirty hours in captivity, however, he found

himself reciting the rosary. At first the words arose in him unconsciously, like an effervescence of the heart, but it wasn't long before he embraced them with intention. The sailboat that had been his dream—and Quentin's rebirth—had become their prison. The Somalis were all around them like a virus in the bloodstream, their incessant chatter, the shine of their weapons, and the stench of their unwashed bodies infecting everything.

For a while, Daniel had maintained the stoical composure he had inherited from his father, planting his feet firmly in the moment and focusing his energies on survival. The sudden appearance of the plane yesterday had even given him cause to smile. The secret message had alerted the authorities. The Navy knew what had happened and where they were. The wheels of salvation were spinning.

But the hours upon hours of stifling confinement in the cabin, punctuated by the occasional gun being waved in his face, had turned his emotions against him in silent mutiny. The worst of it had come in the night when he tried to sleep. He saw his life flash before him, not in an instant, but in slow motion, a cascade of mistakes and failures, poor choices and venial sins.

He saw the way his marriage to the firm—and his underlying quest for his father's approval—had supplanted his marriage to Vanessa, the way he had left her to shoulder the burden of Quentin alone. He remembered the nights he slept at the office to get a deal just right, the Saturdays he spent on the bay entertaining clients and ignoring his family, the meaningless fling he had with Rachel Perkins, one of his paralegals, out of lust and boredom, and the excuses he made—how good he had been at making excuses!—to shut Vanessa up whenever she questioned his priorities.

There was blame to go around, of course. She had her own issues—the anxiety and panic attacks, her obsessive-compulsive tendencies, the tensions with her mother she never quite resolved. But the fault for the mortification of their love wasn't hers as much as it was his. He had taken her for granted, living off the interest of their relationship and drawing from the principal whenever it suited him without regard to the way it made her feel. There had always been a reason for it—making partner, achieving financial security, and aiming for early retirement. But these were placeholders for the missing pieces of his identity, an attempt to answer the question that had beleaguered him since his youth: What does it mean to be a man?

When morning finally came and he opened his eyes to see Liban staring at him, his battered AK-47 resting casually on his lap, Daniel realized that his skin was taut with the residue of tears. He tried to shake off the cords of misery, to hold fast to the hope that rescue was coming and with it the possibility of redemption, but his powers of denial and obfuscation had abandoned him. He mouthed the petition silently: "Holy Mary, Mother of God, pray for us sinners, now and at the hour of our death. Amen."

"Captain," said the pirate called Afyareh, "my men are hungry. It is time for breakfast."

Daniel sat up and glanced at his son, who looked like he had been awake for some time. Quentin spoke quietly. "I'll help you, Dad."

Daniel nodded, grateful for the distraction. "Why don't you get some fruit?"

He left the booth and went aft to the galley, pulling out a tin of oatmeal and setting a pot on the stove to boil. The simple rhythms of food preparation did more to counteract his despondency than all his mental gymnastics in the night. Quentin brought him a bag of mangoes, and they cut them into bowls. If there was one bright spot in the ordeal, it was Afyareh's sense of propriety. He was a rogue like the rest of them, but at least he was civilized.

They ate the meal in shifts of three—an innovation of Afyareh's that prevented overcrowding in the cabin. The pirates handled the food with their hands, except for Afyareh, who used utensils, and all of them gestured their appreciation—a few nods, a word of thanks from the skinny one, Dhuuban, and a quick smile from Sondare, who looked to Daniel like he was fifteen.

Quentin had been the one to pick up their names. He had always had a gift for languages, and he had collected local phrases like souvenirs at their many ports of call. But his facility with Somali pronunciation, uttered as it was in rapid-fire bursts, surprised Daniel. He had addressed the pirates by name at dinner the day before, and they had looked at him in wonderment. Afyareh in particular had been fascinated with Quentin's talent and had spent the evening teaching him Somali words. Quentin absorbed the lessons like a sponge, and repeated the words with such fluency that Afyareh clapped his hands. Only Mas, the pirate with the cut on his cheek, seemed displeased. He sat aloof in the companionway as the sky darkened behind him, cradling his gun as if it were his child.

After everyone ate breakfast, Afyareh ordered his men topside and spelled Liban on watch while Daniel and Quentin took showers and changed clothes. When they were dressed, the pirate beckoned them to come. "You should get some air," he said and led the way to the cockpit.

Daniel blinked away the bright sunshine. The sea was as flat as a bathtub, the swells under a meter in height and the wind barely five knots. The sky was dotted with small clouds, and the air was thick with humidity. Almost immediately, beads of sweat formed on Daniel's brow and his polo shirt stuck to his skin. He sat down beside Quentin and watched Afyareh scan the horizon with his binoculars. He felt a twinge of satisfaction. *He knows they're coming. The only question is when.*

An hour passed, and then two and three. The sun rose in the sky, warming the atmosphere with relentless intensity. After months at sea, Daniel's skin was tan, as was Quentin's. Still, they applied copious amounts of sunblock to ward off the ultraviolet rays. The pirates eyed the lotion with interest, and then, almost sheepishly, they asked to try it.

"They think it will make them handsome like David Hasselhoff," Afyareh explained. "They saw *Baywatch* on satellite TV."

Around noon, Daniel went below and fixed sandwiches and cheese, which the pirates devoured as if they had never eaten before. At the current rate of consumption, he guessed that their food stores would last for another four or five days, as would their fuel supply—long enough to reach the Somali coast. In a strange way, the adequacy of their provisions brought him consolation. The fewer the disruptions, the less likely something would go wrong before freedom arrived.

After cleaning up, they returned to the cockpit and saw a flock of frigatebirds circling on the thermals above them. Guray lifted his gun to shoot at them, but Afyareh shouted him down. When Guray saw that the argument was lost, he went to the bow to sulk. Afyareh sat down next to Quentin and spoke a string of agitated words to Liban. Liban shook his head derisively.

"What was that about?" Quentin asked after a time.

Afyareh hesitated, as if calculating the cost of a truthful answer. Then he shrugged. "He doesn't like black birds. They remind him of the ones he saw when his father died. I told him these are sea birds. Those were Somali crows. He doesn't believe me. He's very superstitious."

Daniel looked at the young pirate. "How it is that your English is so good?"

Afyareh fixed him with an inscrutable look. "I learned it in school."

"You must have had an excellent teacher," Daniel probed.

The pirate's eyes narrowed. "Not good enough."

The response caught Daniel off guard. Something about Afyareh didn't add up—actually, many things. He seemed to have two contradictory personalities: the professional corsair intent on bargaining with their lives, and the gentleman who let them take showers and sprang to the defense of frigatebirds and forced his fellow pirates to eat out of bowls and leave their captives' belongings unmolested. Daniel listened as Quentin chatted with him in a curious blend of English and Somali, trying out new words with Afyareh's encouragement. The pirate seemed to relish the mantle of teacher. *The cultivation came first*, Daniel thought. *Then the criminality. But why? What caused him to lose his way?*

Daniel looked out over the waves and allowed his mind to drift. He didn't know how long it was before he saw the ship, but when his eyes registered the sight, everything else faded into oblivion. He didn't move, didn't speak, just watched the shape grow until he could distinguish the superstructure from the bow and the masts above that. None of the pirates seemed to notice it. Most of them were lounging in the cockpit or on the coachroof, taking in the sun.

It was Mas who saw it first. He shot to his feet and screamed something so violently that spittle flew from his mouth. The other pirates reacted as if Mas had tossed them a grenade. They swung their guns toward the ship, shouting and gesticulating, their faces naked with fear.

Afyareh raised his voice above the din. "Go below!" he ordered Quentin, grabbing his shoulder and shoving him into the companionway.

Liban took Daniel's arm, but Daniel brushed off the pirate's hand. "Don't touch me!" he said angrily, following his son into the saloon.

The pirates clambered down the steps after them and huddled with their guns in every corner of the cabin, looking like sullen teenagers caught drunk at a party. They pointed their Kalashnikovs anxiously out the portholes, as if at any moment commandos might swoop out of the sky and cut them down before they could say a word.

Daniel sat in the booth and put his arm around Quentin. "It's going to be all right," he said, seeing in his son's eyes the precise reflection of his own fears. "The Navy won't do anything foolish. They know how to handle this."

Even as he spoke the words, he wondered if he was right.

PAUL

The SEAL team landed on the *Gettysburg* a few minutes before one in the afternoon. Paul went with Captain Masters and his entourage to meet them in the hangar bay. Masters traded a few words with Frank Redman—a tightly built coil of a man with a lantern jaw, steel-blue eyes, and wavy brown hair—and introduced him to Paul and Alan Rodriguez, Paul's second, who had arrived with a Somali linguist a few hours before. Masters left Lieutenant Commander Cardwell and Ensign O'Brien with the SEAL team while they prepped their weapons and equipment and led Redman and the negotiators to the admiral's cabin in the center of the ship.

Designed to host visiting dignitaries, the admiral's cabin had a private bedroom and bathroom, a lounge and

kitchenette, and an array of flat-screen television monitors, cameras, and audio equipment for videoconferencing.
Masters had designated the lounge to serve as a war room for
the duration of the hostage crisis and reserved the bedroom
for Redman. The SEAL commander dropped his bag on the
floor and donned a headset with a wraparound microphone.
He spoke into the mic, testing the link, then turned toward
Masters and Paul.

"This'll work," he said. "My sniper teams will take positions on the illuminator decks fore and aft. My attack team
is on the *Truman* along with three RHIBs. They'll deploy
when the carrier is in position. We obtained the sailboat's
plans from the shipbuilder in Sweden. We've considered a
number of tactical options, but all of them are high risk.
We'd prefer a negotiated solution."

Redman gave Paul a frank look. "I've never worked with
a negotiator outside my team, but the White House wants
you on point, so that's the way it's going to be. Nevertheless,
this is a military operation. You follow my orders. Is that
clear?"

Paul didn't blink. "I understand the command structure,
Captain, and I appreciate your candor. I'll be candid, too.
I'm not here to offer you gratuitous advice. You're the best
at what you do. I'm the best at what I do. As long as we're
working toward a common goal, I'm on board with you. If at
any point I feel that my advice is being ignored, my team and
I will take the next chopper out of here."

Redman squinted at Paul in surprise. It was a look
Paul had received before from commanders in Iraq and

Afghanistan. They were alpha males, accustomed to deference. But Paul didn't care. However elite their training, they weren't immune to hubris or human error. And they had an institutional bias in favor of force over compromise. For Paul to negotiate effectively, he needed Redman to give him time and stay out of the way.

"Roger that," Redman said at last. "I assume your team is ready?"

Paul nodded. "We have two negotiators—me and Rodriguez here. We also have a Somali linguist on hand to translate. We set up a table with a radio unit and voice recorder. The guys in CIC are going to make a backup recording as well."

The CIC, or Combat Information Center, was the nerve center of the *Gettysburg*, where all of the ship's weapons and communications systems were controlled.

"Very well." Redman surveyed the faces around him. "Our mission is simple—to get the Parkers back *before* the sailboat reaches Somalia. We will not allow the pirates to take them ashore. Is that understood?" When no one spoke, he said, "All right then. Let's get up to the bridge and make ourselves known."

Paul first sighted the *Renaissance* at a distance of five miles. With the sails stowed, its mast was invisible against the haze on the horizon and its hull looked like a buoy bobbing on the cobalt sea. Redman stood beside Paul, looking through binoculars and communicating with his sniper teams as they moved into position. Masters was in the captain's chair, issuing orders to the conning officer.

"Decrease speed to twenty knots," Masters said, "and come three degrees to starboard. I want to approach the sailboat off its stern quarter."

"Full ahead at twenty knots," echoed the conning officer. "Right standard rudder to course 332."

"Decreasing speed to twenty knots," said the helmsman. "Confirm right standard rudder to course 332."

Paul felt the *Gettysburg* slow and heel to port as it carved out the turn. Through his binoculars, he saw the boom and starboard flank of the *Renaissance* come into view.

"Speed is now twenty knots," the helmsman called out. "Heading is now 332, 330 magnetic."

"Very well," said the conning officer.

"Mr. Evans, what's the distance and closure rate?" Masters asked the officer of the deck, a lanky young man hovering over the radar display.

"Five thousand yards, sir," Evans replied, "and closing at fourteen knots."

"Call it out every five hundred yards," Masters ordered.

Evans spoke the countdown with metronomic consistency. At two thousand yards—one nautical mile—Masters decreased the cruiser's speed to twelve knots and adjusted the heading to 329, paralleling the course of the *Renaissance*. Paul could now see the sailboat's cockpit through his binoculars. It was empty. The pirate skiff was trailing behind, tethered to the sailboat's transom.

"There's no one on deck, Captain," said the watch officer.

Masters nodded. "I imagine they saw us some time ago." He turned to Paul. "Why don't I hail them on the bridge-to-bridge and then turn things over to you?"

"Good," Paul said. He took a seat at the chart table, now free of clutter, and picked up the radio handset. Rodriguez was sitting to his right, legal pad open and pen in hand. He would serve as Paul's "coach"—a second set of ears listening for anything Paul might miss. Ali Sharif, the Somali linguist, was standing by the captain's chair, ready to assist.

"One thousand yards," Evans called out.

"This is good for the time being," Redman said.

"All right," replied Masters. "Let's slow down to six knots and keep this distance."

"Aye, aye, Captain," Evans affirmed as the conning officer relayed the orders to the helm.

Masters met Paul's eyes, then held up his own radio handset and pressed the button to transmit. "Sailing Vessel *Renaissance*, Sailing Vessel *Renaissance*, this is the captain of the USS *Gettysburg* a thousand yards off your stern quarter. Do you read?"

Silence fell on the bridge as everyone waited for the response. Five seconds passed, then ten. Masters pressed the button again. "Sailing Vessel *Renaissance*, this is the American warship *Gettysburg*. Please come in. Over."

Suddenly, Paul heard a crackle of static. "Warship, we have hostages," said a male voice in lightly accented English. "They are alive and well. If you want them to stay that way, you will fall back to a distance of four miles and make no attempt to approach."

In an instant, two things happened at once. The watch officer exclaimed, "Captain, there's a man on deck with a gun!" And Redman reported, "Warning shots fired. Single shooter. Dark-skinned male. Probably an AK-47."

Paul leapt to his feet and looked out the window just in time to see the pirate disappear into the sailboat, pulling the hatch closed behind him.

"That was just a tantrum," Redman said evenly. "Agent Derrick, you're on."

Paul's stomach tightened as he picked up the radio. "*Renaissance*," he began, adopting a steady yet soothing tone, "my name is Paul, and I have authority to negotiate on behalf of the United States government. We don't want anyone to be harmed. But the safety of the hostages is your responsibility. We need to talk about how to resolve this so that everyone gets out alive. Over."

He set the radio down and waited pensively for the pirate's reply. In time, the accented voice spoke again. "We will not negotiate until we reach Somalia. If you attack us, we will kill the hostages. Their blood will be on your hands."

Paul pursed his lips. The pirate's deliberate manner of speech, and the quality of his English, indicated both intelligence and education. "What is your name?" he asked. "I told you mine. Over."

"My name doesn't matter. Your government wants something and we want something. If you leave us alone, we will all get what we want. If not, all of us will lose. The choice is yours."

Paul refused to take the bait. "If we're going to talk, I'd like to call you something. Would you prefer I make up a name?"

The pirate took a moment to respond. "You can call me Ibrahim."

"Thank you, Ibrahim. I want to give you a heads-up about what I'm hearing from the Navy. They're not going to let you take the Parkers to Somalia. They're American citizens, and the Navy is not going to abandon them. That means we need to find a different sort of compromise. Over."

An eerie silence followed. Paul waited patiently while Ibrahim considered the ground rules. As lead negotiator, it was his job to convince the pirates that they weren't going to get away with their crime. It was a hard truth for any hostage taker to accept. For that reason it had to be stated early, repeated often, and reinforced at every turn by the guys with guns.

"Ibrahim," Paul said after a while, "are you still there?"

Suddenly, a new voice came on the radio. "*Gettysburg*, this is Captain Parker of the *Renaissance*. My son and I are well. The pirates don't want to hurt us. They will release us as soon as our family pays a ransom. But the negotiation has to happen on land, not at sea. Those are their terms. Over."

Paul nodded at Rodriguez. They had gotten proof of life faster than he had anticipated. "Captain Parker," he said, speaking slowly and clearly, "it's good to hear your voice. My name is Paul, and I'm committed to bringing you and your son home. Unfortunately, we can't let you go to Somalia. We need to negotiate a solution before we reach the coast. Over."

Paul heard the sounds of a scuffle. Then Captain Parker cried out, "No, no, leave us alone! We didn't do anything!" Seconds later, he came on the radio again, sounding scared. "Paul, they're pointing guns at us. They're saying they'll kill us if you don't let us go. Over."

"I understand what they're saying," Paul replied calmly. "But it's against their interest to harm you. They know that as well as we do."

Daniel Parker didn't seem to hear him. "We can work this out. My family will pay them when we get to Somalia. There's no need for violence. Do you read me? We can work this out."

Paul waited a beat before changing the topic. "Captain Parker, how are you for food and water? Do you have enough to eat? If you don't, we can help you with that."

At this point, Ibrahim came on the radio again. "If you want the Captain to stay alive, you will back off to four miles and leave us alone."

Again, Paul disregarded the threat. "How about fuel? Are you running low?"

"We don't need fuel," the pirate said in exasperation. "Go away or the hostages will die."

Paul glanced at Redman and threw the pirate another curveball. "How am I going to do that, Ibrahim? I'm the negotiator, not the captain of the ship. The Navy says they're not going to let you go. I need your help to find a solution that doesn't involve violence. I have a few ideas, but I'm open to yours. How do we deal with this? You tell me. Over."

The silence extended for thirty seconds, then a minute. "Ibrahim, do you read me?" Paul said. "Ibrahim, come back. Over." But there was no response.

Paul put down the handset and faced Redman. "Well, we got proof of life and we got him thinking. I say we pressurize him a bit. Nothing heavy, just something to confirm that we're serious."

The SEAL commander nodded. "Let's put a bird in the air and start shooting with the FLIR." FLIR stood for Forward Looking Infrared, an imaging system capable of recording heat signatures along with ordinary video. Redman looked at Evans. "How long until the *Truman* and *San Jac* arrive?"

"They're scheduled to join us at 22:30 this evening, sir," said the officer of the deck.

"Good. We'll get some Hornets to fly over the sailboat in the morning, and we'll put the RHIBs in the water. We'll tell them we're just doing exercises, but it'll make the point."

Paul shook his head. "The chopper and the flyover are good ideas. But if I'm a pirate and I see boats in the water, I think an attack is imminent."

"We could keep the RHIBs out of sight behind the *Truman*," Masters said.

"What if we offer them something?" suggested Alan Rodriguez. "They don't want provisions or fuel, but what about a secure radio? Bridge-to-bridge operates on VHF. It's audible to everyone for miles around. We could tell them that negotiating over VHF isn't in their interest. That might give us an excuse to show off one of the small boats."

Paul had to suppress a smile. Rodriguez had performed the sleight of hand like a magician, tempering Redman's overly muscular approach while making it appear that he was agreeing with him.

"I like it," Redman affirmed. "I'll get my guys to put some gear together."

"And I'll put the bird in the air," Masters said, picking up a phone and issuing the order to CIC.

Redman faced Paul. "How long before you go back online?"

Paul stood up and looked out the window at the *Renaissance* pitching and rolling on the swells. At a distance of a thousand yards, the sailboat looked like a child's toy alone on the empty sea.

"When they see the helicopter," he said, "I imagine they'll come to us."

VANESSA

Vanessa was in the kitchen making breakfast when she heard the phone ring. It was just after sunrise on the second day after the hijacking, and she was already feeling edgy and claustrophobic. Mary Patterson was sitting across from her at the bar on the island, typing something on her BlackBerry, and Curtis and Yvonne Parker were in the living room chatting with Duke Strong from the Sagittarius Group. Vanessa glanced at the phone sitting in the office nook and then looked at the FBI agent.

"Let them leave a message," Mary said.

Vanessa collected the handset and shook her head. "I don't recognize the number."

Seconds later, she heard the chirp of a new voice mail. She listened to it and took a sharp breath.

"Who was it, dear?" asked Yvonne, walking toward her from the living room. Vanessa's mother-in-law was a regal woman with short white hair, crystalline blue eyes, and porcelain skin that, apart from a few spreading wrinkles, made her look a decade younger than her sixty-six years.

"A reporter from CNN," Vanessa replied with a trace of disdain. She returned to the kitchen and put the phone on the island, replaying the message on speaker. When the recording ended, she said, "This is just the beginning, isn't it?"

Mary gave her a compassionate look. "I imagine the TV crews will be here by lunchtime."

Vanessa sat down on one of the Queen Anne chairs in the living room, her mind whirling like an unsteady top. Her nightmare was about to become national headline news. Skipper padded up to her, and she scratched him behind the ears, grateful for the distraction.

"How do we handle them?" she asked at last.

"The short answer is we don't," Strong replied. A twenty-year veteran of the Bureau and now chief of security at the Sagittarius Group, he was an imposing barrel of a man, with the thick limbs of a rugby player and a face that looked as if it had been chiseled out of marble. "Mary and I will monitor the coverage and let you know if something comes up. The best thing you can do is ignore it."

Mary took the baton from Strong. "We've already maximized the privacy settings on your social media accounts. There's only so much the press can get from public sources. But now would be a good time to bring the people close to you into the loop. They need to know what's coming."

"I'll talk to Bob Rogers at the firm," Curtis said.

Vanessa watched her father-in-law walk to the tall, east-facing windows and retrieve his smartphone from his suit jacket. Once a star linebacker for the Navy Midshipmen, he had filled out in middle age and was a tad on the portly side, but, as Yvonne jested in the British accent she still carried from childhood, he was as formidable as a grizzly bear, and equally friendly.

"I'm going to call Aster," Vanessa said.

She took her iPhone into the dining room and dialed her friend's mobile number. Before the call connected, a thought occurred to her that sent a shiver up her spine. *What if the press finds out about Quentin's suspension? What if they find out about the drugs?* She cut off the call and forced herself to think rationally. The school's records were protected by privacy laws. No criminal charges had ever been filed. The lawyers Curtis hired were bound by confidentiality. The press had no reason to search for skeletons because they were irrelevant to the hijacking.

She shrugged off her misgivings and called Aster again. Before she could complete a sentence, her friend asked what was wrong. Vanessa delivered her account simply, embellishing nothing.

"What can I do?" Aster asked softly.

"Talk to Chad and Emily," Vanessa replied. "I'm not sure when I'll be in again."

"We'll cover your appointments. And I'll cancel the St. Michael's reservation. I don't want you worrying about a thing except your family."

"I already heard from the press," Vanessa said. "They may try to contact you."

"There's no way any of us will talk to them."

Vanessa sighed, borrowing strength from her friend. "Okay. I'll keep you posted."

Aster took a breath. "Keep your chin up. This is going to work out."

Vanessa ended the call and returned to the living room, only to hear the house phone ring again. *Not another reporter*, she stewed silently, but the number had an international exchange. She let it go to voice mail and then listened to the message.

"Hi, Mrs. Parker," said a sweet adolescent voice, sounding worried and embarrassed. "This is Ariadne Wilson in Australia. We've never spoken, but Quentin says he told you about me. We met in the Cook Islands when my family was sailing the Pacific." The girl paused, then forged ahead. "We talk every day now, usually by e-mail. I haven't heard from him in two days, and I'm starting to worry. Have you heard anything? I'd be very grateful if you would call me back."

In spite of her dread, Vanessa felt an unexpected twinge of joy. It was true then, what Daniel had written about Quentin. Something miraculous had happened on the voyage. As a young man, he had always been clumsy around girls, approaching them in awkward ways that invariably backfired. Vanessa knew the names of most of his crushes. They had always been popular girls, and none had returned his affection. Somehow with Ariadne it had been different. Vanessa pressed the "redial" button, hoping the girl was as strong as Daniel suggested.

"Ariadne," she said, "this is Vanessa Parker. I'm afraid I have some bad news."

Ariadne gasped once at the beginning of the story but listened to the rest without comment. When Vanessa finished, she heard the girl crying softly. It was enough to break her heart.

"I'll give you my e-mail address," Vanessa offered, "and I'll send you updates when I can."

"They're going to be okay, aren't they?" Ariadne asked plaintively.

Vanessa spoke with more conviction than she felt. "They're going to be fine."

When the call ended, she looked longingly at her violin. In the swirl of her emotions, she needed an outlet, and music was the surest form of release. But she couldn't play before an audience. It would only increase her stress. She went to the foyer and grabbed her peacoat off the rack, whistling for Skipper to come.

"I'm going for a walk," she said to anyone listening.

She left the house by the back door and walked briskly to the river. Skipper trotted beside her, as if sensing her need for company. The air was chilly but warming, the forest dappled with fall color. She stuffed her hands into her coat pockets and watched a sloop with a red hull navigate the channel toward the Naval Academy Bridge. *Why couldn't they have sailed around the Pacific like Ariadne's family?* she mused. *Why did they have to cross the Indian Ocean?* But, of course, she knew the answer. Daniel had talked about sailing around the world since she had met him, and he had passed along the dream to Quentin.

She didn't stop at the dock like she usually did. Instead,

she followed the riverbank to the edge of her property and then returned through the forest, increasing her pace until she was almost running. She heard Skipper chuffing beside her, his feet clicking on the hard earth. The breeze off the land rustled the trees and sent leaves skittering across the ground. She reached the house feeling invigorated. A swift walk wasn't as effective as Mozart in restoring her equilibrium, but it was a close second.

Mary Patterson approached her when she entered the living room. "We got proof of life," she announced. "Paul Derrick spoke to Daniel. The pirates haven't harmed them."

Vanessa felt relief flood through her. She took off her coat and sat down in the living room across from Curtis and Yvonne. Duke Strong was standing beside the fireplace, typing something on his mobile phone. "Now what?" she asked.

"The Navy is ramping up the pressure," Mary explained. "They've made it clear that they won't let the pirates take them to Somalia."

"What do you mean?" Vanessa asked, not quite comprehending. "What if they don't comply?"

Mary's reply was matter-of-fact. "They don't have a choice."

Vanessa felt a pang of anxiety. "That sounds more like an ultimatum than a negotiation."

For the first time, Vanessa heard Mary measure her words. "The government's principal concern is to ensure the safety of your family. If they go to Somalia, it increases the risk."

Vanessa shook her head. "You said a ransom might be the safest way to end this. It doesn't sound like the Navy is giving that a chance." She took a moment to think. She didn't like this new development. Something about it didn't feel right. She looked at her father-in-law and Duke Strong. "I'd like to talk to the two of you in private." She glanced at Mary. "I hope you don't mind."

"Not at all," the FBI agent said.

Vanessa walked down the hall to Daniel's office and flipped the light switch beside the door. The room was a shrine to nautical history, with old charts in gilt-edged frames, a polished globe and a gimbal compass, an antique sextant, and a bevy of ship models in glass cases. The only concessions to the modern age were the iMac and printer on the captain's desk.

Duke Strong whistled when he stepped inside. "Nice office."

"You should see his father's," she quipped, tossing a glance at Curtis.

When they had taken seats, she got to the point. "I'm concerned about the government's position. I'm grateful for what they're doing, but they're taking a hard line. I don't understand it."

Strong held out his hands. "It's simple, actually. You see this as a personal matter. The government doesn't. They think about it through the lens of policy. Piracy costs the US and other maritime countries billions of dollars every year. They want it to stop. If these pirates get a payday, the incentive for piracy increases. So they're not going to let them get what they want."

Vanessa shook her head. "They don't have a child on

the sailboat."

Strong nodded. "I'm not trying to be cynical. They care about your family. But they're looking at the big picture. The government wants to eradicate piracy and hostage taking. In their minds, the way to do it is to confront the hostage takers with overwhelming force and ask a basic question: 'Do you want to fight and die or put down your weapons and live?'"

Vanessa spoke her next question in a near whisper. "What if the pirates choose to die?"

Strong shrugged. "The entire policy framework rests on the human instinct to survive."

Suddenly, Vanessa felt trapped. She looked out the window at the forest. "So what you're saying is that Daniel and Quentin are pawns in some kind of geopolitical game."

"That's an unflattering way of putting it, but yes," Strong replied.

Vanessa turned to her father-in-law, thinking of his many friends in government. "What if you made a few calls? You could tell them to back down."

Curtis sat statuesque, his hands on the arms of his chair. "If this were just about a ransom, you know we would pay it. But this is bigger than us, Vanessa. They're not going to listen."

"How can you say that?" she demanded. "My *son* is out there. They don't have the right to roll the dice with his life!"

Curtis met her eyes. "My son is there, too," he said softly. "And my grandson."

"Look," Strong interjected, "the SEALs are great at what they do. They got Captain Phillips out. Also, there's a downside to letting Daniel and Quentin reach Somalia. They could end up in the hands of al-Shabaab. That's a scenario you don't even want to think about."

Vanessa buried her face in her hands. She had spent her entire adult life weeding out the imponderables that made her childhood unbearable. She had married a stable man in a stable family—imperfect but predictable. She had achieved academic success in a credible field and joined her best friend in starting a medical practice catering to the low-income and refugee populations in DC—not too lofty, but important enough for personal satisfaction. She had been careful, meticulous, always in the driver's seat. Now everything in her world was spinning out of control. *The SEALs. Somalia. The Shabaab. How did we get to this point?*

She sat up suddenly, possessed of an idea. The only way to defeat helplessness was to take action. She walked back to the living room, her eyes ablaze with purpose. Mary Patterson was standing by the windows, talking on her BlackBerry. She ended the call quickly when she saw Vanessa.

"Everything okay?" she asked.

"No," Vanessa replied simply. "I want to talk to Paul Derrick."

PAUL

Paul was wrong about the helicopter. It evoked no response from the pirates. The Seahawk closed to within half a mile of the *Renaissance* and circled it twice, shooting video, before banking away and taking up station a mile off the sailboat's beam. In the twenty minutes it took to gather the footage, no one appeared on the deck of the yacht or hailed the *Gettysburg* over the radio. The *Renaissance* continued its forward march toward Somalia as if guided by an invisible spirit.

After a while, Paul broke the silence. "*Renaissance*, this is *Gettysburg*, come in. Over."

But no one answered.

After a few more failed attempts, Redman called a conference with Masters and the negotiation team on the bridge wing. The tropical air was stifling—over ninety degrees Fahrenheit—and the humidity off the ocean was so thick that Paul felt like he was breathing underwater.

"I want to know why they're not talking," said the SEAL commander, raising his voice over the wind. "And I want to know how to change that."

Paul met Redman's eyes. "They're not talking because they're holding all the cards. They don't need what we're offering, and they have time on their side. If they reach the coast, they win."

Redman frowned. "You're telling me negotiation won't work?"

"Not at all. What I'm saying is that negotiation is hard to do on a deadline. If the sailboat weren't moving, we could wear the pirates down. Eventually, they'd come to the bargaining table. But as long as they're making headway, they have no incentive to engage us."

"You're saying we need to disable the sailboat."

Paul shrugged. "Disable it or slow it down. Either way, we buy time and reinforce to the pirates that they can't ignore us."

Redman nodded. "We're working on a subsurface infiltration plan to break the propeller and disguise the damage. But I won't send in my dive team until we assess the risk. I need to know how many pirates are on the boat. The visual from the chopper was useless, and I don't see any way to flush them out of the cabin. The sailboat has an AC unit. They have everything they need down below."

Masters looked thoughtful. "What if we put a camera on the radio before we offer it to them?"

Redman raised an eyebrow. "Not a bad idea. I'll get

somebody to take a look at that. Also, we should get someone from the family to send an e-mail to Captain Parker. I doubt the pirates will let him use his computer, but you never know."

"My people will make it happen," Paul said.

Redman nodded. "In the meantime, I want to get closer to the sailboat. I want the pirates to see that we're not leaving. Any objection to five hundred yards?"

Masters shook his head.

Redman faced Paul. "I need you to find a way to get Ibrahim back on the horn. I don't care what you do. Call him every five minutes. Provoke him. Just get him talking. He needs to understand that he isn't in control of how this ends."

It was then that Ali Sharif, the Somali linguist, cleared his throat. He was a quiet man with salt-and-pepper hair and polished ebony skin. "There may be an easier way," he said. "You are right that Ibrahim will not negotiate as long as he is strong. But you are wrong to assume that he will negotiate if you make him feel weak. He is Somali, and Somalis do not compromise. Look at our country—two decades without peace. But we love a good conversation. Ibrahim may talk to you if you have something interesting to say."

Paul was intrigued. "What do you suggest?"

The linguist gave him a wizened look. "How much do you know about Somalia?"

"Clearly not enough."

"Then I will teach you."

✳

As the sun fell toward the molten sea, Paul picked up the radio again and focused all of his energy on the task at hand. "Ibrahim, this is Paul. *Nabad iyo caano*. I don't speak Somali, but my friend Ali here tells me that means 'peace and milk.' We don't have anything like that in English. It's one of the reasons I love the cultures of the East. You invented hospitality."

Paul met Ali's eyes and saw the linguist nod his approval.

"Yaa tahay?" Paul asked, reading one of the phrases he'd scratched out on his legal pad. "I'm curious what clan you're from. We have all these fancy computer systems over here, and they say you're heading to Hobyo. Ali guesses you're Habar Gidir. Is he right? What's your subclan? Are you Sa'ad, Suleiman, or Ayr? Ali tells me you can name your patrilineal ancestors all the way back to Irir Samaale. I understand that's something like thirty generations. I'm ashamed to say I don't know the name of my great-great-grandfather. That's typical in America. We don't think much about the past. Our country isn't very old. Unfortunately, that means we don't always learn from our mistakes."

Paul waited ten more seconds before pressing the button again and speaking into the void. "You may be interested to know that I've read the Quran from cover to cover—not in Arabic, but in English. Ali tells me you probably attended a *duqsi* where you memorized whole suras before the age of six. My favorite passage is from Sura 5: 'If anyone slays a person, except for murder or spreading mischief in the land, it is as if he slayed the whole people; and if anyone saves a life, it is as if he saved the life of the whole people.' A lot of people ignore the significance of that passage, but the Prophet said it himself: 'You won't attain to faith until you love one another. Spread peace among yourselves.' Maybe I'm simple, but I think peace means peace. It seems to me that the violence perpetrated in the name of Islam isn't an expression of true faith. Ali agrees. I'd love to know what you think."

Rodriguez handed Paul a glass of water, and he took a sip, offering Ibrahim an opportunity to respond. He looked around the bridge at the crew of the *Gettysburg*, their faces warmed by shafts of sunlight. It gave him inspiration for his next monologue.

"Ali tells me you can probably quote Somali poetry. He told me that when he was a boy he listened to the elders from his clan recite long verses from memory. He showed me how it's done. Do you know Gaarriye? Ali recited a poem called 'Passing Cloud.' It was quite memorable. I'm going to get my sister some of Gaarriye's work for Christmas. Her name is Megan. She loves that kind of thing."

Paul reviewed his notes. He had circled the word *kinship*, which Ali had repeated often in his tutorial. *I should tell Ibrahim about my family*, Paul thought. *But how do I explain them?* An idea came to him unbidden: *He would understand the carnage. He's probably watched someone close to him die. Perhaps it explains why he risked his life to hijack a sailboat in the middle of the ocean, and why he's now defying the most powerful navy in the world to finish the mission.* Paul was surprised by how deeply this intuition affected him. He blinked and scratched his chin, clearing his mind of distraction.

It was then that Ibrahim's voice came over the radio. "If you have read the Quran," the pirate said, "then you know the story of Iblis in Sura 15."

Paul was so astonished that Ali's gambit had worked that it took him a few seconds to respond. "I do," he said, recalling that *Iblis* was the Muslim name for Satan. "He refused to submit himself to mankind, and God banished him from heaven until the Day of Judgment."

"That's correct," Ibrahim affirmed. "Do you remember how Iblis responded to the curse? What he said he would do to mankind?"

Paul took a breath. "He vowed to subvert our morality, to turn us into monsters."

Ibrahim quoted the sura: "'Because you put me in the wrong, I will make wrong seem good to them on the earth, and I will put all of them in the wrong.' In what way has he touched you, Paul?"

Ibrahim's riddle left Paul dumbstruck. For a long moment, he forgot he was on a Navy ship, forgot he was a negotiator talking to a pirate. His brother's words came back to him from beyond the grave. *This is all your fault!* Kyle had screamed, holding the Beretta in his hands. *You made me do this!* Paul saw the pistol jump, heard the shots ring out, smelled the sick-sweet odor of his father's blood on the carpet, and felt the hollowness in his gut, the horror and grief, as if for the first time.

He took a painful breath and racked his brain for an answer. In the end, he opted for the truth. "Most of my family is dead," he said, struggling to put the psychological lid back on Pandora's box. "That's my confession. What's yours?"

Ibrahim was quiet for a moment. "Death is his signature," he said at last. "I know it well."

Paul saw the opening and went for broke. "There's a way out of this. You know how the sura ends: *Over my servants you will have no authority, except those who put themselves in the wrong.* Let Daniel and Quentin go. Put them on the skiff and take the sailboat to Somalia. Don't compound the evil and invite your own damnation."

Ibrahim matched Paul's solemnity with his own. "If hell is real, I've seen it with my own eyes. Tell the captain of your ship not to come any closer, or he will see it, too."

Paul heard the line go dead. He sat back in his chair and put his hands behind his head, staring at the bundles of wiring on the ceiling. In his career as a negotiator, he could recall only two times when he had developed a personal connection to a kidnapper. On both occasions, the bond had taken weeks to form. With Ibrahim, however, he felt it after a single conversation. *Kinship*, he thought. *It's about soul more than blood. Who are you, Ibrahim? Why do I get the impression that we understand each other?*

Captain Masters interrupted his reverie. "I have a call for you from Brent Frazier. You can talk here, or you can use my office."

"I'll take it here," Paul said, accepting the sound-powered phone from Masters's hand. He walked to the windows and looked out at the sea. The sun had just set, and the sky was burnt orange, like a field of poppies. The sailboat was much closer now. He could see the shrouds bracing the mast and smudges of lettering on the transom spelling out "RENAISSANCE. Annapolis, Maryland."

He put the phone to his ear. "Brent, this is Paul."

"I hear you're making progress," said his boss.

"He's starting to talk, but he's going to be tough to crack. We need more time."

Frazier grunted. "Prince is trying to get approval for the SEALs to disable the sailboat."

"And if he doesn't?" Paul said. "You know we don't work on a timetable."

"We'll cross that bridge when we get to it. For the time being we work off of the Navy's script." Frazier paused. "I have something else for you. It's Vanessa Parker. She wants to talk to you."

Paul absorbed this. "Any idea why?"

"I don't have a clue. But you can probably guess."

"Mary couldn't handle it?"

"She did her best, but Vanessa insisted."

Paul grimaced. It was a complication he didn't need right now. In a barricade scenario, it was highly irregular for the lead negotiator to communicate with the relatives of a hostage. The military was in charge. He was advising the government, not the family, and he had no control over the outcome. But this wasn't really a siege. Nor was it a straightforward kidnapping. He was making everything else up as he went along. Why not this?

"Put her through," he said and waited for Frazier to make the connection.

After a moment, a smooth feminine voice said, "Agent Derrick, I'm very sorry to bother you."

"It's all right," he replied, affecting a genial tone. "Please, call me Paul."

"Thank you," Vanessa said with transparent sincerity. "How are they?"

Paul fixed his eyes on the *Renaissance* as it sailed on into the falling dark. "They're well, as far as we can tell. I talked to your husband this afternoon."

"That's good to hear." She sounded relieved. "Did you speak to Quentin?"

"No. Daniel spoke for both of them."

Vanessa took a breath. "I don't expect there's anything you can do, but I want you to hear this anyway. Whatever they want, my family will pay. We just want Daniel and Quentin to come home."

For a moment Paul didn't know what to say. He glanced at Redman, who was chatting with Masters on the port-side bridge wing. He knew how the SEAL commander would respond. The policy of the Defense Department was inscribed in stone. The Pentagon would rather see a hostage ransomed with blood than with money. That was the only way to stamp out the kidnapping of Americans, or so they said. Paul had other ideas, but it wasn't his place to voice them.

"Vanessa," he said as personally as he could, "I want you to hear me. We will not rest until we reunite you with your husband and son. The team we have here is the best in the world. I know you're scared. I know the waiting is excruciating. If it were my family, I would feel the same way. But I need you to trust me. I promise you—we know what we're doing."

Vanessa allowed the silence to linger and then turned his words on their head. "Do you know what you're asking, Paul?" she said softly. "If I trust you, then that means I hold you responsible for what happens. Maybe we're different, but I wouldn't want that burden."

Paul smiled. He had underestimated her. "I'll keep that in mind," he said, conceding the point. "And I'll see what I can do."

"Thank you," she said again. "That's all I wanted you to say."

ISMAIL

Ismail awoke before first light. The dream had come to him in the darkness and left him with a familiar ache. He saw it again, as he always did, the scene that never seemed to age. The Shabaab camp west of Mogadishu, the parade ground, the derelict barracks, the rusting technicals with their heavy-caliber guns pointed at the earth, the insatiable shouting of the recruits—*"Allahu Akbar!"*—and Yasmin, her tearstained face upturned like a mystic in prayer, as Najiib dragged her away. She had cried out to him, but her words had been lost amid the roar of fighters denouncing their enemies and extolling the virtues of jihad. She had melted into the crowd, and then, suddenly, she was gone—one more shrapnel fragment blown into unremembrance by a land forever at war.

He shook off the sorrow and looked around. His men were scattered about, everyone asleep but Guray, who sat with his rifle and a tin of almonds, watching the door to the Captain's stateroom, which he and Timaha now shared. The sleeping arrangements had been a puzzle, but he and his men knew how to adjust. It was the Somali way, at least that of his generation—adapt or die.

He checked the GPS unit first. They were still on course for Hobyo. The auto-helm was as trustworthy as a desert guide following the stars. *Six hundred miles*, he thought—in English, not Somali. All of the English speaking he had done in the past two days, and the Western music he had listened to, had cleaved his mind like a machete. It astonished him how easily he remembered the patterns of Western speech. His father had drilled the lessons into him from birth, as he had with Yasmin and Yusuf: *Speak Somali with pride, but English for success.*

He nodded at Guray and then opened the weather hatch that led to the cockpit. The sky above was still dark, but the eastern horizon was brightening with the approach of the dawn. He took a breath and went up on deck, crouching behind the helm and taking his binoculars in hand. He scanned the moonlit sea and his heart clutched in his chest. In the night, the Navy ship had moved from a five-o'clock position off the sailboat's stern to a three-o'clock position off the starboard beam. It didn't seem any closer—though in the gloom he wasn't sure—but its stance was more aggressive. He swept the binoculars south and west, and fear shot through him like a shower of sparks.

There were two more ships—one off the port beam and another off the stern.

"Was!" he cursed under his breath, reverting to Somali. He heard Paul's voice like an echo in his brain: *They're not going to let you take the Parkers to Somalia. We need to find a different sort of compromise.* He studied the ships as the night slowly faded. One of them was identical to the *Gettysburg*, but the other—the one off the stern—had a flat deck and a tower off to the side. The truth came to Ismail suddenly. *They sent an aircraft carrier!* In a matter of hours, the Americans had surrounded the *Renaissance* with enough firepower to sink every ship in Somalia's pre-civil-war navy.

Ismail launched himself down the companionway and closed the weather hatch. At the sight of his wild eyes, Guray leapt to his feet, gripping his Kalashnikov.

"Maxaa ka khaldan?" he asked. "What's wrong?"

"There are Navy ships all around us! Wake up the men!" Ismail hissed.

He pounded on the door to the Captain's cabin and heard rustling on the other side. The Captain emerged in sweatpants and a T-shirt, looking worn and disheveled.

"What do you want?" he asked, struggling to control his irritation.

"Come now!" Ismail ordered. "We have a problem."

The Captain followed him into the saloon and stopped short, looking at Guray, Osman, and Mas, who were covering the portholes with their guns and chattering in hard-edged Somali.

"What's going on?" he demanded.

Ismail shoved the binoculars into his hands. "Look," he commanded, pointing out the window. "Your Navy is not listening."

While the Captain surveyed the ships, Ismail roused Timaha from the berth and ordered him to sit beside Sondare and Dhuuban in the dining booth.

Ismail confronted the Captain. "Do you see?"

The Captain nodded. "They told you they weren't going to leave."

Ismail felt the anger growling like a lion inside of him. He grabbed the gun out of Guray's hands. "Do you want to die?" he demanded. *"Do you want to die?"*

The Captain took a half step backward, visibly shaken. "Of course not."

"Then make them go away!"

The Captain hurried to the nav station and picked up the radio, his hands trembling. He fumbled with the controls and pressed the transmit button. "Warship, warship, this is *Renaissance*, come in." He waited a moment and then hailed them again. "*Gettysburg*, this is Captain Parker, do you read?"

Long seconds passed before he got a response. "Captain Parker, this is Paul on the *Gettysburg*. How are you this morning?"

The negotiator's insouciance infuriated Ismail all the more. He aimed the Kalashnikov at the Captain and repeated himself menacingly. "Make them go away."

The Captain glanced at the gun and a stream of nervous words tumbled out of him. "*Gettysburg*, we've sighted two more ships. Why is the Navy escalating the situation? You need to tell whoever is in charge that the pirates aren't going to release us until they get their money. They don't want to harm us, so long as we comply. But if the Navy doesn't go away, they will kill us. Over."

The negotiator's reply was sober. "Are they threatening you, Captain?"

"I am being held at gunpoint. You need to make the Navy understand. We will go to Somalia. We will pay their price. Over."

"I read you, Captain, and I understand your distress. But the Navy is telling me they're not going to let you reach the coast. We don't know what is waiting for you there. Over."

The Captain's voice took on a higher pitch. "You *don't* understand. This is not a game! The Navy is putting us needlessly at risk."

"Captain," said the negotiator evenly, "I want you to listen to me. Your safety is Ibrahim's responsibility. If he kills you, he and his friends will be captured, they will be tried in an American court, and they will be sentenced for their crimes. They could be put to death. On the other hand, if they let you go, we will let them go. They can take your sailboat and return to Somalia."

At this, Ismail's rage bubbled over. He pointed the Kalashnikov at the coachroof and pulled the trigger three times, stitching holes in the wood paneling. In the confinement of the cabin, the gunshots sounded like detonations.

The Captain jumped out of fright. "*Stop it!* This is *madness!*"

"Get out of the way," Ismail ordered, yanking the hand-set away from him. He spoke into the radio. "We are not interested in your deal. We don't want the sailboat, and we're not afraid of your courts. Back off now or you will have to explain to the American media why their countrymen died when they could have been ransomed."

"Good morning, Ibrahim," said the negotiator, not missing a beat. "As I said before, I'm open to ideas. But we're not going to resolve this situation on your terms alone. You need to take care of the hostages. Hurting them isn't produc-tive for you or for us."

Enough! Ismail almost shouted. He pressed the transmit button and pulled the trigger again. The blast echoed in the narrow space and left his ears ringing. "That was a warning," he said, forcing his voice to match the negotiator's calm. "No more talk. Tell the Navy to go away or the Captain will die."

Paul waited a moment before replying. "I'll pass the message along."

Suddenly, all was quiet in the cabin. Ismail stared at the Captain and saw beads of sweat on his brow, the stark terror in his eyes. "Was!" he cursed again. *None of this was supposed to happen! The American troublemakers never should have found us. This is all the Captain's fault.*

But that wasn't really true. It was America's fault, too. The United States was an arrogant bully that treated its superpower status like a license to pick the world's winners and trampled everyone who stood in its way. It was an American admiral who had ordered the slaughter of over fifty clan elders and intellectuals in Mogadishu in June of 1993, many of whom—including Ismail's grandfather, Ibrahim—wanted to help the United Nations disarm General Aideed. The Americans had reacted in horror when Somalis dragged their dead soldiers through the streets three months later. But they had never taken responsibility for the massacre that turned the Somali people against them.

Nor had they learned their lesson, returning a decade later under the guise of the war on terror to support the warlords in fighting the Islamic Courts Union. Of course there were problems with the ICU. But the Courts had brought order to a nation that had known anarchy for half a generation. If only the Americans had given moderates like Adan a chance to marginalize the extremists, Somalia might have found its own path to peace. But instead the US intervened, empowering the warlords who had oppressed the Somali people, supporting the Ethiopians in decimating the ICU leadership, and creating a power vacuum the Shabaab was only too happy to fill. Six years later, the radicals were in control of half of Somalia, launching terror attacks, assassinating politicians, and closing ranks with al-Qaeda. Yet still America soldiered on, acting as if its might guaranteed the righteousness of its cause.

Eventually, Paul came back on the radio. "Ibrahim, I've talked to my commander, and he's going to speak to his superiors. But that's going to take time. These decisions don't happen quickly."

"How much time?" Ismail demanded.

"I don't know. I need you to be patient. In the meantime, the Navy is going to conduct normal flight operations. You might see planes taking off and helicopters in the air. Don't let it alarm you."

This is a diversion, Ismail thought, but he didn't have a choice. "Keep them away from us, or this will end badly."

Then he put down the radio and explained the situation to his men.

The clock in the sailboat's galley ticked away the hours as ponderously as the glaciers Ismail had read about in his father's books. His crew stood by the curtained windows, seized with wonder and dread, as the Navy showed off its near-Promethean capabilities. The helicopters came first, rising off the decks of the ships as the sun rose above the sea. They flew lazy patterns in the air, hovering like dragonflies, dancing minuets, and then disappearing over the horizon, only to return minutes later like emissaries carrying news from afar. They kept their distance, never flying closer than half a mile, but the noise of their rotors drilled so deep into Ismail's brain that he began to pine for silence.

Then came the jets. They shot off the carrier in pairs and climbed into the sky until they were little more than specks in the vast canvas of blue. Occasionally, they descended from the heights and circled the ships like vultures, the scream of their turbines rattling everything in the sailboat that wasn't firmly attached. As the morning turned into afternoon, the flybys increased, throwing Ismail's crew into agitation and triggering a rash of speculations about the Navy's intentions. The men chattered like locusts, weaving their fears into a chorus of paranoia that Ismail was powerless to counteract. He allowed the Captain and Timaha to play their music, hoping it would lighten the mood, but the men were too mesmerized by the naval exercises to listen or care.

Finally, just after three o'clock in the afternoon, the jets returned to the carrier, leaving only the helicopters in the air. It was then that Paul came on the radio again.

"*Renaissance*, this is *Gettysburg*, do you read? Over."

Ismail sat down at the nav station and looked at his men. He saw the lines of apprehension on their foreheads, the doubt in their eyes. Three of them—Liban, Sondare, and Dhuuban—were watching him expectantly, waiting for him to find a way out of the mess. Osman was staring angrily at the radio, as if it were an agent of the enemy. Guray looked nonplussed, his trigger finger twitching on the butt of his gun. But Mas's expression was darker—at once wary and suspicious. His eyes spoke a challenge: *Do you have what it takes to bring this to an end?*

"*Gettysburg*," Ismail replied simply, "what is your answer?"

The negotiator replied with a dodge. "How are the hostages? The last time I talked to Captain Parker he had a gun pointed at his head."

Ismail took a slow breath and played along. "They're well. As I have told you, we have no desire to hurt them. We will let them go as soon as we negotiate with their family. They are the solution to this situation. Your Navy is the problem."

"I understand that," Paul said in an ingratiating tone. "And I'm working on it. I can't give you an answer just yet, but the people in charge are telling me they want to have a conversation. At the same time, they don't want the entire maritime community listening in. We have a secure radio we'd like to use instead of VHF. I need to get a handset over to you. Is that all right with you?"

Ismail furrowed his brow. "What are you talking about?"

"If you look out the window, you'll see a boat in the water with two sailors. They're unarmed and they have the radio. It's easy to use. As soon as we get it over to you, we can talk further."

Ismail picked up his binoculars and pushed aside the nearest curtain. He saw a small craft riding the meter-high waves behind the Navy ship. The sailors were like stick figures at this distance, but they had their hands in the air.

"What is happening?" his men were asking.

"They want to give us a different radio," Ismail replied in Somali. "They want to keep talking, but they don't want anyone else to hear."

Liban was the first to understand. He moved to the window and squinted into the afternoon sunlight. "It's a trap!" he said, shaking his head.

The others followed on his heels and pandemonium ensued. The men began to shout at the Captain and Timaha and denounce the Navy. Osman was most vociferous, spitting out curses like cobra venom, but all of their protestations had the same theme—the Americans couldn't be trusted.

While his men carried on, Ismail took the opportunity to think. They were right to perceive a threat, but they were wrong about its origin. The boat was irrelevant; the Navy wasn't going to attack them with two sailors. The radio was more of a concern. Paul's explanation sounded like an excuse. They weren't anywhere near the shipping lanes. Where were the other vessels that could overhear them? It was more likely that the Navy wanted to use the radio to get close to the sailboat. They couldn't see in the windows, and they had no idea how well his men were armed.

But even that only hinted at the real danger they were facing. Ismail saw it clearly now. The helicopters, the fighter jets, the noise, and the delay in answering a simple question—all of it was strategic. The Navy had no intention of negotiating with them, no intention of letting them go to Somalia to save the lives of the hostages. They were stalling for time, wearing them down, and planning a rescue attempt, just like they did with Garaad Mohammed's boys on the lifeboat with Captain Phillips. The *Renaissance* was three and a half days from the Somali coast. It was more than enough time for the SEAL commandos to mount a stealth attack.

The longer Ismail thought about it, the more convinced he became that talking to Paul was a waste of time. Releasing the hostages without a ransom was not an option. If the Americans wouldn't negotiate on his terms, he would have to force them into it, not by shooting the Parkers, but by co-opting their family to act on his behalf. It was a gamble of monumental proportions. Once he tried it, he could never go back. But he didn't care. He had taken the same risk in fleeing the Shabaab. The only future he wanted was a future with Yasmin. To get there, he had to put everything on the line.

"Shut up!" he exclaimed, getting his crew's attention. His men quieted down and watched him through sullen eyes. "I have a plan," he said and explained himself in Somali. He spoke the story so fluidly, and invoked Gedef's name with such confidence, that he half expected them to swallow the lie without objection. But Mas was Gedef's cousin, and he demanded proof.

"My relatives would never have agreed to that," Mas said. "It's too dangerous."

Ismail stared him down, his heart hammering in his chest. This was a contest of wits he had to win. "Are you calling me a liar? If Gedef wasn't dead, he would tell you himself."

Mas blinked but stood firm. "Swear it in the name of Allah."

When Ismail spoke the blasphemy, he knew his soul was all but lost. "*Wallah hil-atheem*, what I have told you is true."

Mas fell into a brooding silence, and Ismail picked up the radio again. "We are not interested in conversation with your government," he told Paul. "If any boat approaches us, we will shoot it. We are going to Somalia. If you value the lives of the hostages, you will not intervene."

He turned off the unit before the negotiator could reply. Then he looked at the Captain, who was watching him warily. "It is time for a different strategy. I need your help."

III

FRACTURE POINTS

For every action, there is an
equal and opposite reaction.
—ISAAC NEWTON

VANESSA

It was still dark when Vanessa climbed out of bed. She had slept barely two hours the entire night, and she was exhausted down to the marrow in her bones. But it was pointless to lie awake staring at the ceiling and imagining the chess match playing out half a world away. All of it was out of her control—the pirates, the Navy, the negotiation, Paul Derrick. She couldn't believe that life had brought her full circle, back to a place where the ground could shake at any moment, where people with unspoken intentions held the reins of her life. She felt like a child again, like her mother had just announced they were moving to another city for a new man, or a dream job, or a second chance, wrecking whatever sense of home Vanessa had succeeded in carving out for herself since Trish's last flight of fancy—or calamitous failure—compelled her to cut all ties and leave the known world behind.

Vanessa showered and dressed and piled Skipper into

her SUV for the short drive to Greenbury Point, where the Severn River emptied into the Chesapeake Bay. At such an early hour, the street was free of media crews—a mercy after yesterday. Mary had been right. The TV people had shown up just after lunch and stayed until long after sunset. When the first enterprising reporter knocked on the door, Curtis went outside and ordered them to stay off the property. The threat of the law held them at bay, but nothing kept them out of Vanessa's mind. Their presence had haunted her for hours on end, turning her emotional prison into a physical barrier constraining the autonomy she prized more than anything else. She realized as she left the driveway that it was this instinct that had compelled her to rise before the dawn. She needed to feel free again, if only for a few precious minutes.

She parked in the lot at the head of the path and let Skipper loose to scamper and forage, as he always did. The morning sky was low and ponderous, with scudding clouds the color of shale sailing along on a stiff wind. She walked briskly at first and then began to run. She focused her mind on the earth beneath her feet, on Skipper's solitary form in the gray distance, on the sound of the wind in the trees and the river lapping against the breakwater not far away.

At some point she began to sprint. She caught up to Skipper and urged him on with a winded, "Let's run!" The dog dashed to her side, joining her gamely despite his age. They ran together through the forest and around the point to a bench overlooking the wind-tossed bay. It was here that Daniel had brought her in the mad rush of their engagement, here that he had painted a picture of the life they would make, a life with the baby she hadn't wanted to keep, with a house where they could grow old together, with a family—his family—who would care for them as a family should, not out of guilt and obligation like Trish and Ted, but out of love and commitment. It was a pleasant fairy tale, and she had believed it because she wanted it to be true.

She stopped at the bench and took deep gulps of air, her chest heaving beneath her hooded sweatshirt. She looked out at the Bay Bridge and remembered Quentin at thirteen sailing alone on the Sunfish Daniel had bought him for his birthday. He was so comfortable at the helm, so sure of himself, that she had no choice but to indulge his passion for the water, even though she didn't understand it. He was a Parker, as Daniel had often said, and Parkers were sailors. She felt it again—the satisfaction and sorrow of Quentin's transition to adolescence. That was the year he had started to drift away from her, trading Sunday music sessions for afternoons exploring the bay. That was the year he and Daniel had first charted out a course for a circumnavigation.

She started off again at a more leisurely pace, following the wide loop back to the parking lot. Skipper trotted beside her, his tongue dangling. She was so intent on soaking in the silence that she almost didn't feel the vibration of her iPhone in her pocket. By the time she took it out, the call had gone to voice mail. It was Curtis. She called him back.

"What's up?" she said, feeling more stable than she had in three days.

"How far away are you?" he asked.

"I'm at the Point. Is something wrong?"

His reply was guarded. "I don't know."

"What are you talking about?" she demanded. "Did something happen?"

"I can't explain over the phone. Just get here as soon as you can."

Vanessa pulled into the driveway and screeched to a halt behind Curtis's Mercedes-Benz, ignoring the CNN truck setting up a live feed beyond the row of Tuscan pines that shielded the house from the street. A reporter hailed her across the distance, but Vanessa focused on Mary, who was waiting for her on the porch. The FBI agent ushered her into the house. Duke and Curtis were talking in the living room, and Yvonne was on the sofa, paging through an issue of *Architectural Digest*.

"What's going on?" Vanessa asked when they were together again.

"The phone rang a few minutes ago," Mary explained. "We let it go to voice mail, but the caller didn't leave a message. It was an international number. I thought it might be Ariadne, but when I read the country code out loud, Curtis corrected me. The prefix was 881—a satellite phone."

"Daniel!" Vanessa said, making the connection.

Curtis nodded. "It was his number."

"What does that mean?" Vanessa asked in confusion. "Why would they let him call here?"

Curtis's voice took on a note of gravity. "We don't think

it was Daniel on the phone."

Vanessa's imagination went into overdrive. "You mean . . . Why would they . . . ?"

Mary picked up the narrative. "I called my boss in Virginia. He's at the command center where the incident is being managed. They have a direct link to the *Gettysburg*. Derrick was talking to a pirate named Ibrahim. The Navy wanted to deliver a secure radio to continue the negotiations, but Ibrahim cut off the conversation. That was thirty minutes ago. It's late afternoon over there."

"You think Ibrahim called here?" Vanessa asked quietly.

Strong nodded. "That's the only logical inference. But if we're right, this situation is going to get complicated in a hurry—"

Before the security consultant could explain himself, the phone rang again.

Mary was the first to reach the unit. "It's the same number." She held out the handset to Vanessa. "You should take the call. Use the speakerphone. I'll make a recording."

Vanessa stared at the handset like it was a rattlesnake. "You're kidding."

The FBI agent shook her head. "He doesn't know we're here. We need to find out what he wants. Use your instincts. Don't agitate him. Just let him talk."

Vanessa took the phone, struggling to contain her raging nerves. She pressed the "talk" button and turned on the speaker. "Hello?" she said softly.

"Is this Vanessa Parker?" said an accented male voice.

"Yes," she affirmed.

"My name is Ibrahim," the man went on. "I believe you know who I am. Your husband and son are with me. You may talk to them."

"Vanessa," Daniel said, and her heart fell off a cliff. "We're okay. Quentin is okay. They haven't done anything to us." When she didn't respond, he said a little louder, "Vanessa, are you there?"

"I'm here," she finally replied, tears welling in her eyes. There were a thousand things she had imagined saying to him, but she couldn't remember any of them now. Her heart was broken inside of her, yet it was still beating defiantly, like a drowning swimmer clawing toward the light.

"I'm so sorry," Daniel said, his voice thick with emotion. "This is all my fault. I can't imagine how you'll ever be able to forgive me."

The tears spilled down her cheeks. *I was wondering the same thing. But now it doesn't matter. Nothing matters, except bringing you and Quentin home.* "I bought a plane ticket," she said, speaking the words before she could restrain herself. "To Cape Town at Christmas."

His astonishment was as transparent as his feeling. "You did?"

"I played the Beethoven again. From memory." She took a breath, her mind racing on the current of inspiration. "You asked me to do that."

There was silence on the line.

"So you have to make it there," she went on. "Okay?"

"Okay," he said at last, speaking the word like a vow. "It's a plan. Here's Quentin."

"Mom?" Quentin began. "We're all right. Don't worry about us. We'll be fine."

When she heard her son's voice, Vanessa broke down completely. "I'm so glad to hear that, sweetie," she said, wiping her nose. "We're going to find a way to bring you home."

Ibrahim came back on the line. "Mrs. Parker, I want to return your family to you. But there is a price. Five million dollars, delivered to coordinates I will provide. You have until 17:00 hours East Africa Time on Monday, November 14. In addition, you must call off your Navy. We won't release the hostages until we receive confirmation from Paul, the American negotiator, that the ships around us will let us go. Do you understand?"

"That's a lot of money," Vanessa said, feeling the acid burn of dismay. *Five million dollars? Even Curtis and Yvonne don't have easy access to that kind of cash.* "We need more time."

"The deadline is not negotiable," Ibrahim replied. "If you do as I ask, your family will not be harmed. If you fail, they will die. I will call at sunrise tomorrow for your answer."

At once the line went dead.

Vanessa looked at Mary and Duke. "What are we supposed to do?" she asked, feeling like a noose had just been placed around her neck.

"He's given us no choice," Duke replied, his voice grim. "We have to engage."

"I think it's an opportunity," Curtis said. "Until now we've had no influence over the outcome."

"Where are we going to get the money?" Vanessa asked.

Curtis smiled wanly. "Five million is just the opening. He'll come off that figure. It's just a business deal." He gave Mary a hard look. "So long as the government plays along."

The FBI agent tensed. She took out her BlackBerry and punched a number on speed dial. "We shouldn't do anything until we talk to Derrick."

PAUL

Paul stood on the bridge wing of the *Gettysburg*, watching the *Renaissance* through binoculars. The ocean was a mottled turquoise, the late-afternoon sun half hidden by clouds. Forty-five minutes had passed since Ibrahim had signed off abruptly. Paul had tried to raise him again over the radio, holding forth with one monologue after another, but the pirate hadn't replied. Something had changed in the negotiations. Paul had heard a shift in Ibrahim's voice. His last words had sounded like a valediction. Yet the reason wasn't obvious. Paul had talked it over with Rodriguez, but he had offered no insight. Was it a bluff? A challenge? Was Ibrahim daring the Navy to force his hand?

He heard the door open behind him. "Paul," said Captain Masters, "Brent Frazier is on the line again. You can take it out here if you like."

The captain pointed at a handset below the railing.

Paul picked it up. "Hi, Boss. I gather you're aware of the situation."

Frazier laughed dryly. "For once I'm ahead of you. Ibrahim just called Vanessa on the satellite phone. He made a ransom demand. Five million dollars by Monday at 17:00 local time. Either he's stalling, or he's playing the family against us. We don't know which."

Paul was stunned. In his decade as a negotiator, he had never been blindsided by a hostage taker. It was a remarkably uncomfortable feeling.

"As you can imagine," Frazier said, "a lot of people are unhappy over here. MOTR scheduled a call for midnight your time. It'll be Admiral Prince, Amanda Wolff from State, Gordon Tully, the national security advisor and his deputy, Erika Watson, Redman, Masters, you, and me. The White House is looking for an oracle. They want somebody to tell them what the hell they're supposed to do."

Join the club, Paul thought. Then he had an idea. "Amanda Wolff, she's the piracy maven, the one who vouched for me at the beginning, right?"

"Yeah. The way it's looking, you can forget the Christmas card."

"Give me her number," Paul said.

Frazier knew enough not to ask why. He passed along the DC exchange. "Best of luck. You have until the clock strikes twelve to read the tea leaves."

"Do I get to keep the slipper?" Paul quipped, but Frazier had already hung up.

Paul entered the bridge and approached Masters with

his request. Two minutes later, he was on the bridge wing again, listening to the ringtone. It was only eight o'clock in the morning in Washington, but Paul guessed the counter-piracy director was already at her desk. He was right.

"Amanda Wolff," she said, answering on the first ring.

He kept his overture short. "It's Paul Derrick on the *Gettysburg*. Do you have a minute?"

"Of course."

Paul asked the question foremost in his mind: "Have you ever seen Somali pirates negotiate a ransom at sea? I was under the impression that negotiations take place on land."

"It's unprecedented," she replied. "There are only two explanations. Either Ibrahim is using this as a diversion, or he's gone completely off the reservation."

"Spin that out for me. How would he go rogue?"

"It's simple. Pirate organizations have two tiers. The top tier consists of the commanders and investors—almost always old men with means. The bottom tier consists of the young men they send out on missions. The mission com-mander is given clear orders: bring back a ship or don't bother coming back. When the kids show up with a prize, the old men sit around chewing *qat* and talking about how much money they think they can make off of it. They pay someone to negotiate with the shipping company or the family. They drag the negotiation out until they get close to where they want to end up. Then they play bait and switch. They bring in a new negotiator for the final squeeze. Only then do they arrange a drop. If Ibrahim is serious, he and his crew are acting *ultra vires*—beyond sanction. There's no way they can go back now."

Paul absorbed this. "I need some time to think."

"That's what I figured," Wolff said. "I was the one who bought you six hours."

He smiled. "That's kind of you."

"Anytime. And, Derrick? Don't let the White House apparatchiks or the Special Warfare boys talk down to you. They like to throw their weight around, but they need your wisdom more than you need their approval. If this goes down wrong, it's their ass on the line, not yours or mine."

Wolff was nothing if not blunt. When she hung up, Paul put the phone back in its cradle and found Ensign O'Brien on the bridge. "Can you take me someplace quiet? I need to concentrate."

The young sailor nodded. "The fantail. I'll show you the way."

She led him aft from the bridge wing and down a series of ladders to a weather deck where one of the *Gettysburg's* RHIBs hung suspended in netting. They skirted the boat, being careful not to hit their heads, and then descended another ladder to the main deck. They followed a passageway along the outside of the ship to the missile deck—a gray checkerboard housing half of the cruiser's Tomahawk missiles—and then down a final ladder to the fantail.

"Thank you," he said. "I'll find my way back."

Ensign O'Brien gave him a handheld radio. "We'll call you if something comes up."

Paul went to the stern railing and looked out over the *Gettysburg's* wake, watching the water foam and sparkle in the light of the setting sun. The sky was cornflower blue and speckled with clumps of cloud. He inhaled the moist air and remembered his first negotiation class at the FBI Academy, which Brent Frazier had taught. *There's always leverage*, Frazier had said over and over again until Paul found himself dreaming the words in his sleep. *To find it, you have to get into the heart of the subject. What's driving him to do what he's doing? What does he want out of it? Once you know those things, you can guide him toward a resolution you both can live with. Negotiation isn't about us versus them. It's about us collaborating with them to create a scenario in which everybody gets something. That's as true in a hostage crisis as it is in a boardroom. Dignify the subject, even if he's a psychopath. You'll never get anywhere without his help.*

With Ibrahim, there was leverage. Paul could sense it. He wasn't an illiterate desperado or a soulless mercenary doing the dirty work for his Somali paymasters. There was something beneath the surface, something compelling him to risk his life to steal someone else's treasure. If Paul had the luxury of time, he knew he could answer the riddle. But Ibrahim had changed the game. In approaching the Parker family, he had made an end run around the Navy, turning billions of dollars of military hardware into a sideshow. This was precisely the place where leverage evaporated—when a negotiator lost contact with the subject, or the subject escaped the barricade. With one phone call, Ibrahim had made huge strides toward accomplishing both. Or had he? Was it possible that he had gone rogue? If he meant to take the money and run, why hadn't he changed the sailboat's course? It made no sense to sail right back into the arms of his commanders. Then again, he was still days away from the coast. He had time to make a course correction. Perhaps he was waiting for something.

Paul wrestled with the question, gnashed his teeth on it, until he could articulate what his gut told him in words that would influence the heavyweights in Washington. There were those in the government who wouldn't like what he had to say, but he didn't care. Amanda Wolff was right. The politicos needed cover, and he could offer them that. He wasn't a fortune-teller, but he knew people. And Ibrahim, despite the inhumanity of his crimes, was still a member of the human race.

After dinner in the officers' wardroom, Paul spent the evening in meetings, debating the merits of deferring to the Parker family in the negotiation, for the time being at least. He found it easy to convince Rodriguez—he was Paul's protégé, after all—and Masters seemed open to his point of view. But Redman took passionate exception to his proposal.

Paul wasn't surprised. There was a point in almost every hostage crisis at which the tactical commander and the lead negotiator came to loggerheads about next steps. The conflict was usually provoked by the hostage taker's intransigence and the desire of the tactical team to "do something" to resolve the crisis. It was a dangerous moment for the hostages, for tactical action dramatically increased the chance that the good guys would get hurt.

Paul hammered this point home in his discussions with the SEAL commander, citing cases from the CNU's database in which impatience led to bloodshed. Redman listened but didn't bend. "Dammit!" he exclaimed at one point. "We can't allow a bunch of pirates to define the parameters of our mission." Paul tried to persuade him that innovation wasn't the same as capitulation, but the dispute persisted until midnight, when they met in the admiral's cabin for the MOTR call.

Paul and the Navy captains sat at the table in the center of the room, and Rodriguez, Ali Sharif, and Lieutenant Commander Cardwell took seats around the periphery. Paul studied the two flat-screen monitors while an ensign completed a system check. One of the screens displayed a GPS map of the Indian Ocean with position, course, and speed data for the *Renaissance* and the trio of Navy ships. The other screen showed five people sitting in a conference room in front of hanging photos of the president and vice president. *Probably in the bowels of the White House*, Paul inferred. Frazier was there, alongside a hawk-eyed man in uniform—Admiral Prince—and a middle-aged woman in a pantsuit—Amanda Wolff. Paul recognized Gordon Tully, the national security advisor, at the head of the table and guessed that the woman next to him was his deputy, Erika Watson.

"My apologies for the lateness of the hour over there," Tully said in opening. He made summary introductions and then got down to business. "Admiral Prince has just briefed us on the tactical options, and to be frank, they're all bad.

We're still in the dark about the number of pirates. Your snipers say they counted six shadows behind the curtains, but they couldn't be sure. Your attack team could make a subsurface approach, but the pirates are keeping the hatches closed, which means you can't flush them out with tear gas. You could try to disable the propeller, but we don't know how the pirates would react if they figured out the damage was deliberate. The last thing we need is a bloodbath when we still have time for a peaceful resolution."

Tully checked off something on the notepad in front of him. "That brings me to the question of Ibrahim's intent. Agent Derrick, you've talked to him and spent time with dozens of others like him over the years. Is he serious about negotiating with the family?"

Paul leaned forward in his chair, conscious of the displeasure on Redman's face. "Mr. Tully, my interactions with Ibrahim have been limited, so all I can give you is my instinct. I believe he was genuine in approaching the Parkers. Hostage takers who play fast and loose with their words set artificial deadlines and then break them. Ibrahim has made a lot of threats, but the only deadline he's given us is the one for the ransom drop. I can't tell you why he's taken matters into his own hands. But I think he's made that decision."

Erika Watson spoke up. "The admiral tells us you had a conversation with him about religion."

Paul nodded. "We run monologues sometimes to get a subject to engage. My linguist gave me some suggestions, and I improvised. Ibrahim was interested in my knowledge of the Quran. I wouldn't say the conversation was about religion, *per se*. It was about the origins of evil."

Watson wrote something down and then looked back at the camera. "And what impressions did you draw from that exchange?"

Paul took a breath. "I got the sense that he's keenly aware of the moral implications of his actions. If I'm right, then he's rationalizing it somehow. It's human nature. No one deliberately subverts his conscience. My guess—and it's only a guess—is that this is about more than just money to him."

Watson raised her eyebrows. "Are you saying he's motivated by ideology?"

Paul danced around the trip wire. "I doubt it. Ideologues wear their beliefs like a badge. I'm shooting in the dark here, but I'd bet his justification is personal."

Watson didn't disguise her skepticism. "What sort of *personal* justification would satisfy a man like him, if you don't mind me asking?"

Paul didn't miss a beat. "The most powerful motivators are love, loyalty, hatred, and vengeance. Any combination of those would do."

"You make him sound like a romantic," interjected Admiral Prince. "A Somali Jack Sparrow. In the real world, pirates are *hostis humani generis*—enemies of all mankind."

"He may be an enemy," Paul replied. "But that doesn't make him less of a human being."

Redman gritted his teeth. "I agree with Admiral Prince. I think Agent Derrick is giving Ibrahim far too much credit. The man is a pirate. He held a gun to Captain Parker's head and shot holes in the sailboat. He's threatened to kill an eighteen-year-old kid if his family doesn't cough up five million dollars. I don't believe a word he says, and neither should you."

"Captain Redman," said Gordon Tully, "I appreciate your candor. I doubt any of us would dispute your assessment of Ibrahim's character. But what would you have us do?"

Redman's response was direct. "Sir, I'd like permission to disable the sailboat. We can do it under the cover of darkness and make it look like the propeller got tangled in debris. As soon as Ibrahim knows he can't get away, he'll show his true colors."

Tully's eyes bored through the screen. "Has it ever occurred to you that his true colors might include shooting one of the hostages?"

When the SEAL commander hesitated, Paul jumped in. "This morning I would have agreed with Captain Redman. Negotiation requires time, and disabling the sailboat was the least confrontational option. But Ibrahim has given us an opening. If I'm right about his motives, we could get where we want to go without any tactical action."

The national security advisor squinted at the camera. "You're not suggesting we let the pirates get away with the money? That would not only violate US policy, but it would transgress every scruple left in my pragmatic brain."

Paul shook his head. "I'm suggesting we do whatever it takes to liberate the hostages. Then we go after Ibrahim and his crew." He paused. "There's precedent for this. When

Julius Caesar was a young man, he had an encounter with pirates in the Mediterranean. They captured his ship and held him for ransom. He made sure they got the money. But as soon as he was free, he put together a posse and brought the perpetrators to justice. As I see it, that's the safest approach."

Tully laughed sardonically. "I've been in Washington my whole life. I can't remember the last time Julius Caesar was cited as precedent. But I take the point. Amanda, are there legal issues?"

"As long as the capture takes place at sea, we're fine," Wolff replied. "If they reach the coast, it gets more complicated. We have UN authority to apprehend them on Somali soil. But we don't want to anger the government. We're working hard to keep the elections on track for next year."

"With all due respect, sir," Redman interjected, struggling to remain politic, "what if Agent Derrick is wrong? What if all of this is a ruse and Ibrahim has no intention of letting the Parkers go before they reach land? It's been hours since he contacted the family, but the sailboat is still headed to Hobyo. If I'd decided to betray my criminal bosses, I would run as far from them as I could."

"Paul?" Tully said, shifting his eyes slightly.

"I had the same thought," Paul admitted. "I can't explain it. All I can tell you is what my gut tells me. I think he's playing straight."

Tully scribbled on his notepad and then looked back at the camera. "Frank, your concerns are legitimate. But I don't see the harm in giving the family latitude. You can monitor the negotiations. If things go off the rails, we can always disable the sailboat later."

Redman winced. "Sir, if we cede control to the family, it's going to be very hard to get it back. That's human nature, too."

"Granted," Tully replied. "But we're in uncharted waters here—"

"Pardon me, Mr. Tully, Captain Redman," Masters said, "but I'm seeing something strange on GPS." He took a handheld radio off his belt and held it up to his mouth. "Bridge, this is the captain, please check the radar and confirm the current heading and speed of the *Renaissance*."

Paul stared at the wall-mounted display and saw the disparity immediately. When the call started, the headings of the three Navy ships and the sailboat had been identical. Now the sailboat's bearing had changed, shifting slightly to the west, and its speed had increased by over a knot.

"Captain," said a disembodied voice, sounding bewildered. "The sailboat is bearing 298 degrees, forty-nine minutes, at a speed of 7.3 knots. It was bearing 329 at six knots when I last checked." The voice paused. "The watch officer is reporting that the sailboat is no longer pulling the skiff."

All eyes in the admiral's cabin and the conference room eight thousand miles away were riveted on Masters. "At this course and speed, where and when will the *Renaissance* make landfall?" he asked.

The reply came seconds later. "At present course and speed, assuming no set from the current, the sailboat will make landfall twenty-four miles north of Mogadishu at approximately 17:00 East Africa Time on November 14."

Paul made the connection immediately. *That's the deadline Ibrahim gave Vanessa Parker.*

Redman sat back in his chair, frustration written all over his face. He cleared his throat. "As hard as I find it to believe, it seems Agent Derrick's theory is credible. It looks like he's running."

Tully let out the breath he was holding. "That makes it easier. So this is how it's going to go. If the Parkers want to pay, we're not going to stop them. If Ibrahim asks us our position, we tell him whatever he wants to hear. We keep the media in the dark until the pirates let the hostages go. And then we take them down."

DANIEL

The cabin was as dark as a crypt an hour before the dawn, the only light filtering through the portholes cast by the distant stars. Daniel couldn't sleep. He and Quentin were wedged into a bunk barely large enough for one of them, but it wasn't discomfort that was keeping him awake. It was Vanessa, her voice like silk yet pregnant with feeling, speaking words he could scarcely believe. *I bought a plane ticket. To Cape Town at Christmas. I played the Beethoven again. From memory. You asked me to do that. So you have to make it there. Okay?* He didn't know what to do with it, except hold it close.

He watched the rise and fall of Quentin's chest and recalled the day he was born. It was a surprise, just like his conception. He had come three weeks early, and they hadn't been ready for him. The nursery wasn't finished, the crib was still on order, and the law firm wasn't expecting Daniel's absence until the next month. He remembered Vanessa waking in the early-morning hours and putting her hand on his chest. *I think I'm going into labor,* she had whispered, and he had sprung into action, moving like he was a minute late for an interview that would change his life. They made it to the hospital in fifteen minutes flat, but the labor had lasted thirty hours. He could still see the agony on her face when the nurse finally said she was ready to push. She had grabbed his hand and dug her nails into his flesh. *I'm never doing this again,* she said. *Promise me.* And he had. Somehow it didn't seem premature, for both of them were only children. They would pour all they had into the baby. *We had no clue how hard parenthood would be,* he reflected. *But now I can't imagine a world without him.*

Daniel turned his thoughts to the other thing tugging at the edges of his consciousness—the shadow he had seen in the night, creeping stealthily out of the companionway and making its way to the helm. The moon had been obscured by high clouds, but he had seen enough of the figure to determine it was Afyareh—or Ibrahim—whatever the hell his name was today. He had heard buttons being pushed on the autopilot and sensed the turn to port. He had felt the lurch and the sudden surge of power, as if the sailboat had been loosed of a burden. *The skiff,* he had inferred. *He let it go.* Almost immediately, the pirate had slipped back the way he came and disappeared from view.

He couldn't decide if Afyareh's actions were ominous or propitious. The day before had been profoundly distressing. The naval exercises had stirred the Somalis as effectively as kicking a hornets' nest, magnifying the tension in the sailboat until Daniel could almost smell the pirates' fear. Even Afyareh had lost control, wielding his Kalashnikov like a brute. The second time he shot off his gun, the weapon had been so close to Daniel's ear that he hadn't recovered his hearing for an hour.

The terror had climaxed when Afyareh saw something through his binoculars. Daniel still didn't know what it was, but he had watched the Somalis' eyes darken, seen the way they yelped and pointed their guns at the invisible threat. Afyareh had taken command again, soothing them with his golden tongue. But then Mas had challenged him, his eyes laced with sedition. Afyareh had prevailed and Mas had backed down, but the encounter had left Daniel confused, as had everything that happened afterward—the finality with which Afyareh spoke to Paul, his sudden expression of interest in the sat phone, the ransom call to Annapolis, the midnight course change and abandonment of the skiff.

What kind of game was the pirate playing?

Daniel jolted awake to the sound of pounding on the door. He glanced at Quentin and realized he had drifted off. The stateroom was brighter now, the stars gone from the sky. He climbed out of his sleeping bag and slid his feet onto the wood floor. His mind, so sharp in the wee hours of morning, felt addled, as if he had a hangover. He opened the door and saw Afyareh staring at him.

"Wake up, Captain. It's time to call your family again."

Daniel nodded curtly and followed the pirate to the navigation station, ignoring the stares of the other Somalis, who were lounging around the cabin. The stench of unwashed bodies was overpowering, but they had run out of water for showers. What potable water they had left was for drinking only.

He opened the chart table and extracted the sat phone from its case. It was a high-end Iridium model, not much bigger than a cell phone. He punched in the number and turned on the speaker, handing the unit to Afyareh, then sat down in the companionway, his elbows on his knees. Quentin slipped by him and stood in the galley, his hair an unkempt mess.

The line connected and Daniel heard his father's voice. "Hello? Is this Ibrahim?"

"I am Ibrahim," said the pirate. "Who are you?"

"I'm Curtis Parker, the Captain's father. I will speak for the family in the negotiations."

The pirate looked at the ceiling, suddenly lost in thought. "Yes, I remember you. You have a nice watch. Gold, isn't it?"

How did he—? Daniel thought. Then he remembered the day Afyareh explored his stateroom. *Dammit. He must have found the photo album.*

If Curtis was surprised, he didn't show it. "You're well informed."

Afyareh gave Daniel a bemused look. "Are you putting together the payment, Curtis? You have two and a half days until the deadline."

"It's not that simple, Ibrahim. Money doesn't grow on trees. We have no way of raising five million dollars by Monday. The most we can deliver is five hundred thousand. The good news is the Navy has agreed to back off if we can reach an agreement."

Afyareh rolled his eyes. "I have seen the Captain's house and his wife's jewelry. I am certain your family can pay more than that."

Curtis was not moved. "Have you ever heard the expression 'time is money'? Things like real estate and personal property are useless to you. They take months to liquidate. You're asking for cash. Five hundred is the best I can do. The Navy's promise to let you go is worth the remainder."

Afyareh wrinkled his nose, as if he had detected a putrid odor. "I don't like it when people lie to me. Your offer is rejected. You need to work harder."

Without warning, the pirate terminated the call. He shook his head. "Your father is not a very helpful person, Captain. I think next time I will speak to your wife."

You bastard, Daniel thought, wishing he could wring the pirate's neck. He imagined Vanessa sitting in the living room beside Curtis and Yvonne, struggling to hold herself together. Afyareh's perfunctory dismissal of half a million dollars had probably sent her anxiety into the red zone. She hated negotiations. She was the sort of person who paid the asking price or walked away.

He took a breath and composed himself. Afyareh was shrewd; he knew the value of the cards in his hand. He had signaled that he would accept less than the demand, but he had given no indication of how much, leaving Curtis to bid against himself. Still, it was heartening to know that the Navy wouldn't stand in the way. With Curtis at the helm, they would find a way to make a deal.

Afyareh took a seat in the nav station. "How much is life worth?" he said, looking at Daniel. "It's something I have wondered many times. There was a film I saw when I was a boy. My parents didn't want me to watch it, but I did anyway. *Can't Buy Me Love.* Do you know it?"

Daniel nodded but didn't speak.

"I liked Ronald," Afyareh continued. "He knew what he wanted, and he did what it took to get it, even though it ruined him." His eyes glimmered. "Of course, it didn't actually ruin him. He got the girl. It is a paradox. He couldn't buy love, but he could buy friendship. And without that, she never would have loved him. Life is priceless, I think, but money makes everything easier."

The pirate's stomach suddenly growled. "What's for breakfast?" he asked.

Daniel heard the sound of helicopters lifting off as he and Quentin were cleaning up after the meal. The rumble of fighter jets soon followed. The Somalis went to the windows and began to chatter among themselves, as they had the day before. Afyareh tracked the planes with his binoculars and ordered Daniel to turn on some music. While Mick Jagger sang, the pirate toyed with the sat phone and watched the clock as if it were a crystal ball offering him a glimpse of the future.

A couple of hours later, Afyareh punched the "redial" button and set the phone on the table in the booth where he and Quentin were sitting. *It's after midnight on the East Coast*, Daniel almost protested, but the uncompromising look in the pirate's eyes was enough to dissuade him.

"Ibrahim," Curtis said, sounding alert despite the hour. "We've been waiting for your call. You ended our last conversation quite abruptly."

The pirate grunted. "Have you made progress?"

"I can't do anything until you give me a more reasonable number," Curtis replied. "I didn't lie to you. I'm negotiating in good faith. We don't have five million."

Just then, Daniel heard one of the jets approaching. The whine of turbines grew louder until the dishes in the sink began to vibrate. Afyareh held the phone up to the window, allowing the roar to fill the speakers. At last, the jet climbed back into the morning sky and the cabin grew quiet again.

"What was that noise?" Curtis asked, perturbed.

"That is your Navy making trouble for us," the pirate replied. "If you want to do business, then make the Navy go away."

Curtis hesitated. "How am I supposed to do that?"

Afyareh shrugged, as if his request were elementary. "Contact your government. Tell them to fly somewhere else. I will call you back in twenty minutes."

The pirate cut off the call and picked up his binoculars again. He spoke a handful of sentences in Somali, and his men crowded around the windows, watching the sky. While the pirates were distracted, Daniel leaned toward Quentin and whispered, "How are you?"

Quentin glanced around furtively. "I'm worried about Ariadne," he said in an undertone. "The last message I sent her was three days ago."

Daniel almost smiled. *Only a teenage boy would be thinking about a girl when his life is on the line.* "Where's your phone?" he asked. "They haven't disabled the uplink."

"You mean now?" Quentin replied, retrieving the phone from his pocket. "What do I say?"

Daniel looked into his son's eyes and saw a reflection of himself as a young man—all the wonder and confusion and feeling dashed upon the canvas of his heart like a Jackson Pollock painting. He asked the only question that mattered. "Do you love her?"

Quentin blinked, then blushed scarlet.

"Tell her that," Daniel said under his breath. "And tell her to get in touch with your mother."

He caught Liban staring at them and motioned to Afyareh. "My son needs to use the head."

"Yes, fine," the pirate replied and looked out the window again.

While Quentin went to the bathroom, Daniel sat back against the bench and closed his eyes, focusing all of his attention on listening. He could hear the whistle of the jets streaking through the sky and the muted *whump-whump-whump* of the helicopters as they moved around like bumblebees. Curtis had enormous clout in the government, but he wasn't omnipotent. Daniel pictured him on the phone, pulling favors, as he had so many times at the firm. Would the Navy brass defer to him, realizing they had little to gain from provoking the pirates, or would they persist with their shock and awe campaign?

He heard the sucking sound of the toilet flushing, and then Quentin rejoined him.

"Did it go out?" Daniel whispered. When his son nodded, he felt strangely jubilant. *Take that, you sons of bitches!* It was a small victory over the pirates' tyranny, but for the moment it felt like a coup.

"There was something else," Quentin said quietly. "An e-mail from Grandpa. He asked how many rotten apples we took with us."

Daniel felt a chill but didn't change his expression. "What did you say?"

Quentin met his eyes. "I told him seven."

After a while, Afyareh threw the binoculars on the bench and picked up the sat phone. "They're not going away," he spat at Daniel, fury in his eyes. "Your father is playing games with us."

Daniel put his hands out, palms up. "My father is a businessman. He's being straight with you. He can't just wave a wand and make the US government obey. They do what they want."

Afyareh thrust the phone into Daniel's hands. "That is

not *good enough*! Tell Curtis that if he wants us to trust him, he needs to prove that the Navy will not interfere. If the jets are still in the air in"—he glanced at the clock—"thirty minutes, then there will be *no deal*."

Daniel punched the "redial" button on the sat phone, a knot of dread in his gut. "Dad," he began when Curtis picked up, "the Navy isn't complying, and the pirates are getting angry." He conveyed Afyareh's message and the deadline. "Whatever they think they're doing by sticking to their guns, it's having the opposite effect. They need to back off now."

"I let them know that," Curtis said, allowing his frustration to show. "Sit tight."

Daniel spent the next half hour in a state of hyper-alertness. He watched the Somalis as they stared out the windows, cataloging every change in expression and body language and assigning it a value—positive or negative—like some psychoanalytic binary code. For a long time, all of his notations went on the adverse side of the ledger. Frowns and grimaces, tensing muscles, tapping feet, facial tics, muttered denunciations, all were indications of raw nerves and suppressed rage. Then something happened with a suddenness that seemed almost miraculous. Their eyes widened and their shoulders relaxed. Their jaws slackened and their vocalizations took on a lighter tone.

"What's going on?" Daniel asked Afyareh, detecting no

change in the noise outside.

The pirate gave him a triumphant look. "The jets are returning to the aircraft carrier."

Daniel put his arm around Quentin. "Thank God," he exhaled, feeling the relief like a cleansing flood. Somehow Curtis had accomplished the impossible. He had convinced the Navy to pull a punch.

Over time, the mechanical serenade of warplanes and helicopters fell to nothing. The pirates raised their fists and celebrated Afyareh—even Mas, though his contribution was less emphatic.

At last, Afyareh collected the sat phone and called Annapolis. When Curtis answered, the pirate held up the phone to the nearest window. "Do you hear it?" he asked jubilantly.

"Hear what?" Curtis replied.

"The sound of an empty sky." Afyareh allowed the silence to linger, clearly enjoying himself. Then he said, "The Captain told me you were a man of your word. Now I believe him. We will accept three and a half million dollars. I will call again at sunset."

Then he hung up the phone.

VANESSA

Vanessa took long strides up the concourse, pulling her roll-aboard suitcase and looking for her gate. The Ethiopian Airlines flight from Washington Dulles to Addis Ababa was scheduled to depart in thirty-five minutes. She felt an undercurrent of dread, as she always did when she was about to board an airplane. She knew the feeling was irrational. The statistics were overwhelmingly in her favor, as Daniel had often repeated whenever they had traveled. But the fact was that some airplanes crashed. Occasionally, one fell out of the sky. She couldn't imagine a worse way to die.

She glanced at Mary Patterson walking beside her. The FBI agent looked serene, as if the prospect of flying halfway around the world to arrange a ransom drop was something she did all the time. Vanessa was grateful to have company on the journey, but she was equally thankful they wouldn't be sitting together on the plane. She had offered to upgrade Mary's Bureau-sponsored ticket from economy to business, but the FBI agent had declined. It was a blessing. The flight to Africa was thirteen and a half hours, and Vanessa wanted nothing more than to sleep.

The trip had come together at the last minute. Just after four o'clock the previous afternoon, Mary had gotten confirmation from her boss that the government wouldn't interfere if the family negotiated with Ibrahim. With that promise in hand, Curtis had spent all evening crunching numbers and confirming liquidity with his bankers and brokers. As Vanessa suspected, most of his money was tied up in real estate and retirement accounts. But he was not without access to cash. He had extensive lines of credit on his properties, and he had a substantial reserve of dollars and euros stashed in the Cayman Islands that could be wired at a moment's notice to any bank in the world.

Vanessa had contributed what she could—the remainder of the money in Daniel's sailing account and the rest of their depleted savings. When Curtis looked at the amount in surprise, she had confessed, with embarrassment, how much the circumnavigation had impacted their finances. She had offered to draw on her home equity line, but Curtis had refused, leaving Vanessa feeling humiliated. In contrast to Daniel, who had always been a spendthrift, she was a saver. Financial stability was a point of honor. And right now she was anything but stable.

The late-evening hours had been fraught with tension. Curtis had amassed a respectable sum, but they needed Ibrahim to come to the bargaining table. As the phone sat in silence, the minutes ticking away, Vanessa had tried everything to ward off her anxiety. The Bissolotti was so close, but the privacy she needed to play was not. She had turned on music, but it did little to relax her. So she paced in the living room, and took walks with Skipper, and wrote an update to Ariadne, spinning a web of hope to buoy both of them, and listened to Duke Strong's tutorial about ransom delivery, wondering all the while how her blissfully ordinary life had turned into a movie script.

Finally, just after midnight, Ibrahim had called again, but not with a counteroffer. He demanded that the Navy ground its planes. It was an outlandish request, like asking the weatherman to stop the rain. Mary called her boss, and Curtis reached out to his friends at the Pentagon. The government's response was blunt—allowing the family to negotiate didn't mean taking pressure off the pirates. But Curtis persisted, and Frank Overstreet, the assistant secretary of defense, came through, getting Gordon Tully out of bed and putting him on the line with Curtis. After listening carefully, the national security advisor promised to intervene.

That call had ended only fifteen minutes before Ibrahim's deadline. Vanessa watched the time wind down in a state of panic. Her breathing became labored, and her heart thundered in her chest. She went twice to the bathroom, feeling like she might vomit. Then the phone rang again, and Ibrahim delivered the news that the Navy had backed down. Vanessa was so relieved that she felt, for a fleeting instant, a sense of gratitude to the pirate. He might be heartless, but at least he was rational.

As soon as Ibrahim reduced his demand, Strong had

set the wheels in motion for the drop, on the assumption that they would reach an agreement. While the negotiation continued in Annapolis, the delivery would be coordinated in Nairobi. Tony Flint, an erstwhile Force Recon marine and chief of East African operations for Sagittarius, would handle the logistics, but he needed a representative from the family on the ground to assist. Vanessa had volunteered to go, more than anything to get out of the house, and Mary had obtained permission from the Bureau to accompany her.

When they reached the gate, the flight was already boarding. Vanessa walked down the Jetway with Mary, and they parted ways inside the aircraft. She found her seat near the front and collapsed into it, leaning her head against the headrest. She had gotten only ten hours of sleep in the past four nights. Even during her residency, her rest had been more consistent. She had Ambien in her purse, but she hated the thought of using it. As a teenager, she had watched her mother deal with stress with Vicodin, and she had vowed never to resolve her issues through medication. That she now prescribed the same drugs to her patients she found both ironic and irrelevant.

She closed her eyes and dozed for a few minutes, tuning out the sounds of the flight attendants scurrying around the cabin handing out newspapers and beverages. Suddenly, her iPhone rang. She searched for it in her purse. The caller was Ted Collins—her stepfather. *Of all the moments*, she thought. She almost let him leave a voice mail but decided it would only delay the inevitable.

"Hello?" she said, looking out the window at the plane

beside them.

"Vanessa, it's Ted," he said with the papery rasp of an inveterate smoker. "I saw the news. Why didn't you call?"

She thought of a number of excuses, but none of them fit. "There's a lot happening right now. I'm not in a place where I can talk."

He didn't take the hint. "Where are you? Are Daniel and Quentin all right?"

The questions made her bristle. *Since when have you cared about my family? You call twice a year, on my birthday and Christmas. Otherwise, you just send us checks on holidays.* She knew she wasn't really being fair. Ted had taken her in and given her a world-class education, an enviable wedding, and the Bissolotti. But gifts were no substitute for emotional support. He had never been there when she needed a shoulder to cry on. Like Trish, he had left her to navigate the minefield of adolescence on her own.

"I'm on a plane," she said simply. "Daniel and Quentin are okay, for the moment anyway. There's a limit to what I can say. Give me a few days, and I'll tell you more."

It was a promise she didn't intend to keep, but she was desperate to end the call.

Ted, however, blithely ignored her cues. "The media attention is wild. The story is all over the networks. They're saying the Navy is negotiating with the pirates. How are you holding up?"

"I'm hanging in there," she replied a bit testily. "Look, I really have to go."

He cleared his throat. "Let me know if you need anything.

If they want money, I can help. You know that, don't you? Your mother may be gone, but I'm still here."

She heard an odd note in his voice, a hitch of genuine concern, but she didn't know what to think about it. Providence had dealt her a bizarre hand. Born to a dirt-poor beauty queen turned exotic dancer from southwest Virginia, she had lived in squalor for the first decade of her life, never knowing if the power company was going to turn off the lights or the landlord was going to evict them because Trish had spent all her earnings on partying and neglected to pay the bills. Then Ted came along and after him Daniel and Curtis—men who threw money around like life was a giant Monopoly game but who were as stingy as Scrooge when it came to her emotional needs. She had learned to live with them by expecting little from them. She didn't know what to do when they started caring.

"Thanks," she said. "I'll let you know."

When she hung up, she closed her eyes and blocked out everything but the thought of sleep. She felt it when the plane backed away from the terminal and taxied to the runway, when the engines revved and the aircraft rumbled down the tarmac, the overhead bins shuddering and jarring, and when its wings caught the wind and carried them into the sky. She gripped the armrest as the plane climbed through turbulence and only opened her eyes again when they leveled off, the danger of takeoff past. She reclined her seat to its lie-flat position and took two Ambien with a sip of water. This small concession to pragmatism brought her almost immediate relief. Within minutes, she felt her consciousness slipping away like water down a drain, swirling . . . swirling . . .

Until at last it was gone.

When Vanessa awoke, it was dark outside the airplane. She looked out the window and saw the lights of a city strung out like a necklace far below. She called up the map on her entertainment system and saw that they were over the boot of Italy. She watched the lights of Brindisi glitter and asked the flight attendant if dinner was still available. She felt suddenly ravenous. The flight attendant sprang into action, bringing her salad and bread and chicken with rice and asparagus. She declined the offer of wine to avoid dehydration and watched a travel show while she ate. Afterward, she went to the bathroom to brush her teeth, took another Ambien, and fell back asleep.

In the fog of slumber, she began to dream. She was standing in a cemetery in the wet green of April. She knew the place—Cypress Hills in Brooklyn. The marble headstone was nearby, beneath the boughs of a maple tree. The inscription on it read: PATRICIA LEE STONE, BELOVED WIFE AND MOTHER, MAY 5, 1952 TO APRIL 1, 2007. Ted was standing beside her, holding a rose and watching her cry. Words were coming out of her mouth, words she had felt a thousand times but never spoken, the cumulative pain of years, repressed, contained, and finally unleashed on the man who had given her an idyllic end to childhood but never quite loved her like a father.

"Do you know what my earliest memory of her is?" she said. "We were in a club in New York. She never had enough money for a babysitter and always took me to work. I remember her standing in front of a mirror half-naked, putting makeup on her face before she went out to dance. This man came in the room and pulled down his pants. She put a towel over my head and told me not to listen. I was two."

Tears rolled off Vanessa's cheeks. "Living with her was like the circus that never left town. She was always riding high or crashing, spinning delusions about a future Lancelot or lamenting the day when she was the second prettiest girl in Virginia. Do you know how many times she called herself that? 'Miss Alleghany Highlands 1968, runner-up for Miss Virginia.' She was like a perpetual teenager. She never left the age of seventeen."

Vanessa took a breath, then continued her rant. "She never told me who my father was. I asked her for years, but she didn't give me a name. She never told me about her parents or siblings. I didn't know anything about them until the Internet came along, and by then it was too late. She deprived me of family. And what's worse—she never really acted like my mother. I was cooking my own meals when I was seven years old. By the time I was twelve, I was washing laundry and balancing her checkbook. But you know what the crazy part is? Everybody adored her. Everybody treated her like she was special." Vanessa's voice trailed off, and the last part came out in a whisper. "No one paid attention to me."

She looked at Ted and he looked back at her, his hair fluttering in the breeze. He was dressed like he was going to a board meeting—dark suit and tie and wingtip Oxfords. An insurance executive, he was a paragon of consistency and clean living—the opposite of Trish in every way, except for his smoking habit, which he blamed on Woodstock, and his self-absorption, which he didn't see as a fault.

"Are you finished?" he asked at last. "I loved her more than anyone in the world, but I won't make excuses for her. She had a lot of faults. But she's gone now. You have to make peace."

"How am I supposed to do that?" Vanessa asked softly. "She never admitted that she hurt me. Do you know what she told me when I was sixteen? She told me to have as much sex as I liked. I could get an abortion if I got pregnant. She said she would have done it if the laws had been different. Can you imagine telling that to your own child? No wonder I have issues."

Ted shook his head slowly. "She loved you, Vanessa. She told me that many times."

Vanessa wiped her eyes and looked out over the cemetery, shrouded in mist. "Then why did she make me feel like I was a cross she had to bear?"

The dream dissolved into static like the end of an old film reel, and Vanessa slept on as the plane flew over North Africa. She woke hours later to a hand on her shoulder.

"We're about to land," said the flight attendant. "You need to raise your seat again."

Vanessa blinked her eyes, feeling woozy but refreshed. She was still on edge from the dream, but she banished it from her mind and looked out the window, sipping nervously from a bottle of water as the plane descended toward Bole International Airport. The verdant Ethiopian landscape surprised her. The emerald hills and snaking rivers around Addis Ababa had more in common with the Irish country- side than the sun-drenched African savannah she had seen in books and films.

The plane touched down and glided to a halt, taxiing to a spot on the apron a few hundred yards from the glass- encased terminal. Vanessa collected her luggage and met Mary on the tarmac beside an airport bus. The morning air was cooler than Vanessa expected, and the wind blowing off the mountains was brisk. They crowded into the bus with the other passengers—mostly Africans speaking a myriad of languages—and took hold of rubber handles hanging from the roof.

"You look rested," Mary said. "Were you able to sleep?"

Vanessa nodded. "I feel better." She glanced at Mary's BlackBerry. "Do you have reception?"

"It connected right away." Mary lowered her voice. "Ibrahim has come down to three."

Vanessa sighed, at once relieved that they were mak- ing progress and appalled at the outcome that seemed inevitable now. Their target—just under $2 million—was an extortionate sum, more than Trish would have made in two lifetimes. What was worse, the pirates would squander it. Duke Strong had been candid with her. "They'll live like kings for a while—drugs, booze, women, you name it. They'll give some of it to their families. And then when they're broke, they'll look for another ship."

✳

Two hours later, they boarded their connecting flight and found their seats near the back. The plane took off on time and climbed into the tall African sky. The time passed swiftly, occupied by conversation and coffee, and soon they were landing again, this time at Jomo Kenyatta International Airport outside Nairobi. They cleared immigration and proceeded to the curb, where a well-tanned man in jeans and aviator sunglasses introduced himself.

"Ms. Parker, Agent Patterson, I'm Tony Flint," he said, taking off his shades and focusing his startlingly blue eyes on them. "Welcome to Kenya. The car is this way."

He led them across the street to a silver Land Rover and packed their suitcases in the trunk. As soon as they were situated, he navigated the vehicle out of the airport and drove toward the center of Nairobi. Vanessa cracked her window and watched the city pass by. Before long, the thoroughfare became a boulevard swarming with cars and taxis and surrounded by high-rises and green spaces. Apart from the fact that nearly everyone on the street was African, Nairobi looked much like any city in America—at once thriving and decaying and reconceptualizing and rebuilding.

At some point, Vanessa thought to check her iPhone. She found an e-mail from Curtis: Hope you enjoyed the flight. Ibrahim is at 2.5. Duke expects an agreement soon. I'm working on the wire details. Sit tight. We're almost there. She sat back in her chair, grateful, for once, to have her father-in-law at the helm of her future. For all his faults, he knew how to work a deal.

After traversing downtown, they entered a leafy district of bungalows and apartment complexes and turned down a driveway flanked by lush vegetation. They stopped at a gate and Flint exchanged a few Swahili words with a guard, who waved them through. They drove onto manicured grounds and parked outside a stately pink stucco building with wide-paned windows and a terra-cotta roof.

"This is the Muthaiga Country Club," Flint explained, opening the door for Vanessa. "It's comfortable and private. We can check in later. Let's do business first. There's a café in the back."

Vanessa traded a glance with Mary. "I could use a bite to eat."

"Me, too," said the FBI agent, following Flint toward the entrance.

The clubhouse was a throwback to a bygone era, all wood and brass with parquet floors, area rugs, heavy draperies, and antique furniture. Flint led them through the lobby and out double doors propped open to admit the breeze. The courtyard beyond was a sanctuary with jacaranda and flame trees, flowering bushes, and a sprawling lawn abutting a flagstone portico and a swimming pool. They walked around the pool and took seats at a table in the shade of a fig tree.

"So here's the deal," Flint said without prelude. "Ibrahim's deadline is twenty-six hours away. Assuming they reach an accord, Curtis will wire the funds to a bank account we control. I've spoken to the bank manager, and he has cash on hand—all hundred-dollar bills printed after

2005. In the morning, we'll collect the money and package it in a watertight container with a cash-counting machine. The plane will fly out of Wilson Airport. There's a charter company we work with that's very discreet. Flight time to the drop site is under three hours. We'll stay in contact with the pirates until we deliver the package, and then the Navy will take over and retrieve your husband and son. Pretty straightforward."

Only if you make your living trading dollars for lives, Vanessa thought, feeling again the bizarreness of the moment. "How many times have you done this?" she asked.

Flint made no attempt at modesty. "I've organized two dozen drops in Somalia, mostly for hijacked ships but occasionally for kidnapped journalists and aid workers. But all of them were foreigners. This is my first time with an American hostage." He looked thoughtful. "I'll be frank. I'm damn surprised the Navy is taking a backseat on this one. When I was in Iraq, we gave no quarter to kidnappers. It was kill or capture, end of story. Somebody back home must be pulling major strings."

Somebody is, Vanessa thought, but inside she felt a pang of anxiety. She had now heard the same sentiment from multiple experts. Duke Strong's words came back to her: *The government wants to eradicate piracy and hostage taking. In their minds, the way to do it is to confront the hostage takers with overwhelming force.* Mary had toed a softer line, admitting that international kidnappings were often resolved by ransom. And Paul Derrick had seemed genuinely sympathetic to her plea for a peaceful resolution. But the Bureau wasn't in control. And while the Navy had made concessions to allow the negotiations to proceed, the Pentagon had little history of compromise. She recalled Curtis's statement at the beginning, quoting the assistant secretary of defense: *A ransom is not the government's objective.* She glanced at Mary, wondering whether the FBI agent knew something she didn't.

"Is there a menu here?" she asked Flint. "I'd love to see one."

The security consultant stood quickly. "I'll find a waiter."

When he was gone, Vanessa turned to Mary. "He's the third person who's told me that what we're doing isn't in the military's playbook. I need to know that they're going to let this deal happen."

Mary looked suddenly uncomfortable. "I've been assured that the Navy isn't going to interfere."

Vanessa examined the FBI agent carefully, an idea forming in her mind. It was wild and terrifying and exhilarating all at the same time. "That isn't good enough. Not with Daniel's and Quentin's lives on the line."

Mary gave her an empathetic look. "I can imagine how you feel. But we're all on the same side. We're doing everything in our power to bring them home."

"I believe you," Vanessa said, seeing no deceit in Mary's eyes. "But there's a difference. It's personal for me. It isn't personal for them. I need to make it personal."

Mary took a pensive breath. "What do you want me to do?"

ISMAIL

THE INDIAN OCEAN
01°04′26″N, 47°33′55″E
November 13, 2011

Ismail stared at the clock in the galley, watching the second hand make its ceaseless revolutions and wishing he could hurry it on its way. He had never liked waiting. As a young man, he had heard his father say that patience was the truest measure of maturity. But he had disagreed, seeing it as a dress rehearsal for death. *You never get back the days,* he told Adan at the age of seventeen. *I can learn to wait when I'm in the grave.* Tragedy had changed his opinion but not his instinct. There were certain enemies that could only be vanquished with time. But right now he couldn't bear to spend another minute cooped up inside the sailboat.

Neither, it seemed, could his men. As the hours passed, he had heard them grumbling, seen the disenchantment in their faces. Just before sunset, a fight had broken out between Guray and Mas over use of the toilet. The others had quickly taken sides—Osman with Mas, Liban and

Dhuuban with Guray—and Ismail had only been able to arrange a truce after five minutes of shouting. Then, during dinner, Sondare had stumbled into the bathroom and vomited all over the sink, and Osman had launched into a tirade about the food, complaining that it was giving him diarrhea. Ismail had refuted their theories, explaining that they were suffering from cabin fever and seasickness and needed fresh air. But the idea of going topside and facing the Navy's snipers agitated them further.

The only thing that seemed to bring them relief was the promise of payment. So Ismail turned the ransom calls into a spectacle, delivering pre-call predictions, running translations of his dialogue with Curtis—the "mute" button was a wonderful invention—and post-call reports with a forecast of what the Captain's family would do next. Each time he predicted correctly and Curtis raised his offer—first to $900,000, then $1.25 million, then $1.5 million, and most recently to $1.7 million—he endeared himself to the men. It was goodwill Ismail desperately needed to make his gambit work. In time, they would see through his deception and have to make a terrible choice. But that couldn't happen until they had the ransom money in hand. Any earlier and everything would fall apart.

Just before ten o'clock in the evening, Ismail held what he hoped would be his last cheerleading session before he and Curtis reached an agreement. He sat on the bench on the starboard side of the sailboat, and the men crowded into the booth, displacing the Captain and Timaha, who retreated to the galley. Their expressions ranged from eager to jaded to surly, but all of their eyes were on him. He warmed them up with a pep talk and explained that the final steps in a negotiation were the most critical. The family would endeavor to hit the brakes, bringing their last offer up short of their limit, but he wouldn't let them get away with it. He emphasized the point by squeezing an orange into a bowl until it ran dry. Then he picked up the satellite phone and placed the call.

"Ibrahim," Curtis said in greeting. "How are my son and grandson?"

"They are fine, Curtis," said Ismail. "You may talk to them when we have a deal."

"No," Curtis disagreed. "I want to talk to Daniel now."

Ismail hit the "mute" button and translated this exchange for his men.

"Bastard," Osman growled.

Guray seconded this sentiment. "No more talk until the deal is done."

Ismail unmuted the phone. "My men are tired of this negotiation, Curtis. We have been more than reasonable with you. We will not accept less than $2.1 million. I know your family has it. So don't waste my time telling me otherwise. You have seventeen hours left before the deadline."

He terminated the call abruptly and filled in his crew. Afterward, they began to argue among themselves, Liban favoring compromise and Osman making not-so-veiled threats toward the Captain. In the midst of the quarrel, he heard the same phrase repeated a number of times: *laba milyan*—"two million." Ismail resisted the temptation to smile. That was the goal line. He would take $350,000 for

226   CORBAN ADDISON

himself—much less than a commander's share, but enough for his purposes—and he would give each of them $275,000. He hoped it would be sufficient incentive for them to take the leap.

A few minutes later, he called Curtis back. "Are we in agreement?" he demanded.

He was unprepared for Curtis's response. "Ibrahim, I just wired $1.85 million to a bank account in Nairobi. My daughter-in-law is there now. She will collect the cash in the morning and put it on a plane for delivery. That's all we could raise. If you want more, you need to extend the deadline."

Ismail bristled. "I think you are lying, Curtis. I think you are being cheap."

"Then you are a fool," Curtis replied, allowing his emotion to show. "I convinced the Navy to leave you alone. Why would I lie when we're so close?"

Curtis's unexpected move put Ismail in a bind. He was satisfied with the figure. He would still take $350,000 and reduce his crew's per capita share to $250,000. It was more than any of them would make in a decade hijacking ships. The problem was psychological. They were fixated on $2 million. Anything less would make him look weak, and weakness was something he could ill afford.

"That is unacceptable," he said at last. "The deadline stands."

With that he ended the call.

His men peppered him with questions, but he took a moment to think. Their decision had to be unanimous. He had given his men power by inviting them into the negotiations; he couldn't exclude them without undermining his command. There was only one way to get them to accept less than $2 million. They had to feel the urgency of the deal. But he had to persuade them gently. Like a herdsman with his camels, he had to convince them to move on their own.

"The family is toying with us," he said, elucidating Curtis's offer. "I have no doubt we can get two million dollars. But it might take another day or two. I say we wait. We have enough food, and the Navy isn't bothering us. Let's push back until we get the amount we deserve."

The men reacted in predictable ways. Osman pounded his fist on the table. "Two million! No less." Dhuuban and Sondare nodded along. "Two million, two million," they said.

Ismail looked at Liban and then at Mas, holding his breath. His authority as Gedef's successor hinged on what happened next. If they called his bluff and Curtis turned out to be telling the truth, then things could get dangerous very fast. Thankfully, Liban was too smart, and Mas too suspicious, to take his proposition on faith.

"How far are we from the coast?" Liban asked.

Ismail narrowed his eyes. "About a hundred and fifty miles."

"When do you calculate we will make landfall?"

"Just before sunset tomorrow."

This was all the information Mas needed. "I think it's crazy to wait," he said. "You think those ships are going to sit around for another day or two and do nothing to stop us?"

He shook his head vehemently. "I say we take the money and get to the beach as fast as we can."

Ismail crossed his arms, playing the part of jilted commander to the hilt. "You're willing to accept a smaller ransom? What will you tell your family?"

Mas scowled back. "I'll tell them that something is better than nothing."

I couldn't have said it better myself, Ismail thought. He glanced at Osman and Guray and saw that the bravado was gone from their eyes.

Suddenly, Liban said, "I think Mas is right. A smaller ransom is better than a bullet in the head."

Seconds passed and then Osman conceded. "I'm with Mas. Let's do it."

That was the tipping point. The others soon followed suit. Ismail held up the sat phone. "If we take this money, we live with the consequences. Does anyone have a problem with that?"

When no one spoke, Ismail looked at the Captain and Timaha, who were standing in the galley. They were wearing brave faces, but he could see the shadow of fear in their eyes. "We have a deal," he said in English, adopting a friendly tone. "You will be home soon."

Tears welled in the Captain's eyes. "Thank God," he exhaled and wrapped Timaha in his arms.

Ismail allowed himself the luxury of a smile. Against all odds, he had overcome Gedef's death and the loss of the mothership and the might of the US Navy to negotiate a million-dollar ransom at sea, all in a matter of days. It was an unprecedented achievement and would have made Gedef proud. *Yasmin*, he thought, *the devil's work is done. I'm coming for you now.*

Then he called Curtis with the news.

As soon as the ransom terms were fixed and the Parkers were tucked away in their cabin, Ismail offered to take the first night watch and urged his men to get some sleep. They stretched out on the benches and floor spaces and drifted off in minutes, lulled by the sound of the engine and the rocking of the sailboat on the swells. He checked his GPS unit and confirmed their position. The current had set them a few miles south, but that was easy to correct. He made a few calculations and then sat back and waited, working through his plan for the next twenty-four hours until he could recite the sequence by heart, one step after the other, like dominoes falling.

At one o'clock in the morning, he put the sat phone in his pocket, made sure his men were asleep, and then crept to the weather hatch and pushed it aside. He slipped through the companionway and entered the darkened cockpit, staying on the balls of his feet. The gibbous moon was high in the sky, and the equatorial stars were bright despite the humidity in the air. The Navy ships remained on station— the *Gettysburg* off their starboard beam, its twin to port, and the aircraft carrier astern. The SEAL snipers were probably close enough to see him through their night scopes, but not close enough to take a shot, even if they wanted to.

He crouched down and went to the helm, exploring the console with his fingers. He found the button he wanted and pressed it three times. He felt the sailboat turn gently to starboard. Three degrees would offset the drift of the current. It might put them north of the coordinates he had given to Curtis, but the plane wouldn't have trouble locating them. The warships were a dead giveaway.

Ismail left the cockpit and crab-walked toward the foredeck, stepping around winches and coils of line and absorbing the motion of the sailboat in his legs. When he reached the bow, he sat down and filled his lungs with air. He stayed like this for long minutes, listening to the swish-splash of the bow wave and relishing the gift of solitude for the first time in many days.

He saw Jupiter suspended before him like a porch light and Andromeda hovering just above the horizon. He remembered the stories his mother told him when he was a boy, stories of the Sufi mystics who saw meaning in the constellations. *The Prophet forbids us from studying astrology,* she had said, *but the stars are in Allah's hand. They can carry a message.* Ismail traced out the celestial form of the Shackled Woman as the *Renaissance* sailed into her embrace. It was a propitious omen. Somewhere out there Yasmin was waiting for him.

After a while, he took out the sat phone and dialed a Somali number. He had memorized it long ago but used it on only one other occasion—after taking payment from Gedef for the Malaysian cargo ship. He listened to the ring-tone, hoping Mahamoud had been true to his word.

"*As-salamu alaykum,*" said a sleepy voice, using the traditional Islamic greeting.

"Hello, Uncle," Ismail replied in Somali.

"Ismail," said Mahamoud gravely, as if speaking to a ghost. "Are you in trouble?"

More than you could possibly understand, Ismail thought. "I need you to bring a Land Cruiser to a beach near Mallable village tomorrow at sunset," he said. He gave his uncle the coordinates and explained his request in more detail.

Mahamoud was quiet for a long time. Ismail imagined him staring at the floor, brow furrowed, as he had done last September when Ismail had suddenly appeared at his door, seeking shelter from the battle raging in the streets. His uncle was a righteous man, but he was also a political chameleon with friends on all sides of the conflict—warlords, clan elders, Islamists, and government sympathizers. He had prospered as a hotelier in Mogadishu because he had maintained neutrality. It was precisely what made Ismail trust him. In all of Somalia, only Mahamoud could protect him from the Shabaab.

At last his uncle said, "What will you do then?"

If I answered you, Ismail thought, *you would hang up now. But when you look into my eyes, you will see my father and not be able to deny me.* "I will tell you when I am with you."

"What is this number?" Mahamoud asked. "I don't recognize it."

"It doesn't matter," Ismail replied. "Please delete all record of it. I have my mobile. I will call you when we are near the beach."

Mahamoud took a labored breath. "Tomorrow at sunset."

"Thank you," Ismail said sincerely. He looked toward the west and saw Andromeda beginning to set. *"Nabadgalio."*

"Nabadino," his uncle replied and hung up.

PAUL

Paul watched the dawn break from the fantail of the *Gettysburg*. The sun emerged from the sea as a roseate sliver half obscured by a blanket of low-lying clouds. As it rose, it took on shape and intensity until at last it shrugged off its veil and pierced his eyes with shards of light. The ocean it revealed was a millpond. There was almost no wind. It wasn't yet six o'clock, but Paul felt a prickle of sweat forming beneath the collar of his shirt. According to the weather report, the temperature would climb into triple digits by afternoon.

He turned around and looked toward the west, blinking away the sunspots in his retinas. The Somali coast was eighty-five miles away, and the drop site identified by Ibrahim in his last call to Curtis was just four miles shy of the mainland. It was too close for comfort—for Paul and the Navy captains—but there was nothing they could do about it now. Paul had tried to cajole Curtis into stipulating the location of the exchange, but Curtis had made no promises and Ibrahim had given him no opening. Paul had listened to the recordings from Annapolis. The pirate was a gifted negotiator. In another life, Paul would have recommended him for the FBI Academy.

A few minutes later, he left the fantail and climbed the stairs to the missile deck. His limbs felt leaden, weighed down by weariness. He had been awake for the better part of fifty-six hours, talking to Frazier and Mary Patterson, strategizing with Redman and Masters, and going over the recordings with Rodriguez until he could recite them from memory. The SEAL commander was convinced the pirate was running a confidence game. But Paul couldn't square Redman's instinct with the man he heard in his headphones. Ibrahim spoke with unwavering candor. He never hesitated. Even pathological liars had a tell—a faint echo of falsehood. If Ibrahim had one, Paul had yet to discern it.

At the same time, he couldn't explain the phone call the pirate had placed from the bow of the *Renaissance* in the middle of the night. Paul had barely fallen asleep in his rack when Ensign O'Brien woke him to say that one of the Somalis had emerged from the cabin of the sailboat and spoken briefly on what looked like a satellite phone. The SEAL spotter on the forward illuminator deck had caught the moment on an infrared camera, along with twenty minutes of Ibrahim just sitting there like he was in a trance. Redman had sent the video to Admiral Prince, and Prince had arranged another conference with Gordon Tully. The call had turned into a sparring match between Paul and Redman. After listening to both of them, Tully had worked out a truce.

"You're offering me opinions, not fact," said the national security advisor. "I don't like the drop site any more than you do, but when you're running a sting operation—that's the story we're going to feed the press, by the way, a high-seas sting with the ransom as bait—you have to let the other side set some of the rules. Your mission hasn't changed. Get the Parkers out of harm's way and take the pirates into custody. How you do that is your business."

"With all due respect, sir," Redman said, "what if Ibrahim reneges? Once he has the money, what's to prevent him from holding on to the hostages? He could get greedy and ask for more money. He could tell us he won't release the Parkers until he reaches land. He's a pirate, for God's sake. We have no idea what's going on inside his head."

Tully's eyes shifted, but his face didn't change. "Paul?"

"It's a legitimate concern," Paul replied. "But I think a double dip is unlikely. We're sitting on top of him. He knows we won't let him take the hostages to shore. And he's too smart to expect the Parkers to agree to another payment under these circumstances. In my mind, the only way he gets cold feet is if he figures out that the drop is a setup."

"Then you guys are going to have to do a good job selling it to him," Tully said, staring frankly at the camera. "To answer your question, Frank, if Ibrahim reneges, you can take the gloves off. Put your birds back in the air. Disable the sailboat. Make his world a living hell. Do not attempt a rescue without my permission. But do whatever it takes to force his hand."

Redman's shoulders relaxed. "Thank you, sir."

Captain Masters spoke up. "If we stay with the sailboat during the drop, we'll be sitting dead in the water twenty miles from Mogadishu. We're going to have spectators— fishing dhows, skiffs, cargo ships. The *Truman* and *San Jacinto* can give us a buffer. But there's no way to keep this quiet. A lot of people are going to know we're there."

Tully shrugged. "We'll handle the media and the Somali government. You keep the spectators away however you see fit."

After traversing the main weather deck, Paul climbed the long stairs to the bridge. He glanced at the SEAL boats bobbing in the water, like a pod of killer whales. There were three of them with six men each, all clad in black. Redman had brought them over from the *Truman* under the cover of darkness. They were keeping pace with the *Gettysburg* and staying out of sight. If the exchange happened on schedule, only the first boat—with four attackers and two medical corpsmen—would be dispatched to retrieve the Parkers. Conversely, if Ibrahim screwed the pooch, as Redman liked to say, all three boats would form a cordon around the *Renaissance*, diverting the pirates' attention from the SEAL divers who would incapacitate the sailboat's propeller and loop a towline around the keel. The cruiser would then tow the sailboat out of Somali waters, forcing the pirates to surrender or endure an endless purgatory at sea. The plan—which Redman had dubbed "Arachne"—made sense as a last resort, but the SEAL commander's gung-ho enthusiasm left Paul feeling dyspeptic. It was almost as if Redman *wanted* Ibrahim to renege so his team could finally do something.

Paul entered the bridge and found Rodriguez at the chart table going over his notes. Masters was in his chair watching the sea. Redman was standing by the radar display and talking to his men through his headset. When he saw Paul, he signed off and gave the negotiator a hard look.

"Are you ready for this?" he asked, speaking the question almost as a challenge.

Paul ignored the barb and glanced at Masters. "Is CIC on the line?"

Masters picked up the nearest sound-powered phone. "We're ready when you are."

"Let's do it, then," Paul said. He watched as Masters gave the order and took the phone from him. It rang five times before the call connected.

"Hello?" It was Daniel Parker. He sounded more curious than scared.

"Good morning, Captain. This is Paul on the *Gettysburg.*"

Paul heard a scratching noise and muffled speech, as if Daniel had placed his hand over the phone. After a moment, Ibrahim came on the line.

"I will talk to you when we are finished with breakfast," the pirate said.

When the line went dead, Paul started to laugh. "Well, he's feeling like a million bucks. It means he's taken the hook. Now we just have to bury it."

Fifteen minutes later, Ibrahim called back. "As I said at the beginning, we want something and you want something. The Captain's family agreed to give us what we want. So we will give you what you want. We will stop the sailboat four miles from the coast. As soon as we receive the payment and confirm the amount, we will release the hostages."

Paul watched the *Renaissance* knifing through the water five hundred yards away. "That's good news. But I'm curious. How will you release them without your skiff?"

"We will leave them on the sailboat. We have no interest in it. We want the small boat from your ship. We will take that to shore."

Paul furrowed his brow, intrigued by the demand. "Let me talk to the Navy. I'll call you back." He terminated the connection and looked from Redman to Masters.

"Let's go outside," said the SEAL commander, opening the door to the bridge wing and letting in a wave of moist air. When they were alone, he spoke his mind. "I don't like it. It's like giving them a weapon to use against us. Let's imagine Ibrahim is telling the truth and they use the RHIB as a getaway vehicle. My boats have the edge on speed and agility, and we can use the choppers to get in their way. But stopping seven pirates with AKs traveling at thirty knots is going to be far more dangerous for my guys. On the other hand, if he's lying to us, he could easily take the money and make a mad dash to the coast, using the Parkers as a human shield. If we try to stop them, people will get hurt."

Paul frowned. "How is the RHIB any different from their skiff? If they were still towing it, we wouldn't be having this conversation."

Redman's eyes flashed. "We don't seem to agree on anything, do we?"

Paul refused to take the bait. "Look at it another way. What's he going to think if we say no? Right now he's walking on water. He's got almost two million dollars coming to him. We tell him he can't have the RHIB, and he hears we don't trust him. That reminds him of the guns we have pointed at him and the fact that he doesn't like us very much. At that point, he starts to wonder if he can trust us. That kind of logic is more dangerous to the Parkers than giving him the RHIB."

Redman grimaced, his frustration plain. "You should have been a shrink." He turned to Masters. "What do you think, Gabe?"

Masters looked bemused. "You're both overlooking something. Who says we have to give him a fully functional RHIB? My mechanics know those boats inside and out. I bet one of them could fix the engine so it cuts out before they get to the beach."

The light of understanding struck Paul and Redman simultaneously. "It's a perfect trap," Redman said, even as Paul thought, *Leave it to a surface warrior to outwit a SEAL.*

After working out the details, they returned to the air-conditioned comfort of the bridge. Thirty seconds later, Paul had Ibrahim on the line again. "You can have the boat, but we can't bring it over to you while you're moving. We're going to have to wait until you reach the drop site."

The pirate pondered this. "All right. But I want *you* to bring the boat. You will come alone and unarmed. I'll meet you in the Captain's dinghy, and we will make the exchange."

Paul felt a sudden chill. The prospect of a high-seas parley with Ibrahim was at once frightening and fascinating. In ten years of negotiation, he had never met a kidnapper prior to his capture. Afterward, yes, in a courthouse or an interrogation room, but never in the midst of a crisis.

"I assume you'll also come unarmed," he said.

Ibrahim laughed. "My father once said a dishonest person is like a toothless man. No woman will touch him. Here it is different. If I breach your trust, your snipers will put a bullet in my head."

Paul shrugged. "Okay. I'll bring the boat myself." He took a breath, thinking of the deception he was perpetrating. "There's something else. As we approach the coast, we're going to have vessels in the vicinity. The Navy doesn't want spectators, so they're going to clear the area. The other ships will do the work. They won't come close to you, but I don't want you to be surprised."

"What your Navy does is not my concern, so long as they stay away," Ibrahim replied. "If you breach my trust, the consequences will be swift and irrevocable. You will see that I have all my teeth."

I don't doubt it, Paul thought. "I'll call again when we're close to the drop site."

"I look forward to meeting you, Paul," the pirate said and ended the call.

The hours of morning drifted quietly by like jetsam on the current. The mood on the *Gettysburg* was subdued, the gravity of the moment drawing everyone into its sober grip. Conversations were held in low tones. Sailors who usually moved with alacrity adopted a slower step. Paul stayed on the bridge with Redman and Masters, monitoring the many dimensions of activity happening all at once—the preparations of the SEAL small-boat, sniper, and dive teams; the labors of the mechanics to modify one of the RHIBs; and the maneuvers of the *Truman* and *San Jacinto*, sailing in formation like the prongs of a pitchfork to sweep the sea of interlopers.

Around noon, Paul left the bridge, ate a hasty lunch in the officers' wardroom, and went to the CIC—a black-lit warren of computers, wall-mounted screens, and communications equipment—to call Brent Frazier. It was four in the morning in Virginia, but his boss picked up on the second ring.

"Frazier here," he said, sounding wired.

"Are you chewing Nescafé again?" Paul smirked.

Frazier laughed. "For four days straight. If I had a blood test right now, they'd find more caffeine than oxygen. These SEAL guys never sleep."

"I think they're genetically engineered," Paul quipped. "What's the word from Nairobi?"

"I just talked to Mary. The bank rolled out the red carpet. They're back at the hotel preparing the package. They have a turboprop fueled and on the tarmac. They should be wheels up by 14:30 and over the drop site by 17:00."

Paul wasn't surprised. "The guys from Sagittarius are first rate."

Frazier lowered his voice. "Prince is really worried about Ibrahim. He doesn't think the pirates intend to let the Parkers go before they reach the coast. He's been bending Tully's ear about it, and Tully's getting nervous. I have to confess, he's got a point. Think about what happens if Ibrahim reneges. Nobody knows if the sailboat can be towed by the keel. If the tow fails or they have to abort, the *Renaissance* is going to start drifting south on the current. By the time the sun comes up, it'll be off the coast of Mogadishu and within sight of two million Somalis."

Paul felt a churning in his stomach. "What is Prince suggesting?"

"He's pushing the White House to green-light an assault if Ibrahim reneges."

Which would almost certainly lead to the death of the hostages, Paul thought. "Please tell me the president is smarter than that."

Frazier made a noise that was half grunt, half snort. "He is, but he isn't happy about it. He wants a negotiated solution, not an international incident. I spoke to Tully confidentially. He's advising the president to follow your instinct. He was damn impressed by your prediction about Ibrahim going off the reservation. At the same time, he told Prince to put a few options on the table. If you think of any reason you might be wrong—any reason at all—I want to hear about it immediately."

Paul massaged the bridge of his nose, trying to alleviate the headache he suddenly felt. "I'll be meeting with Ibrahim in a few hours. Until then my judgment stands."

"I trust you, Paul," Frazier said. "I know how good you are. But the reputation of the Bureau is on the line. We need a win here."

Not as much as the Parkers do, Paul thought to himself, putting the phone back in its cradle.

At three thirty in the afternoon—15:30 on the Navy's clocks—the *Gettysburg* entered Somali waters and began to close the gap with the sailboat. Redman had proposed a distance of three hundred yards, but Paul, with Masters's support, had negotiated three fifty. A few minutes later, Paul called Ibrahim to finalize the terms of the parley. They agreed to meet halfway between the cruiser and the sailboat in one hour. Paul was concerned Ibrahim would complain about the ship's proximity, but the pirate didn't mention it. *He's not watching us*, Paul surmised. *He's thinking about the money.*

A sailor approached Captain Masters and said, "The VBSS team is ready, sir."

"Thank you, Mr. Richards," Masters replied. He looked at Paul and opened the door to the bridge wing. "I'll show you the way."

The tropical air hit Paul like a blast from a furnace. It felt like summer in Baghdad, but with 90 percent humidity. He put on his sunglasses and followed Masters down the long staircase, trying not to touch the railings—the metal was hot enough to burn the skin. A group of sailors was standing around the RHIB, their faces flushed and their coveralls drenched with sweat. They straightened up when they saw Masters. One of them—a young man with a crew cut—stepped forward.

"Agent Derrick," Masters said, "this is Lieutenant Prescott, the commander of our Visit, Board, Search, and Seizure team. What's the word, Lieutenant?"

"Captain," Prescott said, "we wired a kill switch and a surplus odometer to the engine. She'll go dead in the water after a mile and a half."

Masters looked pleased. "Very good. I'll let you show Agent Derrick the ropes." He shook Paul's hand. "Good luck out there."

When the captain departed, Paul stepped aboard the RHIB with Prescott. The lieutenant made quick work of the tutorial, showing him the control panel, the start switch and throttle, a pair of binoculars in a pouch, and the location of the gas tank in case Ibrahim asked to confirm its contents.

"I'll come with you when they lower the boat," he said, handing Paul a personal flotation device. "That way you won't have to worry about the cables. We'll leave the ladder in place for you to use when you bring back the dinghy. The seas are pretty calm this afternoon. There's a meter-high swell coming from the northeast, but it shouldn't bother you much."

Paul donned the PFD and sat down on the gunwale of the boat in the shadow of the large cantilever davit, hoping to escape the sun. His expectations were dashed. The humidity made the shade irrelevant. He wiped perspiration from his brow and checked his watch—it was 16:02. *Thirteen minutes to game time,* he thought, closing his eyes and breathing steadily to maximize the flow of oxygen to his brain. A memory came to him then—Brent Frazier in a lecture room at the FBI Academy delivering the most poignant lesson of Paul's training.

There comes a point in every negotiation when you wonder whether it's all going to blow up in your face. You're exhausted from sleeplessness. Your hands are shaking from too much caffeine. The on-scene commander is harassing you for taking too much time. The hostage taker is telling you he's going to pull the trigger. And all you want to do is scream at the heavens and pummel yourself for taking such a shitty job. I promise you it will happen. Your faith in the process will be tested. But if you're feeling the heat, then so is the other guy. It's your job to cool things down, buy the guy a beer—so to speak—and convince him that you both want the same thing. The way out of the burning house is through human connection. If you can convince him to trust you, he'll come along when you show him the exit.

The thought of beer gave Paul an idea. He looked at the VBSS team languishing in the heat and asked Prescott, "I know it's last minute, but is there any chance you can get me two dozen bottles of soda in a cooler before I go? Coke, Pepsi, it doesn't matter."

The lieutenant gave Paul a look that said, *Are you kidding me?* But, like a good junior officer, he took the radio off his belt and passed along the request. Five minutes later, a sailor appeared with a Styrofoam container full of Pepsi and crushed ice. Paul rewarded the deliveryman with a soda and passed out bottles to Prescott and his team. They looked at him in surprise, but he waved off their thanks. "We sent you out here to sweat," he said. "The least we can do is keep you hydrated."

In time, the *Gettysburg* slowed to a crawl. Prescott's radio squawked and Captain Masters said, "Ibrahim is in the cockpit of the sailboat. The launch is a go."

Prescott motioned to his team. "Let's get this boat in the water."

The deployment happened so rapidly that Paul barely had time to process it before waves were slapping against the hull. He spread his legs and bent his knees, absorbing the rolling motion of the swell. At Prescott's command, he grabbed the foot ladder the VBSS team tossed over the side and held the boat in place while the lieutenant unhooked the davit cables and started the engine.

"She's all yours," Prescott said when the cables were clear. "Take my radio. You might need it."

Paul accepted the unit and watched the lieutenant clamber up the ladder and disappear over the side. Then he went to the helm and throttled up to half power, angling the RHIB away from the *Gettysburg*. The boat gained speed gracefully, skimming over the surface of the waves. He brought the boat around the cruiser's stern and headed out across the water toward the *Renaissance*.

He was unprepared for the nostalgia he felt being on a powerboat again. It had been fifteen years since his grandfather sold his Bayliner and retired to his home in McLean, a mariner no more. Yet the memories Paul had made on the water with Megan and Grandpa Chuck were some of the most important in his life. It was on the Potomac that he had come to terms with the deaths of his father and brother. It was on the Chesapeake that he had made the decision not to condemn the world but to change it—to save people from their own hands.

When he reached the midpoint between the cruiser and the sailboat, he switched off the engine and allowed the RHIB to bob on the swells. He took out the binoculars and saw a young American in a tank top and board shorts— Quentin Parker—and a thin Somali in a red T-shirt and khaki shorts—Ibrahim—unfold and inflate a compact dinghy. They deployed stairs from the sailboat's transom and set the small craft afloat, attaching an outboard motor. Then Ibrahim jumped into the dinghy, started the engine, and guided it toward the RHIB.

Paul watched in astonishment as the pirate's face came into view. Ibrahim had the boyish features of a late adolescent, yet his dark eyes carried a wizened light. He pulled the dinghy up to the RHIB and leaped across the gap with the surefootedness of a panther, lashing the boats together. Then, suddenly, he was at Paul's side wearing a toothy grin.

"You are not an old man," he said, giving Paul a penetrating look.

"And you have all of your teeth," Paul replied.

Ibrahim sat down nonchalantly. "This is a nice boat," he said, dragging his fingers in the water.

Paul opened the Styrofoam container and held out a Pepsi. "Are you thirsty?"

The pirate looked at the bottle in disbelief. "That is for me?"

Paul nodded, taking a soda for himself. "The rest are for the hostages and your men."

Ibrahim twisted off the lid and took a tentative sip, then downed half the bottle. "I am curious, Paul. Why did you read the Quran? You are not a Muslim."

Paul took a swig of soda, struck by the surrealism of the moment. *I'm sitting with a pirate four miles from Somalia and a few hundred feet from SEAL snipers who are watching us through their scopes. Am I really having this conversation?* He collected his thoughts and gave Ibrahim the only answer that made sense.

"I'm an American. I was in New York on September 11. I wanted to know if the men who took down the towers in the name of Allah were pretenders or true believers."

Ibrahim narrowed his eyes. "What did you decide?"

Paul spoke with great care. "They're parasites. They cloak themselves in religion to empower themselves, but they don't represent the essence of Islam any more than the Inquisitors and Crusaders represented the essence of Christianity."

Ibrahim was silent for a while, staring at the sea. When he spoke again, Paul recognized his words as a quote from the Quran: "'And they have been commanded no more than this: to worship God with genuine devotion; to incline toward truth; to establish prayer; and to practice charity. This is religion right and straight.'"

Paul gave voice to the obvious irony. "If that's true, then why are we here?"

"This is an unholy business," Ibrahim admitted. "But we do what we have to do."

Paul allowed the contradiction to pass. It was a moment for détente, not disagreement. "What will you do with the money?" he asked.

Ibrahim turned reflective. "I will leave this life behind."

"And your men?"

Ibrahim hesitated. "I think they will, too." He searched Paul's face. "When the deal is done, we will let the Captain and Timaha go. That is the truth."

Timaha? Paul wondered but didn't ask. He tilted his head inquisitively. "How can I be sure?"

"'Give full measure when you measure, and weigh with an even balance,'" Ibrahim replied. "I swear on the name of Allah that I will do it."

"I give you my word as well," Paul said, breaking the cardinal rule of negotiation never to lie except to save a life. "Put the hostages on the deck of the sailboat so we can see they are unharmed, and we will let you go. Just promise me one thing."

"Yes?" the pirate asked without hint of mistrust.

"Take the money and make an honest life."

Ibrahim's eyes turned into a mirror revealing Paul's guilt. "*Inshallah*," he said sincerely, "I will do as you say."

VANESSA

The Land Rover raced through the logjam of traffic in Nairobi's business district, careening around buses and delivery trucks, threading through cars and motorcycles, and making a general menace of itself. Tony Flint was at the wheel, laying on the horn and muttering curses; Mary Patterson was in the passenger seat, clutching the center armrest with white knuckles; and Vanessa was in the backseat, holding on to the door handle like a vise and struggling with all her might not to scream obscenities at Flint for wrecking every last vestige of her carefully assembled calm.

After an effortless morning at the bank and the country club, it was inevitable that something would go wrong. The problem had been as prosaic as a defective battery in the radio controller that Flint needed to guide the package to the sailboat. Unfortunately, the controller was from Britain and required a battery that no electronics dealer in Nairobi had heard of. After striking out with the locals, Flint had made a flurry of phone calls to London, begging, pleading, and cajoling the manufacturer for a solution. Eventually, he had talked to the engineer who designed the unit and learned that another battery could be used in its place. Again, however, the technocrats in Nairobi had professed ignorance. All except one—an eccentric young man who ran a used electronics store in Kahawa North.

Unfortunately, Kahawa was on the opposite side of Nairobi from Wilson Airport. In a city like Paris or Washington, DC, that had a beltway around the urban core, this would not have been a problem. In Nairobi, however, all of the highways converged in the city center. They were already seven minutes late to the airport and they still had ten minutes to go—assuming Flint wasn't shading the truth and didn't kill them on the way. Vanessa closed her eyes and tried to imagine she was on a roller coaster. *We're going to get there*, she told herself. *He does this all the time.*

But her apprehension wasn't limited to the car ride. She was about to take a leap of faith that would shock everyone— Flint, the Navy, Paul Derrick, even Daniel. She didn't know if it had ever been done before, but that wasn't her concern. Ever since she had stepped on the plane to Africa, she had been swept up in a whirlwind of fear and freedom. Her routine, with its emotional shelter and physical shackles, felt like a memory from a past life. *They're waiting for me*, she thought. *Daniel and Quentin. I'm not going to let them down.*

When they reached the airport, they took the speed bump with a bone-jarring thud and skidded to a halt outside a nondescript aircraft hangar. A large man with a shaved head opened the hatch and retrieved the package—a watertight crate swaddled in plastic wrap and secured by buckled straps that anchored the parachute and guidance system. Inside the crate were two briefcases stuffed with $10,000 bundles, along with a cash-counting machine.

Flint jumped out and opened Vanessa's door for her, escorting her into the hangar, where a red and white turboprop airplane was waiting for them. "This is Ruan Steyn," he said, gesturing toward the man carrying the package. "He's one of the best bush pilots in Africa. He's never missed a drop."

Steyn gave Vanessa a smile that looked more like a leer. He carried the package to the rear door of the airplane, where a stocky Kenyan loaded it on board.

Flint shook hands with the Kenyan, then faced Vanessa. "After we take off, Charles will drive you back to Muthaiga. I'll call you on the sat phone as soon as the package is on the sailboat."

Vanessa shook her head. "I'm coming with you," she said.

Flint gawked at her in incomprehension. "What are you talking about?"

"I want to see you do it," she replied stubbornly, daring him to refuse.

Flint put up his hands. "That's not the way we do business."

"I'm the client," she retorted. "If you want to get paid, you won't make an issue of it." She waved her hand at the plane. "There's clearly room."

"Vanessa," he said and then adopted a more deferential tone. "Mrs. Parker, I'm not thrilled about the idea because it's dangerous. We're flying into Somali airspace without a flight plan. There are bad guys down there: militias, warlords, Islamists, you name it. Some of them have antiaircraft guns. You never know what might happen."

Vanessa gave him an unyielding look. "I have no doubt that Mr. Steyn will keep us safe." When he hesitated, she spoke from the heart. "Look, Tony, I understand your reservations. But if I were a sailor, I'd be on the boat, too. I know you're going to get proof of life before you make the drop. I want to see them with my own eyes. I don't want to be sitting in a hotel room waiting for a call."

At last, Flint shrugged. "Are you coming, too?" he asked Mary.

The FBI agent shook her head. "This is as far as I go."

Flint angled his head toward the steps. "All right then. Climb aboard."

"Thank you," Vanessa said softly.

Mary wrapped her in an embrace. "I'll see you when you get back. Just think, this will all be over in a few hours."

Vanessa nodded and walked to the plane.

After a short taxi, they took off into the cloudless blue sky, climbing quickly to twelve thousand feet. Vanessa sat in one of the executive seats in the front of the cabin, looking out the window at the vast Kenyan plain and charting the progress of the flight on a monitor beside her. Flint sat a few seats back, punching buttons on the guidance system controller—a laptop with a joystick. He hadn't spoken to her since they left the hangar, but she was too nervous to care. She hated small planes more than anything. In some dark recess of her mind, she was convinced they were going to fall out of the sky.

They flew east toward the Somali border, staying in Kenyan airspace until they left the coast and made a wide northern turn over the ocean. As the minutes passed, Vanessa's thoughts drifted backward in time, like a film reel in reverse. She saw Daniel as he was on the day the *Renaissance* sailed out of Annapolis, heard him whisper in her ear that they would be back soon. So many people had come to see them off—friends, colleagues, journalists, extended family from the Parker clan. As the cameras clicked away, Quentin had cast off the bow line, and Daniel had maneuvered the sailboat into the channel. He had turned then and caught her eye, waving farewell. Guilt had besieged her as she walked away from the pier, guilt for the love and solidarity she didn't feel. She had blamed Daniel for it, as she always did. But in truth, his sins were a kind of consolation, a permission slip to ignore the obvious—that the unraveling of their marriage was her fault as well as his.

She saw it so clearly now, the broken road they had walked, the way their priorities had diverged, like islands drifting apart, until their only commerce was business, the shared responsibility of raising Quentin and managing their assets and deciding where to go on vacation. Their love had gone stale before it grew cold. They had lost the friendship that had joined them in the beginning. The rest had been inevitable—the mercenary Daniel had become, working for the praise of his father because Vanessa had ceased to care; the emotional shell she had developed to protect the privacy of her pain and avert the embarrassment of appearing needy; their infrequent trips to the bedroom and the mechanistic quality of their sex; the affair she was certain he had with that paralegal at his firm; and the emotional bond she had developed with Chad Forrester—how humiliating it was to think about now!—when he offered her sympathy during the uncertainty of Quentin's adolescence.

So much water had passed under the bridge since she had last thought of Daniel with affection that she had almost forgotten what it felt like—what *together* felt like. But suddenly, she wanted it again. She wanted to believe that he was with her, that he wanted to spend the rest of his life with her, that he saw her as beautiful and graceful and worthy of love. She knew there was no way to undo the damage of the past, no way to recover what they had lost. But there was a way to begin again. If he was ready, as he said he was, then so was she. She was tired of being alone.

"Twenty minutes," she heard Steyn call from the cockpit.

At once the plane slowed and began its descent. She looked out at the ocean and marveled at its immensity. It was a world unto itself. If she had been more courageous, she would have joined them in the Seychelles or Bali or New Zealand, as Daniel had proposed in his letters. She would have taken a day trip with them, perhaps even sailed a leg of the journey. But there was always tomorrow. They could sail to the Caribbean or Bermuda. It would require all of her fortitude, but she was willing to go along, if only Daniel would give her the chance.

She saw ships far below, half a dozen of them, their bow waves like arrows in the sapphire sea. The plane descended through a layer of gauzy clouds and continued down, down, down until she could see the ocean swells like ripples on a lake.

"Five minutes," Steyn announced, waving his hand to get their attention. "I see the warships. They're spread out—a couple of miles apart. Looks like they have birds in the air."

Vanessa scoured the ocean but didn't see anything. She glanced at Flint and saw the sat phone in his hand. "I'm ready to make the call," he said. "Any special requests?"

She smiled at his sarcasm. "Actually, yes."

"Why am I not surprised? You want to talk to them," he guessed.

She felt a dam break in her heart. "I want them to see me, too."

Flint shrugged and punched in the number, putting the phone to his ear. "Ibrahim," he began as casually as if he were ordering a pizza. "We have the package. But we need a visual of the hostages before we send it down. Bring them into the cockpit. I'll call back."

Vanessa caught sight of the aircraft carrier miles away. It was extraordinary, really—the assets the Navy had deployed to save her husband and son. She felt gratitude well up in her. Despite her frustrations with the government, she knew the men on the Navy ships cared about what happened to Daniel and Quentin. If they didn't, they never would have come.

"There's the sailboat," Steyn said, banking the plane to give them a better view. "I'm going to bring her down to two hundred feet for the pass."

Suddenly, Vanessa saw it, too, a speck of white beside the gray bulk of another warship. *That must be the* Gettysburg, she thought. *Paul Derrick is on that ship.* The plane descended again until the water looked close enough to touch. She took binoculars from Flint and trained them on the sailboat, her heart pounding in her chest. She saw the mast and the boom and the lettering on the transom and a small boat lashed to the beam. *Where are they?* she thought. *Why aren't they in the cockpit?*

At once, the weather hatch moved, and a dark-skinned man in a red T-shirt emerged from the companionway carrying a gun. He looked into the sky and motioned toward the hatch.

"It's Quentin!" she exclaimed when he appeared. She couldn't believe how shaggy his hair was. He'd never grown it long a day in his life. He was taller than she remembered, and more muscular. For the first time, he looked more man than boy.

"There's Daniel!" she cried when he, too, stepped into the cockpit and put his arm around his son. They waved at the plane, ignoring the pirate beside them.

I'm here! she wanted to shout. *I love you!*

She heard Flint place another call and saw the pirate take a phone from his pocket. "Ibrahim," Flint said, "I have a visual. Give the phone to the Captain. I have someone who wants to talk to him."

Vanessa brought her emotions under control and took the phone from Flint. When she heard her husband's voice, she spoke his name with all the feeling in her heart. "Daniel."

"Vanessa?" he said in disbelief.

"I can see you," she replied as the plane began to bank again.

"My God. How did you . . . ?" She heard his voice trail off and saw him turn to Quentin.

"It's your mother," he said with undisguised wonder.

"Daniel," she said, getting his attention again. "I'm sorry I never came to visit. I should have, long ago. I have so many regrets."

She heard him breathing. "Me, too. More than I can say."

She forged ahead. "I want to come sailing the next time you go offshore. We could take the *Relativity* to St. Thomas. Quentin could bring Ariadne."

"That's a great idea," he said, his voice cracking with feeling. "Let's talk about it later. Quentin's right here. He wants to say hello."

"Mom?" Quentin said when Daniel gave him the phone. "What are you doing here?"

"I had to come. I couldn't leave it to strangers."

Quentin laughed gently. "That's cool. We've missed you."

Vanessa began to cry. She couldn't help it. Her greatest fear—one that had stalked her like a malevolent spirit for so many years—was that she had failed her son, that his childhood travails were her fault because she hadn't stayed home with him, because she had been irritable when he was harder to parent than his peers, because she hadn't known how to connect with him as a teenager except through her music. To see him now so grown up, so poised in the face of danger, and to hear his affirmation meant more to her than anything in life.

She placed her hand against the window. "Can you see me? I'm waving."

She saw him squint, then nod. "Yeah, I see you."

"I see her, too," she heard Daniel say in the background.

"I love you, Quentin," she said softly. "I'm proud of you."

"I love you, too, Mom. See you soon."

Ibrahim took the phone back and sent Daniel and Quentin below. "Mrs. Parker," he said, staring up at the plane as it circled overhead, "as you can see, we have done nothing to harm them. Deliver what you promised, and I will do the same."

"The package is on its way," she confirmed.

"Excellent," the pirate replied and hung up.

Flint took back the phone as the plane banked and began to climb. "It's going to be loud when I open the door. Buckle your seatbelt and stay put until the package is away and the door is closed."

"Two minutes to the drop point," Steyn called out.

"Roger that," Flint said. He turned the handle on the

cargo door, then took hold of it and pulled until the seal broke and the door came off in a whoosh of noise. Warm air rushed into the cabin and sent napkins in the galley swirling. He set the door aside and moved behind the package. "Ready on your mark!" he shouted over the howling wind.

"One minute!" Steyn yelled back.

Vanessa gripped her armrests and looked out the window at the sea. They were high enough now that she could make out the coastline of Somalia painted bronze by the sun. The proximity of land accentuated the gravity of the moment. Without warning, her skin began to tingle and her heart started to race. She slowed her breathing and focused all her energy on resisting the pressure inside of her.

"Thirty seconds!" Steyn yelled. "Fifteen! . . . Ten! . . . Five!" Then: "Go! Go! Go!"

In one motion, Flint shoved the package out of the hatch and secured the door again, bringing a sudden end to the vortex of sound. He returned to his seat and picked up the controller, typing something on the keyboard. "Camera is operational," he called out. "Signal strength is excellent."

Vanessa had two thoughts at once: *I don't want to watch.* And: *I can't bear not to watch.* She slipped down the aisle until she stood behind Flint. She stared at the display in confusion. The video feed was an incomprehensible blur. Then, at once, the camera stabilized, swinging like a pendulum until it came to rest. She saw the sun and the ocean shimmering beneath it.

"Parachute is away," Flint called out, working the joystick. "I have steerage. Full power on the fans. Video is clear and steady. We're on the glide path."

Vanessa saw a cluster of numbers at the bottom of the screen—altitude, ground speed, rate of descent, and wind velocity. The package was at 1,100 feet and falling steadily. Flint zoomed in with the camera until the *Renaissance* came into view, bobbing on the mirrorlike water. She felt a knot in her stomach. It seemed like an impossible target.

"Not much wind today," he said. "It must be hot as hades down there."

She watched, mesmerized, as he guided the package toward the sailboat. She saw Ibrahim in the cockpit with two more Somalis. The resolution improved until she could make out their faces. She stared at the altimeter as it dropped below two hundred feet, then one hundred, then fifty. The pirates reached out their arms and Flint began to count down.

"Five . . . four . . . three . . . two . . . one."

At once the image distorted. Vanessa saw a flash of red—Ibrahim's shirt—then the camera shuddered and the image clarified again. She recognized the base of the helm.

"Bingo!" Flint exclaimed. "Package delivered."

"Congratulations," Steyn said. "Now let's get our asses back to Kenya."

Vanessa let out the breath she was holding and the tension inside her eased. But her work was not yet done. She took a piece of paper out of the pocket of her jeans. "I need the phone again," she said. "I have one more call to make."

Flint made no attempt to hide his annoyance. "You can't call them again until they finish counting the cash.

It's bad form."

She shook her head. "Not them. Someone else."

He threw up his hands and handed her the phone. "Whatever you say."

Vanessa returned to her seat and punched in the number. After two rings, a man came on the line. "Brent Frazier here."

"Special Agent Frazier, Mary said you'd be expecting me."

"Ms. Parker." Frazier sounded piqued. "As you're aware, this is highly unusual."

"I know. But you did it once before."

Frazier took a breath. "I'll patch you through."

She heard a series of clicks and then another man answered. She recognized his voice.

"Hi, Vanessa, it's Paul," the negotiator said. "I hear you're on the plane. How are you?"

She looked out the window at the golden sun, trying to imagine the negotiator on the bridge of the *Gettysburg*. "I'm fine, Paul. It's kind of you to ask."

"What can I do for you?" he inquired.

"I'm calling to thank you. I suspect there were people who didn't want to let us into the negotiations. I don't know what you said or did, but I'm grateful. I'll never forget it."

He took a moment to respond. "You're welcome. I'm glad it worked out."

"You know I spoke to them—to Daniel and Quentin—before we sent the package."

"We saw them in the cockpit," he said. "They looked

good."

"They sounded that way, too," she confirmed. "I want them to stay that way."

"We all do," he replied in a reassuring tone. "It won't be much longer now."

She pictured her son's face, his long mess of hair, the trim form of a man-becoming, and then flashed to her husband, saw the graying stubble of his beard, the light in his eyes, the sturdy legs of a man of the sea. She articulated her request simply.

"I have a message for the Navy and your superiors. Will you deliver it for me?"

Paul hesitated, then said, "Yes, of course."

"Tell them we've done our part. We've done everything the pirates asked of us. Daniel and Quentin are in your hands now." She spoke her final plea with all the passion in her heart. "Bring them home to me, Paul. Bring my husband and son home."

DANIEL

When he left the cockpit of the *Renaissance*, Daniel's mind was on fire. With a single act of bravery and a few kind words, Vanessa had revived the wellspring of his hope. Even in his wildest fancies, he never could have imagined she would fly halfway around the world to make a ransom drop in Somali waters. It made no sense. She was terrified of anything with wings. But she held a special loathing for propeller planes—"mosquito death traps" she called them. There were only a handful of explanations. Either she was high on a drug that eliminated her perception of risk, or she had been lobotomized, or her love for them was more powerful than her fear.

He walked through the saloon and slid into the booth with Quentin, oblivious to the stares of the pirates all around. He couldn't care less about them now. They were like a sickness that had run its course. He gave his son a look of amazement.

"She said she'd come with us to St. Thomas. She said you could bring Ariadne."

Quentin shook his head. "She must be smoking something."

Daniel laughed out loud. "I know."

Liban stepped toward them. "No talk."

Daniel felt liberated. "Your money is coming. What difference does it make?"

"No talk," the pirate repeated menacingly.

"Fine," Daniel said with a shrug.

He heard a high-pitched buzzing noise and looked toward the cockpit, where Afyareh and Guray and Osman were standing, watching the sky. The noise grew more distinct. It was clearly a propulsion system of some kind. When the sound reached a fever pitch, he watched, rapt, as the pirates extended their arms and began to shout excitedly. Then, in an instant, they took hold of a container with black straps and an apparatus with strings attached. The strings bowed, and Guray and Osman grabbed the parachute, bundling it into a ball.

As one, the pirates in the cabin descended on the cockpit, blocking Daniel's view. With their attention diverted, Daniel resumed his conversation with Quentin.

"Did Ariadne respond to your e-mail?" he whispered.

Quentin nodded. "It was the longest thing she's ever written me."

Daniel looked into his son's eyes. "What did she say?"

Quentin blushed in embarrassment. "It's personal, Dad."

"I know," Daniel said with a smile. "I've been there."

Quentin pondered this, then said eagerly, "She wants to come for a visit after we get home. She graduates at the end of this month, and she's looking at colleges in the US. What do you think?"

The question, and its underlying assumption, took Daniel by surprise. He had spent the past five days in the hostage bubble, hoping that rescue would come. He hadn't given serious thought to what that salvation would entail—the end of the circumnavigation; the uncertain fate of the *Renaissance*; the return to the daily grind with its hour-long commute, war-room meetings, and late-night deal-making; the pressure he was under to take over the firm when Curtis retired. Even after all they had suffered, he didn't want to abandon the sea just yet. He wanted to be with Vanessa again, but the rest he would just as soon leave until May. Quentin, however, seemed to have made peace with an early homecoming. It was Ariadne's influence, no doubt. Now she was all he could see.

Daniel shelved his misgivings and gave his son the answer he wanted to hear. "That sounds like a good plan. I think your mother is going to like her a lot."

"They're talking already," Quentin replied. "Mom's keeping her updated."

Daniel was about to reply when the pirates returned to the cabin with the container.

"Move, move," Liban said, forcing them into the back of the booth.

Afyareh set the container on the floor and placed two

metal briefcases and a cash-counting machine on the table. He opened the briefcases, unveiling stacks of one-hundred-dollar bills bound by rubber bands and arranged lengthwise in rows. He picked up a bundle of bills. "I didn't trust Curtis at first," he told Daniel, "but he came through. He is a man of his word."

It's not your money, you bastard, Daniel thought. *My father worked hard for it.* Somewhere deep inside him, though, Daniel knew that wasn't quite right. Curtis had been born into privilege; he had inherited the law firm from his father in the mid-1980s when military contracts—their stock in trade—had been exploding; he had invested his earnings in real estate and profited handsomely from the boom before heeding the early warnings about a crash and liquidating his riskiest holdings. His success was as much a product of genetics and environment as effort and enterprise. If he had been born in Somalia, he could have ended up just like Afyareh, stealing other people's money.

The pirate removed the rubber band and fed the bills into the counting machine, which shuffled them and spit them out with startling speed. "Ten thousand," he said. He began to count the stacks, keeping a running tab in English and Somali. The first briefcase held one hundred stacks, each of which he handled, fanned to make sure all of the bills were genuine, and then put back in its place. Every so often, he fed a stack through the machine.

After examining the last stack, he smiled. "One million dollars," he said, closing the briefcase and setting it aside. His crew rehearsed his words in Somali: *"Milyan oo doolar . . . milyan oo doolar.*"

Afyareh repeated his routine with the second briefcase—numbering the bundles and running random stacks through the machine. Halfway through, he picked up the pace, as if the counting had become a formality. "Forty-one," he said, fanning the bills. "Forty-two . . . forty-three . . ."

As he was nearing the end, Daniel heard the warble of the sat phone. The pirate took it out of his pocket and shook his head dismissively. "They can wait," he said, turning off the phone and picking up the next set of bills. "I don't like to be rushed."

A minute later, something happened that took everyone by complete surprise. A mechanical noise came from across the water. Its pitch was low at first, but it rapidly escalated to a piercing whine. Then the whine took on a percussive beat, a *whump-whump-whumping* that swept over the sailboat like the waves of a gale. The sound meant only one thing: a helicopter was taking off.

The pirates reacted as if they were under attack, screaming at each other in confusion. Only Afyareh had the presence of mind to look out the window. He bellowed something in Somali, a rictus of hatred twisting his face. Like wasps stirred from their slumber, the pirates moved to the windows, their voices blending together into an angry chorus of unintelligible words.

Daniel pulled Quentin close and felt him trembling. He called out to Afyareh, demanding an explanation, but the pirate ignored him and picked up the VHF radio.

"What are you *doing*, Paul?" he shouted into the

handset. "This was not our deal!"

Daniel watched him, terror-stricken. *Dammit!* he thought, unable to comprehend how their fortunes could have turned so quickly. *What is the Navy doing?!*

After a moment, he heard the negotiator's voice. "Ibrahim, I tried to call you on the sat phone, but you didn't answer. You don't need to worry. Our radar picked up a couple of boats launching from the beach. We're sending the helicopter to keep them away. Over."

Afyareh translated Paul's words into Somali, but his men weren't pacified. They pointed their guns at the windows and hurled epithets at the departing chopper.

"That's not acceptable, Paul," Afyareh replied in a threatening tone. "If you want the hostages to be released, you need to put the helicopter back on the ship now."

"Ibrahim," the negotiator replied in a soothing voice, "our agreement hasn't changed. The helo is a precaution for the safety of the hostages. We don't know why the boats just launched. We don't know who's driving them or what they're carrying. The helo isn't going to stop you from reaching the beach. I made a promise I intend to keep."

When Afyareh passed along the translation, his men separated into three camps. Sondare and Dhuuban fidgeted with their hands, looking agitated and afraid. Guray, Osman, and Liban flexed their muscles and held their weapons belligerently. Mas, however, fixed Afyareh with a wilting stare. He said something in Somali that made the others look at him in bewilderment. Then everyone started talking at once. There were shouts and fists pumped and guns knocked around as Afyareh and Mas faced off in a vociferous war of words.

"What's happening, Dad?" Quentin whispered, his voice riddled with fear.

"I don't know," Daniel replied. "If they start shooting, use the table for cover."

After what seemed like an eternity, Afyareh seemed to regain control of the situation. The pirates started nodding and gesturing like troops at a rally, all except Mas, who stared out the window sullenly, muttering to himself and cradling his gun.

Daniel gave Quentin a squeeze. "I think we're okay."

It was then that Afyareh did something that shocked him to the core. He lifted his gun off the bench and swung it toward them, shoving the weapon in Daniel's face. Quentin cried out in fright, but the sound barely registered in Daniel's ears. His mind ceased to think, his body went rigid, and his world shrank to the size of the gun barrel and the wooden stock and the finger on the trigger.

"What do you want?" he managed to say.

"They are not listening to me," the pirate replied, his eyes burning. "You will make them listen. Or you will die."

PAUL

Paul watched the Seahawk sail away toward the thin slip of land dividing the setting sun from the glowing sea. As the rotor noise faded, he turned his gaze once again to the *Renaissance*, floating only 250 yards away. On Redman's orders, Masters had used the *Gettysburg*'s bow and stern thrusters to creep closer to the sailboat while the pirates counted the ransom money. With binoculars, Paul could now see every inch of the sloop, except for the cabin, which remained obscured by curtains. He had strong reservations about the SEAL commander's aggressive stance, but Redman had overruled him when he had aired his disquiet in a private conference in Masters's cabin.

"Come off it, Derrick," Redman said. "Ibrahim now has the hostages *and* the ransom money. In poker, that's four of a kind. He's not going to let the Parkers go unless he knows we have a straight flush. Ten thousand tons of Navy-grade steel says we do."

"That's not the way he's going to see it," Paul objected. "He knows we have snipers. Parking this ship on his door-step is an invitation to doubt us. And if he doubts us, he's going to escalate."

"I'm not interested in psychotherapy," Redman replied, exasperated. "I'm here to rescue the hostages. He's dragged this on long enough. He needs to know this is the end of the road."

Paul had objected again when Redman ordered the helicopter to chase away the boats—probably curious fishermen—launching from the beach. But the SEAL com-mander hadn't budged, agreeing only to permit Paul to issue a warning over the phone. When Ibrahim didn't answer, Paul knew what was going to happen next. Ibrahim's eruption hadn't surprised him, nor did the silence that now enveloped the bridge. *We fueled their fears*, he thought. *They're returning the favor.*

Suddenly, the captain's phone buzzed. Masters picked it up and listened briefly. "It's Daniel Parker," he said to Paul. "He's asking for you."

Paul shot Redman a look that said, *This is exactly what I meant.* "Captain Parker," he said in a friendly tone, "how are things over there?"

"Paul!" Daniel said, sounding breathless and afraid. "You have to *do something*. You have to get the Navy to *listen*. If the chopper isn't back on the ship in five minutes, they're going to kill us."

Paul steeled himself against the empathy he felt for

the Captain. This was a moment when he had to be firm. "Daniel, I need you to calm down. Who's saying that to you? Is Ibrahim saying that? Because that isn't the deal we arranged."

"Yes, it's Ibrahim," Daniel croaked hoarsely. "But the others are with him."

"Have they processed the contents of the package?" Paul asked.

"They were almost finished when the chopper took off," the Captain replied, quieting down a bit. Suddenly, Paul heard the distinctive clatter of rifles being loaded. "*Stop it!*" the Captain shouted. "Put the guns *down*! Paul, they're pointing their guns at us. You have to do something *now*."

Paul locked eyes with Redman. "Captain, I hear what you're saying. I want you to tell Ibrahim that I'm going to talk to the Navy. I need him to be patient. The chopper is miles away now. It's going to take time to get it back on the ship."

"Okay, okay," Daniel replied and repeated the message.

At this point, Ibrahim came on the line. "Your five minutes is now four. I am not the one breaking our agreement. If you do not act quickly, the Captain will die."

When the connection terminated, all eyes in the bridge turned toward Paul and Redman.

"He's bluffing," the SEAL commander said. "If he kills Captain Parker, there's no chance he'll reach the mainland with the money."

Paul nodded. "I agree. But it means he's getting close to the edge. I strongly advise you to land the helicopter. It wasn't part of the deal."

Redman turned to the officer of the deck. "Mr. Evans, what is the status of the boats you saw?"

"Sir, the vessels are no longer closing. Range is two and a half miles."

Redman pointed his binoculars toward Somalia. The sun had set minutes before, and the afterglow was quickly fading, ushering in the first stars of evening. He turned to Masters. "Can you patch me through to the helo?"

Masters picked up the phone and gave the order to CIC. Seconds later, Paul heard the pilot's voice come over the audio system. With concise questions, Redman confirmed that the boats were skiffs carrying fishing nets and buoys, that there were no weapons visible, and that both vessels had ceased their forward movement. Redman thanked the pilot and hung up.

"Let's get the bird on the deck," he said. "Call the *Truman* and ask Captain Ellis to put one of his choppers on standby. I don't like the boats sitting there, but I can't make them leave." He faced Paul again. "Get Ibrahim back on the line and tell him to look out his window."

Thank God, Paul thought, punching the "redial" button on the sat phone. The pirate answered immediately, and Paul relayed the message. Ibrahim grunted and told him to wait. Paul watched out the window as the Seahawk returned from the west, skimming low over the water. The helicopter made a tight circle around the cruiser and then descended to the deck in a riot of sound.

"Do you see it?" he asked Ibrahim when the rotor noise

diminished. "It's powering down."

The pirate didn't mince words. "We want the helicopter inside the ship."

Paul put the phone on mute and spoke to Redman. "He wants us to put the bird away. I think we should do it. We have the chopper from the *Truman* if we need it."

"What is he going to ask for next?" the SEAL commander growled. "The Navy band to play while he sails off into the sunset?" He glanced at Masters. "Put the Seahawk in the hangar bay. But that's it. That's the last concession I'm prepared to make."

With a nod, Paul unmuted the phone and passed along the news.

There was a moment in every negotiation when Paul realized that the outcome was no longer in his hands, that everything he had been working toward came down to a choice on the part of the hostage taker: to accept something as a hedge against the possibility of getting nothing—or worse, being imprisoned or shot to death—or to cast off all moral restraint and press for unconditional surrender. Smart kidnappers always settled for something. The ones Paul worried about were the fools, the mentally deranged, and the ideologues who interpreted death as martyrdom.

Paul had no doubt about the category to which Ibrahim belonged. The young pirate was the most capable villain he had ever encountered. He was a dynamic negotiator with a nimble mind, both courageous and calculating in the face of risk. He knew when he had leverage to exercise and when he had reached the limits of his power. He had never accepted the full burden of compromise, always pushing the Navy to meet him in the middle.

For this reason, Paul felt little fear as he watched the dusk fall over the sea. He sensed the tension around him like static in the air, heard it in the hushed voices of the sailors as they busied themselves with routine tasks, saw it in the creases on Gabe Masters's forehead. But he was largely immune to it, as was Frank Redman. It was intriguing that the two of them, having clashed so often in the heat of the crisis, had reached the same conclusion: that Ibrahim was about to concede.

It took the *Gettysburg*'s ground crew fifteen minutes to move the helicopter into the hangar bay. When Masters confirmed that the Seahawk was secure, Paul called Ibrahim again. The phone rang and rang without answer. After ten rings, he thought about using the radio again but decided against it. The transmission would be audible to anyone with a VHF receiver and a line of sight to the cruiser at sea or on land. After the twentieth ring, Paul frowned. *This isn't like him. What's going on?*

At long last, Paul heard the click of a connecting call. "Ibrahim," he said preemptively, "the helicopter is inside the ship. It's time to make the exchange."

When the pirate replied, Paul knew that something had changed. Perhaps it was the timbre of his words, or perhaps it was the words themselves—spoken in accusation, not conversation—but Paul sensed the tremor like a seismograph picking up an earthquake.

"You moved the ship," Ibrahim said.

Paul felt a surge of adrenaline and dread. "What are you talking about?"

"You know what I mean. My eyes do not lie."

"It's getting dark," Paul said, deflecting the truth. "Things look different at night."

Ibrahim would have none of this. "You have betrayed our trust. You must move the ship. We will not release the hostages until you are one mile away. You have five minutes to comply."

The line went dead.

Paul felt a shock of fear. He glanced at the clock—it was 18:13—and then at Rodriguez, who was sitting at the chart table. He saw the doubt in the negotiator's eyes. He turned toward Redman, preparing himself for a battle he had to win. "He's serious this time. This isn't a bluff."

Redman's face looked like chiseled marble in the darkened bridge. "Let's talk outside," he said. When Paul and Masters joined him on the bridge wing, he spoke succinctly. "His position is a violation of terms. He got the drop and counted the cash. Now he's having second thoughts."

"You're wrong," Paul rejoined. "I met with him. I looked into his eyes. He was willing to trust us as long as we trusted him. Now he thinks we broke the covenant. In his mind, all bets are off."

"Precisely," the SEAL commander retorted. "Which is why negotiation is no longer advisable. It's time to demonstrate to him that he doesn't have a choice."

Paul's heart dropped. "You don't get a man to climb down from the ledge by surrounding him with guns. You convince him that living another day is better than the alternative. We should agree to move the ship if he releases Quentin Parker."

Redman stared him down. "Your advice is duly noted, but the way I see it, Ibrahim has reneged. I don't have authority for an assault, but I can turn up the heat. It's time for Arachne."

"Frank," Masters broke in, surprising Paul, "we've known each other a long time. I have enormous respect for your team. But Paul is right. Ibrahim is in a dangerous place. If we go tactical, he'll see it as preemptive. There's no telling what he'll do."

"Are you saying we should move the ship, Gabe?" Redman demanded. "Because that's not the way we do business. We don't let our adversaries dictate terms."

"I agree," Masters said. "But this isn't about us. It's about two American sailors in harm's way. If ever there was a time to tread lightly, it's now."

Redman looked flummoxed. While he could ignore Paul's objections, he couldn't dismiss the opinion of a naval officer equal to him in rank. As Paul watched, the SEAL commander checked the time and made a snap judgment.

"I'll grant Ibrahim's request if he puts Quentin Parker in a life preserver with a safety light and sends him overboard. We'll pick him up in one of our RHIBs." He paused, looking between Paul and Masters. "But I'm not going to tolerate delay. We have spectators and we're drifting toward Mogadishu. He can have ten minutes to think about it. If he doesn't meet the condition in that time frame, we're doing it my way. Is that clear?"

Paul came within a hairsbreadth of saying, "I don't deliver ultimatums," but the flash of iron in Redman's eyes convinced him otherwise. The SEAL commander had given him breathing room. It was scarce, yes, but he had to make it work.

He got Ibrahim on the phone again and explained the counteroffer. He heard staccato bursts of chatter in the background, all in Somali.

"You're changing the bargain, Paul," the pirate said, interrupting him. "You moved the ship while we were counting the money. Why did you do that? To bring your snipers closer so they can kill us? I remember a lesson my father taught me. If a merchant says he'll bring you ten camels but he only brings nine, you pay him for the nine and demand the last one for free. You broke our trust. We aren't going to pay you for the tenth camel."

Paul didn't react. "Ibrahim, moving the ship wasn't part of our agreement either. We can renegotiate, but you need to give us something in return. You lose nothing if you let Quentin go. You can hold on to the Captain until we're far enough away for comfort. That's the best I can do."

"You're not listening, Paul," the pirate said, growing strident. "The one who breaks trust has the obligation to restore it. If you had not moved your ship, we would be on the beach by now and the hostages would be in your hands.

You moved your ship. It is your duty to move it again."

Paul looked out at the night, struggling to control his racing thoughts. *I need more time. I have to find a way to reach him again.* "Ibrahim, do you recall what you said when we first spoke? You want something, and I want something. You have what you want—a bunch of money and a boat that will take you to the beach. You're almost home. I still don't have what I want. We need to help each other get to the goal line. Take some time to think about it. I'll call you back in ten minutes."

"No!" Ibrahim snarled, losing all pretense of control. "You think because you have bigger guns, because you are American and we are Somali, you can make us bend? Read your history. That's the same arrogance that brought down Corfield and Garrison. Our guns are pointed at the hostages. Back off or we will eat them like meat. Do you hear me? *Back off or we will eat them like meat!*"

Corfield and Garrison? Paul thought, his mind processing at light speed. *Garrison is the American general who presided over the Battle of Mogadishu in 1993. But Corfield?* For some reason the name sounded familiar. He searched his memory and then it came to him—a footnote in the brief Frazier gave him. Richard Corfield was the British officer charged with putting down an anticolonial rebellion led by Mohammed Abdullah Hassan, a Somali mullah, in 1913. When Corfield's Camel Constabulary engaged Hassan's Dervishes, Corfield perished, after which Hassan penned a poem celebrating his demise.

"Ibrahim," Paul said, allowing a hint of desperation into

his voice, "please listen to me. I can't do this on my own. I need you to help me—"

At once he realized he was talking to himself. The line had disconnected.

"Shit!" he exclaimed, slamming the phone against his palm.

"He's made his decision," Redman said harshly. "I'm sending in the boats."

Paul disregarded all decorum. "Did you not hear what he just said? We don't have leverage anymore. The Parkers are in danger. We need to move this ship back *now*!"

"Agent Derrick," Redman countered. "I've watched you play footsy with these assholes for nearly a week, and look where it's gotten us." He toggled on his headset. "All units, this is Arcturus—"

"Frank," Masters interjected before the SEAL commander could give the order. "You agreed to give him ten minutes. He has eight left. He might change his mind."

Redman swore under his breath. Then just as quickly he regained his composure, conscious, no doubt, of the many young sailors staring at him. "All units, stand by," he said into his microphone. He looked at the clock on the bulkhead. It read 18:22. "Eight minutes then," he barked and opened the door to the bridge wing, disappearing into the night.

For Paul, watching the seconds count down opened up a wormhole into the past. All at once he was in the house in Annandale again, listening to the march of the wall clock as Kyle contemplated what to do with the gun in his hand. He saw the whole story playing out before him, like a cord unraveling—the years of insults his brother had endured; the way his father had mocked his drawings and ridiculed his interest in drama, calling it a "refuge for fags and sissies"; the humiliation Kyle had suffered when his father read his private journal at the dinner table, exposing the feelings he had for a boy in his class; and the final shame—being forbidden to attend his senior prom because he wouldn't go with a girl. That was the moment when Kyle had finally cracked.

Paul remembered how the house had stood in the gray light when he and Megan pulled into the driveway after football practice. He could still smell the fresh paint on the door when he opened it and heard shouting coming from the back of the house. Megan reacted quickly, leaping into the fray to take up Kyle's defense, but Paul stopped and listened, weighing the gravity of the confrontation. His father and brother had fought before, but the outcome had never been in doubt. This time, however, he heard in Kyle's cries something more sinister and dangerous.

He remembered the scene as it was when he reached the den: his mother, Ellen, weeping on the sofa; John and Kyle screaming at each other in front of the fireplace; and Megan waving her arms and yelling at her father to leave her brother alone. His mother pleaded with Paul to do something, and he tried to intervene. But Kyle shoved him aside with a strength that shocked him.

"Get out of the way, Paul!" he shouted. *"This isn't your fight!"*

For long moments, father and son traded expletive-laden barbs, and then, at once, Kyle's face went rigid and his hands curled into fists.

"You think I'm a mutant, you sack of shit? Here's a mutant for you!"

Before anyone understood what he was doing, he took the poker from the fireplace and slammed the butt against John's head. As his father fell to his knees, Kyle slipped the pistol out of his ankle holster and pointed it at him.

"Get up!" he hollered, his voice shredding from the strain. *"Be a man! You made me what I am!"*

In the seconds that followed, the world seemed to hover in suspension. Paul heard his mother crying, heard Megan begging Kyle to put the gun down, but he blocked all of it out, focusing instead on two things—the clock on the wall and his brother's face. He knew in his gut that Kyle was on the brink, but he also understood that there was a way back and that it hinged on a choice. In pulling the gun on his father, Kyle had begun to sever his ties to the future, but he wasn't all the way gone. He could still choose life over death.

Just as Ibrahim could still choose.

Paul watched the bridge clock with mounting dread. 18:24 . . . 18:25 . . . 18:26. He trained his night-vision binoculars on the *Renaissance*. In the falling dark, the portholes were cutouts of light. He saw shadows moving beyond the curtains. Something was going on between Ibrahim and his men. In the last two calls, he had detected a subtle shift in the pirate's language. For days, Ibrahim had spoken on behalf of his crew, using "I" language, as if he were in complete control. After the helo took off, however, his speech had been dominated by "we" language. Paul clenched his teeth. *We have no clue what the other Somalis are like. What if someone else is making a power play?*

The minutes continued to tick away—18:27 . . . 18:28 . . . 18:29—but the sat phone and the radio remained silent. Suddenly, the door to the bridge wing opened and Redman appeared again.

He looked at Paul. "I spoke to Admiral Prince, and he agrees with my assessment. We've given the pirates innumerable chances to do the right thing, and they're still dragging their feet. At this point, action is imperative. Doing nothing will endanger the hostages as much as doing something." He pointed at the clock. "Their ten minutes are up. Arachne is a go."

For an instant, Paul considered lodging a final objection, but he knew it was pointless. A knot formed in his stomach, and the muscles in his neck and shoulders tightened until his body felt like it was bound in a straitjacket. He watched the sailboat through his binoculars, bobbing on a sea of iridescent green, as Redman issued the orders to his team.

"Gray One, Two, and Three, Red One and Two, this is Arcturus. Execute Arachne. Gray Team, keep your distance to seventy-five yards. Light up their world, but keep your weapons safe. Do not fire even if fired upon. Red Team, good luck and Godspeed."

Paul watched the SEAL boats throttle up. They rounded the bow of the *Gettysburg* in a cluster and headed quietly across the water. At the midpoint, the boats on the wings fanned out and the lead boat slowed to a crawl, approaching the *Renaissance* cautiously. Thirty seconds later, they reached their stations, surrounding the sailboat in a triangular embrace. In an instant, they painted the yacht with blinding light.

Redman spoke into the radio. "*Renaissance*, this is the *Gettysburg*. We mean you no harm. We had an agreement. We want you to honor it. Let the hostages go and we will let you go. Over."

For a long moment, nothing happened. Paul imagined the SEAL divers moving stealthily under the black water, their propulsion vehicles and rebreathing systems leaving no trace of their passage. When he first explained Arachne, Redman had predicted that his team would need twelve minutes to complete the insertion, disable the propeller, secure the towline to the keel, and return to the cruiser. Paul watched the clock, hoping the gambit would work. He tried to get into Ibrahim's head, but it was an impossible leap. *How are you going to end this? What choice are you going to make?*

The gunshots when they came sounded like firecrackers in the night. There was a long burst—at least seven shots in rapid succession—then silence again.

Immediately, the watch officer exclaimed, "*Shots fired! Shots fired on the* Renaissance*!*"

Paul felt the clutch of panic. Then his reflexes engaged

and he lifted his radio handset and binoculars off the chart table, wrenched open the door to the bridge wing, and raced to the railing, barely conscious of Redman and Masters behind him.

"*Ibrahim, this is Paul!*" he shouted into the radio, zeroing in on the sailboat with his binoculars. "*We had a deal! Don't do this!*"

He heard nothing in reply.

He grabbed the external phone off the hook and spoke to CIC. "This is Derrick. Patch me through to the *Renaissance*."

The pulsing ring of the sat phone reminded him of the flatline on an EKG. He heard more gunfire from across the water—this time a four-shot burst—then more silence.

"*Pick up the damn phone!*" he yelled when no one answered. "*This is madness!*"

Suddenly, he was aware that there were people around him. Everyone was talking at once. Redman was on the radio with his boat team and snipers, trying to get a handle on what was happening. Masters was deploying his Seahawks and requesting backup from the *Truman* and *San Jacinto*. An officer with a video camera was taking footage of the scene. A few sailors were speculating in whispers.

Then came the last round of shots—a cluster of three. Unlike the earlier bursts, these were deliberate, as if the shooter had taken careful aim.

At that moment, the wormhole opened up again, and Paul was in the den in Annandale all those years ago. He saw his brother babbling like a child, mucus dripping from his nose and mixing with his tears, as he waved the gun around. He heard his father's pleading, his sister's shouts, his mother's sobbing, and his own words of desperate reason. Then the moment came when Kyle made his choice. His expression hardened and his irresolution vanished. *This is all your fault!* he cried. *You made me do this!* He pulled the trigger twice and watched his father fall. Then he turned the gun on himself.

Paul stared at the sailboat as the old wound reopened in him. Moisture came to his eyes and bewilderment crowded his heart. *Why, Kyle?* he cried into the depthless well of the past. *Why, when you had so much to live for?* Then the time warp closed, and Paul confronted the awful truth of the present. *Why, Ibrahim? Why, when you swore to me you wanted peace?*

It took Paul a moment to register what he was seeing. Bodies were pouring out of the sailboat, bodies with thin limbs and colorful clothes holding guns and moving with the zeal of the terrified. They leaped over the gunwales and into the Navy RHIB, firing their weapons into the dark. Paul saw Ibrahim's red shirt and the flash of a briefcase in his hands. And then he, too, was over the side. The RHIB's engine came to life with a throaty roar. And then they were off, racing for the coast.

The exodus happened so fast that even Redman took a second to react. "Gray One, secure the sailboat," he ordered. "Gray Two and Three, take down the RHIB. Seahawks inbound to support. Weapons free. Weapons free. Fire if fired upon."

As Paul watched, two of the SEAL boats peeled away from the sailboat and churned up the water in pursuit of the pirates. At the same time, the third boat approached the *Renaissance* from the stern. A pair of SEALs dressed in black vaulted into the cockpit, cradling their weapons. One of them disappeared into the cabin, then returned a second later, waving his arms wildly and shouting something into his radio that Redman repeated for all to hear.

"Cas-evac. Cas-evac. Hostages are down. Repeat, hostages are down."

ISMAIL

THE INDIAN OCEAN
02°09′11″N, 45°41′58″E
November 14, 2011

As Ismail fled the sailboat, he felt like he was in someone else's body. His eyes were seeing, his muscles pumping, his fingers gripping a briefcase and a gun hot from the firing. But he sensed them from a distance. His ears felt like they were stuffed with cotton. All he could hear was a piercing ring that faded in and out, at once near and far away. His thoughts, too, were a chaotic jumble of impressions, as if his mind were a shattered mirror, reflecting the world in pieces.

Everything was scrambled. Everything was inverted. The night sky was dazzlingly bright. His men were jostling him, their mouths forming words, but he understood none of it. A pair of feet—*his* feet—cleared the gunwale and landed in the Navy boat. A pair of hands—*his* hands—flipped the starter switch, rammed the throttle to its stop, and yanked the wheel hard to port, aiming at a gap between the lights. Somewhere beneath him he felt the vibrations as the boat tore across the dark water, leaping the swells, but they were dampened somehow, as if the floor were made of jelly.

The only thing right side up and rightfully his was the crushing weight of pain. The wheel of time had spun the past into the present. The djinn of his first victim—the boy he had killed in the camp at Lanta Buro—had become an avenging angel, snaring him in a trap he had laid with his own hands. It was the curse of war. His father had warned him of it. He who lives by the gun shall also die by it.

He saw the black-hulled speedboats converging on him, their torches glowing like white fire in the night. He saw his men huddled in the bottom of the boat, firing wildly toward the light. As the ringing in his ears began to fade, he heard the angry hum of bullets slicing the air around him. He ducked for cover but felt no fear of the living, only the dead. The living could take nothing from him that had not already been taken. The dead, however, held the power of judgment.

He guided the boat like a serpent, fouling the Navy's aim. He focused on Venus, shining like a beacon above the horizon. The beach wasn't far now. Mahamoud was waiting for him there with a way of escape. His uncle would know what to do with the money in the briefcase he had salvaged from the abattoir of the sailboat. Mahamoud would know how to find Yasmin.

It was then that Ismail's men started to die. Guray was the first to get hit. He cried out and clutched his neck, then slumped over and fell into the sea, disappearing into the darkness. Liban came next. Liban, the faithful—the only one whose loyalty had never faltered, even at the end. Two bullets tore a gaping hole in his chest. He tried to shoot back, but his wounds were too great. As his breathing slowed, he clutched at the sky, as if begging Allah for mercy.

At that moment, the pain in Ismail's soul opened into an abyss. He saw the faces of the dead swirling around him—the faces of those he had killed and those he had loved and watched die. There were many whose names he never knew, fighters from the African Union and Hizbul Islam he had fought in the war. But some of them had names. Their graves were the record of his ruin.

Adan, his father, in the schoolyard in Medina.

Samatar, in the training camp at Lanta Buro.

Yusuf, his brother, on Maka al Mukarama Road.

Gedef, his mentor and protector, on the high seas.

Daniel Parker, captain of the *Renaissance*.

Quentin Parker, like Samatar but with white skin.

Guray, whose life had been a tragedy from the beginning.

And now Liban, his companion and friend.

The horror was greater than Ismail could bear. He let loose a primal scream and turned the helm hard over, driving straight at the speedboat that had killed Liban. Bullets shredded the air like shrapnel. One whizzed by his ear, another ricocheted off the control panel, but none hit him. The speedboat swerved to avoid them and then joined its twin on the other side, racing toward the coast.

Ismail looked to the west. The mainland was a black scar beneath the starlit sky. He drove the boat toward it, taking evasive maneuvers but always pressing ahead. He heard the helicopters in the sky and saw their spotlights spearing the air. They swept over him and lit up the dark sea. He felt the downdraft from the rotors, felt the thunder of their presence, but he refused to surrender. Instead, he yanked the helm back and forth, trying to dodge the beams.

All at once, he heard a noise that made no sense. The engine of the boat coughed and sputtered, then quit altogether, as if struck by an unseen hand. As the boat slowed in the water, rising and falling with the waves, he flipped the starter switch over and over again, trying frantically to reengage the engine. He heard his men shouting at him, begging him to fix the problem, even as they fired a hail of bullets at the monsters in the sky.

Suddenly, he heard a voice boom across the water. "Throw your weapons into the water and put your hands above your head. Your boat has been disabled. Cease your fire or you will be shot."

In an instant, Ismail understood everything. The Americans had betrayed him not once but twice—in moving the warship closer without warning and in giving him a broken boat. They had never intended for him to reach the beach with the ransom money. They had given him a rope to hang himself. He felt rage welling up in him along with despair. They were liars, all of them—even Paul, who brought him Pepsi and quoted from the Quran. As perfidious and corrupt as he was, Mas had been right. *I was a fool to trust them*, Ismail thought. *They only meant us harm.*

He saw the choice before him with stark clarity—to die a warrior's death or accept capture by the Navy and trial and imprisonment in the United States. He saw the gun at his feet, felt the adrenaline flowing in his veins. All he had to do was pull the trigger and the Americans would end his misery. But then he saw the faces of Dhuuban and Sondare staring back at him. They were just kids, like Samatar and Yusuf and Quentin Parker, their sins far less grievous than his. They hadn't murdered or deceived anyone. They didn't deserve to die.

He heard himself speak in Somali: "It's over! Do as they say!" Then he threw his gun over the side and raised his hands into the night.

He was completely unprepared for what happened next. As the nearest speedboat approached with men in black brandishing automatic weapons, Mas turned and pointed at him, shouting a single word at the top of his lungs. It was an accusation at once true and false, and it pierced Ismail's heart with more precision than a sniper's bullet.

"Shabaab!"

"Shabaab!"

"He is Shabaab!"

VANESSA

Vanessa stared at the phone in her hands like it was a living thing. She pressed the "redial" button again and listened to the maddening ring. *Pick up, Ibrahim!* she thought, trying with all her might to hold herself together. *What are you doing?* It was just after seven o'clock, nearly two hours after the drop. The cabin of the plane was as quiet as a graveyard. Flint was looking at her, his expression unreadable. She'd had the same exchange with him after each call.

Vanessa: "Why aren't they answering?"

Flint: "They're probably still counting the money."

Vanessa: "How long can it possibly take?"

Flint: "You need to be patient."

But patience was the furthest thing from her mind. Her thoughts were a whirlpool dragging her into the darkness. Something wasn't right; she could feel it. Daniel and Quentin should have been released by now. The nightmare should have been over.

She dropped the phone in her lap and looked out the window at the moonlit African plain, struggling against the gnawing pains in her chest. There was nothing she could do to stop the panic when it reached this stage. It was like a runaway train barreling down a mountainside.

She reclined her seat and closed her eyes, focusing all of her attention on breathing. She felt her diaphragm contracting and relaxing, heard the air passing through her nose. When she locked in the rhythm, she allowed her mind to drift. She imagined herself picking up the Bissolotti, placing the bow on the strings, and launching into Schumann's "Träumerei." She visualized the music filling her heart like a concert hall and chasing away the demons. In time, the pressure in her chest subsided.

"How much longer until we land?" she asked Ruan Steyn as calmly as she could.

"Forty-five minutes," Steyn called from the cockpit.

Vanessa lifted the sat phone again and tried the *Renaissance* without success. She punched in Brent Frazier's mobile number next, hoping he would have an update, but he didn't answer either. She blinked in confusion. She had spoken to him just before the drop. Why wasn't he available? She called Mary's BlackBerry. The FBI agent had promised her it would never be out of reach. She waited and waited, but all she heard was a chorus of endless rings.

She felt the chill begin like a wintry trickle beneath her collar. There had to be a benign reason for the silence. *It's going to be all right,* she reassured herself. *We did everything they asked.*

At last, Steyn announced their descent into Nairobi. Vanessa fastened her seatbelt and watched the lights of the city grow closer. The plane flared over the runway and landed smoothly, taxiing to the same hangar from which they had left. When Steyn shut down the engines, Flint opened the door.

"We'll call them from the office," he said with an unconvincing smile.

Vanessa collected her purse and stepped out of the plane. She saw Mary standing beside the Land Rover. The FBI agent walked toward her, then pulled up short, as if unsure how to make the approach. Vanessa saw the trail of mascara beneath Mary's eyes and stopped dead.

"What's wrong?" she exclaimed, her resistance crumbling. "What *happened?*"

Mary gave her an ashen look. "There was a shooting," she said in an unsteady voice. "Daniel is dead. Quentin is in critical condition. He's in surgery now."

For a moment, Vanessa just stood there, too stunned to speak. Then the shock gave way to horror, and her body began to shake. *"No! Oh God, no!"*

Mary wrapped her in a fierce embrace. "I'm so sorry," she whispered. "I'm so sorry."

In an instant, Vanessa's suffering turned into anger. *"Why?"* she screamed, pushing Mary away. *"Tell me!"*

"I don't know," Mary said softly. "No one knows."

Vanessa's eyes flashed. "Get me on that ship! I don't care what it takes. *I want to see my son!*"

Mary's bottom lip quivered. "The Navy has some of the

best surgeons in the world. They're doing all they can for him."

"That's not *good enough*!" Vanessa shrieked, feeling helpless and cornered. *"Get me on that ship!"*

Mary looked at her compassionately. "I wish I could."

Just as quickly, Vanessa's anger transmuted to despair. She sank to her knees and began to weep. She heard voices shouting inside her head, like a great assembly of her detractors. Trish, in Quentin's first year: *You're too serious to have a child. You need to lighten up.* Ted, when Quentin started to see a therapist: *I always thought the kid was strange.* The detective at Annapolis PD: *Did you have any idea your son was into drugs?* Then her own voice rose above the rest: *If you don't get your act together, Vanessa, he's going to be as messed up as you are.* The prophecy spoken a thousand times by her shame had finally come true. She was married to a dead man she had just started to love again, and her son was hovering on the brink, his body riddled with bullets.

Mary put a hand on her shoulder, but she shrugged it off. She didn't know how long she stayed on the hangar floor. It could have been minutes or hours, she didn't care. She saw nothing, heard nothing, felt nothing except the vertigo of falling and the humiliation of failure. She was a disgrace. Everything in her world was meaningless apart from Quentin's life.

At last, the raging storm of her emotions began to relent, leaving her exhausted and empty. Through her tears she saw Mary's outstretched hand. She took it and climbed to her feet, allowing the FBI agent to lead her to the Land Rover.

Tony Flint opened the door for her, looking mortified. "I'm sorry, Vanessa. I never thought . . ." His voice trailed off as he closed the door behind her.

She settled into the seat and wiped her eyes with her sleeve. She saw Mary slide in beside her and felt the Land Rover accelerate out of the hangar. She had so many questions. But only one of them mattered right now. "How long has Quentin been in the OR?" she asked quietly.

Mary turned toward her, her eyes limpid in the shadows. "I spoke to Paul half an hour ago. All he could tell me was that Quentin had been airlifted to the *Truman* and that he was in surgery. Paul was about to take a helicopter to the carrier. He said he'd call as soon as he could."

Vanessa felt the ache of grief in every inch of her body. *Paul Derrick. The best negotiator in the FBI. How could he have failed? How could all of them have failed? The Navy, the SEALs, the entire apparatus of the government? How could the whole thing have gone so horribly wrong?*

"Are the pirates dead?" she asked in time.

"Two of them were killed," Mary said. "The rest were captured. They'll be tried in federal court. I expect the government will ask for the death penalty."

Vanessa shook her head. *They don't deserve a trial. They deserve a hanging.* "And Ibrahim?"

Mary met her gaze. "He survived."

Vanessa remembered the pirate's final words to her: *We have done nothing to harm them. Deliver what you promised, and I will do the same.* She wanted to lash out at him then, to claw his face with her fingernails and pluck out his eyes.

You're a liar! she thought. *You're a liar and a murderer. Death is too decent for you. Whatever it takes, I will watch you burn.*

PAUL

The Seahawk carrying Paul and Rodriguez landed on the *Truman* at 19:51, an hour and twenty-two minutes after the shooting. The aircraft carrier, darkened for nighttime operations, was a hive of activity and noise. Men in helmets and goggles were moving about the flight deck, tending to helicopters and jets gearing up for flight. The aircrewman collected the negotiators' duffel bags and led them across the amber-lit deck, around the tower, and down two flights of stairs to a hatch that opened into the ship.

The *Truman* was under way again and heading out to sea, its massive propellers driving it across the water at over thirty knots. Paul suspected that as soon as the ship emerged from Somali waters, the Navy would launch a squadron of planes to offer air support to the battle group during the long trip around the Horn of Africa. No one knew exactly how the Somali government and the world community would react as news of the incident spread, but Paul was certain it would generate controversy and dominate headlines for weeks.

He and Rodriguez followed the aircrewman into a cramped waiting room, where they were greeted by a thirty-something African-American officer dressed in gray and blue coveralls.

"I'm Commander Adrian Johnson, the JAG attorney on the admiral's staff," he said. "I'll be your liaison for as long as you're aboard." Johnson gestured at a female sailor beside him. "This is Ensign Miller. She'll take your bags to DV Row, where you'll be staying. We have a post-incident briefing at 22:00. Until then, we're free. Where would you like to go?"

"Take us to the hospital," Paul said. "I want to see Quentin."

In the aftermath of the shooting, his mind had become a haunted place, stained with memories he couldn't shake. Daniel Parker: *Paul, they're all pointing their guns at us. You have to do something now.* Ibrahim: *I am not the one breaking our agreement. If you do not act quickly, the Captain will die.* And Vanessa Parker from the skies: *Bring them home to me, Paul. Bring my husband and son home.* Paul had lost hostages before, but never had the failure felt so personal. None of them had taken him back to the house in Annandale. None of them had reminded him of Kyle.

He followed Johnson out of the waiting room and into the warren of the ship. Below the flight deck, the carrier was a world unto itself. As on the *Gettysburg*, the levels, decks, and compartments on the *Truman* were organized in a triple-coordinate system intended to demystify the ship's layout. The carrier, however, was so colossal and its innards so labyrinthine that the bull's-eye plaques offered little more than ornamentation. Soon Paul lost all sense of space and distance and trailed the JAG officer like a pack mule.

"Where are the pirates?" he asked.

"The SPs are being sanitized in the medical bay," Johnson replied, using the official shorthand for "suspected pirate." "We'll admit them to the brig as soon as they're scrubbed. We set aside classrooms for the interrogations. Your friends from the Bureau are chomping at the bit."

Of course they are, Paul thought. *Ibrahim and his crew just shit on the entire United States government. They're going to hit them with a sledgehammer. Besides, they've been cooped up in this floating anthill for the past five days. This is their chance to do something.*

He glanced at Rodriguez. "I think you should go make friends with the boys from New York. I want an inside track on the interview process."

Rodriguez nodded. "I'm happy to babysit."

"How long before the pirates are extradited?" Paul asked Johnson as they walked down a long corridor studded with oval hatches.

"The wheels are already in motion for Justice to take the ball," the JAG officer replied. "As soon as we get to Djibouti, we'll put them on a plane and send them Stateside."

"What about the SEALs? They're going to need to deliver statements."

Johnson looked Paul in the eye. "Captain Redman and his team will participate in the investigation as the needs of justice require. But their involvement in this incident is highly classified. For the sake of national security, their names will never be divulged nor the precise nature of their duties revealed to the public."

The pirates aren't the only ones being sanitized, Paul mused. *Redman may never face scrutiny. Unless* . . . The thought struck him like an epiphany. *Unless the truth comes out in the legal proceedings.*

He filed the idea away and trailed Johnson into the hospital. The lobby was at once sterile and surreal. Doctors, nurses, and corpsmen scurried about, looking at charts and attending to the sick. Patients waited for treatment in chairs along the wall. A receptionist directed traffic from behind a counter with a sliding-glass window. It felt like the emergency room intake in an urban hospital. Paul found it hard to believe he was on a ship in the Indian Ocean.

Johnson greeted the receptionist. "Andrea, I need an update on the status of Quentin Parker. Can you find me someone who assisted with the cas-evac?"

"Dr. Hancock!" the woman called out, hailing a middle-aged man in a lab coat talking to a young nurse. "Weren't you on the flight deck when the casualties were brought in?"

The doctor nodded gravely, as if he'd just seen a ghost. "I brought the boy down myself. I was in the Trauma Bay when they brought his father in."

Johnson turned to Paul. "Dr. Hancock is our senior medical officer. He can answer your questions." He waved to Rodriguez. "I'll take you to the classrooms."

When they left, Hancock gave Paul a poignant look. "I don't understand. The last we heard they were about to be released. Now this." His eyes moistened and he looked away. "I'm sorry. It's just that my son is the boy's age."

Paul felt a stabbing pain in his stomach. *Kyle was eighteen, too.* He shook his head, struggling to remain impassive. "I wish I could give you a reason."

"Bastards," the doctor said under his breath. "I hope they rot in hell." He shook his head and collected himself. "So what can I do for you?"

Paul thought of Mary meeting Vanessa in Nairobi. The knife twisted in his gut. "I need something to tell the family. They'll want details."

Hancock angled his head. "Let's find a place to talk."

Paul followed the senior medical officer down a series of hallways to a room with two gurneys, an array of medical equipment and filing cabinets, and track lights on the ceiling. Both gurneys looked like they had been recently used.

"This is the trauma bay," Hancock explained. "It's where we do stabilization care. When the helicopter landed with the boy, I had a team on the flight deck. The corpsman on the chopper had already intubated him to get him breathing again. He had an entry wound here—" He put his hand on his chest slightly to the right of his sternum and about two inches below the clavicle. "He also had a flesh wound with tissue damage below his right shoulder. He was losing consciousness and bleeding internally. We brought him down on the elevator. By the time we got him here, he was unresponsive."

Hancock walked to the first gurney. "Our surgeon—Dr. Alvarez—made a scan with the ultrasound and saw that he was in cardiac arrest. The bullet had punctured his heart, and the blood had leaked into the pericardium, causing a tamponade. Dr. Alvarez made an incision in his chest and stopped the bleeding. He massaged the heart, bringing it back to rhythm, and put chest tubes in to manage the lung injury. Then he prepped him for the OR."

The doctor pointed toward the wall. "They're in there now. It'll be another hour or two before we know the outcome. About the time we sent the boy into surgery, they brought his father in." Hancock took a belabored breath. "The damage was severe. He'd been shot half a dozen times in the chest and head. Part of his skull was missing. There was nothing we could do. The wounds were not survivable." His voice dropped almost to a whisper. "I was the one who pronounced him dead."

Paul steeled himself against the sorrow and recalled the gunshots. In the first round, he had heard six or seven shots in a rapid burst. They must have been aimed at Daniel. There were four shots in the second round and three shots in the last round. If Quentin had only two wounds, as Hancock indicated, that meant that whoever shot him missed at least once and possibly twice. In such close quarters, it made little sense, unless the gun malfunctioned or the shots were fired in extreme haste. He made a mental note to mention the enigma to the investigators.

"What did you do with the Captain's body?" Paul asked.

"We treated him like a soldier," the doctor replied. "We put his remains in a Conex box for the trip home. They'll take him to Dover. His family can collect him there."

Paul met Hancock's eyes. "Can I see him?"

The doctor nodded, gesturing toward the hallway. He led Paul to a utility elevator and stepped inside. "We put him in the hangar bay for ventilation."

Seconds later, the doors opened on a cavernous space bustling with sailors performing maintenance on a trio of fighter jets. Hancock walked toward one of the massive flight elevators that stood open to the air. Off to the side Paul saw a polished aluminum container with an American flag draped over it. A sailor stood beside it. He came to attention when Hancock approached.

"At ease," the doctor said. "Give us a few minutes."

"Yes, sir," the sailor replied, walking away.

"Take your time," Hancock said. "I'll be back shortly."

Paul knelt beside the container and put his hand on the stripes of the flag—red for courage, white for innocence. He choked up at the thought of the broken body inside.

"I'm sorry, Captain," he said softly, daring to hope that wherever Daniel was he could hear him. "This never should have happened." He blinked away the tears. "Your son is in good hands. I'm going to do what I can to make it up to him. I promise you that."

He stood up again and felt a surge of anger. He clenched

his hands into fists and looked out at the sea, glistening beneath the moon. *Dammit, Ibrahim! What the hell were you thinking?*

An hour and a half later, Paul was back in the Trauma Bay, pacing the floor like a caged beast. He kept looking at his watch, as if the act of checking the time could speed up the clock. Finally, at 21:42, the door opened and Hancock entered with a Hispanic man dressed in stained blue scrubs.

"Agent Derrick," Hancock said. "This is Dr. Alvarez, the ship's surgeon."

Alvarez nodded perfunctorily. "I have good news and bad news. The good news is he's alive and stable. We repaired his heart and lung and gave him a blood transfusion from our Walking Blood Bank. The bad news is he's comatose. It's likely that his brain was deprived of oxygen before we got his heart beating again. We won't know how severe the anoxia was until he wakes up again."

"When will that be?" Paul asked.

The surgeon shook his head. "It could be a day, it could be a week or two, before his cognitive functions start to return. We'll transport him off the ship within forty-eight hours. I understand his family is in Annapolis. I recommend sending him to Georgetown for acute care and Medstar NRH for rehab."

Paul tried to stay optimistic. "What are the odds he'll make a full recovery?"

Alvarez regarded him candidly. "I can't say with any certainty. Brain injuries are very hard to predict. But he's young and otherwise in good health. He could make a comeback."

It's not much, but it's something for Vanessa to hold on to, Paul thought. "What about his memory? Will he remember what happened?"

The surgeon's expression turned thoughtful. "If you're asking if he'll be able to talk to you about the incident, I have no idea. It depends on the state of his brain."

It was then that Paul remembered something. "Do you know how many bullets hit him?"

"There were two," Alvarez replied. "We found one lodged in his chest. The other one entered and exited through the soft tissue in his upper arm."

Paul shook the surgeon's hand. "Thank you. I mean it." Then he turned to Hancock. "Where can I make a phone call? I need to contact his mother."

"That would be CDC," the doctor replied. "I'll take you there."

Calling Vanessa Parker was one of the hardest things Paul had ever done. Guilt seared his conscience like a brand. For some reason he thought of Michelangelo's *The Last Judgment*. He felt like the damned man holding his face in his hands while devils dragged him into the underworld. When Hancock handed him the phone in the black light of the CDC—the nerve center of the carrier—he closed his eyes, cleared his mind, and allowed intuition to guide his words.

Mary Patterson answered her BlackBerry on the second ring. "Hello?"

"It's Paul," he said darkly. "Is she there?"

Mary inhaled audibly. "It's for you."

Paul heard a sniff and then Vanessa came on the line, her voice discordant with weariness and grief. "Paul? Is he alive?"

"Yes," he answered. "He's in the ICU, but he's stable. The doctors saved his life."

She began to cry. It was awhile before she spoke again. "How bad are his injuries?"

Paul passed along Dr. Alvarez's assessment, imbuing his tone with confidence. When he finished, he heard silence on the line. He tried to imagine what she was thinking. The shock had worn off in the hours since the shooting. She was a physician. She had prepared herself for the worst. But the truth carried a burden all its own. Quentin had survived, but his life had become a question mark. It was a terrible load for a mother to carry.

Eventually, she broke the spell. "What happened?" she whispered. "Why did they do this?"

He took a breath and let it out. "I don't know yet. But I'm going to find out."

"Okay," she said simply.

He softened his voice and spoke from the heart. "Vanessa, when I asked you to trust me, you told me that trust entails responsibility. You're right. If you need someone on our side to blame, then blame me. I didn't bring them home."

If he was looking for absolution, she didn't offer it. Instead, she said, "When can I see him? I'll go anywhere. It doesn't matter."

"It should be soon. I have the senior medical officer here with me. He can tell you more."

He handed the phone to Hancock and sat down on a swivel chair, looking around the CDC at the marvels that allowed the Navy to peer into the reaches of sea and sky and define a thousand different threats. They were nearly omniscient, these sailors with their godlike instruments and computer arrays. But there was one gaping omission in the data. None of their devices could penetrate the human heart. None of them had signaled a warning when Ibrahim and his crew were on the verge of murder. It had taken a human to see it, and another human to ignore it.

Dammit! Paul thought for the hundredth time. *Damn it all to hell.*

A few minutes before 22:00, Commander Johnson collected Paul and led him on another disorienting trip through the *Truman* maze to a classroom not far from the brig. Paul almost laughed when he saw all of the G-men milling around. The place was a petri dish of pent-up testosterone. He caught sight of Rodriguez and Ali Sharif talking to a naval officer. He walked in their direction but was stopped by a tall man with salt-and-pepper hair. *SSA*, Paul inferred, eyeing the younger men trailing behind him. *He wears his hubris like cologne.*

"I'm Supervisory Special Agent Steve Pressley from New York," said the tall man, thrusting his hand into Paul's. "I'm in charge of the investigation. This is Tom Hicks and Alfonso Rubio from our extraterritorial squad. We've already obtained initial statements from the SPs. It's disturbing stuff. I'm sure you'll be fascinated to hear it."

"Of course," Paul said, hiding his concern. If Pressley's team had obtained statements from the surviving pirates in under three hours, they must have been cutting corners, searching for a narrative. That could mean only one thing— they were feeling pressure from on high. He recalled Brent Frazier's words: *The reputation of the Bureau is on the line. We need a win here.* Now, without a rescue story to deliver to the media, the definition of a "win" had changed. The government needed a scapegoat.

Commander Johnson summoned them to attention. "Gentlemen, take a seat, please."

When everyone was situated, a man with white hair and a regal bearing took the podium. "I'm Admiral Wilson, commander of the Strike Group. As all of you know, just before 18:30 today, the Somalis who hijacked the SV *Renaissance* opened fire on the hostages, killing Daniel Parker and critically wounding his son, Quentin. Pursuant to the decision of the interagency in Washington, the Justice Department will spearhead the response to the incident. The changeover will take place as soon as we get the pirates and the sailboat to the port of Djibouti. We're currently thirty-eight hours away. The *Gettysburg* will take somewhat longer to deliver the sailboat."

He surveyed the men in the room, looking many of them, including Paul, in the eye. "I'm sure all of you understand the gravity of these events. Piracy on the high seas is a scourge our nation has battled since its inception. But the cold-blooded murder of one of our citizens and the attempted murder of another—an eighteen-year-old boy—while in commission of an act of piracy are crimes of profound moral turpitude. The United States will stop at nothing to bring these malefactors to justice. Special Agent Pressley and his team from the FBI have begun the process of questioning them. He is going to brief us on his progress." Wilson held out his arm, inviting Pressley to the podium.

"Thank you, Admiral," Pressley said. "Like all of you, I'm deeply saddened by what happened here today. We gave the hijackers every opportunity to resolve the standoff peacefully. Unfortunately, there are some in Somalia who despise the freedom we hold so dear. We were unaware until this evening that those elements were present aboard the sailboat. But after conducting initial interviews, it is clear that the murder of Daniel Parker and the attempted murder of Quentin Parker were acts of maritime terrorism. The leader of the pirates, Ismail Adan Ibrahim, also known as Afyareh and Ibrahim, is a member of the East African terror group al-Shabaab."

Paul was thunderstruck. He had met with Ibrahim—or Ismail, whatever his name was—face-to-face. He had looked into the pirate's eyes and seen a sincere desire for resolution.

Ismail had quoted the Quran, yes, but not with the zeal of a militant. He had spoken with erudition beyond his years. Whatever Pressley was saying could not possibly be true unless Paul had utterly misjudged the pirate, in which case it would be better if he just turned in his badge now.

"Excuse me, Agent Pressley," he said, "that's a very interesting theory. But I spent the last five days talking to Ibra—*Ismail*—and I saw no hint of the person you're describing. I've dealt with the Taliban in Afghanistan and JTJ and ISIS in Iraq. When I met Ismail, I met a hostage taker, not a jihadist. I would stake my career on that assessment."

Pressley's eyes flashed with irritation. "Agent Derrick, I respect your experience and your contributions, but I was the one who conducted the interviews." He held up a legal pad. "Ismail admitted his association with the Shabaab. The other pirates gave us the story. There was a scuffle. They tried to stop him, but he persisted. Ismail didn't deny any of this. He accepted responsibility. Unless you have reason to believe he would make a false confession, you're mistaken."

Paul gave Pressley an incredulous look. "I want to talk to him. I don't mind if it's off the record, but I want to talk to him now."

The SSA stared at Paul as if he had grown a second head. "With all due respect, the CNU has no role in the investigation. This is my case, and I won't allow meddling."

Paul turned to Admiral Wilson. "Admiral, as I understand it, the pirates are in the Navy's custody until we reach land. That means that Agent Pressley's team is acting under your authority in conducting the interviews. I have no desire to interfere with his investigation. I want to nail the bastards to the wall as much as anyone. I'm simply asking for the chance to speak to Ismail in person before this ship reaches Djibouti and to ask him if these extraordinary allegations are true."

The admiral looked at Commander Johnson. "Adrian, do I have the authority?"

Johnson nodded, his eyes alive with intrigue. "Yes, sir, you do."

The admiral regarded Paul candidly. "You impressed the hell out of Gabe Masters. That's good enough for me. Go ahead and talk to him. Just don't make me regret it."

Paul let out the breath he was holding. *If Masters had been in command instead of Redman*, he wanted to say, *we wouldn't be here right now.*

An hour later, Paul sat alone in the classroom next door, a camera mounted on a tripod next to him and a digital recorder at his feet. All of the overhead lights were off, leaving most of the room in shadow. The only illumination came from a table lamp resting on a desk nearby. Paul had arranged the furniture with care, creating a space for conversation, not interrogation. It was often thought that the key to extracting information was to maximize the suspect's discomfort. In fact, the opposite was usually the case. The more a suspect felt esteemed, the more likely it was that he would speak freely.

Paul heard a knock at the door. Seconds later, Ismail entered the room, escorted by the brig's Master at Arms and the Special Agent Afloat from the Naval Criminal Investigative Service, or NCIS. The pirate was dressed in green scrubs, his hands and legs in shackles and his head covered with a hood. The Master at Arms led him to the seat across from Paul while the NCIS officer documented the encounter with a handheld camera.

"I'd prefer to keep him in cuffs," the Master at Arms said to Paul.

Paul shook his head. "No cuffs. He's not a threat to me."

The Master at Arms raised an eyebrow but complied, removing the manacles and hood. Beneath the hood Ismail was wearing earmuffs and work goggles blacked out with tape. *They really don't want him to know where he is*, Paul thought as the Master at Arms uncovered the pirate's eyes and ears. Ismail blinked and looked around the room, focusing on Paul. His eyes were bloodshot and his expression blank. As soon as he took a seat, the NCIS agent pressed the "record" button on the mounted camera and retreated with the Master at Arms to a corner of the room.

"Your name is Ismail, not Ibrahim," Paul began in a casual tone. "It seems there is a lot about you that I don't know."

The pirate looked at him opaquely. "Ibrahim was my grandfather," he said slowly. "He was killed in an airstrike ordered by General Garrison in 1993, along with many other Somali elders who wanted peace. They were willing to work with America, and they believed America would work with them. I made the same mistake. Your country is not interested in peace unless it is on your terms."

Paul met his eyes. "I'm sorry to hear that. I'm not proud of many things my country has done. But that isn't why you're here, is it? You're here because a man is dead and his son—a boy about your age—is fighting for his life. What would your grandfather say about that?"

Ismail remained impassive. "He would tell you what he told my father. Trust is like fire. When it is respected, it keeps the body warm in the night. When it is mishandled, it destroys everything in its path. I am here because you violated my trust. It seems I would be here no matter what."

The RHIB, Paul thought. He stepped around the landmine. "So you're a member of the Shabaab. You're an Islamist. You hate America because of wars we've fought in Muslim lands."

The pirate stared back at him implacably. "I am a Muslim. I believe that there is no God but Allah and that Muhammad is his prophet. I fought for al-Shabaab in Kismayo and in the Ramadan Offensive in Mogadishu. You know what I think about America."

Paul noticed his use of the past tense. "Were you working for al-Shabaab when you hijacked the sailboat? Is that why you changed course from Hobyo to Mogadishu?"

"What do my men say?" Ismail asked.

"They say you were Shabaab all along," Paul replied. "They say they obeyed you because you threatened to turn them over to the Amniyat."

For the first time Paul saw the shine of emotion in the

pirate's eyes. "You should believe them," Ismail said at last. "They are good boys. They didn't want this to happen."

"Does that mean you lied to me?" Paul asked, lacing his tone with indignation. "You were going to take the hostages ashore even with the ransom deal?"

Ismail folded his hands in his lap, his face a mask again. "We lied to each other, Paul. We did it for our own reasons. But your lie is what brought us to this place."

"So you shot them?" Paul demanded, venting his outrage. "You picked up your gun and shot Daniel and Quentin Parker. Is that what you're telling me?"

The pirate's expression didn't change. "I warned you, Paul. I warned your government. You didn't listen. You brought this on yourself."

Paul leaned forward, piercing Ismail with the intensity of his gaze. "Do you know what they're going to do to you? They're going to crucify you. They're going to run you up a flagpole and make a public example of you. Do you want that? Do you want to put your family through that?"

Something about what Paul said struck a nerve in Ismail. He saw it happen, saw the almost imperceptible twitch in the pirate's facial muscles. It was the tell he was looking for. Ismail was wearing a disguise. Paul knew it as surely as he knew his own soul. But what the disguise was concealing— and why the pirate had chosen to wear it—he couldn't say. Moreover, in the Bureau's infinite wisdom, it wasn't for him to find out. It was Pressley's case now, and the man from New York had no interest in a mystery, only in assigning blame. What Paul needed was a proxy, someone to pick up the spade and dig with ruthless determination until the truth couldn't hide anymore.

He needed Megan.

He looked into Ismail's eyes and spoke his valediction. "I hope you find yourself a good lawyer. God only knows how much you're going to need it."

IV

RICOCHETS

Halt at the abodes and weep over
the ruins and ask a question:
"Where are the loved ones?
Where are their camels gone?"
—MOHYUDDIN IBN 'ARABI

PAUL

The snow was soft and white as goose down falling from the clouds. Paul felt the edges of his skis beneath him, carving smoothly through the powder, back and forth, with metronomic consistency. The double black diamond run through Black Bear Glade was as steep as it was narrow, like an arrow shaft through the evergreens, but Paul felt no fear. He was alone with the mountain and the snow. His eyes were open and blood was flowing through his veins. He was alive, and that was all that mattered.

At the bottom of the glade, he made a hard turn and dropped into a tuck, flying down the slope like a ball shot from a cannon. Out of the corner of his eye, he saw a skier fall in the middle of Osprey, another expert run. And then in a blink he was past and the solitude returned. He focused all of his attention on the present. He felt the sting of freezing wind on his cheeks, fought the lactic acid burning in his thighs, heard the sizzle of his skis on the snow. For a moment, a precious glimmer in time, he felt the melancholy retreat and he was glad that he had come.

When he reached the base of Grouse Mountain, he saw Megan by the lift, clad in red and white like a cardinal in a winter forest. She gave him a little wave as he slid to a stop, spraying her boots with snow. He lifted his goggles and wiped the moisture from his eyes.

"This place is a shrine," he said, smiling at her like they were twenty again and tearing up Snowshoe and Killington. "I'm sorry I never came before."

"You're here now," she replied. "That's all that matters."

He poled with her toward the lift and caught an express chair to the top, sitting back against the cushions as the chair took flight. They climbed through curtains of snow, enjoying a companionable silence. His breathing slowed, and his heartbeat took on a normal cadence as the rush of adrenaline faded. After a while, he spoke the question he'd wanted to ask ever since he accepted her invitation to spend Christmas with her in the Rocky Mountains.

"How is Ismail? The Bureau's pretty much shut me out of the loop."

It was strange but true. After sailing with the *Truman* to Djibouti and witnessing the FBI take custody of the pirates, Paul had boarded a military transport flight back to the United States. A few days later, two agents from New York had taken his statement and then disappeared into the ether, never returning his calls or e-mails. The blackout wasn't completely surprising. The Bureau was highly compartmentalized, and after his showdown with Steve Pressley on the carrier, the investigators weren't going to do him any favors. Still, it felt like an affront, as close as he was to the case.

Megan brushed snow out of her face. "The jailers tell me he's a model inmate. He keeps to himself and does what he's supposed to. I'm just glad he's in maximum security. There's a rumor going around that al-Qaeda was behind the hijacking. He's gotten threats."

Paul shook his head. *The media are so gullible*, he thought. A few days after the shooting, someone in the government had leaked the Shabaab connection to the press, igniting a firestorm of speculation among reporters and pundits about terror on the high seas. It was a diversion, pure and simple. No one—neither the FBI nor the news agencies—had yet corroborated Ismail's story about fighting for the Shabaab, and no radical group had claimed responsibility for the incident. Whoever was behind the leak wanted one thing: to keep the spotlight off the government long enough to allow some other tragedy to replace the *Renaissance* in the headlines.

"I'm glad your partners let you represent him," Paul said. "I was afraid they would balk."

"The timing was right," Megan replied. "We just wrapped up a couple of big cases." She grinned. "It wasn't that hard to convince them. Trials like this don't come along very often."

Paul heard the undercurrent of enthusiasm in her voice. Ever since law school, she had been a passionate opponent of the death penalty, for reasons both moral and personal. Of all the offers she had received after her Supreme Court clerkship, she had accepted the position at Mason & Wagner because they supported the Innocence Project—an organization working to exonerate wrongfully convicted individuals—and handled death penalty appeals on a pro bono basis. Ismail's case, although expensive to try, was a win-win for the firm, with massive media exposure and the prospect—always enticing to defense lawyers—that there was more to the shooting than the government claimed.

Megan knocked her skis together, sending puffs of snow into the air. "I was more concerned that Ismail wouldn't agree to it. I expected him to be suspicious, but he just seemed surprised. The judge asked him about my relationship to you, but he didn't blink. He took the offer."

Paul glanced at her. "He didn't have much choice. It was either you or the public defender." He paused. "Does he talk about me?"

Her eyes glimmered. "You know I can't answer that. But I heard from the jailers that he drinks a Pepsi every day. He likes it better than jailhouse tea."

Paul laughed wryly. He had never felt more conflicted about a human being than he did about Ismail. The thought of the pirate evoked a witches' brew of perplexity, sadness, curiosity, and rage, along with a subliminal sense of guilt. Part of him wondered whether, in referring the case to his sister, he had betrayed the Parker family.

Megan seemed to read his mind. "How is Quentin?" she asked gently.

He looked out at the mountain. "Mary says he's making progress. They moved him over to rehab after he started breathing on his own. His faculties are coming back, but the doctors don't know if he'll make it all the way. It's impossible to tell with a brain injury."

Megan nodded slowly. "And Vanessa?"

He shrugged. "I don't know. I haven't spoken to her since Daniel's funeral."

The Parkers had held the memorial service the Sunday before Thanksgiving, and Paul had almost not attended. For days, he had debated with Mary Patterson whether it would disturb Vanessa more to see him in person or to know that he hadn't come. At the last minute, he deferred to his colleague's intuition and joined her at St. Mary's Parish in Annapolis. The sight of the closed casket surrounded by pictures of Daniel nearly wrecked his composure. He sat in the back of the sanctuary and tried not to think about the way the mural of stars on the ceiling reminded him of the *Gettysburg*.

He first glimpsed Vanessa across the sea of pews. She was younger than he expected and prettier, her skin as pale as porcelain and her red hair partially hidden by a wide-brimmed hat. She received the condolences of the mourners gracefully, but he saw the strain on her face, the sheen of tears in her eyes. When she took her seat, he couldn't contain his anger. *All of this was avoidable*, he thought. *If only Redman had listened to me, if only Ismail hadn't pulled the trigger, Daniel would be alive, Quentin wouldn't be in the hospital, and this woman wouldn't have to put on a brave face and pretend she isn't shattered.*

After the service, he escaped the church before the receiving line formed and drove with Mary to the cemetery. They arrived at the grave site before the others and stood in the shadow of an oak tree as a cold rain started to fall. In time, Vanessa appeared and took her spot beside the grave with Curtis and Yvonne—Paul knew their faces from the photos he had seen in the media. The priest made brief remarks, and then the mourners fled the soggy knoll to take shelter in their cars.

It was then that Paul approached Vanessa.

"You're Paul, aren't you?" she guessed, searching his face with her green eyes. "I wondered if you would come."

The emotion of the moment nearly rendered him mute. Both of them had crossed continents and oceans to save Daniel and Quentin. Yet all of their efforts had come to nothing in the end. He took her gloved hand in his and allowed his pain to show. No words were adequate; none even seemed appropriate. He spoke because he had to, and because she deserved it. She deserved so much more.

"Your husband was a courageous man," he said, struggling to steady his voice. "I came to honor him. I also came to tell you that I'm sorry."

She wiped a tear from her cheek. "You gave us a chance. You didn't pull the trigger."

Her pardon sounded hollow in his heart. It didn't matter if she didn't blame him. He blamed himself. "If there's anything I can ever do for you or Quentin," he said, leaving the offer open-ended. He couldn't imagine why she would take him up on it, but he made it to show that he cared.

She managed a small smile. "Thank you," she said, squeezing his hand before turning away.

Megan's voice snapped him out of his trance. "We're at

the top."

He shook off the memory and skied off the lift, sliding to a stop. He took a breath and exhaled a plume of vapor. The snow-filled air smelled of spruce and pine. "What's wrong with Simon?" he asked, trying to lighten the mood. "How can he spend a day like this at the lodge?"

Megan gave him an ironic look. "What can I say? He's a photographer. He wanted to take some shots in black and white."

"His loss," Paul said. "Where to?"

"Let's do something together. How about Raven Ridge?"

He looked out at the valley below, veiled by the falling snow. "Beat you to the bottom," he said, digging in his poles and pushing off.

Her laughter sounded like chimes in the quiet air. "Not a chance," she replied and kept pace with him all the way down.

That evening, Paul dressed in gray jeans and a dark cashmere blazer—his attempt to blend in with the Beaver Creek elite—and took the elevator to the hotel lobby to meet Simon and Megan for dinner. They were staying at the Ritz Carlton in Bachelor's Gulch—a paragon of neo-rustic luxury chic with the exposed beams and stacked stone of a hunting lodge and the cozy intimacy of a Swiss chalet. As with most things in Megan's orbit, it was out of Paul's league, but he had declined her offer to pay for his room. He might be a public servant, but he wasn't a pauper.

He walked down the hallway toward Buffalo's, expecting to see Simon chatting with the hostess and Megan checking her watch. *Strange*, he thought when he didn't see them. His sister was nothing if not punctual, and he was a few minutes late, as he intended. Despite Megan's assurances that he didn't look out of place, he felt like Jack at the banquet in *Titanic*, an ordinary Joe in a better man's outfit thrust into a world of privilege he despised and admired at the same time.

He took a seat at the bar and ordered a martini. Five minutes passed, then ten. He checked his BlackBerry, but she hadn't called or texted him. He finished his drink and ordered another. He caught a few glances from an attractive woman at the other end of the bar and worried that the bartender might pass him a note with a room number. It had happened before, and once he had given in to the temptation. It was an experience he didn't wish to repeat.

After fifteen minutes, he decided something must have come up. He asked for the check, thinking he would order room service, but then he heard her voice. He looked up and saw Megan walking toward him, dressed in a sleeveless black shift and high heels.

"Where's Simon?" he asked, greeting her with a kiss on the cheek.

"He's not coming," she replied in a tone that made plain her distress. "Let's sit down."

The hostess led them to a table by a plate-glass window

overlooking the snowy patio. A waiter soon followed with their menus. He told them the special for the evening—something with antelope that sounded extravagant—and handed Paul the wine list.

"Bring us a bottle of Romanée-Conti La Tâche, 2005," Megan said.

"An excellent selection, madam," the waiter replied and then left them alone.

Paul raised an eyebrow, studying her closely. "Why do I get the impression that you just ordered the most expensive wine on the list?"

"Because I did," she said simply. "I'm putting it on the room. It'll go on his card."

Paul set his menu aside. "You don't have to talk about it if you don't want to," he said, though his words were a formality. She was an open book to him, as he was to her.

She fingered her napkin, and he noticed she wasn't wearing her wedding ring. "There was another reason he didn't want to ski today," she explained. "I caught him Skyping with one of his students. I asked if he was sleeping with her. He didn't deny it. I blew a gasket. I told him I would leave him unless he ended it. He went home this afternoon. I don't know if he's coming back."

Paul's stomach clenched. "I'm sorry, Meg."

She took a sharp breath. "He promised me he'd never allow his . . . *recreations* to interfere with our relationship. I was foolish enough to believe him. It's *Christmas*, for God's sake."

Paul nodded, at once infuriated that Simon could hurt her so blithely and glad that she had finally rebuked him.

"You can always stay with me," he said with a touch of humor. "It's just a step below this place."

Her lips curled into a smile, but the sorrow didn't leave her eyes. "Seriously, though, are we just a couple of misfits, or is marriage impossible today?"

He looked at her reflectively. "Nana and Grandpa Chuck wouldn't have won an award for marital bliss. But they built a life together. They were there for us."

Megan looked out the window at the still-falling snow. "It's funny. I always thought their relationship was boring. Now I envy them. They made it fifty years. Can you believe it?"

The waiter appeared with their wine. Megan's eyes lit up when she tasted it. "Exquisite," she said. When their glasses were full, she made a toast. "To you, Paul. You're the only person in the world who's never let me down."

Paul took a sip of the wine. It was exceptional, but he found it hard to enjoy, given the drift of his thoughts. He pondered whether to voice them, then decided there might never be a better time.

"That's not quite right," he said softly. "I have let you down."

She stared at him blankly and he took the plunge.

"I drove to Annandale the other day. I was sure someone had demolished the house, but it was still there. The only thing different was the paint."

"Don't," she said, shaking her head pensively. "It's not relevant."

He gazed at her intently. "What if it is, though? What if we've been living the past twenty-five years trying to undo what happened that day?"

"Paul, that's enough," she said, her wineglass trembling in her hand.

But he didn't seem to hear her. "The thought struck me out there on the *Gettysburg*. In all this time, we've never talked about it—"

She interrupted him. "*Paul!* That's enough."

Silence descended upon the table. He looked at her face, so precious to him, and saw the raw vulnerability there, the wound inside that had never properly healed. *It wasn't your fault*, he wanted to say. *Kyle made his own choice.* But he honored her request and left it alone.

He took another sip of the wine. "This is really good. I'll thank Simon the next time I see him." He watched as the levity brightened her eyes. "So how much did this penance cost him, anyway?"

For an instant she looked sheepish. Then she grinned. "Guess."

"A thousand?" When her grin broadened, he said, "Two?"

She shook her head. "Three. And we're only getting started."

He smiled at her and picked up his menu, thinking of ordering the antelope. "Remind me never to get on your bad side."

❋

The next morning, Paul awoke to a text message from Megan. Sorry for the drama last night. Thanks for always being there. I'm ready to hit the slopes whenever you are. XXOO.

He was about to reply when his BlackBerry rang. He saw that the caller ID was blocked. "Give me a break," he said, taking the call with a barely intelligible grunt.

"Paul, it's Brent," Frazier said. "I apologize for the timing, but we have a situation. A couple of American aid workers were kidnapped from the Dadaab refugee area in northern Kenya. We think they were taken over the border into Somalia."

Paul leaned back against his pillow, feeling a headache coming on. "And here I thought you were calling to wish me a merry Christmas." He let Frazier squirm, then twisted the thumbscrews. "You know I'm in Colorado? On vacation. With my sister."

"I'm sorry," Frazier said, sounding contrite. "But we need you. Two months ago, the Kenyans sent troops into Somalia to fight al-Shabaab, a battle the US is actively supporting. If the radicals get hold of the hostages, we could have another Nick Berg on our hands."

Paul massaged his forehead. "Then find them and get them out. I'm sure Frank Redman would be happy to do it."

He heard Frazier breathing. "I know the last month has been hard for you. It's been hard for all of us. But if mistakes were made, they weren't your fault. You did your job."

You're damn right, Paul thought but didn't say. "I appreciate that, Brent. But it's two days before Christmas. Book me a ticket on the twenty-sixth. If you need someone now, send Rodriguez."

Frazier hesitated. "Gordon Tully's the one asking. What do I tell him?"

Paul's reply came out uncensored. "Tell Tully I'm not his bitch. The next time he gives an on-scene commander authority to ignore my advice, I'm walking out. On second thought, don't tell him that. Tell him I'm on vacation."

With that, Paul cut off the call. He went to the window and pulled back the curtains, allowing sunlight to stream in. The mountain was a winter wonderland—everything white except the sky. It was going to be a bluebird day on the slopes.

He sent a text to Megan. Not a problem, Sis. You know I love you. I'll meet you at the lift in an hour.

VANESSA

The examination room at Small World Family Medicine was as friendly a place as Vanessa could imagine in the world of health care. Its warm lighting and soft blue and yellow hues evoked a spring sunrise; its blown-up photographs of smiling children—one from each continent—reflected the inclusiveness of the practice; its crayon drawings, all done by child patients, set a tone of vitality and life, not disease and death. There were toys for toddlers in a bin on the floor, a frosted window admitting natural light, a fern spreading branches below the windowsill, and all of the medical implements were hidden away in cabinets. Yet she often wondered what her refugee clients thought of it. Most of them had arrived in the United States with little more than the clothes on their backs. They were accustomed to noisy clinics in squalid camps where the pressure of humanity was overwhelming. The examination room, by contrast, was a manicured oasis of tranquility. After more than a decade of practice, she still couldn't decide whether the effect was jarring or reassuring.

What would Halima say? she thought as she scanned the questionnaire in front of her. The girl was eighteen, the first-born of five children, only three of whom were still alive. Born in Darfur in western Sudan, she was Muslim but not Arab, which made her a target for the ethnic cleansing perpetrated by the Sudanese government. In late 2003, soldiers had burned her village to the ground, killing her father and two brothers. Her mother had fled with Halima and her sisters to the Kakuma refugee area in Kenya, where they lived for seven years until they were resettled in the United States.

Halima had been fortunate. She was smart and industrious and had acquired a decent command of English in the camps. She was also blessed with a hardy disposition and had survived chronic malnourishment and two bouts of malaria with little sign of long-term distress. In the initial evaluation, Vanessa didn't have time for a physical. She focused on building rapport and determining whether there were any acute issues like infections or parasites that required immediate attention.

"Your health is good," she told the girl. "We need to run tests on the samples we took. But you should be pleased."

"*Subhanallah,*" Halima said, her large eyes sparkling. "Thanks be to God."

Vanessa escorted the girl to the lobby, where her mother was waiting. "I'd like to see you again in a couple of months. The receptionist can give you an appointment."

Halima smiled. "You are very kind, Dr. Vanessa. Stay well."

As soon as she left, Vanessa's carefully constructed façade began to crack. She walked quickly to her office, locking the door behind her. Her grief was like a tropical squall. She never knew when it would arise and how hard it would blow. She kept tissues in her pockets for the occasions when she came unglued in public. But those moments were rare. In the past two months, she had become a virtual hermit, seldom venturing beyond her house, her practice, and Quentin's recovery room, first at Georgetown Medical Center and now at Medstar National Rehabilitation Hospital. She knew that the sooner she returned to a normal rhythm, the sooner her heart would begin to mend. But solitude was safe. People were unpredictable. Most of the time she wanted nothing more than to be left alone.

After a minute or two, the worst of the storm passed. She looked at her watch. She had an hour before she had to be at the hospital, and the drive wouldn't take more than thirty minutes. She closed her eyes and concentrated on breathing. She had to be strong for Quentin. The interview would be an ordeal. He had agreed to do it, and Dr. Greenberg, his neuropsychologist, had given him permission, despite the gaps in his memory. But the FBI was relentlessly thorough. Vanessa had spent two days with the investigators, and more than once their questions had left her in tears.

She opened her eyes again and saw the letter sitting beside her computer. It was Daniel's last, sent the day they sailed from the Seychelles. Reading it had become a daily pilgrimage for her. It was a paean to Quentin and a vision of the person he could become again if only his brain would heal.

Dearest V:

We're about to depart for Réunion. We've had an extraordinary week in the Seychelles. All of the islands were memorable, but La Digue was in a class by itself. It's a paradise of sun and sand and sea, worlds apart from the noisome frenzy of the modern jungle that we know so well. On La Digue, the soul doesn't huddle in self-protection. It opens its wings and takes flight.

The place brought out the truest essence of our joy. Quentin spent most of his time climbing the endless granite boulders that line the beaches and protrude into the water, creating swimming pools in the surf. I wasn't adventurous enough to follow him, but I had the time of my life strolling barefoot across the sand and watching him scale the monoliths and stand at the highest peak, a silhouette against the sky.

You know better than anyone how much I've struggled with fatherhood. You know the doubts that have haunted me, the fear that Quentin would inherit the worst of my insecurities, that I would, by demanding too much of him, turn him into a spineless drone, a people-pleaser terrified of risk, as I've been for most of my life. Until this trip, those fears seemed not only justified but certain to come true.

No more. The boy who once crawled like a caterpillar has become a butterfly. He is alive, Vanessa. I've never met anyone more alive than he is. He is beautiful and strong and intelligent and capable. He could sail the rest of the way on his own and I don't doubt he would make it home.

I give you more credit for this than I take myself. He sees the hearts of others like you do. He feels deep empathy for pain. There once was a day when I struggled to love him. Today, I look up to him. I wish I were more like he is. Maybe I will be someday. But even if I never make it, I am comforted that in this way, at least, I haven't failed. I haven't failed our son.

Where will he go? Only time will tell. But I believe that the stories he will pass on to his children will be greater than the story I'm telling you now. He's as close to bulletproof as a man can get in this life. Nothing can hold him back. He's learned to rise above his fears.

See you soon, I hope. Perhaps Cape Town?

—D

Vanessa set down the letter, thanking Daniel again for this talisman of hope in the blackest hours of her night. The thought came to her, as it had many times before, that it was almost as if he had known what was coming. It was ridiculous, of course. But she couldn't help wondering if an angel had touched him that morning in the Seychelles. Someday she would read the words to Quentin. Someday he would remember the way his father was at the end. The letter was a more fitting epitaph than anything she could write.

She stood up and collected her things, saying good-bye to the staff. Aster met her in the hallway and saw the dried remnants of her tears. She gave Vanessa a long hug.

"Are you comfortable with this?" she asked. "Is he ready to answer questions?"

A few minutes ago, Vanessa might have said no. But the letter emboldened her. "I think he is."

Aster gave her a poignant look. "Are you ready?"

Vanessa nodded. "I've come this far, haven't I?"

"My mother always told me that strength is a choice. Be strong."

Vanessa smiled. *I'd rather be bulletproof. Like my son.*

On the drive into Washington, Vanessa turned on Bach's *Brandenburg Concertos*, but her mind drifted backward across the days and weeks since Quentin had returned to the United States and been admitted to the ICU at Georgetown. It had been a long and painful road to get him to the point where he could sit for an interview with federal agents, to the point, indeed, where he could understand what happened to him and why he needed to answer their questions at all.

Vanessa had remained at his bedside for days, watching as he slowly woke up from the coma. After the full battery of tests, the neurologists had confirmed what the military doctors suspected: he had suffered temporary anoxia—or oxygen loss to the brain—as a result of cardiac arrest brought on by the tamponade in his heart. The prognosis, however, was unclear. No one had been able to say with any certainty how the injury would affect him. So Vanessa asked them not to try.

The first three weeks had been a waiting game—excruciating at times, exuberant at others. He learned how to breathe on his own, how to swallow food, how to take thoughts out of the cloud of confusion and forgetfulness and form words again. Vanessa played his favorite piano music in the background—Chopin, Liszt, Schubert, Rimsky-Korsakov, Debussy. She read him stories and poetry and Ariadne's daily e-mails. To Vanessa's astonishment, the Australian girl took his injuries in stride, pressing in with support instead of disappearing into the woodwork. The effect her words had on him was almost hypnotic—steadying his soul and illumining his eyes.

After four weeks, his doctors had discharged him from acute care and moved him across town to NRH, where an award-winning team of therapists helped him recover his mental acuity, long-term memory, and motor skills. The more alert and energetic he became, the more the past took shape in his mind and the more he regained muscle control—maintaining balance while standing upright, walking over uneven surfaces, holding a toothbrush, dressing and feeding himself.

But there had been bumps in the road. Quentin's capacity for language, his ability to make decisions—known as "executive function"—and his memory of the days preceding the shooting were significantly impaired. At first he seemed unaware of his disabilities. But the more his body and mind healed, the more agitated he became about his limitations. He was especially disturbed by his aphasia and amnesia. When he struggled to string words together in a sentence or identified another blank spot in his memory, he would pace his room like a tiger, muttering to himself. Sometimes when Vanessa came to visit, he refused to talk to her.

For Vanessa, however, the hardest part wasn't the stuttering pace of Quentin's recovery; it was the depression into which he slipped when she confessed to him that his father was gone. He had asked about Daniel many times, but Vanessa had dissembled as if he were a small child. "He's not here right now," she told him. After a week of rehab, Dr. Greenberg cautioned her against extending the illusion too far. So she summoned her courage and told him the truth. His response confirmed the worst of her fears. She watched in agony as his face fell and his mouth hung open, as the light faded from his eyes and he lapsed into a different kind of coma—a coma of the heart.

For two days he lost all interest in human interaction. He stayed in bed, wrapped in blankets, and ignored everyone. Music didn't soothe him. Neither did Ariadne's messages. Vanessa interrogated his therapists, searching for a way to save him. They told her to be patient and to give him space; he would return to her in time. At some point she realized that he wasn't just struggling with grief. He was struggling with guilt—that he had survived and that he couldn't remember how Daniel died.

It was then that she had an epiphany: for Quentin to escape the tunnel, he had to find a way to bury his father on his own terms. So she retrieved Daniel's postcards and letters and read them aloud to Quentin. The postcards were a travelogue of their port calls in the Caribbean, Panama, and the South Pacific. Daniel had written his first letter on Rarotonga, in the Cook Islands, after Quentin met Ariadne. As Vanessa revived Daniel's memories, speaking them with her own voice, they became like threads in a tapestry, weaving together the narrative of Quentin's redemption.

He started to talk again, to add to Daniel's stories, filling in details that his father had omitted. He asked Vanessa to read the Rarotonga letter twice and then told her about Ariadne—about the days they had spent circling the island on mopeds and hiking across its mountainous spine, about the nights they had walked on the beach beneath the stars, talking about everything in the world. His therapists informed her that his openness was a symptom of his brain injury. But she regarded it as a gift. For the first time in his life, she had an unobstructed window into his soul.

A week later, in a therapy session with Dr. Greenberg, Quentin had started to talk about the hijacking. His memories were inchoate and disorganized, but the neuropsychologist encouraged them, evaluating the consistency of his story and his capacity for answering questions. In time, the doctor told him about the investigators who wanted to talk to him. Quentin agreed to an interview, and Dr. Greenberg made the arrangements.

Upon reaching the hospital, Vanessa parked in the garage and walked through the lobby to the elevator. Soon she emerged on Quentin's floor and strolled down the hallway to his room. Dr. Greenberg met her at the door. A jovial man with a balding head and a scraggly beard, he looked more like a lumberjack than an expert in brain medicine. But he was as sharp as they came.

"He's in good spirits," the doctor said. "He really wants to do this. I'm going to limit the initial session to half an hour. I've made that clear to the agents. They can explore his surface memories, but I don't want them to go too deep until we see how he responds."

"Where will you be?" Vanessa asked, feeling a twinge of anxiety.

"I'll be down the hall. If at any point you feel uncomfortable about the way it's progressing, you can terminate the interview." He touched her shoulder. "It's going to be all right."

When he left to get the investigators, Vanessa opened the door and found Quentin sitting upright on the bed, watching television. He was dressed in jeans, sneakers, and a Naval Academy sweatshirt, his long hair pulled back in a ponytail.

She kissed him on the forehead. "Hi, sweetie. How are you today?"

He stared at her a moment before smiling. The therapists called it "brain lag"—the second or two his mind required to adjust to something new. "Hey . . . Mom," he replied, hesitating slightly between words. "I'm good . . . I want . . . to get this . . . over with."

"I know you do," she said warmly. "You're going to do fine. Just take your time. There's no need to rush. It's okay if you don't remember something."

His eyes shifted to the bed, and he rubbed the hem of his blanket, as he did when he was nervous or upset. "I will . . . tell them . . . what I know."

Vanessa placed a chair beside him and arranged two more at the foot of the bed. Then she turned off the television and took a seat, squeezing his hand. A minute later, she heard a knock at the door, and Dr. Greenberg brought in the agents. She knew them from her own interview. Ben Hewitt was a Harvard-educated attorney who had left a lucrative job in New York "to do something good for a change." Carlos Escobido was Hewitt's opposite—a hard-charging, chain-smoking detective from the Bronx who had busted drug dealers and Mafia dons before 9/11 prompted him to join the feds and hunt terrorists. Both were dressed casually in shirts and slacks. They shook Quentin's hand and took a seat, placing a digital recorder on the bed.

Hewitt took the lead. "Quentin," he began, "I want to tell you how sorry we are for what you've gone through. We're going to make this as easy as we can—a few questions today, maybe a few more tomorrow. Is that all right with you?"

Quentin processed this. "I will tell you . . . what I remember."

"That's all we ask." Hewitt sat back and folded his hands. "Do you recall when the pirates came aboard the sailboat? Can you tell me about that?"

As Vanessa watched, Quentin turned away from Hewitt and stared at a spot on the wall. "It was night," he said with a frown. "Or morning . . . It was dark. I was . . . on watch . . . I fell asleep. I heard shots . . . then my dad came . . . from below. We didn't fight."

"How many were there?" Hewitt asked as Escobido made notes.

"Seven." Quentin grimaced and closed his eyes. "I know . . . their names." Suddenly, he blurted out, "Mas." He thought some more. Then: "Liban . . . Their leader was . . . Af . . . Afyareh."

Hewitt waited a few seconds before asking, "How did you know Afyareh was in charge?"

"He told us," Quentin replied. "And . . ." He looked lost in thought. "And . . . we saw . . . the way he talked . . . to the others. He spoke English . . . he . . . *negotiated* . . . with the Navy."

With deftness and a gentle touch, Hewitt led him through the major events in sequence: the arrival of the *Gettysburg*, then the *Truman* and *San Jacinto* the next morning; the planes and helicopters the Navy put in the air and then grounded after Curtis—"Grandpa," in Quentin's words—intervened with the government. When Hewitt inquired about the ransom negotiations, however, Quentin drew a blank. Vanessa watched him wrestle with himself, saw his brow furrow and his shoulders tense. She traded a glance with Hewitt and shook her head almost imperceptibly.

"Why don't we change gears?" he said, taking her cue. "With the time we have left, let's focus on Afyareh. Is that okay with you?"

The muscles in Quentin's face relaxed. "Okay."

Hewitt softened his tone. "Did Afyareh ever point his gun at you?"

Quentin looked into the distance again. "I don't . . ." For a moment he seemed confused, then his expression clarified and his eyes filled with sadness. "Afyareh . . . pointed his gun . . . at my dad. He said—" A tear spilled down Quentin's cheek. "He said, 'Do you . . . want to die?'"

Vanessa took a breath and held it, transfixed by her son's words. She imagined the scene—Daniel's hands flying into the air; Afyareh shouting his threats; Daniel pleading with the pirate not to shoot; Quentin watching the confrontation, at once horrified and afraid. She felt the rage again, stirring in her gut. Then, in an instant, her anger branched out and encircled her heart like a malevolent vine, blocking out the light. There at the core of her something else began to grow—hatred.

Hewitt made a note to himself. "Those were his exact words: 'Do you want to die?'" When Quentin nodded, he asked, "Do you recall when he said that?"

Quentin began to fiddle with the edge of his blanket again. "There was a . . . boat that came . . . No, that was . . . another time . . . The ships were nearby . . . He was angry . . . He wanted them . . . to go away . . . I don't . . . I don't remember when that was."

Sensing Quentin's agitation, Hewitt became gentler still. "Was it during the day or at night?"

Quentin closed his eyes and clenched his jaw, trying to work out the puzzle in his mind. Seconds passed in silence, and then, without warning, he swung his legs over the side of the bed and stood up. He was wobbly at first, but he stabilized himself against the wall and refused Vanessa's offer of assistance. She watched him like a hawk as he rounded the bed, worried that he might fall. But he stayed on his feet, taking steps as hesitant as his speech, until he stood by the window and looked out at the winter sky. He touched the glass and faced Hewitt again.

"I don't know . . . if it was . . . day or night. When I remember . . . I will tell you."

ISMAIL

The dream came to Ismail again in the night. He saw the parade ground in the midday heat, the earth beneath the stomping feet of the Shabaab fighters sparkling like desert quartz. The sky above was so pure that it looked as if it had been painted blue and glazed by the sun. He was standing in a line with the others—mostly boys, but a few girls, Yusuf on his left, Yasmin on his right. The contrast between his fifteen-year-old brother and seventeen-year-old sister could not have been starker. Tearstained and hunched over, Yusuf looked like an old man. Yasmin, on the other hand, stood like a warrior princess, her head erect and her eyes aglow with scorn.

Dressed as she was in a flowing gold *abaya*, it was no surprise that Najiib spotted her from across the camp. All of the other girls were swaddled in black from head to toe. Black was the safest color for a woman in Mogadishu, but Yasmin didn't care for the monochromatic palette of the

Islamists. "God made the world colorful," she liked to say. "A woman should reflect that."

She didn't blink when Najiib examined her through his designer sunglasses, his black headscarf blowing in the wind. She stared straight ahead, her eyes boring holes through the Shabaab militiamen who had raided their school, murdered their father and three teachers, crammed as many students as they could into their technicals, and delivered them to the camp as "new recruits."

"What is your name?" Najiib asked as the noise of the fighters filled the air around them.

Yasmin ignored the question, and Najiib glared at her. "Are you deaf? Do you not hear me? It is unlawful for a girl to disrespect a man."

When Yasmin answered him, her tone was fraught with bitterness. "It is also forbidden to murder a believer, yet you do not think twice about killing a righteous man."

Najiib stared at her, calculating how to respond. At last, his lips curled into a devilish smile. He turned to the militiamen and laughed. "The girl has religion; it is good." His men laughed with him. He faced her again. "I have killed many men. Which of them was righteous?"

She pronounced her father's name reverently. "Adan Ibrahim Abdullahi."

Najiib's expression became deadly serious. "Adan Ibrahim Abdullahi. He was an apostate, an enemy of the *mujahedeen*. He was warned and he did not repent. I ordered his assassination."

Suddenly, Yasmin's defiance crumbled. She broke down and began to cry silently.

"You are related to him, aren't you?" Najiib said, taking hold of her chin. "Yes, I see the resemblance. You are his daughter."

Terror gripped Ismail. He wanted desperately to intervene, but he knew it would only endanger them. He had heard about Najiib in whispers spoken by the men of Mogadishu. Some called him "Azrael"—the Angel of Death. Apart from Godane, the elusive emir of the Shabaab, there was no *mujahid* more dangerous in all of Somalia.

"What is your name?" Najiib hissed.

"I am Yasmin Adan Ibrahim," she finally admitted.

Najiib smiled again. "*Ha.* It is wise to be honest with me." He took her by the arm. "Come, I will show you the righteous path."

"*No!*" she said, struggling against him. "Leave me alone!"

But Najiib only tightened his grip. He dragged her out of line and into the pandemonium of the parade ground. Ismail saw her turn and shout to him, her headscarf unraveling in the wind. And then, in a flash, she was gone.

Ismail awoke with a start, unsure for a moment where he was. The truth came to him in sensations—the coarseness of the blanket on his skin, the hard mattress pressing against his back, the concrete walls marking out the boundaries of his cell. He was in America, in the maximum-security block of the Chesapeake Correction Center, in the hands of a justice system he would never escape.

He rolled out of bed and stood on the cold floor facing east. He didn't know what time it was exactly, but the lights weren't on yet, which meant it was before 6:00 a.m.—time to observe the *Fajr* prayers. He went through the motions from memory, reciting the *takbir*, folding his hands over his chest, bowing and touching his knees, kneeling, prostrating and touching his forehead to the ground, sitting with his legs bent to the side, reciting Sura *al-Fatiha*, standing again, and so on.

When the ritual was finished, he sat on the edge of the bed and thought about the dream. It always ended the same way, with Yasmin melting into the crowd of *mujahedeen*—his last glimpse of her. But there was one more memory that he had always wondered about, a flash of yellow from the Land Cruiser that passed by just as he pointed the gun at Samatar. Had she seen him kill the boy?

He felt the shame again, like a noose around his throat. If she saw him, what did she think? She wasn't there to see what came before it: the commander who had delivered the boy to the militiamen, casting him on the ground and kicking him in the stomach; the Shabaab fighter who had picked Yusuf out of the lineup and thrust an AK-47 into his hands, ordering him to kill the deserter; the way Yusuf had nearly fallen to pieces in fear; the way Ismail had stepped forward, taking the gun from his brother, and put on a show for the commander, shouting, *"Allahu Akbar!"* with the zeal of a jihadist, then turning the gun against Samatar and saving Yusuf's life.

He shook his head forcefully and focused on Yasmin. Where had Najiib taken her? West to the stronghold of Baidoa? South to the port of Kismayo? Or to somewhere in the interior, to a village of herdsmen and farmers lost in time? Najiib had almost certainly married her, for she was beautiful, and it was the practice of the Shabaab commanders to take their pleasure with captured girls. But had he brought her into his household under the formal rule of *nikaah*, or had he used the loophole of *nikaah misyar*—the traveler's marriage—to have his way with her and then cast her aside, divorcing her with a declaration and taking no obligation for her future? It had been almost three years since the school attack. Anything could have happened. Yet Ismail clung to the hope that Najiib was too proud and too libidinous to let go of a catch like her. He had to believe that. To believe otherwise was to admit defeat.

At six o'clock, the lights came on, and Ismail went to the door of his cell, waiting for his breakfast. "Morning, friends," said the jailer—a portly man named Richie—as he and his second—a short man everybody called Longfellow—carried the trays up the stairs and distributed them to the inmates. Ismail's cell was third in line on the second floor of the block.

Longfellow greeted him with a half smile. "Chicken and vegetables," he said, sliding a tray through the open port. "And tea with enough sugar to kill a diabetic. As the Frenchies say, 'Bon appétit!'" The jailer turned away and then thought of something. "What the hell does Afyareh mean anyway? Sounds like an Arab sheikh."

"It's a nickname," Ismail replied. He was always deferential to the guards, and they rewarded him for it, treating him kindly and doing him favors like bringing him sweets and turning his bland tea into something approaching proper *shah*. "It means 'agile mouth.' My men called me that because I speak English and Arabic as well as Somali."

Longfellow laughed. "A regular pro-di-gy," he said, emphasizing each syllable of the last word. "Someday you'll have to tell me how you got mixed up with a bunch of pirates." He swung the port closed. "Eat fast. They're coming for you at seven."

An hour later, after Ismail finished breakfast, mopped his cell, and took a shower in the stall on the main floor, Richie came for him. The jailer put him in irons and led him to a bank of elevators and down to a holding cell in the transfer area. He found his court clothes laid out on the bench: a gray pinstripe suit, white shirt, blue tie, and black dress shoes and belt, courtesy of his attorneys. It was the fanciest outfit he had ever worn, and every time he put it on it gave him the illusion—for a moment, at least—that he was somewhere other than in an American jail, standing trial for murder.

He changed out of his orange jumpsuit and waited on the bench for the sheriff's deputies to collect him. A few minutes later, they appeared and escorted him to the van. He was the only one attending the hearing. His men had already entered into plea bargains with the government, promising to testify against him in exchange for lighter sentences. They were being held in another jail—he didn't know where. According to Megan Derrick, his lawyer, their stories were consistent, which didn't surprise him. As soon as Mas had spoken the accusation on the ocean, he knew they were going to point the finger at him. But it didn't matter. He knew what he had to do. In a strange way, their accusation was a gift. It gave him additional leverage with the government.

The ride to the federal courthouse in Norfolk took forty-five minutes. The deputies parked in the rear lot and led him inside, handing him off to the US marshals, who put him in their holding tank until everyone had assembled for the hearing. When the time came, a gray-haired old marshal with a lopsided smile took him upstairs to the courtroom. It was the most ornate chamber Ismail had ever seen outside a mosque, with an ornamental ceiling twice as high as an ordinary roof, giant windows with red curtains, decorative lamps and stonework and oil portraits on the walls, and dark wood everywhere in the gallery, around the judge's bench, and at the tables before the bar.

Megan was waiting for him on the defense side, along with a coterie of associates and paralegals. She greeted him with a hug and he replied with a smile. There had been moments, especially at the beginning, when he wondered if he could trust her, but he had seen no hint of deception in her. She was intelligent and forthright and extremely capable. Everyone from the judge to the US attorneys to the marshals respected her. And unlike her brother, Paul, she came with no strings attached.

Soon after Ismail found his place at the defense table, the judge's law clerk stood up and knocked his gavel three times. "All rise! The Honorable Chief United States District Judge Marian Philips McKenzie presiding. Please be seated and come to order."

Judge McKenzie appeared and walked to the bench, scaling the steps and taking a seat in the middle of three high-backed chairs arranged beneath the seal of the United States. She was a handsome black woman with a moon-shaped face, a prominent forehead, and compassionate eyes.

"In case you're wondering," she began, "the magistrate is out on sick leave. I'm handling my own arraignments." She looked at the assistant US attorneys, Clyde Barrington and Eldridge Jordan, over her horn-rimmed spectacles. "Is the government ready to proceed?"

"The government is ready, Your Honor," said Barrington.

The judge turned to Megan. "Is the defense ready?"

Megan nodded. "We are, Your Honor."

"Very well." The judge turned to Ismail. "Mr. Ibrahim, as your attorney has no doubt informed you, the government has filed a Superseding Indictment in your case, naming you as the sole defendant. Ms. Derrick has waived formal arraignment, but I'm going to read the charges into the record before requesting your plea. Is that clear?"

Ismail stood and said, "Yes, Your Honor."

He listened as the judge rehearsed the litany of crimes of which he was accused—piracy under the law of nations; conspiracy to commit hostage taking resulting in death; hostage taking resulting in death; conspiracy to commit kidnapping resulting in death; kidnapping resulting in death; conspiracy to commit violence against maritime navigation resulting in death; violence against maritime navigation resulting in death; the use, carrying, brandishing, and discharge of a firearm during a crime of violence resulting in death; assault with a dangerous weapon on federal officers and employees; and murder and attempted murder within the special maritime and territorial jurisdiction of the United States.

The magnitude of the charges made Ismail's head spin. He struggled against the weight of guilt. In the days after the shooting, there had been times when it had overcome him, stabbing his heart like a dagger. As time had passed, however, the remorse had resolved into a cold ache. No matter what happened—even if Quentin made a full recovery—it would never leave him. The boy's blood and that of his father were a permanent stain on his soul.

When the judge finished the recitation, she focused on Ismail again. "Mr. Ibrahim, how do you plead to these charges: guilty or not guilty?"

Ismail spoke the words despite the pain. "Not guilty, Your Honor."

"The government has also filed a notice of intent to seek the death penalty should you be found guilty on any of the charges for which such a punishment is permissible under law. Has your attorney explained this to your satisfaction?"

"Yes, Your Honor," Ismail intoned.

"Thank you, Mr. Ibrahim," the judge said, and Ismail sat down again.

The judge next took up the matter of the trial date.

Megan objected when she suggested June, but the judge allayed her concerns by promising to consider a continuance if the government didn't move quickly in producing relevant documents and witnesses. She set the trial for June 18 and scheduled a motions hearing for March 2 to handle any disputes about the scope of discovery, including the inevitable question of national security.

"Are there any other matters that I need to take up at this point?" she asked the attorneys.

"No, Your Honor," said Megan and Barrington at the same time.

The judge nodded. "Very well. This case is adjourned."

When Judge McKenzie departed the bench, Ismail looked toward the back of the courtroom and caught sight of Vanessa. He recognized her from the photo album on the sailboat. He met her eyes and saw the suffering in them, the depthless well of her sorrow. He remembered standing beside Daniel and Quentin as the plane flew overhead, remembered seeing her hand on the window and catching a glimpse of her red hair. The words he had spoken to her echoed in his head: *We have done nothing to harm them . . . nothing to harm them . . . nothing to harm them.* He wanted to tell her that he had meant it, that he never wanted this to happen. But he knew it wouldn't assuage her pain. Nothing would.

Megan touched his shoulder. "We need to talk."

"Okay," he said, following her to a windowless conference room on the way to the lockup. They took seats at a table, and Megan took out a pad and pen.

"A June trial means we have a lot of work to do," she said. "The statements you made on the *Truman* are damning. I'm going to move to suppress them, and I'm going to attack the indictment. But I'll be frank with you—I'm not going to get much relief. Unless something changes, they're going to hang you with your own words. I've said this before, and I'll say it again: I don't believe for a second that what happened out there is as simple as your crew claims. I don't think the Shabaab has anything to do with it. What really happened, Ismail? I can't help you unless you help me."

He met her eyes. The more he was around her, the more she reminded him of Paul. "I told you before. We had a deal, and we intended to honor it. But the Navy broke its word."

She shook her head. "That's not good enough. I can dredge up every mistake the Navy made—and believe me, I plan to—but they didn't shoot the hostages. *You* did. At least that's what your crew says. You've never directly admitted it, but you haven't denied it either. This isn't a game, Ismail. You're rolling the dice with your life."

"What does it matter?" he asked, regarding her frankly. "I have no defense to the piracy charge. You told me yourself: the minimum sentence is life in prison."

"I can't believe I'm hearing this," she exclaimed. "Prison or not, life is very different from death. They want to execute you. If that's what you want, that's your choice. But I'm not going to help you commit suicide. Either tell me the truth, or I'm going to ask the Court to get you another lawyer."

He looked away, feeling profoundly conflicted. Like her brother, she was gifted at persuasion. But she couldn't fathom the calculations running through his head. His life was over. He knew he would never spend another day in freedom. There were only two things he wanted anymore: to rescue Yasmin and avenge the destruction of his family. There was a chance—albeit remote—that he could achieve both objectives at the same time. But for the gambit to work, he needed Megan's help.

"If you want to know what happened on the sailboat, I'll tell you," he said quietly. "I did it. I pulled the trigger. Are you happy now?"

Megan sank into her seat. "Okay," she replied with a trace of sadness. "I can live with that. But I need you to tell me why. Were you intoxicated? Were you under duress? Did you have a psychotic episode? You could have made your escape and left the Parkers unharmed."

He shook his head. "The reason doesn't matter."

Her eyes flashed. "You're far too intelligent to believe that. If you were coerced or your capacity for rational action diminished, we could establish a defense to the murder charge."

He stared at a dark spot on the table, an imperfection in the grain of the wood.

When the silence became uncomfortable, she said, "What's going on here, Ismail? Why do I get the sense that I'm being manipulated?"

He looked up at her again and felt a flutter of déjà-vu. He needed her to trust him, just as he had needed Paul to trust him. Everything depended on it. "I can't tell you the reason. Not yet. But I will tell you. I need you to accept that."

She returned his gaze without blinking. "I'll do that on one condition. I want to know how all of this started. I want access to your family. I want the jury to know who you really are."

In an instant, Ismail's guilt metastasized into shame. He thought of his relatives scattered across the globe. He was certain that all of them knew about his father's death. The clan networks were like gossip chains, disseminating news almost as rapidly as the modern media, and far more personally. To them Adan was a hero and a martyr, a man who had made the ultimate sacrifice for his country. The last thing Ismail wanted to do was to tarnish his father's honorable name.

He held his breath until he began to feel light-headed. Then he made his concession. "My father is dead. I'm certain my mother is, too. I have an uncle in Minneapolis, an aunt in London, and an uncle in Mogadishu. I suggest you talk to them."

"What is the name of your uncle in Minneapolis?" Megan asked.

He spoke the name in a whisper. "Farah Said Ahmed."

YASMIN

The Juba was low again, a latticework of water ribbons meandering between green banks, but at least it was still flowing. There had been times in the past year when the river had nearly disappeared into the sand. The rains of the *deyr* had brought an end to the worst drought in anyone's memory, but by November they were gone and the heat had returned, parching the land again.

Yasmin knelt in the shade of a broad-limbed *higlo* tree and dipped her jug into the water. When it was full, she stood and strapped it to her back, looking out across the river toward the horizon. The desert was a patchwork of yellow earth and green scrub, broken by the occasional cluster of deep-rooted trees—feathery acacia, flat-topped *qudhac*, and majestic *damal*. The sky was a dusty blue and sprinkled with small clouds.

The village where she had lived for almost three years now was in the hinterlands of southern Somalia, equidistant from the port of Kismayo and the Kenyan border. It was a hardscrabble town of herdsmen and the merchants who served them, thriving in the good years when the rains came and the camels and goats and cattle grew healthy and fat and brought strong prices at the market, and struggling to survive when the rains failed and the livestock starved and the waters of the Juba slackened and grew brackish. It was worlds apart from urban Mogadishu and light-years from cosmopolitan Nairobi, where Yasmin had spent her early childhood.

"Are you finished?" Fatuma asked from her perch at the base of the *higlo* tree. "I'm hungry."

Yasmin regarded her with a mixture of irritation and compassion. Fatuma was always in need of something to eat these days. She was eight months pregnant with Najiib's child.

"Ha," Yasmin said. "Yes. Let's go."

She rearranged the fabric of her hijab and helped Fatuma to her feet, leading her to the gate in the wall and the court-yard beyond. The house where Yasmin lived with Fatuma, Najiib's first wife, and Jamaad, his *habaryaro,* or aunt on his mother's side, was made of cinder block and had a covered porch and a tile roof—rarities in a village mostly comprised of mud huts. But there the luxuries ended. The windows were open to the air. The concrete floors were only partially covered with rugs. The toilet was a hole in the ground with ceramic footrests. And meals were cooked on a camp stove.

Jamaad waved from the porch, beckoning Fatuma to sit with her while Yasmin prepared lunch. *How our fortunes have reversed*, Yasmin thought as she went to the kitchen and heated a pot of water. When Najiib brought her here years ago, she had been the privileged one, the object of his desire, and Fatuma had been shunted to the side, the wife who couldn't make a baby. But then time had passed and Yasmin, too, had failed to produce a child. They had grown as close as sisters during the long months of their barrenness, vowing that if Allah smiled on one of them, they would never let it come between them. But then Fatuma had conceived and everything had changed. Suddenly, Yasmin had become the pariah, forced to serve the mother-to-be of Najiib's son. On his last visit, Najiib had spoken it like a prophecy: Fatuma would give birth to a boy.

Yasmin put spaghetti in the pot, diced some vegetables, and sautéed them in a pan with *hawaash* spices and goat meat left over from yesterday's dinner. As she worked, she tried to buoy her spirits by reciting poetry in her mind, as her mother had taught her to do.

Al-Shafiʻi: *If in your heart you are content, then you are equal to those who possess the world.*

Saʻdi Shirazi: *No man has the ability to number his numberless blessings.*

Rumi: *Keep silence, that you may hear from that Sun things inexpressible in books and discourses. Keep silence, that the Spirit may speak to you.*

But God didn't speak to her; the verses of the poets didn't lift her up. Instead, as the minutes marched on and the aroma of Somali spices filled the air, she found herself slipping into the well-worn rut of despair. This life she was living was a lie in of all its particulars, a miserable shell of alienation and abuse. She was the prisoner of a man who had murdered her father and so many others in the name of the faith she so cherished. Her soul was in exile, her hope all but gone, its only remnant a tendril of memory, a few words spoken by her brother in the back of a technical on the first day of blood and fear: *If they separate us, keep your phone,* Ismail had whispered. *I will find you.*

She had held on to her mobile, just as he said, secreting it in her undergarments and hiding it from Najiib and Jamaad and Fatuma until she acquired a plastic bag with a watertight seal and found a place to bury it—in a seam of dirt between the roots of the *higlo* tree. Every month she rose in the middle of the night and recovered the phone, bringing it into the house and refreshing the battery with Jamaad's charger. Each time she sent a text message to Ismail's old number, praying he would reply. But her inbox was always empty. After years of silence, she imagined he was dead, but she continued the ritual because she could think of nothing better to do.

She had given thought to escaping many times. The danger, however, was immense. The Shabaab controlled all of the towns for a hundred kilometers in every direction. Their spies were everywhere; even the most humble beggar could be an informant. The roads, too, were crawling with Shabaab fighters, bandits, thieves, and now Kenyan soldiers notorious for taking liberties with Somali women. Even if she could manage to evade all of them, she would almost certainly succumb to the elements. Without a local's knowledge of watering holes or an animal to provide milk, she would die of thirst in less than a week, assuming she wasn't mauled by a lion or struck by a cobra. The Dadaab camps in Kenya were two weeks away by foot.

When she finished preparing lunch, she served the spaghetti and chutney with *chapatti*—Indian flatbread—to Jamaad and Fatuma on the porch and ate by herself across the yard in the shadow of one of the *higlo* tree's overhanging limbs. The isolation gnawed at her, scavenged for stray scraps of joy like a vulture picking apart a carcass. She had always been social by nature. When she and Fatuma were friends, at least she had a companion. Now she was an outcast, no better than a servant. *Hooyo*, she thought, imagining her mother's face, *if God honors those who keep the faith, why is Aabbe dead? Why am I here? Where are Ismail and Yusuf? Where are you?*

"Yasmin," Jamaad called from the porch, holding up an empty glass that had been filled with water. "I'm thirsty. Please get me something else to drink."

Yasmin left her plate on the ground and fetched Jamaad a Coke from the refrigerator. Powered by a small generator, the fridge was one of the few modern conveniences they had in the house. When she handed Jamaad the bottle, the woman said to her, "I received a text from Najiib. He has promised to visit as soon as the baby is born."

"Good," Yasmin said, plastering a smile on her face and returning to her spot by the wall. How she hated the mask she had to wear to disguise the truth—that she loathed Najiib with all of her heart. When she met him, she had been a girl of seventeen with her father's love for learning and her mother's compassion for the poor. She had been chaste, uncorrupted by a man. Then in a single day Najiib had torn her world apart, defiling everything she considered good. Yet he didn't hate her; he fancied her. And he wanted her to fancy him. How many times had he said that he wanted *her* to bear his son? He had turned her life into a wretched contradiction, and his return promised only suffering.

She could see it now: the joy on his face when he heard the baby's cry, the presents he would give to Fatuma to reward her for her gift—gold jewelry and embroidered silk and Ray-Ban sunglasses and a new iPhone, the very icons of the West the Shabaab claimed to despise. Then after Fatuma was feted and asleep, he would come to Yasmin's room and pour out his lust upon her, treating her like a common whore. He would leave her in pain, but he wouldn't notice or care. She was whatever he wanted her to be. In Najiib's world, he was his own plenipotentiary.

Allah was just a figurehead.

When night came, Yasmin made sure that Jamaad and Fatuma were comfortable before retiring to her room with her kerosene lantern. She owned only one book: a copy of the Quran in Arabic. She opened the volume and traced the flowing lines of the second sura, finding her favorite passage. She knew the words by heart, but she read them out loud like a prayer: "'Our Lord! Do not lay on us a burden greater than we can bear. Forgive us for our sins. Have mercy on us. You are our Guardian.'" Then she closed her eyes, turned out the lamp, and went to sleep without taking off her clothes.

Hours later, she woke again and listened carefully for sounds of movement in the house. Satisfied, she rose in the darkness and crossed the floor barefoot, slipping silently out the front door and across the courtyard. She couldn't use the gate; it was padlocked. Instead, she went to the *higlo* tree and pulled herself up onto one of the limbs. She sat perfectly still, all of her senses attuned to the night sounds she knew so well—the cicadas, frogs, and nocturnal birds, and the soft murmuring of the river. She heard nothing amiss. The village was quiet.

In time, she slid across the limb and dropped down on the far side of the wall. She reached between the roots and uncovered the bag with her mobile phone. After powering on the unit, she saw that the battery had just enough life to find a signal. Her heartbeat increased when she checked her messages. As always she was disappointed. The last message in her inbox was from her mother the day before the school attack. She had texted Khadija many times over the years but never received a reply. Her mother's silence meant one of two things: either she was dead or she had disappeared into the underground to escape the Shabaab.

Yasmin went to the river's edge and sat on the bluff, looking at the stars. She saw Orion in the west and the Southern Cross to the south. She remembered the many nights her father had taken her and her brothers up on the roof in Mogadishu and taught them the constellations. *Your ancestors once read the heavens like you read a map,* Adan had said. *It's a skill you should have. You never know when you're going to need it.*

She could have spent all night there in the company of creation. But she stayed only five minutes before typing a message to her mother: Hooyo, I'm alive. I need your help. And one to Ismail: Are you out there? I'm still waiting.

Then she climbed the *higlo* tree and returned inside to charge the phone.

MEGAN

The winter air felt like dry ice on Megan Derrick's skin. It was as if the gunmetal sky had frozen solid around her, drawing all the warmth from her body. She huddled deeper into her parka, pressing her gloved hands into the pockets and wincing at the sting of the wind on her cheeks. *Why does anyone live here?* she wondered as she waited for the car to arrive. *Why did the Somalis—a desert people—choose this city to establish the largest diaspora community in North America?*

Before long, she saw a silver Toyota Yaris turn into the hotel entrance. The man behind the wheel was too large for the subcompact automobile. He had to climb out in stages, bending his head, extricating his legs, and rolling forward before standing. He was at least a foot taller than she was— six and a half feet, she guessed. His face was almond brown, his eyes dark and thoughtful, and his goatee a frame for a mouth that didn't look like it smiled often.

"Ms. Derrick, I am Farah," he said, his words as stark

as the look he gave her. "There is a place we can talk not far from here."

She slipped into the passenger seat and watched him fold his body back into the car. Finding him had been easy enough. One contact had led to another until five degrees of separation reduced to one—a friend who taught at the Elliott School of International Affairs; the Senior Somalia Desk Officer at the State Department; an imam at a prominent mosque in Minneapolis; and, finally, a relative from Farah's subclan who lived on his street. The challenge had been to convince him that the Ismail Adan Ibrahim she represented was actually his sister's son. He denied it resolutely until, with Ismail's help, she named his patrilineal ancestors going back four generations. At that point, his resistance dissolved and he agreed to meet with her.

"Is it always this cold?" she asked, warming her hands on the dashboard vents.

He pulled out onto the street. "The winter is hard, but it is a good place to raise a family."

"How many children do you have?" she inquired, making conversation.

"Three. And you?"

"I've never had kids." She spoke the admission easily after years of practice, but still she felt the weight of it in her heart. It hadn't been a conscious decision as much as a consequence of the life she had chosen—the work that never ended, like an express train with no stops; the cases and clients that piled up, every one a person, a family, a company in need; and the men she had dated and the one she had finally married, all equally yoked to their professions. Sometimes when she saw a mother cuddling a baby or pushing a child on the swings, she wished for a moment that she could take her place. But then she remembered the mountain of her responsibilities, the people who were depending on her, the lives hanging in the balance, and the moment always passed—though the ache never quite disappeared.

When Farah lapsed into silence, Megan sat back and watched the city pass by. Soon skyscrapers gave way to apartment buildings, strip malls, and residential neighborhoods—the placeless fingerprint of suburbia. After a while, Farah pulled up to a parking gate outside a building with glass storefronts. He waved to the attendant and found a spot in the busy lot.

"This is a Somali mall," Farah said. "There are a few in the city. I own this one."

She surveyed the mall and the many customers milling about in shops and restaurants. "Looks like a good investment."

"It was," he affirmed without inflection.

After extracting himself from the car, he led her into a hallway lined with stalls—a mall within the mall. All manner of goods and services were on display, some Western, some Somali: fabrics, shoes, electronics, mobile phones, accountant advice, travel assistance, and a wide variety of food. The air was redolent of cooking oil, grilled meat, and spices. She followed him into a café with a handful of tables along the wall. He greeted the young Somali vendor with a gregarious grin.

"The samosas are excellent here," he said. "As is the tea.

It is my treat."

"Thank you," she replied, unzipping her parka.

A few minutes later, they took seats at a table in the back with a plate of deep-fried pastries and mugs of Somali tea. Farah waved at the food. "Please eat. I will talk."

She nodded and took a bite of a samosa. It was piping hot and delicious.

"I wasn't prepared to receive your call," he began, his tone flat. "I saw the news reports about the hijacking, but I didn't follow the story. My clan has never been involved in piracy." He spoke the word with distaste, revealing the wound to his pride. "Ismail is the firstborn son of my younger sister, Khadija. I knew him when he was a boy— when his family lived in Nairobi—but I haven't seen him since they returned to Somalia. I was certain he was dead. That is why I didn't believe you when you called. It is still hard to believe."

"Why did you think he was dead?" Megan asked softly.

Farah glanced at the vendor, who was talking on his mobile phone. He lowered his voice and asked a question of his own. "What did he tell you about the Shabaab?"

Megan's pulse quickened. She had asked Ismail a dozen different ways about his association with the Islamists, but he had declined to elaborate. "As his lawyer, I can't tell you what he's said. But I'd be very grateful if you would tell me what you know."

Farah's nose twitched. "The story has many dimensions."

"Take as long as you want," Megan said, picking up another samosa.

Farah fixed his expressionless eyes on her. "There are many who deserve blame for what happened, but Adan, his father, is the first. He was foolish to take his family back to Mogadishu. If they had stayed in Kenya, Ismail and Yasmin would be at university, and Yusuf would be graduating from secondary school. They could have been doctors, lawyers, businesspeople. But Adan had this silly dream. He wanted to open a school in Mogadishu. He wanted to be a part of the rebirth of Somalia."

Yasmin, Yusuf, Megan thought, taking out a pad and pen. *Where are they now?*

Farah looked away from her, as if remembering. "To understand what I'm about to tell you, you need context. In the year 2000, the world powers created the first transitional government in Mogadishu. Many Somalis believed that change was in the wind. I did not. The warlords still ruled the streets. I advised Khadija to stay with the children in Nairobi. But Adan wouldn't allow it. He knew the new president. He was convinced the war was about to end." Farah's eyes clouded further. "People have been saying that for twenty years, and still the war goes on."

Megan nodded. She had spent much of the past month struggling to make sense of the internecine bloodshed, political machinations, and international interventions that had defined Somalia since the fall of the nation's long-standing dictator, Siad Barre, in 1991. It was like trying to disentangle the knot of the Israeli–Palestinian conflict. The grievances were so numerous and entrenched in a past so complex that every time she felt she was about to unlock the mystery of it, the key slipped through her hands and she found herself suspended again in a fog of incomprehension.

"They got a house in Bulo Hubey, not far from the airport," Farah went on. "It was the safest neighborhood in the city—always under government control. But Adan's school was in Medina, where there was fighting. To his credit, he had formidable friends. His brother, Mahamoud, is a man of great influence in Mogadishu. For years his friends were a shield around him. But then the Shabaab came and defeated the warlords. They ignored the old rules—the bribes and favors that made Mogadishu work. Their goal was domination. Even Mahamoud couldn't control them."

Mahamoud, Megan wrote on her pad. *I need to talk to him.*

Farah sipped his tea. "It was remarkable to see how quickly the Shabaab gained ground. We Somalis have always been moderate in our religious views. Extremism is not native to our soil. It is an import from Arabia and Afghanistan. The Islamists exploited the dislocation caused by the war. They did what the government failed to do: they brought law and order to the streets and gave businesses a chance to flourish again." He held out his hands. "The people were tired of the fighting. They gave the Shabaab what they wanted—power. That was when they took off the mask. They started punishing women for going outside without a headscarf. They amputated the hands of thieves, stoned people accused of adultery, recruited soldiers by force and bribery, and silenced dissent with the gun. Adan was one of the dissenters. He continued to teach English and science in his school. I admire that about him. What I don't admire is the way he exposed his family to reprisal."

When Megan finished off the last of the samosas, Farah said, "Would you like more?"

"No, thank you," she said. "I enjoyed them, though."

Farah glanced at the boy behind the counter again and then folded his hands on the table. "I saw it coming even here," he continued. "The Shabaab put pressure on the transitional government until the Ethiopians who were propping it up grew weary and left the country. That was early 2009. The African Union stayed behind, but they were weak. I talked to Khadija every week. I told her to take the children back to Nairobi. But she wouldn't leave without Adan, and Adan refused to leave."

Farah took a breath, and for the first time Megan saw a flicker of emotion in his eyes. "It didn't take the Shabaab long to control most of Mogadishu. That spring, they attacked Adan's school. They shot him in front of the children and took the older students away to fight with them. Ismail, Yasmin, and Yusuf were among them. My sister worked as a nurse at Medina Hospital. She was there when it happened. I talked to her the next day. She was beside herself. She'd spoken to Mahamoud, and he said there was nothing he could do. The Shabaab was a black hole."

Megan sat back in her chair, spellbound by Ismail's story. *They murdered his father in front of him? They kidnapped him?* The memories from her own childhood came to her unbidden—the explosion of the gun in Kyle's hands, her father crumpling to the floor, the wall behind him spattered with blood, the cordite hanging in the air, her mother's screams. She forced them out of her mind.

"What happened after that?" she asked quietly.

Farah blinked. "My sister escaped from the city. She went to my father's house in Merca, but it wasn't safe. He found her transport to the Kenyan border. She walked the rest of the way to Dadaab."

Suddenly, Megan's horror became astonishment. "You mean his mother is *alive*?"

Farah nodded. "I talked to her yesterday."

My God, Megan thought. She had pressed Ismail about why he was so certain that Khadija was dead, but as on so many other points he had refused to give his reasons. She searched Farah's face and saw a hint of moisture in his eyes. "Is there a way I can speak to her?"

Farah put out his hand. "If you give me your pen, I will write down her number. She works as a nurse in the Dagahaley refugee camp."

Megan made no attempt to hide her elation. After he scrawled out the digits on her pad, she asked, "Did you ever find out what happened to Yasmin and Yusuf?"

"Yusuf was killed in the fighting," Farah answered. "I don't know what happened to Yasmin." He was quiet for a long moment, and then changed the subject. "When is Ismail's trial?"

"It's scheduled for June," she said. "Will you testify? The jury needs to hear your story."

He looked down at the table. "I will have to think about that."

She understood his reticence. To make public his association with Ismail would bring his family into disrepute. Still, she urged him on. "Please do. He needs your help."

"There are things I do not understand," Farah said in a voice just above a whisper. "He escaped from the Shabaab, but he didn't flee the country. Why did he stay? And why did he get involved in piracy? It flies in the face of everything Adan and Khadija raised him to believe."

Megan spoke carefully. "To be honest, I don't understand it either."

Farah gave her a pointed look. "So he didn't tell you." He scratched his chin thoughtfully. "There is a saying in Somalia that a person is like a bush. It looks safe on the outside, but on the inside it's home to snakes and scorpions. I suppose that is a kind of explanation."

I'm not so sure, Megan thought but didn't say. *I think he had another agenda. He still does.*

ISMAIL

Longfellow's voice rang out in the empty gymnasium where Ismail was playing basketball. "Your lawyer is on her way up. She says it's important." When Ismail gave him a crestfallen look, the jailer grinned. "Don't worry, you'll get your time."

Ismail nodded and took a final shot. The ball bounced off the backboard and rattled around the rim before falling through the net. Every prisoner in the maximum-security block got an hour of free time at some point during the day, and Ismail had developed a regimen that gave him a little bit of everything—ten minutes of pushups, sit-ups, and calisthenics, ten minutes of shooting hoops, ten minutes for a shower, and thirty minutes for reading the newspaper, searching for stories about Africa and the Middle East. He relished the daily ritual and was loath to lose a minute of it.

He met Longfellow at the door and put his hands out, wrists flush, and his feet shoulder-width apart, allowing the jailer to cuff him. Seconds later, Richie buzzed the cell block

door, and Longfellow led him down the hall to the conference room. After the jailer removed his handcuffs again,
Ismail sat down at the table and waited nervously for Megan
to appear.

He had been dreading this visit for two weeks, ever
since their conversation at the courthouse. He was sure it
had to do with Farah. He felt the butterflies in his stomach,
the cord of shame around his neck, weakening his resolve.
For three years, he had had no contact with his family, apart
from Mahamoud. In that time he had committed crimes
that his relatives would never understand. His hands were
covered in blood, his heart choked by it. Yet he was a part
of them, joined by the bonds of clan and kin. He couldn't
dismiss them even if he wanted to.

In time, Longfellow opened the door again and let
Megan in. She greeted Ismail with a smile and took a seat
across from him. "I met with your uncle," she began, and
Ismail clenched his jaw, steeling himself against the guilt.
"He told me about the Shabaab attack on your school. It
makes sense of a lot of things. He also told me the most
extraordinary news." She paused, examining him through
empathetic eyes. "Your mother is alive. She's in a refugee
camp in Kenya."

Ismail was unprepared for the emotions that overcame
him, the tears that clouded his eyes, and the trembling
that seized his hands. On the night he absconded from the
Shabaab, running from the heartbreak of Yusuf's death,
Mahamoud had told him of Khadija's visit and the advice
he had given her to flee to Kenya and call him when she got

there. He had never heard from her again. Logic suggested the reason—she never made it out.

"How can that be?" Ismail asked in a near whisper.

"Her family helped her," Megan replied and passed along the details Farah had shared.

Ismail's mind raced. *Why didn't she call Mahamoud when she got to Dadaab? He promised to look for news of us.* In a flash he intuited the answer: because Mahamoud was Habar Gidir and she was Abgal—rival clans whose twenty-year struggle for control of Mogadishu had turned the once-proud city into a bombed-out vestige of civilization. After Adan was assassinated, her family had told her not to trust Mahamoud, and she had gone along with them because she was afraid.

Megan reached out and touched his hand. "Farah gave me her number. I spoke to her this morning. She would love to hear from you."

Ismail's humiliation knew no bounds. "You told her I'm here?"

"It doesn't matter," Megan said. "She loves you."

He stared at the table, riven by indecision. Words came to him from the past—the charge Khadija had given him when the Shabaab infiltrated Medina and began to threaten Adan: *If anything ever happens, don't let Yasmin and Yusuf out of your sight. You are the eldest. They are your responsibility.* He had gone to the ends of the earth to honor her request, but he had failed.

"Here is her number," Megan said, sliding a piece of paper across the table. "I put money in your account. You can call her whenever you want."

He looked at the number and then pushed the paper away. "Not yet," he said.

"Why?" Megan asked, her bewilderment plain.

He shook his head, focusing on the wall. *I don't want to explain.*

After a long pause, Megan took the paper back. "You do what you want, but I'm going to meet her. I need to hear her story."

He said nothing for a long moment, wrestling with his shame. Then he spoke the only words that mattered. "When you see her, please tell her that I'm sorry."

MEGAN

The dusty airstrip was shimmering in the desert heat when Megan stepped off the plane. The blast of hot air hit her like a wave, causing her skin to tingle and her forehead to bead with sweat. It was only nine in the morning, but already the temperature in the Kenyan border town of Dadaab had passed ninety degrees. The contrast with Minneapolis was surreal. Only one week ago she had stood like an icicle in frozen air that seemed to have blown straight from the North Pole.

She followed a motley crew of humanitarian workers across the tarmac to a gravel lot filled with white SUVs emblazoned with the logo of UNHCR, the UN refugee agency. They waited there for a flatbed truck to deliver their luggage from the World Food Programme plane that had flown them in from Nairobi. When the truck arrived, Megan grabbed her suitcase and bundled into an SUV with a trio of aid workers—Europeans, by the sound of it—for the ride to the UN compound.

For the first time since she took Ismail's case, she felt like she was starting to understand—not everything, by any means, but some things, the context that gave birth to the tragedy. The threadbare tale the young Somali had told the FBI on the *Truman* was a canard. The Western media had embraced it uncritically because it reinforced their bias against Muslims and paranoia about terrorism. But they had it exactly backward. Ismail wasn't a follower of the Shabaab; he was their victim.

She had sensed the fallacy from the beginning. In their initial meeting, she had given him a test, asking him to describe the Parkers. He was taciturn at first, but she urged him on with gentle questions and got him talking. She paid close attention to his mannerisms, cataloging facial expressions, body language, and inflection, and detected none of the pathologies of a cold-blooded killer. He talked about Daniel and Quentin with respect bordering on affection, recounting Quentin's facility for Somali words, Daniel's glossy photo album, and the music Quentin had played over the sailboat's stereo system using his iPhone. Afterward, she wrote in her notepad, *Paul was right. He's not who he says he is. But then who is he? And why is he putting on a masquerade?*

The enigma was bewitching. As the weeks had passed and the government had divulged more details about the shooting, Megan found herself enthralled by the case, puzzling over it at all hours of the day and night, often at the expense of her paying clients. Ismail had confessed to pulling the trigger, but he refused to tell her why. He had reinforced, not contradicted, his crew's allegations about the

Shabaab, but he made no attempt to behave like a jihadist. There was only one explanation that made any sense: he was playing a high-stakes poker game with an objective she had yet to identify.

She looked out the window as the SUV entered Dadaab—a haphazard warren of dirt roads, decrepit dwellings, and ramshackle shops. Everyone she knew had warned her against making the trip—everyone except Paul, who understood the reasons behind her near-fanatical devotion to her death penalty clients. She had called him before she booked the ticket. He hadn't admitted it directly, but she knew that the kidnapping of the American aid workers was the reason he left Colorado before the New Year. He had given her two pieces of advice: "Make sure you vet your security team, and watch your back in the camps. If anything doesn't feel right, get the hell out of there."

She studied the faces of the locals. Most were ethnic Somalis—the men wearing Western shirts and pants, and the women wrapped in colorful *abaya*s and headscarves that left only their faces, hands, and feet exposed. They regarded the UN vehicle with wary eyes. From the research she had done, she wasn't surprised. In the past century, the Somalis had seen their land carved up by Britain, France, and Italy, parceled out in peace treaties to Ethiopia and Kenya, invaded by the Ethiopians—with American support—and used as a battleground in the proxy war between the United States and al-Qaeda. Even when the international community offered aid, it often came with geopolitical strings attached. It was little wonder the average Somali had a jaded view of the West.

After a few minutes, the SUV arrived at a security gate flanked by fortified concrete walls and manned by stern-faced guards with machine guns. The guards checked their IDs and let them through the gate. When they entered the compound, Megan realized that the walls were only the first of many barriers erected to keep the militants at bay. Inside the gate was a vast network of smaller compounds, each with its own fencing, security gates, and armed sentries.

When they reached the UNHCR compound, a guard escorted Megan and her companions on foot to a final checkpoint—a security post with a metal detector.

At last, she entered the compound and saw a Kenyan man standing in the sun beside a hedge of rainbow-colored bougainvillea. "Ms. Derrick," he said in accented English. "I am Peter Mburu with External Relations. Welcome to Dadaab."

"This place is a fortress," she replied, shaking his hand.

He smiled easily. "It is unfortunate but necessary. There are four hundred thousand Somalis in our camps. Most are refugees. A few are not. We don't take chances." He gestured toward a bungalow with flowering plants all around. "Come. Let's talk about your mission."

He led her into an office with a fan blowing at full power. He sat down at a desk, and she took a seat across from him. "I looked over your security arrangements. Your fixer, Baraka, is trustworthy, but I don't know the drivers he hired. Are you sure you want to go to the camp? If you can spare another day or two, perhaps we can arrange for Khadija to meet you here."

Megan shook her head. "She's expecting me today. Besides, I have hearings in the US next week. Baraka told me not to worry. He's going to come along."

Peter shrugged. "When is he bringing the vehicles?"

"Ten o'clock," she replied.

Peter checked his watch. "Good. We have enough time for your security briefing."

When the time came, Megan walked with Peter to the car park and waited for Baraka to arrive. Standing there in the scorching heat, her collar stained with sweat, she felt a tremor of apprehension about the journey she was about to make. The Dagahaley refugee camp was the northernmost outpost in Dadaab, a forty-minute drive from town and only fifty-five miles from the Somali border. According to Baraka—a Kenyan fixer recommended by a journalist friend in Nairobi—they would travel in two light trucks with an armed escort of four police officers. But his assurances only went so far. The drivers and officers were strangers to her, and she was paying them a pittance—by American standards at least. Even if they were honest, she found it hard to believe they would risk their lives for her.

A few minutes later, a pair of Toyota HiLux pickups pulled into the lot with two Somalis behind the wheels and three Kenyans in military fatigues crammed into one of the cabs. The lead driver climbed out and smiled at her through crooked teeth.

Megan narrowed her eyes. "Where is Baraka? He said he would be here."

"No problem, no problem," the man said. "Baraka busy. I am Omar. I work with him. We go?"

Her eyes flashed. "That's not good enough." She took out her iPhone and called the fixer. "Omar is here," she said when he answered. "Where are you?"

"I'm sorry, my friend," Baraka said. "Something came up. Omar will take care of you."

"You promised to come," she retorted. "You also promised me four officers. I see only three."

"The other one wasn't available," Baraka replied smoothly. "Don't worry. You will be okay."

She almost said, "This is my life you're talking about," but she knew it was futile. She had been to Africa half a dozen times—to Cape Town and Victoria Falls with Simon and with Paul, years ago, to climb Kilimanjaro. When it came to making plans, nothing ever happened the way it was supposed to. She looked at Omar. His teeth reminded her of Stonehenge. She couldn't tell if he was grinning at her because he was friendly or nervous. She hesitated a moment longer but never considered backing out. She had learned long ago that fear was a choice she didn't have to make. *Sometimes you have to live on the edge*, she thought, gripping the strap of her rucksack. *The fall is far, but the view is much better.*

"Fine then," she told Baraka. "If anything happens, it will be your fault." She ended the call and faced Omar. "I want the other truck to lead and you to stay close behind."

"No problem, no problem," said the Somali.

She turned to Peter, who was staring at her with concern. "I'll text you my brother's phone number," she said. "If there's an emergency, give him a call. He'll know what to do."

They departed the compound by the side gate and left Dadaab behind. The road to the camps was nothing more than a dirt track into the desert, badly rutted and choked with dust. The view out the windshield reminded Megan of a watercolor painting—the sky washed out by the feverish heat, the earth pale and red like an old scar. She saw a few hardy trees in the distance, their crowns peeking above the horizon, but the rest of the vegetation was low-lying scrub, gray-green against the featureless backdrop of dirt, rock, and termite mounds.

She watched the lead truck as it bounced along, trailing a cloud of dust. Her iPhone was in her hand, the text message to Peter already sent and another prepared, this to Paul in case Omar turned on her. Her senses were on hyper-alert, taking note of the driver's every movement, every variation in the landscape, every smudge on the horizon that might be the plume of an intercepting vehicle.

As time passed, the gap between the lead truck and theirs slowly widened. She told Omar to speed up, emphasizing her wish with her hands. A few seconds later, he turned the wheel and took a spur road, accelerating over the uneven ground until the shocks of the truck were overwhelmed by the jarring and juddering.

"What are you doing?" she demanded as the lead truck vanished into the scrub.

"This faster," he replied, grinning at her.

She clenched her teeth. Baraka had explained the rationale behind the convoy—the lead truck was supposed to sweep the road for explosive devices and scout for an ambush while her truck followed in its path. Omar's improvisation had put her in danger, but she could do nothing about it. She sat back and forced herself to relax, remembering something Grandpa Chuck had told her before she and Paul climbed Mount McKinley: *No matter what happens, always keep your wits about you. The things that scare us most in life almost never come true.*

In this case, the old man was prophetic. It wasn't long before the spur became a sidetrack and intersected with the main road again. They fishtailed in a soft patch of dirt and closed to within a few car lengths of the lead truck. Megan exhaled audibly and put her iPhone in her pocket.

"See?" Omar said, the smile still etched on his face. "No problem."

In time, Megan saw an assemblage of structures in the distance—a few administrative buildings and a vast array of tents and huts bordered by stick fences. They passed a signpost bearing the emblems of international aid organizations and approached a walled compound with razor wire. The guards at the gate refused to let the trucks in but beckoned Megan to follow them on foot.

"Call when finished," Omar said. "We go home."

A matronly Somali woman was waiting for her beyond the gate, a bottle of water in her hands. She was dressed in an emerald-green *abaya* and a white headscarf that framed a cherubic face—wrinkled and fleshy around the edges, but still lovely despite her age.

"*As-salamu alaykum,*" Megan said, using the formal Islamic greeting.

"*Wa alaykumu s-salam,*" Khadija replied, beaming brightly. She handed Megan the water and spoke in clear yet accented English. "You must be thirsty after the drive. I'm so sorry you had to come all this way to see me. It is a tense time."

"I understand," Megan replied, taking a swig of the cool water.

"Come," Khadija said. "We can talk in my room."

Megan followed her down a path to a dormitory-like building with a thatched roof and half a dozen doorways screened by fabric. Khadija doffed her sandals outside one of the doors and held back the screen, allowing Megan to enter. Megan sat on one of two beds and looked around. The room was simple but colorful with fabrics draped on the walls and a fan circulating air.

Khadija took a seat across from her, her eyes clouding with emotion. "I still can't believe that Ismail is alive. Though what he has done . . . I can't understand it. Is he well?"

Megan smiled softly. "I have a photo of him." She took out her iPhone and found the picture she had taken of Ismail before his first court hearing, after greasing the wheels with the marshals to get the phone inside the lockup. The lighting wasn't great, but Ismail cut a nice figure in his new suit.

She handed the phone to Khadija, and the woman began to cry quietly. After a while, she said, "He is my son, but he is different. His eyes are hard. There is much pain in him."

"Will you tell me about him?" Megan asked tenderly. "The way he was before."

Khadija blotted her eyes with a tissue. "Ismail is his father's son—passionate, loyal, and stubborn. When he was growing up, he had no interest in childhood. He read all of Adan's books by the age of fifteen. He memorized the Quran in Arabic. He was fiercely protective of his brother and sister. Once when he was twelve, Yasmin was stung by a scorpion. Adan and I were at the market, and the children were home alone. He carried her to the hospital, running all the way. He saved her life."

Somehow, none of this surprised Megan. "Farah told me what happened to Yusuf. But he didn't know about Yasmin. Do you?"

Khadija's eyes took on a faraway look. "The Shabaab treated girls differently from boys. Some were used to support the fighters, but most were given away in marriage. Yasmin was beautiful. I imagine one of the commanders claimed her." She stared at her hands. "After they were taken, there were so many times I wanted to try to find them. But I couldn't. It was too dangerous."

Megan asked her next question delicately. "What would you have done if you *had* tried?"

Khadija hesitated. "I would have texted them. They

all had mobile phones. Maybe the Shabaab took them, but maybe not." She folded her hands, her lip quivering. "I don't know what I would have done if they had replied. But at least . . . at least I would have known they were alive."

Megan saw the lacuna immediately. "They never texted you?"

Khadija shrugged. "I wouldn't know. I gave my phone to Mahamoud, my husband's brother. He told me I needed to disappear. He promised to destroy it."

Megan made a mental note of this. "Did you stay in touch with Mahamoud?"

"Not after what happened to my husband." Khadija frowned, as if searching for the right words. "Somali clans are like families. Before the war, we got along. We married across clan lines. We had friends from many clans. But the war has torn us apart. When I left Mogadishu, my father told me to cut all ties to Adan's clan. He said his relatives would stay in touch with Mahamoud."

Megan waited a moment before asking her next question. "Do you have any idea why Ismail would have gotten involved in piracy?"

Khadija answered with quiet conviction. "I have never known a boy more honorable than Ismail. There must be a reason. But what? I can't imagine it."

Megan softened her voice. "Do you know what could have driven him to kill?"

Khadija closed her eyes. "There is a saying of the Prophet Muhammad, peace be upon him, that all creatures are God's children and the ones dearest to God are those who treat his children best. That was Ismail when I knew him. But the Ismail in your photo . . . I don't know." She opened her eyes again. "Farah told me about the boy he shot. How is he? I pray for him every day."

Megan gave her a sanitized answer. "He's improving. But it's taking time."

Khadija looked at her inquisitively. "Farah said you are representing Ismail in the courts for free. If he did this terrible thing, why are you helping him?"

Megan held her expression steady. *If I told you, you wouldn't understand.* At once, she questioned herself. *She's seen death. Perhaps she would.* Her mind flashed to the photograph she kept in her desk drawer at the office, the one she had taken of Kyle at his easel, working on a still life of roses—the wispy brown hair falling into his eyes, the dash of a smile, like a secret to be shared, the gaze that never lingered long, the product of a restless mind. She felt the sorrow again, like a wound that never stopped bleeding. She steeled herself against the pain and offered Khadija a partial truth.

"I want the public to hear the whole story, not just the part the government wants to share. I also happen to think that execution is immoral. It doesn't cure the wrong; it compounds it. Ismail could make something of the rest of his life, even in prison."

Khadija looked back at her, her eyes glistening in the light. "There is a verse in the Quran that talks about retribution. But it also contains a promise. If anyone remits the penalty by way of charity, it is an atonement for sin. I'm not sure that applies to you. But I would like to think it does."

Megan reached out and touched her hand. "That's kind of you to say. Before I left, Ismail gave me a message for you. He asked me to tell you that he's sorry."

Khadija shook her head slowly. "I will always love him. But if he owes me an apology, he will have to tell me himself."

VANESSA

The morning dawned as gloomy as the shadows in Vanessa's heart. She went about her routine with the zeal of a convent novitiate, but her mind was crowded with distraction. The hot water in the shower woke her up but didn't soothe her. Her cappuccino tasted bitter. Even the Bissolotti sounded discordant, though she played Rachmaninoff's *Vocalise* and Paganini's twentieth caprice without error. It was Quentin who was haunting her, filling her soul with a melancholy she couldn't seem to break.

It had been twenty-two days since his discharge from NRH. She had spared no expense in preparing for his homecoming—framing photographs from his travels, putting fresh sheets on his bed, tuning the piano, buying him a new Sony PlayStation and a suite of the hottest video games. She had hoped that bringing him home would accelerate his recovery, but the effect had been just the opposite. Instead of liberating him, the house had trapped him in a mausoleum of memories, confronting him on all sides with reminders of his father's death and his own disabilities.

The stairs he had once taken three at a time he couldn't climb without holding the banister. The wood floor that he used to skate across on socks he had to cross in rubber-soled shoes to keep from slipping. The boats down at the dock were off-limits, as was the dock itself. The PlayStation and piano were like Kryptonite; he didn't touch them and refused to tell her why. One of his therapists had explained it to her. He was afraid his fingers were inadequate to the task. In his mind, it was better not to try than to suffer the discouragement of proving himself right.

The depression overcame him within hours of stepping foot in the door. He retreated inward and shut out the world, sleeping until early afternoon, ignoring his therapy, sitting on the sundeck under blankets watching the river pass by, and ignoring Vanessa's increasingly anxious attempts to engage him. She tried all the strategies that had worked in the hospital, but nothing seemed to help. Music irritated him, as did Daniel's letters. Even Ariadne's e-mails didn't buoy his spirits. After three weeks, Vanessa was convinced she was losing him.

She put the violin back on its stand and ran her hand over the piano, recalling the sonatas they had practiced together on weekends and occasionally performed for family and friends. *Will he ever play again?* she thought. She caught herself and shook her head. *Don't go there. You have to be strong for him.*

She ate a breakfast of eggs and toast and answered the

door when she heard the knock. Curtis and Yvonne were standing on the porch. She ushered them inside. She was dreading the day ahead, the hours she would spend with Curtis driving to the courthouse while Yvonne looked after Quentin. She didn't have the energy for conversation. In the aftermath of the shooting, relationships had become tedious. Everyone meant well, but no one understood. She didn't need sympathy or flowers or meals or phone calls. She needed her son to come back to her.

"How is he, dear?" Yvonne asked, giving Vanessa a hug.

"He's asleep," she replied without elaborating.

Yvonne nodded. "Of course. Don't worry yourself. We'll be fine."

Platitudes, Vanessa thought. *How tiresome.* She put on a brave face and gathered her coat.

When she turned around, Curtis cleared his throat and met her eyes. "Yvonne had an idea. It's a good one. I think you should listen to it."

Everyone has an idea, Vanessa thought, regarding him in annoyance.

Yvonne took a pensive breath. "That's right. I've been thinking it might be helpful if he had a friend his age. I can only imagine how isolated he feels."

Vanessa winced. *When he left on the voyage, his only friend was a drug peddler. And Hans nearly ruined his life.* She tried not to be patronizing. "Who do you suggest?"

Yvonne took a breath. "What if you flew Ariadne over? She's finished with school now. Quentin told me they talked about it before . . . the incident."

Vanessa was taken aback. "When did he tell you that?"

Yvonne traded a look with Curtis. "Just the other day, dear. When you were at work."

Vanessa turned away and walked to the window in the living room, hiding the tears in her eyes. What had she done wrong? Why would her son talk to his grandmother and not to her? She balled her hands into fists. She didn't realize that Yvonne had followed her until she spoke from a few feet away.

"You're a wonderful mother, Vanessa. You're doing everything you can for him. But you can't save him. His therapist told me something the last time she was here. He needs a new North Star. He needs someone to build him a bridge into the future. You can walk with him there, but I don't think you can show him the way."

Vanessa hugged herself to ward off her despair. "What makes you think Ariadne can do it?"

Yvonne touched her arm softly. "I don't know if she can. But isn't it worth a try?"

The miles between Annapolis and Norfolk passed quickly beneath the wheels of Curtis's Mercedes-Benz. Mercifully, Curtis filled the air with music instead of words. Vanessa watched the blur of scenery and tried not to think about Yvonne's suggestion, tried not to think about anything but Mozart's ebullient Violin Concerto No. 3. Whenever her mind drifted toward Quentin, she imagined herself playing the concerto, her bow dancing on the strings of the Bissolotti. In this manner, half an hour disappeared, and after it forty minutes with Brahms, an hour with Mendelssohn, and finally Beethoven, before Curtis turned off the stereo and allowed her to finish the trip in silence.

At a quarter to ten, they emerged from the Hampton Roads Bridge-Tunnel and drove into downtown Norfolk. The courthouse stood on the corner of Brambleton Avenue and Granby Street, a monolith of stone beneath the granite sky. They parked in a nearby lot and used the side entrance, passing through security and taking the brass-and-wood elevator to the third floor. The courtroom was across a marble lobby and through swinging double doors robed in time-worn Virginia pigskin—trivia Curtis had shared on their first visit. They took seats in the back and waited for the judge to appear.

Vanessa looked around at the faces in the gallery and smoothed her skirt to keep her hands from fidgeting. In contrast to the last hearing, the media were largely absent. She recognized a couple of journalists along with Agents Hewitt and Escobido from the FBI, but she didn't see any of the network reporters who had tried to get a statement from her after the arraignment. The rest of the spectators looked like lawyers and government officials—a potpourri of dark suits and self-important expressions.

Then there was Ismail. Every time she saw him she felt the wound again, and the hatred. She stared at the back of his head, drilling holes in his skull, as if she might reach into his brain and demand answers: *Why? Why did you murder my husband? Why did you try to kill my son?* As the seconds passed, her questions stirred the cauldron of her rage. *Your time is coming. They're going to bury you in an unmarked grave.*

"All rise!" the law clerk intoned, his gavel echoing in the vaulted chamber.

Vanessa stood with Curtis as Judge McKenzie ascended to the bench. She looked over her glasses at the attorneys. "Counsel, I've read your motions and memoranda. I will rule on the motions to dismiss on the briefs. With the time we have, I'd like to discuss the scope of discovery. Ms. Derrick?"

Vanessa watched as Megan walked to the podium. Under any circumstances, the trial would have been surreal. But Megan's decision to defend Ismail against the crime her brother had tried so hard to prevent was nothing short of bizarre. Whose side was she on?

"Thank you, Your Honor," Megan began, her diction crisp and her voice clear. "This case presents the Court with a difficult dilemma. Is our justice system beholden primarily to the interests of national security, or are we beholden to the truth? The government has been generous in its disclosure of all unclassified information. We now have a fairly good bird's-eye view of what happened before and after the shooting. But there is a whole universe of classified information they have kept from us, secrets that relate to the 'why' of what happened—the decisions made by the government at all levels, including the special-operations forces. The United States has placed the entire blame for this tragedy on the shoulders of a twenty-year-old man. They are asking this Court to impose the ultimate penalty. The least they can do is allow their own actions to be scrutinized."

The judge frowned. "The obligation of this Court is to assess whether the government can prove beyond a reasonable doubt that your client committed the crimes alleged. We are not in the business of apportioning blame. What is the exculpatory value of the classified information?"

Megan held out her hands. "I won't know it until I see it, Your Honor. All I know is that seven Somalis were holding two Americans hostage on the sailboat. My client negotiated with the Parker family to pay a ransom in exchange for the release of the hostages. The ransom was, in fact, paid. The government agreed to let the Somalis go per their agreement with the family. Then, minutes later, the shooting started. What I want to know is why? The other Somalis have made allegations about my client's motives. But their story doesn't square with the events. What's missing from the picture is what the Navy did immediately before the shooting. What decisions were made in the chain of command? And what actions were taken in response to those decisions? If the government precipitated the violence, the jury needs to know that when they assess my client's state of mind."

"Your Honor," interjected Clyde Barrington, "the government is not on trial here."

"You're quite right," the judge affirmed. "Still, Ms. Derrick has a point."

As the lawyers continued to spar, Vanessa watched them in disgust. The elaborate pageantry of the legal system seemed absurd in light of the simplicity of the crime. What did it matter what the Navy did or neglected to do, or what Ismail was thinking when he pulled the trigger? All that mattered were the bullets that shredded the bodies of the two people she was closest to in the world. She stared at Ismail again. *You did this to them, you son of a bitch! You and no one else!*

She felt a sudden burning in her throat, like she was about to vomit. She stood up and walked quickly out of the courtroom, her heels clicking on the polished marble floor. By the time she reached the restroom, the bile had stopped churning, but her heart continued to race. She sat down in a toilet stall and closed her eyes to block out the light, taking deep breaths until the sensation passed. *I don't think I can take five more months of this,* she thought.

After a while, she left the restroom and walked to the window at the end of the hall, looking out over the Norfolk skyline. She saw her reflection in the glass, the drawn look in her eyes. Before long, she heard footsteps behind her.

"Are you all right?" Curtis asked.

"I'm okay," she managed.

He stood there for a moment in silence, then spoke with a depth of feeling she had never heard before. "We're very different people, Vanessa. But my heart is broken, too."

It was her instinct to push him away, not to let him near the bloody mess of her pain. She had been that way since childhood, keeping people at bay. Why let them in when they were almost always a disappointment? But something in Curtis's tone drew her into the light. She turned around and saw that his arms were open to her. She hesitated, searching his face, and then stepped into his embrace. The empathy she felt was as inviting as it was unexpected. It wouldn't last—nothing ever did.

But, for a moment at least, she didn't have to stand on her own.

That afternoon, after they returned from the hearing, Vanessa took a drive into Annapolis. Quentin was working on strength exercises with his physical therapist—an event that usually sparked anger in him, both irrational and justified—and she needed space to cleanse her mind. She parked in the garage off Main Street and walked down the hill to the docks. A late-winter chill was in the air, but the clouds had parted and sunlight was streaming through.

She bought a latte from City Dock Coffee and followed Randall Street to the Naval Academy. She entered the campus by the main gate and strolled along King George Street to the river. Just beyond the Visitors' Center was a small patch of green space with a brick promenade. She took a seat on one of the benches and closed her eyes, allowing the sun to suffuse her skin with warmth.

Her heart was full of bitter sludge. She could feel it sloshing around inside, choking her with its stench. She hated the venom almost as much as she hated Ismail. In spite of everything the world had thrown at her, she had always managed to stay positive, find a goal, and fixate on it until the past disappeared around the bend. But the strategy wouldn't work this time. She had no ambitions within reach. She couldn't bring Quentin back if he wouldn't talk to her.

She couldn't redeem her marriage; Daniel was gone. She had never felt so tormented, so irredeemably lost.

It was then that she had an idea. She resisted it at first, thinking up all manner of excuses why it wouldn't accomplish anything. But the more she thought about it, the more it took root in her. It wasn't a panacea, but it was a place to start.

She left the Naval Academy and walked briskly around the circle. She saw the tall spire of the church in the distance. She hadn't been to mass since the funeral. She hadn't wanted to face the incessant questions, the endless condolences. It was easier just to stay away. Besides, she had never been much of a Catholic. She had converted when she married Daniel, but she had never met God in church. She attended mass because it was part of her routine. Confession, on the other hand, she had grown to cherish. It was a catharsis she now craved.

The door of the church was open when she tried it. She entered the sanctuary and looked around for one of the priests. She saw Father Minoli by the altar, tending to a display of votive candles. He was a gentle old fellow with a piercing wit and a deep reservoir of wisdom. He was also a longtime friend of the family and had presided over Daniel's funeral. She walked softly up the aisle beneath the Gothic arches and the starry sky and waited until he noticed her.

"Ah, Vanessa," he said, turning around. "It's so good to see you. How is Quentin?"

She looked into his kind eyes, framed by bushy eyebrows. "He's not doing so well," she replied, surprising herself with her transparency.

The priest looked at her with compassion. "I'm very sorry to hear that. Your mother-in-law told me the transition home has been rough."

She swallowed the lump in her throat. "I don't mean to bother you, but do you have time for a confession?"

"Of course," he said. "I'm always here for you."

She went to the confessional and took a seat in the box while the priest settled in on the other side of the partition. She organized her thoughts and crossed herself. "In the name of the Father, Son, and Holy Spirit, my last confession was in October before . . . all of this happened."

She didn't make it any further before the tears came. *Pull yourself together*, she commanded, exhausted of crying. *This is embarrassing.* But the sorrow refused to abate. For a moment she considered abandoning the confessional, but she wasn't a stranger here. She could never run far enough. With no place else to go, she spoke the truth.

"I've told this to no one, but I feel wrath in my heart. I feel it when I see the man who killed Daniel. I feel it when Quentin struggles to find the right words, when he stares out at the river at the boat he used to sail, when I see the sadness in his eyes. I'm afraid, Father. I don't know what will become of him. I feel despair. I don't know where to go for hope."

When she fell silent, she wiped her eyes and waited for the priest to respond. As the seconds multiplied, she wondered if he was asleep. Then she heard the whisper of his voice and realized he was praying. In time, he delivered his exhortation.

"My daughter, you are not alone. Remember our Blessed

Mother who watched her son suffer as you have watched Quentin. Consider the path she walked to forgive those who took his life. Remember the redemption that came about. And have faith that redemption is possible for Quentin and for you, however unlikely it may seem."

Father Minoli's words hit Vanessa in the gut. They were right and wrong at the same time. She mouthed the contrition, received the absolution, and left the church through the back entrance, walking down the path to the courtyard. The gardens were aglow in the afternoon sunlight. She strolled beneath the bare trees and wrestled with herself. She wanted redemption but not forgiveness. Mary was a saint. What she had accomplished wasn't possible for mere mortals.

The compromise came to Vanessa suddenly. It was possible that she could have one without the other. At least, as Yvonne said, it was worth a try. She checked her watch. It was morning in Melbourne. Ariadne would be awake.

She took out her iPhone and placed the call.

YASMIN

The Juba was a ghost snake in the night, the ripples in the moving water coruscating in the light of the moon like the scales of a black mamba. It was long after midnight, and the village was as quiet as the sky. The only sounds Yasmin could hear were the susurrations of the river, the chirping of frogs, and the lonesome calls of a nightjar somewhere in the black distance.

She stooped at the river's edge and filled her jug with fresh water, her thoughts alternating between worry and prayer. Fatuma had been in labor now for more than two and a half days, and the baby had yet to crown. She was a hardy young woman, the daughter of desert nomads, but even she had limits, and she was beginning to fade. Jamaad was at her bedside along with a midwife named Fiido from the village. Yasmin had offered to serve as Fiido's assistant. She was beyond exhausted, but her comfort was irrelevant. The only thing that mattered was keeping Fatuma and the child alive.

She walked quickly through the gate—unlocked for three nights now—and crossed the yard to the house. Fatuma was laboring in the living room surrounded by lanterns and incense, the mattress beneath her stained dark with blood. Yasmin placed the water beside Fiido, who dipped a towel into it and blotted Fatuma's forehead. The girl was lying on her side in the fetal position, her body trembling with muscle spasms, her hands clutching at her distended belly.

Yasmin sat down beside Jamaad and looked at Fatuma. The suffering in the girl's eyes was transparent. In the first twenty-fours hours, she had moved about and breathed with rhythm and talked through the pain like any mother about to give birth. By sunset on the second day, however, her movements had slowed, her eyes had lost focus, and her contractions had diminished until they vanished altogether. There was no question in Yasmin's mind. The baby's head was too large for the birth canal. They needed to get Fatuma to a hospital immediately. But Jamaad wouldn't hear of it. She had rejected the idea as soon as Yasmin raised it, heckling her for her lack of faith. "The doctor's knife would burn her womb," she had said. "God will bring the child when he is ready."

But the child didn't come. As the hours passed and darkness gave way to dawn, Fatuma stopped moving entirely. Yasmin felt the anger building inside of her. She wasn't trained in medicine, but Khadija had taught her all about childbirth, even inviting her to observe a delivery at the hospital in Medina. Yasmin had paid careful attention when Fiido performed the episiotomy, and she had seen the mistake. The incision Fiido made in Fatuma's perineum was clumsy and blunt, neither properly placed nor large enough to widen the cervix, not with all the scar tissue left over from Fatuma's circumcision. Yasmin wanted to say something about the scar tissue, to suggest a second cut with a different placement, but she knew Fiido wouldn't listen to her, and neither would Jamaad.

The circumcision was the problem, Yasmin knew, just as it was for many Somali mothers. It was an ancient practice, handed down from the Egyptians to the modern day because the culture demanded it. At once a purification ritual and a prophylaxis against fornication, nearly every Somali girl underwent the procedure in preadolescence, spreading her legs on a table in a clinic or on a rock in the bush, feeling the fire of the blade as it pared away her intimate flesh, and then the piercing of the needle—or the thorns if no needle was handy—as the circumciser sewed together her vagina, leaving a hole no larger than a pen for urine and menstrual discharge.

Yasmin was a rarity in Somalia—she had never been cut. But she had seen pictures of an infibulated vagina in her mother's medical books. In her mind, the cruelty of the practice was matched only by its senselessness. Circumcision offered no medicinal value to women. Yet its dangers were manifold—hemorrhaging, infection, septicemia, urinary blockage, complications with menstruation—and its consequences for society were devastating. It made childbirth a greater risk to a woman's health than war. After seventeen years in her mother's house, Yasmin hated the practice almost as much as Khadija, but not quite—Khadija had been circumcised.

When the sun rose above the windowsills, coloring the grim scene in the living room, Yasmin gathered the courage to confront Jamaad. "She needs a doctor," she said, trying to maintain a respectful tone. "The baby is stuck in the birth canal."

Jamaad frowned with displeasure. "What do you know about giving birth? I've had four children, all of them in my own house. Why are you worrying when you should be praying? You are behaving like a *kafir*—an unbeliever."

Yasmin bristled. Nothing irritated her more than ignorance masquerading as wisdom. "Why do we live in a house if not to keep out the heat and the wind? Why do we lock our gate if not to keep out thieves? God doesn't do these things for us. He gives us minds so we can do them for ourselves."

"Silence, foolish girl!" Jamaad ordered. "You speak of what you do not understand."

Yasmin turned to Fiido and saw the fear in the midwife's eyes. Jamaad was like queen mother in the village. But Yasmin was Najiib's wife, and that gave her a privilege that Fiido didn't have. She glanced at Fatuma lying pitifully on the bloody mattress and her anger boiled over.

"She needs medical attention!" she exclaimed. "It has been nearly three days, and the baby is not coming. This is *Najiib's* child. What will he think when I tell him you let his wife and son suffer?"

Now Yasmin's words struck home. Jamaad blinked once

and her expression became obsequious. "There is no need for that. We will take care of Fatuma, *inshallah*." She turned to Fiido. "Call Geelle. We will take her to the hospital at Marere. I will pay him for petrol."

The midwife nodded and took out her phone. Ten minutes later, Geelle—the only villager prosperous enough to own an SUV—pulled his battered Land Cruiser into the courtyard and opened the hatch while Jamaad, Fiido, and Yasmin lifted Fatuma on her mattress and carried her to the truck. Jamaad slid into the front seat, and Fiido and Yasmin climbed into the back with the water canister and a handful of towels.

The 120-kilometer drive to Marere was nearly as interminable as the labor itself. The road was little better than a camel track, and without air conditioning the Land Cruiser turned into a furnace in the sun. Yasmin helped Fiido blot the girl's skin, her lips moving in the silent rhythm of prayer: *Oh God who grants laughter and tears, who created male and female, who has promised a second creation, a resurrection of the faithful, please give Fatuma and the baby life and not death this day.*

But her ministrations didn't seem to help. By the time they crossed the river a few kilometers north of the town of Jilib, she could barely detect Fatuma's pulse. The girl's eyes were closed, her fingers as limp as wilted flowers. Fiido told Geelle to speed up, but he could only go so fast without risking an accident. In desperation, Yasmin stretched herself out on the floor and held the girl's hand as the truck jounced along, reciting the words of the Quran into her ear and willing her to live. But Fatuma didn't respond. She just lay there like a rag doll, lifeless, unbreathing.

At long last, they pulled up in front of the hospital. Jamaad jumped out and ran into the building, returning a minute later with a Somali woman in an orange *abaya* and eyeglasses—one of the doctors, Yasmin guessed. Geelle threw open the hatch of the SUV, and all of them lifted Fatuma's mattress and carried it into the hospital. The doctor summoned a few nurses and moved Fatuma onto a gurney, pushing her quickly into the operating room. Jamaad tried to accompany them, but a nurse stepped into her path and directed her to a waiting room down the hall.

Yasmin followed her with Fiido and Geelle, the bitter taste of dread in her mouth. She knew what was going to happen. It was inevitable now. She was furious with Jamaad for her pride and superstitions and with Fiido for her fear. Both of them were complicit in Fatuma's fate, as was the circumciser who had cut her as a child. But Yasmin wasn't as concerned about assigning blame as she was about Najiib. He was coming home any day now, expecting to meet his firstborn son. It would have been difficult enough to intro-duce him to a daughter—a possibility he had refused to consider. But to bring him a stillborn child? It would drive him mad with rage. He would give Jamaad a tongue-lashing, but she wouldn't bear the brunt of his fury—Yasmin would.

Before long, the doctor appeared again, her eyes liquid with sorrow. "I'm sorry," she said, shaking her head. "The girl didn't make it. Her baby also is dead."

Jamaad began to wail, and Yasmin buried her head in

her hands. She had spent the past three years in relative peace and safety, protected from the war by the remoteness of the village and from the famine by Najiib's largesse. She had concentrated on surviving, holding out hope that Ismail would come for her. Her safety, however, had always been contingent on Najiib's favor. She had disappointed him once—by failing to give him a son—but her beauty and Fatuma's pregnancy had shielded her from the fallout. Now with Fatuma and the child gone, she was completely exposed. All she had left to offer him was her body. It was a threadbare covering. He would tire of her eventually, and then he would discard her. Or perhaps he would remember how much he had hated her father, and he would kill her.

No, Yasmin told herself. *I won't let him. There is another way.* The time had come to take matters into her own hands. Even if the risk was great, she had to find a way to escape.

PAUL

The United Airlines flight from London touched down at Dulles airport a few minutes ahead of schedule. Paul gathered his duffel bag and backpack and shuffled off the plane, following the crowd of passengers to the immigration hall. He passed through passport control and customs without delay and hailed a taxi to Arlington. It was the first time he had been back on American soil since December.

The negotiation to secure the release of the American aid workers had been grueling, but the Somali kidnappers—some had taken to calling them "land-based pirates," though Paul considered the term an oxymoron—had played by the book. The cat-and-mouse game of demands, delays, threats, and obfuscation had ground ahead with the momentum of a millstone, slow but inexorable. There had been no surprises, no handoff to the Shabaab. The deal would have been done and the ransom delivered but for the last-minute decision by the authorities in Washington that the older of the hostages was suffering from a heart condition and required immediate medical attention.

Just like that, Paul and his team of negotiators had been pulled off the case and the job turned over to a squadron of Navy SEALs—the golden boys of DEVGRU, Paul was sure, though he couldn't confirm it. The SEALs had planned and executed the raid with extraordinary precision. They had parachuted into Somalia under the cover of darkness, converged on the bush camp where the aid workers were being held, killed a dozen pirates in a shootout, and carried the hostages to a Blackhawk helicopter for the trip back to Kenya. The operation had confirmed two things for Paul: first, that the SEALs were masters at what they were trained to do, and second, that even the masters require favorable conditions for a successful mission, conditions that were never present during the *Renaissance* hijacking.

Four months had passed since the shooting on the sailboat, but Paul had never stopped thinking about Ismail and the Parkers. In his flights of fancy, he imagined himself walking in Megan's footsteps, reading her case file, sitting in on her interviews, and attending every hearing from start to finish. But he couldn't do that. The dictates of law and professionalism required that the barrier between them remain impregnable. Paul was a government agent and a material witness. Megan was the government's nemesis and bound by the rules of confidentiality. To avoid a conflict of interest, their spheres had to remain separate until the jury delivered its verdict.

The taxi dropped Paul off outside his apartment

building—a brick and glass high-rise without a hint of personality. He lugged his bags into the lobby and took the
elevator to the tenth floor. His apartment was at the end
of the hall. He stopped on the threshold, struck by the
thought: *Is this really where I live?* It was a typical Beltway
flat—efficient but soulless, with two bedrooms, a bathroom, a living room, and a kitchen. Its crowning feature was
a miniature terrace with a view of the Kennedy Center across
the Potomac River. He heard Megan's words echoing in his
head: *This place is a dump.* He shrugged. *Fair enough, but
what other option do I have?*

He tossed his bags on the couch and went to the piano
by the window, sitting down on the bench and closing his
eyes. Usually when he did this a song came to him: Gershwin
if he was cheerful, Billy Joel if he was nostalgic, Chopin if he
was melancholy, and so on. This time, however, he drew a
blank. It wasn't that the moment lacked a soundtrack, rather
that he was too distracted to think of one.

He had something in his duffel bag that he had to
deliver, something the Bureau's legal attaché in Nairobi
had given him before he left Kenya. He had almost refused,
inventing an excuse to avoid seeing her again, but his mouth
hadn't formed the words. Before he knew it, the wooden
chest was in his hands and the memory of Vanessa's face
seared on his conscience.

Better to get it over with, he thought. *It's not going to get
any easier.*

He extracted the chest from his bag and took the elevator to the garage. His Audi A5 coupe was in his parking

space, just as he'd left it. He climbed in and punched her address into the GPS system, then sped out of the lot and onto the George Washington Parkway. It was a Sunday afternoon and the roads were blissfully free of gridlock. He took the Arland Williams Memorial Bridge into DC and headed east, crossing the Anacostia River and merging onto Interstate 295 to Maryland. His navigation system said the drive to Annapolis would take forty minutes.

He planned to make it in thirty.

Half an hour later, he turned onto Norwood Road and counted mailboxes. He found her house at the end of the street and pulled up beside a row of Tuscan pines. *Now this is a home*, he thought, taking in the stately Cape Cod and the verdant grounds all around. He locked his car and walked down the cobblestone drive to the grape arbor and the front porch, carrying the chest in one hand. The sun was bright in a sky the color of blue jay feathers, and the air carried the first hint of spring.

He knocked twice and prepared himself for an awkward greeting. He hoped the visit would be brief, but he wasn't about to control the conversation. He was at her mercy. He had failed her and her family in a spectacular way. It was a debt he could never repay.

He heard the deadbolt retract, watched the door swing open, and then she was there, staring back at him. She was wearing white jeans and a turquoise top that brought out the green in her eyes.

"Paul," she said quizzically, leaving the obvious un-stated: *What are you doing here?*

A golden retriever skittered around her feet, its tail wag-ging. He knelt down and scratched the dog behind the ears, grateful for the distraction.

"That's Skipper," she explained, a touch softer. "He's everybody's friend."

"I should have called first," he said, standing up again. "I just got back into the country." He looked into her eyes. "I have something that belongs to you."

When he held out the chest, she inhaled sharply. "Is that . . . ?"

He nodded. "It was Daniel's."

She took it from him and turned it over slowly, rubbing her thumb across the brass engraving plate. Paul knew the inscription by heart. It read:

To my son, Daniel, who grew up dreaming of life
on the Golden Hinde. May you find fair wind
and following seas. Bon voyage. —Dad

"It's from Zanzibar," she explained. "His father gave it to him before they cast off."

She lifted the lid with trepidation, as if she were opening Daniel's casket. A stack of blank paper and a pen were on the bottom beneath handwritten pages folded and standing on edge. Paul hadn't read them out of respect, but he was sure the FBI agents who had combed over the *Renaissance* had examined them thoroughly before declaring them immaterial to the investigation.

She fingered the pages, lost in thought. Then she realized that Paul was still standing on the porch. She gave him a sheepish look. "I'm sorry. Please come in."

He trailed her through the foyer and into the spacious living room. The inside of the house was as manicured as the outside, balancing the earth tones of the furniture and floor with splashes of color in the artwork on the walls. There were windows all around. The house was like a prism, drawing in the light. Yet there was something missing from the scene. It was too quiet.

"Would you like coffee?" Vanessa asked, placing the chest on the island.

"That's kind of you," he replied. "But I've had enough caffeine in the past few months to keep me awake for the rest of my life."

She gestured toward the couch and took a seat on a wingback chair. "You were out of the country?" she asked, making conversation.

"Kenya," he replied, contemplating whether to elaborate. *Screw it*, he thought. *She can handle it.* "I don't know if you saw the story of the aid workers taken into Somalia."

She looked away and played with her hands. "You got them out."

He shook his head. "The SEALs did."

She winced painfully, thinking no doubt of what might have been. For an extended moment, she wavered on the edge of a decision, struggling with her emotions. He saw the question coming a mile away. He couldn't avoid it. She had asked it once before.

"Tell me what happened out there, Paul. Please. I need to know."

He took a breath, wrestling with the conflict between his personal feelings and professional obligations. A part of him wanted to tell her everything—Ismail's promise on the RHIB, the faith he had invested in the pirate, Redman's contrary instinct, the creep of the *Gettysburg*, closing the distance to the sailboat, the pirates' delay in releasing the hostages, his sense that something had shifted between Ismail and his men, the last explosive exchange over the radio, and Redman's fateful decision to send in the small boats. But until the trial, he was sworn to secrecy. Besides, what purpose would his story really serve? It wouldn't give her closure. It wouldn't explain what had happened on the sailboat. That was what she ultimately wanted to know. Anything less would only increase her misery.

"There are some things I can't say right now," he told her. "But I'll be candid. I'm not satisfied with what we know. Something happened out there, something only the people who were on the sailboat can explain."

Her eyes glistened with moisture. "You mean Quentin."

He saw the danger in the question—the trip wire that could send her spiraling into self-recrimination. He stepped over it gently. "There were others there, too."

She fidgeted in her seat, her distress plain. "Have you lost hostages before?"

"Three of them," he said. "I could tell you their names, what they looked like, who their families were. I live with them every day."

"Did it always happen the same way?"

He answered her implicit question. "In the other scenarios, the kidnappers were jihadists. They wanted to make a statement. This case is different. I don't think ideology has anything to do with it."

She stood from her chair and went to the window, staring out at the yard. Seconds passed in silence, and then she looked at him again. "Why is your sister representing him?"

He spoke candidly. "Because I asked her to."

"Why?" Vanessa asked softly.

It was the other unavoidable question. He gave her an honest answer. "I can't tell you how awful I feel about what happened. You deserve justice. Your family deserves justice. Whatever Ismail did, he should be punished for it. That's the government's job. But there are flaws in the system. People in power, even good people, sometimes allow their pride to get in the way of the truth. Someone needs to make sure that doesn't happen. That's where Megan comes in."

Vanessa's face was a picture of damaged grace. "I suppose I can accept that," she said. Then she brought the conversation to a close. "I appreciate you coming all this way. It was kind of you to bring back the chest."

"Of course," he replied, walking with her toward the door. He wanted to inquire about Quentin, but he had the sense that the timing was wrong, that it was too personal a subject at such a fragile moment. He decided to call Mary

Patterson from the car.

It was then that he noticed the piano standing in the corner. He stopped in his tracks. "That's a Bösendorfer. I've never seen one outside a concert hall."

"It is," she confirmed, sounding surprised. "Do you play?"

He nodded and walked toward the instrument, admiring the craftsmanship. He saw the sheet music arrayed upon the stand. It was Chopin's Nocturne in E Flat Minor, Op. 9, No. 2. "That's one of the loveliest pieces ever written for the piano," he said with a trace of a smile. "Every time I play it I wonder if it came from another world."

He glanced at Vanessa and was taken aback by her reaction. All of her guardedness was gone. She stood there looking at him until the silence became uncomfortable. Then she spoke words he never expected to hear: "Will you play it for me? I would love to hear it again."

For a time he didn't move, just stared back at her, bewildered by the feelings swirling inside of him. It wasn't the request, touching as it was. It was the intimate way she had asked it, the tenderness in her voice, the way the light fell on her face, lifting the veil of her pain and revealing the woman behind it. He wasn't prepared for the beauty he saw in her. He didn't want to look away.

"I'd be honored," he finally said. He took a seat on the bench and extended his hands above the keyboard. To his astonishment, he felt them trembling. He couldn't remember the last time he had been nervous. Was it the piano? The nocturne? The way Vanessa was looking at him? He closed his eyes and shut all of it out, the way his mother had taught him to do when he was a boy. It was her gift to him, this alchemist's instrument, these eighty-eight notes that could take the slugs of lead thrown by the world and turn them into nuggets of gold. The piano had been his escape in the darkest days after the killings. It had spoken for him when he had no words to say.

He rested his fingers on the keys and began to play. The nocturne transported him, as it always did, giving him the sense that he was floating through the clouds, liberated from all constraint. But the Bösendorfer wasn't a passive partner. It added a crystalline clarity to the register, a featherlight touch to the action—especially in the trills and runs—that elevated the experience into a new realm. For four minutes, it was like he was somewhere else, somewhere perfect, where Daniel Parker was alive again, and Quentin was whole, and Vanessa's heart wasn't shattered in a thousand pieces, and Megan wasn't driving herself into oblivion to save her clients from Kyle's fate, and he wasn't so lonely, a failure at everything that mattered most.

When he struck the last note, he opened his eyes and saw Vanessa's tears. Then he saw something that took his breath away. Quentin was standing there beside her, watching him play. He had never seen the boy up close. He had his mother's upturned nose and rounded chin, the shape and symmetry of her eyes, but his hair was darker and his irises were hazel, not green. He walked toward the piano, a slight hitch in his step, and put his hand on the case.

"You play well," he said evenly. "I am . . . impressed.

What is . . . your name?"

Paul stood and offered his hand in greeting. "I'm Paul. It's nice to meet you."

The boy stared at him in puzzlement, then his eyes fell, as if he was thinking. At last he looked up again. "You were there . . . weren't you? I recognize . . . your voice."

Paul nodded. "Yes."

The boy took his hand and shook it firmly. "Thank you. I wish . . . my dad could be here . . . to thank you, too."

Paul heard Vanessa crying softly behind her son. Her hand was on her lips and she was staring at the floor. He blinked back his own tears. He couldn't recall a time when he had been so moved. "You're welcome," he managed, not knowing what else to say.

"May I?" Quentin asked, gesturing at the piano.

"Of course," Paul said, stepping aside and allowing the boy to take a seat. He looked at Vanessa and saw the wonderment on her face. It came to him that this was the first time Quentin had played since the shooting. *My God*, he thought. *Let him remember. Let his notes be true.*

And they were. Every single one. Quentin played the nocturne in his own way. He was a genius, his mastery of the keyboard far superior to Paul's own. The longer he played, the more expression he put into the music. At the end, when the long run of sixteenth notes took him into the upper part of the register, his face transformed and he began to smile in a lopsided way. It was like a light had come on inside of him. He looked different, as if his spirit had awakened from sleep.

After the last note was played, he turned to his mother

and said, "Mom, I can still . . . do it. I haven't forgotten . . . how to play."

Vanessa started to laugh and cry at the same time. She walked toward the bench and wrapped her arms around him. "I know, honey," she whispered. "It's beautiful."

The moment was so rich with private emotion that Paul had to look away. He wandered across the living room to the glass doors that led out to the deck, taking in the yard and the pool and the forest and the boat dock and the river glittering in the sun. Soon he heard Quentin begin another nocturne—"Clair de Lune" by Debussy. As the notes filled the air with their inimitable grace, the thought came to him: *Daniel, wherever you are, I hope you can hear this.*

VANESSA

When she closed the door behind Paul, Vanessa felt like she was walking on water. Quentin had moved on to Grieg's magisterial *Notturno*, a piece she loved for its melodic texture and technical virtuosity. His touch wasn't as flawless as it used to be—there were places in the rapid trills where his rhythm was slightly out of joint—but the imperfections didn't matter. The sound was miraculous to her ears.

She walked slowly into the living room, hoping to preserve the moment, but Quentin was so focused on the keys that he didn't notice her. She took a seat on the Belgian wingback and watched him from across the room. The passion in his eyes was almost as intoxicating to her as his proficiency. It had been years since he had played with such feeling. It was like he was twelve again, taking lessons twice a week and devoting every minute he wasn't in school or on a sailboat to studying the great composers. The piano had been his first love, even before the sea. To see him rediscover it—especially now with his future hanging in the balance—was almost too wonderful for Vanessa to behold.

When the song ended, she clapped softly and dried her eyes. "You play so well. Ariadne is going to love listening to you."

Quentin regarded her thoughtfully. "Would you like . . . to join me?"

The question caught Vanessa off guard. It wasn't that she hadn't considered it—as he played she had eyed the Bissolotti longingly, but she hadn't wanted to impose. "We don't have much time," she said, checking her watch. "Her flight lands in an hour."

"'Beau Soir,'" he insisted. "It will take only . . . three minutes."

"An appropriate choice," she said with a smile. *How beautiful an evening this is going to be.* She walked to the violin and placed the instrument beneath her chin. "Whenever you're ready."

He met her eyes and nodded once. Then he began to play.

The international arrivals hall at Dulles airport was bland, boxy, and boring, but Quentin wasn't paying attention. He stood just behind the barricade, his hands in the pockets of his leather jacket, his weight distributed evenly between his sneakers, and a sloppy grin on his face. Vanessa stood beside him, feeling giddy. Something had happened inside of him, something of seismic significance. Looking at him now, she barely recognized the depressive curmudgeon she had lived with for nearly a month. *Paul Derrick*, she thought in amazement. *Who would have thought that he would bring us such a gift?*

At the same time, she felt slightly anxious. She had spoken with Ariadne and her mother at length, making sure the girl understood what she was getting into. She had described Quentin's injuries, given her a primer on amnesia, and outlined his ongoing therapy, all in an attempt to temper her expectations. But Ariadne hadn't hesitated. As she put it, the "medical gene" was in her DNA—her father and grandfather were anesthesiologists, and her uncle was a chiropractor. She guessed that she would end up in medical school eventually, though she was in no rush to decide. To Vanessa, Ariadne's self-assurance and maturity were a good omen, but they weren't a guarantee. The girl had her whole life ahead of her. Was it really possible that she could still love Quentin in spite of his disabilities?

Vanessa watched the steady stream of passengers exiting the customs area, looking for Ariadne's face. Quentin was the first to see her. He called out to her, and she turned toward him with a brilliant smile, dragging her suitcase around the barrier to meet him. She threw her arms around him and held him tightly, kissing his cheek. Then she turned to Vanessa and gave her a spontaneous hug. In an instant, Vanessa confirmed three things about her: she was a spark plug; she was her own woman; and she was real. Her outfit was as cute as she was—a formfitting pink sweatshirt and skinny jeans. But she wore almost no makeup, and her long golden hair was pulled back in a clip.

"Thanks so much for bringing me over, Mrs. Parker," she said, her accent adding a mellifluous timbre to her words. "I'm so excited to be here."

"We're delighted to have you," Vanessa replied, liking the girl immediately. "And please, call me Vanessa. Mrs. Parker is Quentin's grandmother."

She led the way out of the terminal and down the walkway to the parking garage, listening to Quentin and Ariadne talk like they had known each other their whole lives. If the girl cared about his halting speech, she didn't show it. She picked up the cadence naturally, modulating her own words to match his rhythm. The effect she had on him was mesmerizing. She drew him out of his shell, and he started to speak with more confidence. She was affectionate without being clingy, holding his arm loosely and resting her head on his shoulder in a way that was almost sisterly. *Maybe Yvonne was right,* Vanessa thought. *Maybe Ariadne will help him find his way into the future.*

That evening after the teenagers turned in—Quentin in his bedroom upstairs and Ariadne in the guest quarters— Vanessa poured a glass of wine and took the Zanzibar chest to her favorite chair. She was exhausted from a day of surprises, but her soul felt lighter than it had since the shooting. She had no idea what Daniel had written in the folded pages, but whatever it was she could handle it. Her son was no longer dead to the world. He was coming back to life.

The chest was heavier than she remembered. The wood was a dark red-brown—somewhere between walnut and rosewood. She placed it in her lap and opened the lid, bracing herself as she unfolded the pages. She saw the familiar salutation—*Dearest V*—and the date scrawled at the top—*November 7, 2011*. Her heart clutched in her chest. He had written this on the same day he wrote her the letter about La Digue. She glanced at the second page and saw the blank space at the bottom where his signature would have gone. Her mind raced with speculations. If he stopped writing in midstream, why didn't he discard it? There was only one reason to keep the letter—he meant to finish it.

She returned to the first page, her heart galloping in her chest. *I can do this*, she thought. *I can get through this*. She began to read.

> *Dearest V:*
>
> *Is love like the body? Does it begin to die the day it is born? Is it like the breath of transcendence you feel when the Bissolotti is in your hands—evanescent, a chasing after the wind? Were we fools when we put on our rings, when we made our vows and pledged our lives to one another, when we spoke of a fidelity that would endure to the grave? Is every married person a fool? These are the questions that rattle around in my head when all I can see is water and sky and white sails. Maybe I have too much time to think. Perhaps*

the silence is driving me crazy. Or maybe not. Perhaps it's brought me back to sanity.

Why are we such strivers, you and I? What have we gained by the endless hours of our toil? What have we been trying to prove? That we can master our own universe, control our own destinies, rise above the tide of mediocrity we see all around us? We have a beautiful house, a vacation property, advanced degrees, and enough money to live as comfortably as any family needs. Yet what good is any of it if we're miles apart in our hearts?

I take responsibility for those miles. I didn't have a clue who I was when I met you, or when I said "I do," or when we welcomed Quentin into the world. I didn't know what love would require of me. I pretended to understand it, put it in all sorts of fancy philosophical terms, but when it came down to the dirty diapers and the sleepless nights and your emotional needs, I couldn't handle it. I followed in my father's footsteps, working hard and providing. That was my mantra, my excuse to embrace the rat race I told you I hated. I became a slave to a necessity I had invented—a slave by choice—all because I didn't know how to give.

Where do we go from here? I've been wondering that, too. Does it make any sense to talk about beginning again when so much water has passed under the bridge? What do we do with our history, with our sins? Father Minoli would say that we confess them and

*receive absolution. Maybe it's that simple with God,
I don't know, but it isn't simple with human beings.
Nothing is ever really washed away. Our memories
bind us to our pain, our regret, our failures, and those
of everyone else who has hurt us. What does contrition
really mean in a world full of scars? Is it even possible
for one person to forgive another for the hurts he has
caused?*

*If it is, I'd like to tell you that I'm sorry. For
everything.*

Vanessa closed her eyes and allowed the letter to fall
from her hands. She breathed in the stillness, giving the
grief its place, and then she stood and went to the patio
door, slipping out into the night. The air was cold but not
bitter, and the stars were out in force, twinkling at her
across the infinite distance. She followed the path lights
down to the dock. The wood planking creaked beneath her
feet as she strolled to the end and sat down, dangling her
legs toward the water. The lamps of the Naval Academy
Bridge glittered like a necklace in the dark.

She let her mind move with the current, ignoring the
chill needling her skin. She saw her past like a river behind
her—the chutes and narrows of childhood, the rapids of
marriage and parenting, and the cataracts of the past few
years, culminating in the shooting. She pictured Quentin
asleep in his bed and Ariadne in hers. She remembered the
laughter they had shared, the love they couldn't hide even
if they tried. She shook her head and put her thoughts into

words, speaking them out loud on the off chance that some-where he might be listening.

"I don't have the answers," she said softly. "But I'm sorry, too."

V

PROOF OF LIFE

We know what dark persuasions
dwell in the soul of man;
for we are closer to him
than his jugular vein.

MEGAN

MOGADISHU, SOMALIA
March 20, 2012

From a height of five thousand feet, the Somali coast looked burnt yellow and bone straight, its scarred hills and sandy swales spilling down into the trackless blue of the Indian Ocean. Megan watched out the window of the vintage DC-9 as the plane descended toward Mogadishu. She had put the trip together at the last minute with assistance from her journalist friend in Nairobi. She had never intended to set foot on Somali soil. It was one of the most dangerous countries in the world and no place for an American woman traveling alone. But Mahamoud had given her no choice.

It had taken her a month to reach him on the mobile number Ismail had provided. Apparently, he had been traveling, putting together the financing for a new hotel venture, and he had left his Somali phone at home. After some cajoling, he had suggested they meet in Mombasa, which was fine with her. She had always wanted to visit the seaside town. But then his plans had changed while she was still in the air, and he had returned to Mogadishu early. She had received the text message when she landed in Nairobi. It was unwelcome news, but fitting in a way. Ismail's life was on the line in her country. It was only fair that she be willing to risk her life in his.

The ground rose up to meet the plane, and then, with a shudder, they were down. As they taxied to the terminal, Megan turned on her iPhone and tried to connect to a network. Her carrier had assured her that she would be able to roam on her American SIM card. It was strange— Somalia didn't have a US embassy, but its telecom system was compatible with her phone. Then again, she thought, in this globalizing world, technology was the new diplomacy.

When her phone didn't connect right away, she selected a network manually. She tried to text Mahamoud, but the message didn't go through. After three more attempts, she tried calling him, but the line didn't connect. *So much for worldwide coverage.* She looked out the window at the tall fences and razor wire surrounding the runway. Beyond the fences were thickets of green scrub and bronze bluffs that led down to the sea. She saw a trio of white UN planes on the tarmac and a drab-green African Union personnel carrier driving along a perimeter road. The airport was located on a heavily guarded military base operated by AMISOM—the African Union Mission to Somalia. It was the safest place in the country. Outside the base, all bets were off.

Suddenly, her iPhone chirped. She read the text message on the screen: Ku soo dhowow SOMALINET lambarkaagu waa 25297260709. Please call 111 for assistance. She debated with herself, then dialed the help line. A man answered. He spoke to her briefly in halting English—just long enough to ask her where she was from—and then he hung up abruptly. Seconds later, her phone rang. She took the call as the plane stopped outside the small terminal.

"Your phone is working now," said a male voice in impeccable English. "Welcome to Somalia. You are from America, is that right?"

The question raised a red flag in her mind, but she needed her phone to work. "I have a US SIM card. I was told it wouldn't be a problem."

"Of course," said the voice. "Where are you staying? At the airport or in town?"

"Why does that matter?" she asked with a growing sense of unease.

The man persisted. "I'm just trying to have a friendly conversation. What kind of work do you do? Are you with a private contractor or the government?"

What the hell is this? she thought. She scratched the microphone on her jeans and said, "You're breaking up." Then she ended the call and turned off the phone.

She took a deep breath and tried to slow her hammering heart. She remembered an article she had read on the Internet about the security situation in Mogadishu. While the Shabaab had abandoned their bases in late 2011, they hadn't really left the city. Instead, they had adapted into a terrorist organization specializing in assassination and kidnapping. She felt a stab of dread. *I bet the guy I just talked to was with Shabaab intelligence. Welcome to Somalia, indeed.*

She wrapped a scarf over her head in keeping with the local custom and followed the line of passengers—all Somalis—down the ramp and across the tarmac to the terminal. The sky was tropical blue, the air balmy and redolent of the sea. She saw waves breaking on the shore not far away.

"Ms. Derrick," said an African man in a loose-fitting shirt and baggy pants. "I'm Manny with SKA. Come with me."

She nodded, grateful that the logistics company had agreed to meet her planeside. The Kenyan journalist had outlined her accommodation options in Mogadishu—three compounds within the AMISOM base and two guesthouses just outside the walls. Megan had gone with SKA because they operated the airport and offered en suite security arrangements for trips into town.

She trailed Manny into the chaotic terminal building. There seemed to be little order to the immigration process. Some passengers were milling around, talking on mobile phones. Others were sitting on benches or standing by the wall, as if waiting for something. The rest had formed haphazard queues behind a row of booths manned by officials stamping passports. Manny took Megan into a room just off the arrivals hall. A portly Somali man asked for her passport and examined it with care.

"Why are you here?" he asked, staring at her as if she were a mental patient.

"I am meeting a friend," she answered, following the advice of the journalist to be minimalist in sharing information with anyone in Somalia.

"She is staying with you?" the man said, and Manny nodded. "Please make sure she doesn't do anything foolish." He handed Megan's passport back and dismissed them with a wave.

After purchasing a visa at one of the immigration booths, Megan followed Manny out of the terminal and across a parking lot thronged with vehicles and people. A number of Somali men eyed her strangely, but the women looked away. Manny directed her to a minibus and opened the sliding door.

"What did he mean by making sure I didn't do anything foolish?" she asked, taking a seat.

"You are an American woman," Manny replied. "That means you are a target. They don't want an incident. It's bad press."

She smiled grimly and looked out the window as they pulled out of the lot. "Can I borrow your phone? I need to make a call."

Manny handed her his mobile, and she punched in Mahamoud's number. Ismail's uncle answered on the first ring. "What happened to your phone?" he asked.

"It isn't working."

"I will get you a new one. We can meet in one hour. I will tell Manny the location."

"Where?" she asked, feeling a sliver of apprehension. *And how do you know Manny?*

But Mahamoud didn't answer. He had already hung up.

❋

In contrast to the UN compound in Dadaab, the SKA facility had no trees, no flowers, and no landscaping. It reminded Megan of military barracks without artillery and soldiers. The structures were mostly white shipping containers standing on concrete blocks, with cutout windows and doors and air-conditioning units attached to the roof. She checked in at the office and left her bag in her room—a spartan affair with a single bed, a small bureau, a TV, and a writing desk. Then she went to the gate and waited for Manny, who had promised to pick her up again after running an errand.

Eventually, she saw the minibus and climbed in. "Where are we headed?" she asked.

"To a place near the beach," Manny replied nebulously. "It's not far away."

She frowned. "How did Mahamoud get there? He lives in town."

"He knows everyone," Manny replied. "He goes where he likes."

She sat back and took in her surroundings. The compound was located on a dirt road that circled the airport like a running track. They rounded the end of the runway and passed a graveyard of rusting vehicles, many mutilated by explosives. After a while, they made a turn and climbed a hill through a dense thicket of scrub. When they emerged from the brush, Megan saw the blue of the ocean stretching out before her. A man was standing at the top of the hill, holding two folding chairs. He was tall and imposing with a henna-dyed beard and dark sunglasses.

Manny pulled to a stop. "I will wait here," he said.

When Megan climbed out, the man with the sunglasses gave her a thin smile. "I am Mahamoud. You did not bring a recording device?"

She shook her head. It was one of the ground rules he had established before the meeting.

"Good, because this conversation is not happening. I don't know you and you don't know me. I am only here because of my regard for Ismail and his father." He held out his hand. "Come. There is a place nearby where we can talk."

He led her across a scree of rocks and sand to a coral jetty that jutted out into the sea. He opened the folding chairs and gestured for her to take a seat. "If we had met in Mombasa, I could have offered you tea. Here the view will have to do."

"It's beautiful," Megan said, watching the waves crash upon the jetty, sending spray high into the air. "I can't say I expected it."

He nodded. "You are American. When you think of Somalia, you think of Black Hawk Down and pirates and starving babies and al-Shabaab. Your perspective is incomplete."

An interesting entrée, she thought. "What's missing from the picture?"

Mahamoud looked at her frankly. "We are—the ordinary people of Somalia. And our past. This city was once the jewel of the Indian Ocean. We had restaurants and cinemas and sports facilities and great buildings that stood for hundreds of years. Someday it will be a jewel again."

She narrowed her eyes. "I don't mean to be blunt, but it's hard to see much hope in the news."

He shifted in his seat. "No, the media only cares when a bomb goes off. They don't talk about children playing in the streets, teachers training them in English and computer skills, people coming home from the diaspora and starting businesses. Mogadishu is like a phoenix rising from the ashes."

"I talked with Farah in Minneapolis. He wasn't so sanguine."

Mahamoud raised his eyebrows. "Farah has made his home in the United States. He will not build this country's future. It is people like my brother, Adan, who will build it."

She made her objection as delicately as she could. "But Adan is dead, killed by the same madmen blowing themselves up in the streets."

Mahamoud gave her a sagacious look. "Adan took a great risk, but his death was a kind of victory. He said it many times. Evil can't be defeated until it is brought into the light. The attack on his school unmasked the Shabaab more effectively than any argument he could make."

"I doubt his wife and children see it that way," Megan replied quietly.

Mahamoud stared out at the sea. When he spoke again, his tone was more personal. "Every victory has a cost. That is the lesson of history. No cause is vindicated without sacrifice. And sometimes—as much as it hurts us—we have to pay the price with blood."

Megan grimaced. *If you asked the militants who killed Adan, I bet they would say the same thing.* But she kept her thoughts to herself. "Khadija came to you after the attack.

What did you tell her?"

"I told her to leave the country immediately. She had cousins in Nairobi. She could stay with them and claim asylum as she and Adan had done when the war began. I also told her not to search for the children. Parents who try to negotiate with the Shabaab almost always end up dead." He paused. "I never heard from her again. I don't know what happened to her."

Megan watched his face as she disclosed the news. "She's in Kenya. I met with her last month."

His mouth went slack in astonishment. "Khadija is alive?"

"She's a nurse in Dadaab," Megan explained and filled him in on the details.

He held out his hands. "I suppose I'm not surprised. Her father never thought much of me."

"Did you try to find the children?" Megan asked.

Mahamoud nodded. "Ismail and Yusuf were easy enough to trace. They joined a unit that went south to Kismayo and fought Hizbul Islam for control of the port. After that, the Shabaab massed its troops outside Mogadishu and mounted an offensive during the holy month of Ramadan. Yusuf was killed in the fighting. That's when Ismail made his escape."

Megan leaned forward in her chair. "Do you know where he went after that?"

"Yes," Mahamoud said matter-of-factly. "He came to me."

She smiled. *I was hoping you would say that.* "Tell me about it."

He recounted the tale without embellishment. Ismail had come to him in the night, evading his guards and vaulting over the wall around his hotel. Mahamoud had awoken to a soft knock at the door of his cottage. With the fighting going on in the city, he had expected to see his security chief, but instead Ismail had stumbled in, bedraggled, bloodstained, and mumbling incoherently about Yusuf. Mahamoud had cleaned him up, calmed him down, and extracted bits and pieces of the story.

Their unit had made an advance against AMISOM's position on Maka al Mukarama Road, the artery connecting the airport to the city. They had faced off against tanks, armed only with mortars and Kalashnikovs. Ismail had taken shelter behind a jeep, trying to shield Yusuf from the carnage. But one of the tank rounds had landed close to their hiding place. Ismail had blacked out from shock. When he awoke, he found his brother lying beside him, his head nearly gone.

As Megan listened, she tried to keep Ismail's story separate from her own, but she found it impossible. When she pictured Yusuf, she saw Kyle instead. She turned away from Mahamoud and gazed out at the sea, enraged at a world that devoured children with impunity. She felt a newfound solidarity with Ismail. She embraced the humanity of it even as she saw the risk it posed. To save him from the needle, she had to remain objective. And she would. She would contain her emotions. But she would fight for him like she had never fought before.

"What did you do after you took him in?" she asked.

"He stayed with me three days," Mahamoud answered.

"I told him about his mother and gave him clothes and a cell phone. Then I drove him out of the city. There was only one place I thought would be safe. There is a camp for internally displaced people about twenty kilometers from here run by Dr. Hawa Abdi and her daughters. I left him there with money for a bus ticket to Kenya."

"Did you hear from him again?"

Mahamoud shook his head slowly. "Not until I received your call."

For the first time, she heard a false note in his voice. "He never tried to contact you?" she persisted, eyeing him carefully.

His expression remained opaque. "No."

"Do you have any idea how or why he would have gotten into piracy?"

"When he came to me, he was damaged. I don't know what was going on in his mind."

I think you're lying to me, but I have no way to prove it. "Is there anyone else who might know?"

Mahamoud shrugged. "Perhaps someone at Hawa Abdi's place. They have an office in Nairobi. You could call them when you get back."

Megan took a slow breath, conscious of the gamble she was about to make. "You said the village is only twenty kilometers away. Can you take me there?"

He laughed wryly. "My security team would never agree to it."

"Why is that?"

He took off his sunglasses and gave her a piercing look.

"Ms. Derrick, the revival I told you about is happening only in Mogadishu. The Shabaab still rules the rural areas. If you show your face outside the city, you will have forty-five minutes at most before they come for you."

Memories cascaded through Megan's mind—the aid workers captured in Dadaab and the SEAL mission that freed them; the stranger who called her on the plane and interrogated her about her plans; the Internet video she had seen of Nick Berg's beheading in Iraq. She didn't doubt that Mahamoud was right about the danger. But she couldn't go home without the truth. Ismail was rotting in a cell, on trial for capital murder. If he joined the pirates purely for the money, the jury would probably deliver him to the executioner. But if he was lured or coerced in some way, they might show him mercy.

"Is there anyone who can take me there safely?" she asked.

Mahamoud looked at her as if she were insane. "You can't be serious."

She didn't blink, just stared back at him.

Eventually, he sighed. "If you want to go to Afgooye, talk to AMISOM."

YASMIN

March 21, 2012

Najiib came home on the dusty road two weeks after Fatuma and the baby died. The villagers greeted him with shouts and waves as his technical meandered through the streets, not because they loved him, but because they knew what he could do to them if he decided they were subversive. If his men caught them chewing *qat* or smoking cigarettes or listening to Western music or a soccer game on the radio, they would be beaten with a bullwhip. If their wives or mothers or daughters went outside without a head covering, they would be arrested and flogged. If they were accused of adultery or promiscuity, they would be stoned to death. If a spy reported that they had disparaged the Shabaab, they would be executed without trial. If they were caught conspiring with the government, they would be beheaded in public. The villagers cheered Najiib because his power over them was absolute.

Yasmin was in the kitchen preparing lunch when she heard the noise. It was faint at first, a murmur wafting along on the breeze. As the seconds passed, however, it increased in volume and merged with the sound of an engine and squealing brakes. *He's here*, Yasmin thought, running to her room and putting on her hijab and veil. After delivering a plate of rice and chutney to Jamaad, she walked to the gate, reciting the names of God in her mind to ward off the dread: *Allah, ar-Rahman (the Compassionate), ar-Rahim (the Merciful), al-Malik (the Ruler), al-Quddus (the Pure)* . . .

Then he was there, the technical nosing into the yard, his men—four of them this time—in combat fatigues, holding their guns skyward, their faces swaddled with scarves so that only their eyes were showing. Najiib was sitting in the driver's seat dressed in a crisp white shirt and sunglasses, his scarf as black as the desert on a moonless night. She went around to his door and stood in silence. She never spoke to him unless he initiated the conversation. The one time she had tried he had slapped her for disturbing his thinking, leaving her cheek bruised for a week.

He opened the door and stepped out, undoing his scarf and taking off his sunglasses. He was a handsome man with a hawk nose, thoughtful eyes, and a beard that he trimmed obsessively. *"As-salamu alaykum,"* he said as his men spilled out of the truck and went about securing the property. He turned to Jamaad, who had abandoned her food and walked halfway into the yard. "Is Fatuma inside?"

Yasmin let Jamaad handle the explanation. She had encouraged her to tell him about Fatuma ahead of time, but Jamaad had disagreed, arguing that he would handle the news better in person.

Jamaad stammered for a moment and then blurted out a half-truth: "There was a problem with the pregnancy. Fiido was here. We did everything we could. We took Fatuma to the hospital in Marere, but she and the baby died."

For a long time Najiib stood rooted in place. Then he turned away and grabbed his gun from the truck. He walked out the gate, taking the path down to the river. Yasmin didn't move. She was an expert at reading his moods. She knew that anything she did while he was in such a state would be interpreted as a provocation. Jamaad was not so savvy. She followed in Najiib's footsteps, recounting in a tearful voice how hard she had tried to save his child.

The burst of gunfire shocked Yasmin like an electrical wire. Still, she didn't move. *Did he kill her?* she thought. *Could he possibly have murdered his own aunt?* Then she heard the woman shrieking—not in pain but in fright—and let out the breath she was holding. Seconds later, Jamaad ran into the yard again, looking terrified. She brushed by Yasmin and vanished into the house.

It was awhile before Najiib reappeared, but Yasmin waited for him submissively, ignoring the heat of the sun and the perspiration collecting on her skin beneath her *abaya*. Eventually, he walked through the gate and stopped before her. "Did it happen as she said?" he asked.

"Yes," she replied, knowing that the truth would only incite him further.

He searched her face and then grunted, "My men are hungry."

When he walked away, she returned to the kitchen and

calculated how much food she needed to prepare. She didn't have enough rice to feed five men, but she had plenty of corn for grits. She also had fresh goat meat and milk from the market and frozen mangoes that she could thaw. It was a good meal, probably better than they had eaten in a long time. It would satisfy their bellies and, if she was lucky, it would temper Najiib's anger.

She heard his men bantering and laughing in the yard. *He didn't tell them about the baby*, she surmised. It made sense. Najiib lived in a cocoon of secrecy. Everything she knew about him she had gathered from observation or hearsay in the village. No one knew where he went when he wasn't home. There were rumors about a training camp on Badmadow Island near the Kenyan border and of a base in Baraawe on the coast, but no one had seen them. People whispered that he had spent time with the *mujahideen* in Afghanistan, but they didn't know any details. Even his role in the Shabaab was shrouded in mystery. Everyone feared his power, but no one was certain whom he answered to in the organization. His nickname was enough to fuel endless speculation—"Azrael," the harvester of souls.

She served lunch to the men in the shade of the *higlo* tree and ate inside with Jamaad, who had ceased her simpering and now sulked in disgrace. Yasmin knew she would have to tread carefully for a few days until the woman regained favor with her nephew. But she didn't intend to bear with Jamaad much longer. In the days since Fatuma died, she had sketched out an escape plan and started squirreling away provisions around the house. If the rains of the *gu* didn't

fail as they had last year, they would offer her the chance—
however slight—to disappear.

That evening after supper, Yasmin drew water from the river
and scrubbed herself with soap until she could no longer
smell her sweat. Then she put on her nightclothes and went
to her room. She lit incense candles in the corners, drew a
curtain across the window, and massaged rose oil into her
skin. She knew he would come to her when his men were
asleep. What she didn't know was how rough he would be.
She read from the Quran, but the words didn't soothe her
nerves. She waited on edge, trying to relax. The tenser she
was, the more it would hurt.

He appeared around midnight, a shadow in the doorway. She stood up when he approached. He took her hair
in his hands and rubbed it between his fingers. She could
feel his desire like an aura around him. She was sure he had
consorts in the camps, but his feelings for her were unique.
Every time he came to her he spoke the same line of verse.
This time was no exception.

"You are more beautiful than rain in the season of
drought," he said.

As always, she said nothing in return, just stared at his
chest until he bade her to look at him. She stood still while
he undressed her and lay back against the bed, concealing
her shame. Though she had spoken the vows before the
imam and two witnesses, her marriage was a fraud. She was

his conquest, not his wife. Most of the time she didn't think about what he had stolen from her. But in these intimate moments, when his body was against hers, the pain was too great to resist.

She saw their faces like frames in an old film reel—Adan smiling at her through his spectacles as he delivered his daily lessons; Khadija discussing poetry with her on her bed; Ismail playing music on his computer and dreaming about university; and Yusuf, sweet Yusuf, drinking life in like a sponge. She had loved them without reservation, unlike her clan, which had spawned so much bloodshed, and her country, which had never known peace in her time. But her family was gone, all because the man whose smell now filled her nostrils had decided that her father was an enemy of God.

When at last Najiib was spent, he rolled over on his back and stared up at the ceiling. She ignored the discomfort in her loins and waited patiently, expecting him to speak, but he said nothing. His silence was an ominous sign. It meant that she hadn't pleased him, or that he had come seeking more than gratification. In time, he sat up and proved her intuition correct.

"Fatuma was weak," he said quietly, looking into her eyes. "You are not weak. But what good is strength if you have an unfruitful womb?" He leaned close and whispered into her ear, "It is time for you to give me a son. Or I will find another who will."

MEGAN

Three days after her meeting with Mahamoud, Megan hitched a ride with Manny to the office of the AU/UN Information Support Team—AMISOM's public affairs division—on the other side of the airport base. The morning sun was like a torch in the sky, bleaching the ground white. It had taken some persistence to find transport to Hawa Abdi Village, but she had been fortunate enough to meet Isra, a lovely Somali-Kenyan woman, who had come to her aid and arranged a military convoy for her.

Manny dropped her off outside the IST compound, and a Ugandan soldier opened the gate for her. She knocked on Isra's door, and the young woman opened it with a smile. "Come in," she said in English, ushering her into the room. "Here is your body armor."

Megan took the heavy green vest and slipped her arms through the loops, cinching the belt around her chest. The vest was fitted with steel plates capable of stopping high-powered bullets—in the best case, at least. In the worst case—multiple shots at short range—they would slow them down. Megan was only mildly reassured. If she got shot, no hospital in Mogadishu would operate on her. They would medevac her to Nairobi, and she would probably die on the way.

Isra handed Megan a matching helmet. "You can wait to put this on," she said. She made a call on her mobile phone and spoke a few words in Somali. Then she put on her own body armor, grabbed a second helmet, and looked at Megan. "Are you ready to go?"

Megan nodded, struggling to suppress her nerves. She had cheated death before, climbing some of the tallest mountains in the world, skydiving over the desert and the ocean, and bungee jumping into the New River Gorge. But extreme sports lacked the malevolence of human beings. *Am I really doing this?* she asked herself rhetorically, knowing the answer full well. *Yes, I'm doing this. If I leave a stone unturned and Ismail ends up buried in the earth with Kyle, I'll never forgive myself.*

She followed Isra to an SUV and sat quietly during the ride to the AMISOM car park. The driver left them beside a line of armored vehicles, all painted green with tinted windows and enormous tires. "This is our Casper," Isra said as a soldier opened the hatch of one of the vehicles and motioned for them to climb in. "You should put your helmet on now."

Megan donned the helmet and scaled the steps, taking a seat at the center of the cabin. The Casper was large enough to accommodate twelve passengers, together with a driver and navigator and a doorman at the rear. For this ride, however, she and Isra were alone. As soon as they settled in, the driver started the engine and the vehicle lurched forward with a growl, falling in between two attack vehicles armed with roof-mounted machine guns.

The convoy left the base by way of the main gate. The airport road soon gave way to an urban jungle of dirt lanes, cinder-block houses, apartment buildings, shops with color-ful advertising painted on the walls, and telephone poles with wires so tangled they looked like birds' nests. Megan watched the people with a wary eye, wondering how many of them had connections to the Shabaab. Most paid no attention to the convoy, but a few stopped to watch. She shuddered when a man in a doorway took out his mobile phone and placed a call. *It's nothing*, she told herself. *He couldn't possibly have seen me.*

They made halting progress through the warren of streets, hampered by traffic at every turn. At last they reached a roundabout at the top of a hill and the traffic thinned out. The Casper picked up speed and whisked them through the outskirts of the city and into the rural hinterlands, slowing only to circumvent huge craters in the roadway—the result of erosion and IEDs, Isra explained.

Megan looked out at the pristine desert sky and tried not to think about Shabaab assassins and roadside bombs. She saw a herd of camels in the distance, their hides a shade or two darker than the yellow clay beneath their feet. A herdsman in a long-sleeve shirt and *ma'awis*—a male sarong—was keeping them moving toward the road.

She pointed them out to Isra. "Where are they going?"

"They are headed to market. Some will be slaughtered for meat. Others will be sold to Arabia. The Somali camel herd is the largest in the world."

After a while, the convoy braked to a halt outside an iron gate with a sign that read: HAWA ABDI VILLAGE: KEEPING HOPE ALIVE. Two men pushed the gate aside, allowing them to enter. The driver parked the Casper between a sprawling pink bougainvillea bush and a three-story building with terraces and a Greek revival façade. The doorman opened the hatch and let them out.

"I think you are safe here," Isra said. "You can take off your body armor."

Megan glanced around the well-kept grounds and saw children playing beneath the limbs of an acacia tree. "Okay," she agreed, feeling a modicum of relief. Her shoulders were sore from the vest, and she felt silly wearing the helmet over her scarf.

A cheerful-looking woman in a black *abaya* greeted them. "I am Dr. Munira," she said in thickly accented English. "This is my team." She swept her arm toward a cluster of Somalis behind her—two smiling women, covered but not veiled, and two sober-looking men, one carrying a clipboard and the other an AK-47. "This way, please. Our time is limited."

Megan followed the doctor through another gate and across a courtyard to a house with a tile veranda. Dr. Munira gestured toward a leather couch, and Megan and Isra took seats.

"How long do we have?" Megan asked.

Dr. Munira spoke frankly. "Thirty minutes. Any more and the risk will be too great."

She offered them bottles of Coke—glass, not plastic—and sat beside them on an ottoman. "It is good that you sent a photo," she began. "I recognized Ismail right away, but I didn't know his real name. When he was here, he went by Ibrahim. He was one of many young men who came to the camp at that time. He understood medicine, so we put him to work at the hospital. We had thousands of people to care for, and more were always coming. He never talked about his past, but I knew he had been involved in the fighting. Sometimes his eyes would lose focus and he would slip away. I never saw him smile, but he was trustworthy and kind. I was sad that he didn't stay."

A hospital volunteer suffering from post-traumatic stress, Megan thought. *Now that's a story I can tell the jury.* "Where did he live when he was here?"

"He stayed in the camp with Ahmed, one of our maintenance men. I talked to Ahmed, and he is willing to speak to you." Dr. Munira exchanged a few words in Somali with the man holding the clipboard, and he placed a call on his mobile phone. After a brief conversation, he said something that made the doctor frown. She gave Megan a frustrated look. "He promised to meet us here, but our generator just went down. He says he cannot come."

"Is there anyone else I can talk to?" Megan asked, resisting the urge to look at her watch. "I need to know what Ismail did while he was in the camp."

Dr. Munira conferred with her team for a moment. "I'm

certain there are other people who knew him, but finding them would take time. Ahmed is your best contact. I can arrange for you to speak with him by phone after you return to Mogadishu."

Megan shook her head. "It would be better if I talked to him in person. Is he far away?"

Dr. Munira addressed the man with the gun. He didn't look pleased. The doctor turned to Isra. "If we take her, will AMISOM provide security?"

Isra shook her head. "They are only responsible for our transport."

Dr. Munira faced Megan again. "I have no way to guarantee your safety in the camp. We are careful about the people we let stay here, but we don't know what ties they bring."

Megan took a breath and let it out slowly. She remembered the day she and Paul had tried for the summit on Mount McKinley. It was late in the climbing season, and their guide had told them there was a 50 percent chance that a cold front could move in while they were on the peak, blocking their retreat. The alternative was to wait for a clear day that might never come. They didn't hesitate, and the weather held, affording them an unforgettable view.

"I'll go with you," she said, an idea forming in her mind. "But I need a few more Coke bottles."

The path to the generator led through the densest mass of humanity Megan had ever seen. The camp was like a temporary city with compact dwellings made of corrugated metal and tarpaulin stretching as far as the eye could see. There were people in every direction, faces old and young, children scampering about in the dirt, white-haired men in *kufi* caps sitting cross-legged and talking with animation, teenagers tending stalls with goods on display, middle-aged women hunched over cooking pots, and aging women with long faces and wrinkles taking shelter from the sun.

As Megan walked along with Dr. Munira and her retinue, everyone turned and stared. She broke the spell by handing out Cokes—one to a girl who touched her sleeve; another to a grizzled old man who gave her a wan smile; a third to an adolescent boy who crossed his arms until he saw what she intended; and the last to a young mother with a baby in a sling. Her munificence softened the mood, and some of the people started to wave and smile. Others, however, gave her withering stares.

Eventually, the doctor led her into a grove of mango trees. "This is our Camp David," she said. "It is where Dr. Hawa and the elders gather to sort out problems. Ahmed will meet us here."

She dispatched the man with the clipboard to an outbuilding not far away, and he returned with a bespectacled man of indeterminate age—Ahmed. The maintenance man peered at her, then sat down in the shade. Megan sat across from him and the others formed loose arcs on either side.

"I will interpret for him," said the doctor. "Please hurry. We have only ten minutes."

Megan fixed her gaze on Ahmed. "Do you remember a

young man named Ibrahim who worked at the hospital? He was here at the end of 2010."

When Dr. Munira translated the query, Ahmed spoke a string of words in rapid-fire Somali.

"Yes," the doctor answered on his behalf. "He remembers Ibrahim. He was a good boy, but he didn't stay long. He doesn't know where he went."

Megan pressed in. "Can you tell me how he left the camp and who he left with?"

"He was like many other boys," Dr. Munira said after Ahmed replied. "He just decided to leave. He might have gone with some others, but Ahmed doesn't know. Ibrahim didn't talk very much."

Megan changed direction. "Did he ever talk about his parents or his brother or sister?"

Ahmed thought about this, then nodded. Dr. Munira translated. "He once talked about his sister. He wanted to find her."

Yasmin, Megan thought, sitting up straighter. "What else did he say about his sister? Did he know where she was?"

Ahmed spoke a burst of Somali, and the doctor said, "He doesn't know anything else."

Sensing her time was short, Megan put her ultimate question on the table: "After Ibrahim left the camp, he went to Hobyo and became a pirate. Do you know why he might have done that?"

Dr. Munira gave her an inscrutable look. "I'm not sure you should ask that."

Megan didn't blink. "If he knows the answer, it could help Ismail."

"All right," the doctor sighed. "But he may not like it." She translated the question in a gentle tone, like a mother breaking bad news to a child.

Megan was unprepared for Ahmed's reaction. He jumped to his feet, barked something at her, and stomped out of the mango grove, disappearing into the outbuilding.

"What just happened?" she asked, shaken by his departure.

"It is what I expected," said Dr. Munira. "Piracy is forbidden in Islam. It is also dangerous. The pirates are bad men. If Ahmed knows anything about it, he would never admit it."

Megan looked into the doctor's eyes. "Do you know anything about it?"

Dr. Munira hesitated. "Around that time, I heard rumors of young men in the camp telling stories about ships and ransoms. I don't know what made Ismail travel to Hobyo. But if the rumors were true, perhaps he went with those boys."

But that doesn't explain why, Megan thought, exasperated by the chasm that remained in her understanding. *According to everyone who knew him, it went against the grain of his character.*

After a moment, Dr. Munira asked, "Do you know if Ismail ever found his sister?"

Megan shook her head. "I don't think he did."

"So many sad stories. Sometimes I wonder if we have

forgotten the meaning of peace." The doctor looked at her watch. "Your time is up. We need to go back."

Megan stood and followed Dr. Munira out of the trees, flanked by Isra and the doctor's entourage. She saw the hospital in the distance and trudged toward it. For some reason, the thought of Yasmin stuck in her mind. She had the sense that she was missing something. Ismail had been taciturn about his past during his time in the village. But he had let one thing slip—his desire to find his sister. That he had dropped his guard suggested that she loomed large in his heart. Megan thought back to her conversation with Mahamoud and realized with a start that she had overlooked something. She took out the mobile phone he had given her after their meeting and called his number.

"Ms. Derrick," he said brusquely. "Are you still in Mogadishu?"

"No," she replied. "I'm at Hawa Abdi Village."

For a moment he didn't speak. Then he surprised her with a compliment. "I didn't think you would go. You are a brave woman—foolish, but brave."

His generosity emboldened her. "There's something I didn't ask you before. I need to know about Yasmin. I'm wondering if Ismail left the village because he wanted to find her."

Mahamoud was silent again, breathing. At last, he said, "We will talk when you get back."

"Where?" she asked, electrified by the possibility of a breakthrough.

"I will come to you."

✳

A few minutes after noon, the AMISOM convoy reentered the airport complex and trundled down the dirt road to the car park. Megan took off her helmet and body armor and wiped the sweat from her brow. When the Casper rolled to a stop, she climbed out and gave Isra a grateful hug.

"We made it," she said. "Thank you for everything."

Isra smiled. "I'm glad we could assist." She pointed at a minibus idling on the fringes of the lot. "I think your ride is here."

Megan turned in surprise. Sure enough, Manny was waiting for her. Her heartbeat quickened when she recognized Mahamoud in the back. She bid Isra farewell and walked to the minibus.

"Where are we going?" she asked Ismail's uncle, taking a seat in the front.

His reply was cryptic. "I thought it would be nice to take a stroll on the beach."

Manny pulled out of the car park and took the perimeter road around the airport. They passed the graveyard of disabled vehicles and turned into the tangle of brush. Halfway up the hill, Manny braked to a stop and let them out at the head of a rugged path that led down to a beach strewn with seaweed. Megan saw the coral jetty in the distance, jutting out into the bay.

"After you," Mahamoud said.

Megan stepped carefully around rocks and vegetation and walked out onto the sand. The breeze off the ocean was strong, taking the edge off the midday heat. She strolled beside Mahamoud without a word, watching the waves curl into thunderous lines of sparkling white. Eventually, he began to speak.

"What I am about to tell you is for you alone. Do you understand?" When she nodded, he continued. "Ismail left Hawa Abdi's place in November 2010. I heard from him again in April. He called from a Somali number. He said he'd gotten some money and wanted me to take care of it. I didn't ask questions. I put the money in a bank account in Nairobi. It's still there."

Ismail's cut from a prior ransom payment, Megan deduced. "How much was it?"

"Twenty-five thousand dollars. The next time I heard from him was last November. He called from an international number. I've since learned it was a satellite phone."

Dear God, Megan thought. *He called from the* Renaissance.

"He said he was in trouble," Mahamoud went on. "He asked me to bring a Land Cruiser to a beach twenty miles north of here at sunset the next day. He told me he was bringing six men."

A chill ran down Megan's spine. There were seven pirates on the sailboat. That meant Ismail intended to release the hostages. Then another, more dreadful possibility dawned on her. Or he premeditated their murders. She shook her head. When Ismail called his uncle, he had no motive to kill the Parkers. *Dammit*, she thought, *I wish Mahamoud could testify. But the government would charge him as an accessory.*

"Did you do what he asked?" she asked softly.

Mahamoud nodded. "I was there. I saw the warship through my binoculars. After the sun went down, I lost sight of it. But then the lights went on. I don't know what they were, but they were very bright. I saw the mast of the sailboat above the water. After a few minutes, the lights started moving. Then I saw helicopters in the air. That's when I left the beach." He took a breath. "I looked back from the bluff and saw a boat in the water surrounded by lights. I couldn't see detail, but I guessed Ismail was on it. I read the story the next day on the Internet."

Megan pondered this. She had deposed Captain Masters and the *Gettysburg* sailors and received affidavits from the SEAL team in lieu of depositions. All of them had mentioned the floodlights, but none had given much detail. "Did you hear the gunshots?" she asked quietly.

Mahamoud shook his head. "The surf was loud. I heard nothing."

"Why are you telling me this? I asked you about Yasmin."

Mahamoud looked out at the sea. "Because I believe Yasmin is why he did it."

Megan stared at him, transfixed. "What do you mean?"

"When Ismail came to me after Yusuf died, he told me what happened to her. He was obsessed with finding her. I almost offered to help, but then he told me the name of the man who took her. I couldn't do it. It would have been a suicide mission. I took him to Hawa Abdi's place instead."

Megan's head spun in the vortex of revelation. "What man?"

"His name is Najiib," Mahamoud replied darkly. "He is a killer and a ghost. But his story isn't important. What matters is Ismail. He wanted to know if Najiib might release Yasmin for a sum of money. I told him I didn't think Najiib would negotiate, and that even if he would, it would take more money than we could ever afford. When I said that, I wasn't thinking about piracy."

The epiphany hit Megan with explosive force. "That's why he went to Hobyo," she whispered. "That's why he hijacked the *Renaissance*. He wanted to buy her freedom."

Mahamoud exhaled. "I think so."

The transformation from victim to victimizer, Megan thought. *At last I understand.* "You said you almost offered to help him. What did you mean?"

Mahamoud took a mobile phone out of his pocket and punched a few buttons. "I took this from Khadija before she left Mogadishu. See for yourself."

Megan saw a text message on the screen. She read the words in disbelief. "Hooyo, I'm alive. I need your help." The date was January 29, 2012. The sender was Yasmin.

"This was only two months ago!" Megan exclaimed.

"There were others before it," he said. "I received them all."

Tears gathered in Megan's eyes. "Do you know where she is?"

Mahamoud shrugged. "Somewhere in the south, I suspect. I can't be sure."

She read the message again. "Is there anything you can do—?"

He interrupted her. "There is nothing. If I tried, I would be killed."

Megan felt a pang of despair. "Should I tell him?"

"That is your decision. I don't know what I would do."

She watched a tall white bird swoop down and land on the water in front of them. "Why didn't you tell me any of this before?"

Mahamoud met her eyes. "Because it wasn't relevant. I thought you were just another rich American trying to soothe your conscience by helping a poor Somali. When you risked your life going out to Hawa Abdi's place, I saw how much you care."

Thirty minutes later, Megan locked herself in her room at SKA and paced the floor, thinking about Ismail and Yasmin. The crimes Ismail had committed were unspeakable, but his devotion to his sister was pure. She thought about Paul and wondered what he would have done in the same situation. *He would have come for me,* she decided. *He would have gone to the ends of the earth.* She shook her head angrily. There had to be a way to help Yasmin. Whoever Najiib was, he wasn't omnipotent.

She sat down on her bed and opened her laptop, connecting to SKA's wireless network. There were forty-five new e-mails in her inbox. She scanned the headers and saw one from Kiley Frost, her senior associate. The subject line read: *URGENT—FBI Lab Reports.* The message had a bevy of attachments. *Finally!* Megan exulted. *We've been waiting forever for these.*

She opened the e-mail and read the summary. A graduate of Vassar and Harvard Law, Kiley had never been one for hyperbole. So when Megan saw that she had underlined three phrases and ended the last paragraph with a triple exclamation point, she knew the scientists at Quantico had stumbled onto something big. She read the words twice, then three times, and her heart began to race. Why was it that progress always seemed to come in waves?

Kiley had written:

After analyzing the trajectories of the bullet holes on the sailboat and the rifling on the recovered slugs, the Lab determined that there were five clusters of shots. Clusters One and Two (a three-shot burst and a single shot into the coachroof) happened sometime earlier and came from the same gun. The Lab noted that Ismail (a.k.a. Ibrahim) fired a single shot while transmitting over the radio on November 11 and inferred that the warning shot was Cluster Two. They inferred that Ismail probably fired Cluster One around the same time.

The Lab next determined that Cluster Three (the seven-shot burst that killed Daniel Parker in the navigation station), Cluster Four (a four-shot burst into the coachroof), and Cluster Five (the three-shot burst that wounded Quentin Parker in the dining booth) happened very close together. The Lab concluded, however, that Clusters Three and Four came from a <u>different weapon</u> than Cluster Five and that <u>none of these clusters</u> came from the weapon that fired Clusters One and Two.

Based on this, the Lab concluded that either the person who killed Daniel and then proceeded to fire four bullets into the roof changed weapons before shooting Quentin, <u>or there were two shooters</u>!!!

ISMAIL

Life in the maximum-security block was like a tunnel without end. The only way to endure it, Ismail found, was to set aside all thought of the outside world—the world of sunshine and color, wind and rain, land and water and air and freedom—and abide in the interior of the soul. Time, as Adan used to say, quoting the Sufi poet Shabistari, is an imaginary point that is ever passing away. The real truth is inward: *Being is the sea; speech is the shore; the shells are letters; the pearls knowledge of the heart.*

As the days turned into weeks and the weeks into months, Ismail adopted the rhythm of jail life as his own. He focused on living in the present, strengthening his body through exercise, centering his mind through prayer, and waiting patiently for the right moment to take the only action left to him, an action that would either redeem or destroy him. If he failed, everything he had done would be meaningless. If he succeeded, neither prison nor death could hold him.

The time was coming, and soon. The stars had begun to align. He had seen the story in the newspaper, a mere footnote amid the headlines about the Arab Spring in Yemen and sanctions in Iran, but to him an immeasurable gift. His leverage had doubled, perhaps tripled, on account of it. But he wasn't quite ready to exercise it. The hook Mas had given him required longer to set. He needed to let its barb sink so far into the minds of his government masters that their certainty about his guilt and associations would seal the legitimacy of his offer. This was especially true now that he knew his mother was alive. It wasn't just Yasmin's life he held in his hands. It was Khadija's, too.

Ismail heard a knock at the door of his cell. "Lunch is over," Longfellow said, opening the slot and waiting for Ismail's tray. "Your lawyer is coming for a visit."

"When?" Ismail asked, relinquishing the tray.

"Fifteen minutes," the jailer replied.

She met with Mahamoud, Ismail guessed. *She wants the truth. But I can't give it to her. Not yet.*

When the time came, Longfellow reappeared and put Ismail in shackles. With the jailer's hand on his arm, Ismail shuffled down the stairs and across the block, his chains jingling. Richie buzzed the door and let them into the hallway. Megan was already in the conference room waiting for him.

"Afternoon, ma'am," Longfellow said. "Cuffs or no cuffs?"

"No cuffs, please," Megan replied, and the jailer complied, ushering Ismail to the table.

"I'll be outside," Longfellow said and closed the door behind him.

"How was Mombasa?" Ismail asked as Megan took out her notepad.

"I met him in Mogadishu," she replied, giving him a bemused look.

He stared at her in astonishment. "You went to Somalia?"

She nodded. "I also went to Hawa Abdi Village. I know who you are, Ismail. I know why you went with the pirates. You didn't go because you wanted to get rich. You went because of Yasmin."

Ismail stiffened in shock, her words reverberating in his head. He tried to think of a way out, but all paths led to the same dead end. She had turned the tables on him. By her grit and determination, she had taken away the reins.

"I know something else," Megan went on. "I know that Daniel and Quentin were shot with different weapons. The evidence from the sailboat proves it. I don't think you were the only shooter. I think something happened out there, something very different from what you and your confederates told the government. I'm your attorney, but I'm not a mercenary. I need you to tell me the truth."

He searched her eyes and knew that he was trapped. The feeling enraged him. "You don't understand!" He slammed his fist on the table. "This isn't the time!"

Longfellow opened the door to check on them. "Everything all right?"

"We're just talking," Megan said evenly.

The jailer frowned. "Keep it down then."

When they were alone again, Megan regarded Ismail coolly. "What don't I understand?"

Ismail closed his eyes and opened them again, instinct vying with emotion for control of his will. He couldn't afford to lose her goodwill. He had to do something. She had forced his hand. "What did Mahamoud tell you about Yasmin?"

She leaned back in her chair. "He told me about Najiib."

"Did he say anything else?"

"She's alive," Megan said quietly.

His heart skipped a beat. How many nights had he dreamed of her in the pirate camps and on the ocean? How many times had he imagined the day he would bring Mahamoud the money and ask him for help? He folded his hands to steady them. "How do you know?"

Megan smiled. "Mahamoud has your mother's phone. She sent text messages."

Ismail put his head in his hands as his heart tumbled end over end in the euphoric current. After a time, he made his decision. His sister had survived three years in the clutches of the Shabaab. There was no promise of tomorrow. The time to act was now.

"I want to talk to the government," he said. "I want to make a deal."

Megan looked confused. "You mean Barrington? I doubt he'll be interested in a plea."

"Not the US attorney. The United States."

He sketched out his plan, and Megan's eyes widened in astonishment. "This is unbelievable. Is this what you've been holding out for?"

He allowed his silence to speak for him.

She shook her head. "The Justice Department isn't

going to like it."

"The right people will listen," Ismail insisted. "I need you to find them."

Megan pondered this quietly, then her lips spread into a conspiratorial grin. "If I do this for you, I want the truth about what happened on the sailboat. No more games."

Ismail nodded. "As soon as they do it, I will tell you."

The meeting took place four days later in a conference room at the Norfolk branch of the Naval Criminal Investigative Services, an obscure redbrick building on the expansive grounds of the Norfolk Naval Station. There were six people present—Ismail, Megan, Ezra Brown, the US attorney for the Eastern District of Virginia, Zach Carver, a senior official from the Justice Department, Sabrina Redford, the undersecretary of state of something or other, and a gray-haired man with pasty skin who introduced himself only as "Bob from the intelligence community."

Ismail was dressed in his suit, not his orange jumper, and his hands and legs were unbound. He looked at each face around the table, conscious of the gravity of the moment. He relished the feeling of being in the driver's seat again, but he had no illusions. They could take everything away from him in an instant. They were bureaucrats, politicians, and spooks who operated in circles of influence he could only begin to imagine. He knew they distrusted him and suspected that they loathed him. He would never succeed by appealing to their compassion. He had to convince them that cooperating with him was in the interest of the United States.

When Megan nodded for him to go ahead, he spoke in a low tone. "Mohamed Abdullah al-Noor, also known as Abu Warsaame Abdi, Azrael, and Najiib—the Shabaab's chief enforcer and one of the founders of the Amniyat. I can give him to you. But I want something in return."

Bob put his arms on the table, focusing his clear blue eyes on Ismail. "Mr. Ibrahim, you'll forgive me if I'm skeptical. The last known photograph of Najiib was taken in July of 2008. His trail has gone cold. We've heard rumors but none of them are confirmed. For all we know he's dead."

Ismail didn't flinch. "That's exactly what he wants you to believe." Megan handed him a printout of a news story, and he put it on the table. "On February 9 of this year, Godane appeared in a video with Ayman al-Zawahiri and pledged allegiance to al-Qaeda. The Shabaab is now the world's problem. They have proven their ability to commit acts of terror outside Somalia. They will continue to disrupt the Somali government and destroy anyone who stands in their way. Najiib is behind their campaign of assassination. I know that from personal experience."

Ismail took a breath and steadied himself. Then he told Adan's story.

When he finished, Bob scratched his chin. "Even if you saw Najiib in May of 2009, that was three years ago. How do you know where he is now?"

Ismail gave him a thin smile. "Because Najiib took my sister." He described the scene in detail, just as he remembered it, and watched as their eyes caught fire in the light. "I know Yasmin is alive. I'm confident she's still with him."

Bob looked dubious. "But you don't know that for certain."

Ismail shook his head. "Not yet. But I can confirm it."

"How?"

Memories swirled in Ismail's mind. "When they took us to Lanta Buro, I knew they would separate us. I told her to hide her mobile phone. That's how I would find her. She still has the phone."

Ismail saw something shift in Bob's expression. This was the moment he had been waiting for, the pivot point in the negotiation. During his time with the Shabaab, he had heard whispers about the wizardry the Americans could perform with a mobile number—the way their satellites could geolocate a phone even when it was powered down, hijack it with spyware, and transform it into a homing device. To get what he wanted he had to give them the number. But first they had to agree to the exchange.

"She is expecting to hear from me," he went on. "If I text her, she will tell me about Najiib. But the text must come from a Somali number. An international number will make her suspicious."

Bob nodded. "We can make that happen."

It was the reply Ismail expected. "Do you remember the story of the genie?" he asked. "Rub the lamp and make three wishes. Before you get the number, I want three guarantees."

Bob tilted his head. "Let's hear what you have to say."

Ismail put the full weight of his heart behind his words.

"I want you to right the wrongs Najiib has done to my family. You can't bring back my father or my brother, but you can save my sister and mother. I want you to help Yasmin escape from Somalia. I want you to give her and my mother permanent resident status in the United States. And I want you to give them the reward posted on the Internet—three million dollars for Najiib's location. You can do what you like with him."

Zach Carver from the Justice Department was the first to speak. "Are you planning to ask for a reduced sentence? Because I can tell you that's going to be very hard to do."

Ismail shook his head. "Whatever the jury decides, I will accept."

Carver traded a look with his colleagues. "I think we should talk about it."

"Give us a few minutes," Bob said, standing up and ushering the others out the door.

Ismail listened to the clock on the wall and thought about how strange it was that he was sitting in an office in Virginia negotiating with the American government about Yasmin and Khadija's future. How many times had he nearly been killed by bullets and bombs? How many nights had he spent counting the distant stars and struggling not to despair?

He glanced at Megan seated beside him. "How did I do?"

She tilted her head. "Now I know what Paul meant. You're a natural."

It was ten minutes before the others returned. "Mr.

Ibrahim," Bob said, sitting down again, "the immigration hurdles are easy to overcome, and Ms. Redford assures me that the State Department will authorize the reward. Your sister is the challenge. Even if she is in duress, she is not a US citizen. We won't put our people at risk. We can help her as soon as she leaves Somalia. But we can't get her out."

Ismail feigned a look of frustration. He had anticipated this response, but he needed them to believe he was making a concession to cement the agreement. "If that is all you can offer me, then I need time to persuade her. And I need you to promise me that you will do nothing with the information I give you that would endanger her or any other innocent person."

"That's not a problem," Bob said smoothly. "But there's a condition to the deal: you can't talk about it with anyone other than your lawyer. That includes your mother and sister. You can't tell them why we're helping them. If you talk, we walk. Understand?"

Ismail nodded his assent.

Bob took a smartphone out of his jacket. "I'll take down the number when you're ready."

Ismail looked deep into his eyes. "The last time I made a deal with your government, they betrayed me. I want some assurance that you're not going to do the same thing. I would like to know your real name. I'm certain it isn't Bob."

The intelligence specialist looked startled but recovered quickly. "I can't tell you who I am. But I can tell you this: I just talked to Gordon Tully, the national security advisor. He approved the deal."

Ismail raised an eyebrow, making every effort to sound reasonable. "Why should I trust him?"

Bob displayed a trace of mirth. "Because he speaks for the president of the United States."

Ismail glanced at Megan and saw her nod. "Okay," he said and recited the digits from memory. "This is the message you must send: *Qosol, are you there? I'm sorry it's taken so long. I need to know where you are and if you are still with him. Madaxa.*"

Bob peered at him quizzically. "What are 'Qosol' and 'Madaxa'?"

"They are nicknames. I called her Qosol, which means 'laughter.' She called me Madaxa Adag, which means 'hard head.' Often she just said Madaxa."

Everyone around the table chuckled. Then Bob read the digits and the words back to him to confirm their accuracy. "How long do you think it will take her to respond?" he asked.

"I don't know," Ismail said. "But she will respond, *inshallah.*"

Bob met his gaze. "I hope you're right."

VANESSA

Vanessa sat in her office finishing up her notes from Halima's physical. It had been a heart-wrenching hour for the Sudanese girl. If not for the camaraderie Aster had offered her, she might have left the practice in tatters instead of tears. The first time Vanessa had confronted female genital mutilation in her examination room it had left her speechless and horrified. After more than a decade of caring for refugees, however, she had come to expect it, though the anger it inspired always felt fresh.

Some cultures were worse offenders than others. If a girl came from East or West Africa, there was a good chance she had been circumcised. Sometimes she had lost only the foreskin of her prepuce, sometimes her prepuce and her clitoris. Occasionally, however, the cutter had disfigured her entire pubic area, removing the prepuce, clitoris, and labia minora, and stitching together the labia majora until 90 percent of the vaginal opening was blocked by skin and scar tissue. In most cases, the mutilation could be repaired. But therein lay the rub. Girls who had been circumcised saw it as a part of their cultural identity and essential to their womanhood. When they discovered the truth that they were actually in the minority, that, in fact, the vast preponderance of the world's women still had their sexual organs intact, they reacted with disbelief, then confusion, then grief.

Halima had been no exception. Vanessa had gone over everything else with her first before introducing her to Aster and letting her friend tell her story. Every time she heard it, it gave her chills. Circumcised at the age of eight in an Eritrean clinic, Aster had suffered painful cramping, urination issues, and abdominal bloating throughout her adolescence until, finally, in college she had met a doctor who had explained the cause of her suffering and offered to restore her body to its natural state. It had taken her months to decide, but she had gone ahead with it, and it had changed her life. Aster showed Halima before-and-after pictures of the reversal procedure and held her hand when she cried, reassuring her that everything she was feeling was appropriate and necessary and that she would get through it. Then she had walked her back to the waiting room and handed her off to her mother.

"What do you think she'll do?" Vanessa had asked when the girl was out of earshot.

"She's strong," Aster said. "I see it in her eyes. She'll be back."

"What will she tell her family?"

Aster shrugged. "It will be hard at first. She won't convert them. But she will convert her sisters and bring them when they're old enough. And when she has daughters of her own, she'll tell them the truth and protect them. That's the way cutting is going to die. One generation at a time."

Vanessa focused again on the form in front of her and signed her name, sliding the sheet into Halima's file. Then she returned the file to the records room.

Chad Forrester met her in the hallway, wearing his trademark grin. "Are you going to make it tonight?" he asked. "Aster and Abram are coming."

The spring garden party, she thought, cringing internally. *Thank God I have an excuse.* "I'm going to Norfolk. I won't be back in time."

Chad looked disappointed. "Another court hearing?"

"Yes," she lied. "I'm sorry."

He shrugged. "How is Quentin's therapy going?"

"He's doing well," she replied breezily. "But I really have to run."

Before he could respond, she slipped by him, grabbed her jacket and purse off the desk, and walked to the parking lot. For weeks now, he had been making subtle overtures toward her, inquiring how she was doing, asking after Quentin, and offering to cover her patients whenever she had an appointment. He had never been inappropriate, but she knew his intentions. He had been attracted to her for years. Their dalliance during Quentin's early adolescence hadn't progressed beyond a few lingering embraces, but she knew he wanted more. Now Daniel was gone, and he was taking delicate steps toward the opening, assuming, no doubt, that her mourning couldn't last forever. About that he was right. But the rest was fanciful. She had no interest in him.

On the drive to Annapolis, her iPhone rang. When she saw Ted's name on the screen, she took a heavy breath. He had called her every week for the past four months, asking whether she needed any help and when he could come down and see them. She had made up a dozen excuses to postpone the inevitable, but she knew she couldn't delay much longer.

She connected the call. "Hello?"

"Vanessa, it's Ted," he began. "How are you?"

She shuffled through a few responses, but all of them felt disingenuous. Finally, she opted for candor. "We're doing well. Quentin's making steady improvement."

He coughed and cleared his throat. "That's wonderful to hear. Is there anything I can do to help you? You know I'm always here if you need anything."

She caught the unmistakable subtext: *I'm old and bored with retirement, and you and Quentin are the only family I have left. I'm tired of being shut out.* "I know," she said and then took the leap. "Listen, if you still want to visit, this would be a good month. Our calendar is pretty clear."

He was quiet for a moment. "That's kind of you. Unfortunately, I'm going to Europe for a couple of weeks. One of those tours, you know. How about May?"

"That would be nice," she replied, almost meaning it.

"I'll check my schedule and send you a few options."

She smiled in spite of herself. *Same old Ted. Unless he's overseas, the only thing in his date book is golf.*

"It'll be good to see you," he said with feeling. "I'll bring something for Quentin."

"Just bring yourself," she said, knowing in her heart that she'd done the right thing.

Twenty minutes later, she turned onto Norwood Road and drove through the canopy of trees to the end of the lane. It was just before one in the afternoon on the kind of dewy day in early spring that always made her feel like she was witnessing the birth of the world. The sky was as blue as a robin's egg, the daffodils were smiling at her from their beds, and birds were warbling in the trees. Despite the gravity of the trip she was about to take, something in her felt like singing along.

She pulled into the driveway and saw Paul Derrick waiting on the steps. Dressed casually in jeans and a bomber jacket, he looked more James Dean than J. Edgar Hoover. She told him as much when she greeted him.

"I feel like a monkey in a suit," he said with a laugh.

"What does the Bureau think about that?" she asked, opening the front door.

"We're a mutual toleration society," he replied. "They tolerate me and I tolerate them."

She led him through the living room and out onto the back deck. She saw Quentin and Ariadne down at the dock cleaning out the *Relativity*. She smiled. In less than a month, the Australian girl had managed not only to revive Quentin's dreams of sailing but also to convince him that he could get out on the water this spring. The effect had been transformative. Where before he had lamented his therapy, now he engaged it aggressively. He had found his old knot board in the attic and practiced his bowlines and hitches, tuning his fine motor skills. He had also been playing the piano nonstop. There were moments when Vanessa resented Ariadne's closeness to him, but they didn't last for long. The girl was too likable to begrudge.

"Do you think he's ready for this?" Paul asked, standing beside her.

Vanessa inhaled softly. "It was his idea. I couldn't say no."

Paul checked his watch. "We should get on the road soon. Ben Hewitt is meeting us at five."

Vanessa nodded and started down the path to the river. "Do you sail?" she asked.

He shook his head. "My grandfather had a Bayliner. We used to go boating on the weekends. I always thought sailing looked too complicated."

She gave a wry laugh. "That makes two of us. I don't get as seasick on a powerboat." She stopped on the sundeck and waved to Quentin. "It's time to go. We don't want to be late."

"It's my fault," Ariadne said. "I lost track of time." She stowed the rag she was using to polish the wood and stepped onto the dock.

"Hi, Paul," Quentin said, standing up. "Did they let you . . . bring the recordings?"

Paul nodded. "I have them with me."

"Good," the boy replied. "This is Ariadne. She's coming, too."

"Pleasure," Paul said, greeting the girl. He turned to Vanessa. "Shall we?"

They reached the Norfolk Naval Station in three and a half hours, Paul leading in his coupe and Vanessa following with Quentin and Ariadne. She had deep reservations about Quentin's idea. It was one thing for him to answer questions about the shooting in a sterile environment, another thing to revisit the crime scene and listen to the tapes of the negotiations in hopes of triggering his memory. She had tried to dissuade him, even lobbying Dr. Greenberg to forbid it. But the neuropsychologist had demurred, opining that Quentin could decide for himself. It was her fault. She shouldn't have told him that the *Renaissance* was back in the United States. He had been obsessed with it ever since.

When they pulled up to the security checkpoint, Ben Hewitt and another man climbed into Paul's car, and the guard let both vehicles through the gate. The naval station sat on an immense parcel of reclaimed waterfront and contained an airport, a seaport, and a collection of buildings large enough to be a small city. After a few minutes of driving, they stopped beside a row of hangars not far from the wharf, where half a dozen ships were tied up.

Vanessa saw the *Renaissance* standing on its keel between

two hangars, supported by jacks and surrounded by a chain-link fence. The sight of it turned her stomach. She looked at Quentin in the mirror and saw his somber expression. She couldn't fathom what he was thinking. It was on this boat that he had traveled the world and watched his father die. It was on this boat that he had spent the best and worst days of his life.

They left the SUV and walked with Paul, Hewitt, and the third man—Hewitt introduced him as Fred Matheson from NCIS—to a gate in the fence. Matheson removed a padlock and swung the gate open, admitting them to the enclosure. Vanessa watched as Quentin walked toward the sailboat and ran his hand over the hull. His eyes were hooded, his look indecipherable.

He moved to the ladder propped against the transom. "I'm going to . . . need some help. My balance . . . isn't great."

Paul stepped forward to stabilize him.

"Is this really what you want?" Vanessa asked as he put his foot on the first rung.

He nodded. "It's the only way . . . I will remember."

He made his way up the ladder, step by tentative step. When he reached the top, he swung his leg over the side and slipped into the cockpit, sitting on the portside bench. Paul climbed up after him, then Vanessa and Ariadne, and finally Hewitt and Matheson.

Vanessa stood behind the helm for a moment, taking in the sweep of the coachroof and the silent mast and boom. *It feels like a ghost ship*, she thought. *Whatever benevolent spirit it had is gone.* She sat down on the starboard bench and looked away from the piercing afternoon sun.

Suddenly, Quentin began to speak. "I remember sitting here with Afyareh . . . before we saw the first warship. He taught me to say things . . . in Somali. We saw some frigatebirds . . . flying above us. Guray wanted to shoot at them . . . but Afyareh wouldn't let him. He said Guray was afraid . . . because they were black. Guray was superstitious."

Vanessa was unprepared for the turbulence the story aroused in her. At the same time it affirmed one of her assumptions about the pirates—their penchant for wanton violence—and subverted her impression of Ismail. She realized with discomfort that she had come to picture him as a cartoon villain. It was a caricature inspired by emotion, not a portrait grounded in fact.

"Do you remember any of the words he taught you?" she asked.

Quentin narrowed his eyes, thinking. "Sailboat is *doon*. Sail is . . . *dhoofnay*. Table is *miiska*. Girl is *gabar*. Beautiful is *qurux*. There were . . . a lot of words."

She shook her head, astonished by his faculty for language. "Why did he teach them to you?"

"I asked him to," Quentin replied. "He was good to us . . . before the Navy came. He let us listen to music . . . and take showers." He fixed his eyes on Paul. "Can we go below now?"

"I'm ready if you are," the negotiator replied, extracting a digital recorder from his pocket.

"Freddie and I are coming with you," Hewitt said. "We need to tape the conversation."

"Do you mind if I stay out here?" Vanessa asked, troubled by the thought of entering the place where Daniel died. She knew the FBI had cleansed the boat and removed all vestiges of the shooting, but she didn't want to feed the demons in her imagination.

Quentin shrugged, and Paul gave her a look that said, *I'll take care of him.*

"Can I sit with you, Vanessa?" Ariadne asked, moving closer to her. Vanessa nodded. The girl had an uncanny sense for what people needed. She took Ariadne's hand and held it gratefully.

The negotiator slid the weather hatch open and looked into the sailboat. "Just a minute," he said and entered the cabin, sliding back the curtains from the portholes. He poked his head out again and helped Quentin down the steps. Vanessa held her breath, worried that he was walking into a psychological ambush. But he handled it without incident, following Paul past the galley and into the dining booth. She could see their bodies through the hatch, but she couldn't see their faces.

When Agents Hewitt and Matheson settled in across from them, Quentin spoke again. "This is where we sat most of the time . . . after the Navy came," he said, his voice quieter but still audible to Vanessa. "This is where . . . we slept at night."

"Do you remember anything else about the day before the *Gettysburg* came?" Paul asked. "Did anything significant happen?"

There was a long pause, then Quentin said, "There was

a . . . dispute about the food. Mas thought we had poisoned it . . . because Osman got diarrhea . . . after eating peanut butter sandwich crackers. Mas pointed his gun at us. Afyareh told him that Osman . . . was allergic to peanuts."

"Tell me more about Mas," Paul said. "What was he like?"

Quentin's reply was steadier. "He wasn't kind to us . . . like Afyareh. He didn't speak English. He had a scar . . . on his cheek. He and Osman were friends. But he didn't like Afyareh."

"What do you mean he didn't like him?"

"I remember them arguing," Quentin said. "I don't know . . . what it was about."

"Was that before or after the ransom negotiations?"

The query stumped Quentin. "I think it was . . . when the planes were in the air. I'm not sure."

"Did you know the *Renaissance* changed course in the middle of the night? It happened soon after Afyareh made contact with your family."

"We changed course?" Quentin asked, his bewilderment plain.

"When the *Gettysburg* arrived, the sailboat was on a course for central Somalia," Paul said. "After the course change, you headed toward Mogadishu. The pirates didn't mention that?"

"No," Quentin replied.

"All right. Let's go to the recordings. Since our time is limited, I'm going to focus on the last communications between Afyareh and your grandfather before the ransom was agreed to, and between Afyareh and me before the shooting. You let me know if you think of anything."

Vanessa looked into the sky and tightened her grip on Ariadne's hand. Her heartbeat increased to a drumbeat and anxiety gnawed at the edges of her consciousness. *If Quentin can do this, you can, too,* she told herself, pushing back the fear. Suddenly, she heard Curtis's voice. The conversation was a series of torrid exchanges separated by static and clicks.

[Click]

Curtis: Ibrahim. How are my son and grandson?

Ismail: They are fine, Curtis. You may talk to them when we have a deal.

Curtis: No. I want to talk to Daniel now.

[Static]

Ismail: My men are tired of this negotiation, Curtis. We have been more than reasonable with you. We will not accept less than $2.1 million. I know your family has it. So don't waste my time telling me otherwise. You have seventeen hours left before the deadline.

[A click, then a pause, then another click]

Ismail: Are we in agreement?

Curtis: Ibrahim, I just wired $1.85 million to a bank account in Nairobi. My daughter-in-law is there now. She will collect the cash in the morning and put it on a plane for delivery. That's all we could raise. If you want more, you need to extend the deadline.

Ismail: I think you are lying, Curtis. I think you are
        being cheap.

Curtis: Then you are a fool. I convinced the Navy
        to leave you alone. Why would I lie when we're
        so close?

Ismail: That is unacceptable. The deadline stands.

[A click, then a pause, then another click]

Ismail: I talked to my men. We are willing to accept
        $1.85 million.

Curtis: That is good news, Ibrahim. We have a deal.
        Please provide the delivery coordinates.

Vanessa heard a different kind of click and realized Paul
had turned off the recording. She watched her son through
the companionway, willing him to be strong.

"We were in the galley . . . when that happened," Quentin
said. "The pirates were in the booth. They talked together a
lot . . . during that conversation. I remember they were . . . *agitated* when Grandpa said he could only pay $1.85 million."

"Was Afyareh in charge of the conversation?" Paul
inquired.

"All of them were talking. They reached . . . a decision
together." He was quiet. "I think Mas had something . . . to
do with that. Yeah, Mas and Afyareh talked."

"Did Mas guide the decision?" Paul asked.

"No," Quentin said. "Afyareh was . . . in control."

"Did he ever lose control?" the negotiator pressed gently.

The cabin was silent for an extended moment. "I don't
know," Quentin finally said, sounding exasperated. "I still

can't remember . . . what happened at the end."

"That's all right," Paul said calmly. "You're doing a great job. The next recording happened after the ransom was delivered. Are you ready for it?"

Quentin's response was a notch quieter. "Yes."

Paul pressed "play" and the recording began.

[Static]

Ismail: What are you doing, Paul? This was not our deal!

Derrick: Ibrahim, I tried to call you on the sat phone, but you didn't answer. You don't need to worry. Our radar picked up a couple of boats launching from the beach. We're sending the helicopter to keep them away. Over.

Ismail: That's not acceptable, Paul. If you want the hostages to be released, you need to put the helicopter back on the ship now.

Derrick: Ibrahim, our agreement hasn't changed. The helo is a precaution for the safety of the hostages. We don't know why the boats just launched. We don't know who's driving them or what they're carrying. The helo isn't going to stop you from reaching the beach. I made a promise I intend to keep.

[Static]

When Paul turned off the recorder, Vanessa's mind was swarming with questions. What were the boats that had launched from the beach? Were they connected to the pirates? Why had she never heard about the helicopter before? On multiple occasions, she had asked the FBI for more information, but no one had mentioned it. What else had the government withheld from her? Lastly, why did Ismail's voice sound different? Beneath his usual belligerence, she had detected a trace of fear. What was he afraid of? The Navy? The helo? Or something else?

After a moment, Quentin began to speak again. Vanessa had to strain to hear him. "I remember that conversation . . . *vaguely*. It's like there's a cloud . . . in my head. There was an argument, I think. I remember shouting . . . but I don't know who was doing it." He thought for a while longer. "I remember my dad saying something . . . about using the table as cover if they start shooting."

Vanessa listened as Paul sought to elicit more information about Afyareh and Mas, but all of Quentin's replies were variations of "I don't know." Each time he confessed ignorance he sounded more agitated, as if the blank spots in his memory were a personal failing, not the result of brain injury. Vanessa wrestled with her instincts, longing to intercede but knowing that Quentin would react badly. After a moment, she decided to follow Dr. Greenberg's example and let her son stand on his own.

"There's another series of exchanges," Paul said. "The last one. But I'll only play it if you want me to. What you've done today is admirable. There's no shame in stopping now."

"I don't want . . . to stop," Quentin replied gravely. "I need to finish this."

"Okay," Paul said. "Here goes." He pressed the "play" button.

[Click]

Derrick: Captain Parker, how are things over there?

Daniel: Paul! You have to do something. You have to get the Navy to listen. If the chopper isn't back on the ship in five minutes, they're going to kill us.

Derrick: Daniel, I need you to calm down. Who's saying that to you? Is Ibrahim saying that? Because that isn't the deal we arranged.

Daniel: Yes, it's Ibrahim. But the others are with him.

Derrick: Have they processed the contents of the package?

Daniel: They were almost finished when the chopper took off.

[Clatter of rifles being loaded]

Daniel: Stop it! Put the guns down! Paul, they're pointing their guns at us. You have to do something now.

Derrick: Captain, I hear what you're saying. I want you to tell Ibrahim that I'm going to talk to the Navy. I need him to be patient. The chopper is miles away now. It's going to take time to get it back on the ship.

Daniel: Okay, okay.

Ibrahim: Your five minutes is now four. I am not the

one breaking our agreement. If you do not act quickly, the Captain will die.

[Click, then a pause, then another click]

Derrick: Do you see it? It's powering down.

Ismail: We want the helicopter inside the ship.

[Static]

Derrick: We're going to put the helo away. It shouldn't be long now.

[Click, then a pause, then another click]

Derrick: Ibrahim, the helicopter is inside the ship. It's time to make the exchange.

Ismail: You moved the ship.

Derrick: What are you talking about?

Ismail: You know what I mean. My eyes do not lie.

Derrick: It's getting dark. Things look different at night.

Ismail: You have betrayed our trust. You must move the ship. We will not release the hostages until you are one mile away. You have five minutes to comply.

[Click, then a pause, then another click]

Derrick: Ibrahim, I can get the Navy to move the ship, but I need you to give me something in return. Put Quentin in a life preserver with a safety light and send him overboard. We'll pick him up—

Ismail: You're changing the bargain, Paul. You moved the ship while we were counting the money. Why did you do that? To bring your

snipers closer so they can kill us? I remember a
lesson my father taught me. If a merchant says
he'll bring you ten camels but he only brings
nine, you pay him for the nine and demand the
last one for free. You broke our trust. We aren't
going to pay you for the tenth camel.

Derrick: Ibrahim, moving the ship wasn't part of
our agreement either. We can renegotiate, but
you need to give us something in return. You
lose nothing if you let Quentin go. You can
hold on to the Captain until we're far enough
away for comfort. That's the best I can do.

Ismail: You're not listening, Paul. The one who
breaks trust has the obligation to restore it. If
you had not moved your ship, we would be on
the beach by now and the hostages would be
in your hands. You moved your ship. It is your
duty to move it again.

Derrick: Ibrahim, do you recall what you said when
we first spoke? You want something, and I want
something. You have what you want—a bunch
of money and a boat that will take you to the
beach. You're almost home. I still don't have
what I want. We need to help each other get to
the goal line. Take some time to think about it.
I'll call you back in ten minutes.

Ismail: No! You think because you have bigger guns,
because you are American and we are Somali,
you can make us bend? Read your history.

That's the same arrogance that brought down
Corfield and Garrison. Our guns are pointed at
the hostages. Back off or we will eat them like
meat. Do you hear me? Back off or we will eat
them like meat!

Derrick: Ibrahim, please listen to me. I can't do this
on my own. I need you to help me—

When silence descended again, Vanessa realized that
her hands were shaking. Her stomach felt as if it had been
put through a blender. She didn't know where to direct her
anger. She heard Ismail's words in an echo chamber. *You
moved the ship . . . moved the ship . . . moved the ship. Back
off or we will eat them like meat . . . eat them like meat . . . eat
them like meat.* She wanted to scream out loud, but she didn't
know where to direct it—at the government or at the pirates.
Ismail had demanded money for lives, and she had paid him
every last dollar. That was supposed to end the standoff. But
it hadn't. The deal had broken down while she was still in
the air. Daniel was dead because of it, and Quentin would
probably never be the same. Someone needed to pay. But
which party was ultimately to blame?

The sound of Quentin's voice wrested her from her tail-
spin. "I remember there were *lights* . . . and more shouting.
But it's like . . . a fog. I can't see it . . . I don't *know*."

At that moment, Vanessa felt pain in her fingers.
Ariadne was crushing her hand like a vise. Her cheeks were
pale as a ghost and stained with tears. Vanessa extracted
her hand and wrapped her arms around the girl. Ariadne's

warmth steadied her heart.

"It's okay," she heard Paul say inside the cabin. "You've done everything you can."

"No," Quentin said in an anguished voice. "I *have* to remember." Then something came to him. "*Wait!* I remember something . . . Afyareh said to my dad. He said, 'You make them listen . . . or you will die.' I don't remember when . . . but I think it was at the end."

Quentin's words brought Vanessa's wrath into focus. It didn't matter that Ismail had taught him phrases in Somali or rescued a few frigatebirds or shown him kindness before the Navy came. The government might have made mistakes, but they hadn't turned the sailboat into a slaughterhouse. She remembered Ismail standing in the cockpit of the *Renaissance* as her plane passed overhead. She pictured him in the courtroom, his eyes soulless, calculating. There was a host of things she would probably never understand about what had happened. But she understood this much.

Ismail deserved to die.

YASMIN

The night was as black as the wings of a crow as Yasmin scaled the *higlo* tree and dropped down on the far side of the wall. The sky was overcast for the first time in months, and the air carried a hint of humidity. After the devastating drought and famine the year before, the clouds were a propitious sign. They meant the rains were coming. The *gu*—the lifeblood of the Somali nation—would not fail again.

She extracted the bag with her mobile phone and sighed with relief. The zipper was as tight as she had left it. After Jamaad, moisture was her greatest adversary. If water got into the bag, it would destroy the phone and sever her last connection to the outside world.

She turned the unit on and saw that the battery was dangerously low. She could only use it for a minute or two before she would have to take it inside and charge it again. Suddenly, the phone warbled in her hands. The electronic noise sounded impossibly loud in the quiet night. She searched the shadows along the riverbank for movement, but all was still.

She looked back at the phone and saw a notification on the screen. She had a message from an unknown number. She was sure it was a mistake. The sender probably thought she was someone else. Or her carrier was reminding her to add airtime to her dwindling account. She had long wondered what she would do when her balance ran out. The only way she could get more airtime was to steal money from Jamaad's secret stash and buy it in another village. But that plan had two fatal flaws. If money went missing from the jar, she was the only suspect. And a road trip meant paying for petrol. Even if she invented a pretext, Jamaad would never allow her to shop alone.

Yasmin opened her inbox and selected the new message, scanning it without thought. When the words finally registered, she stared at the screen in shock. After three years of waiting, three years of keeping the phone hidden and preserving the battery, sending messages into the void, she almost couldn't believe the message was real. But the salutation didn't lie. It was from Ismail!

He had written in English: Qosol, are you there? I'm sorry it's taken so long. I need to know where you are and if you are still with him. Madaxa.

She typed her reply in haste, cursing her wobbly fingers. I'm still with him. I'm in a village in Middle Juba. What do you want me to do?

When she sent it, she tried to temper her expectations. His message was two weeks old. She didn't know where he was or how soon he would receive her reply. She listened to the gurgle of the river and the chirping of the frogs. *I've waited this long*, she told herself. *I'll survive a few more days.* Then she had another thought. *I need to silence the phone.* She opened the settings menu and disabled the sound. A moment later, she felt the phone vibrate in her hands. She nearly dropped it in surprise.

Is he there now? Ismail asked. If not, when will he come back?

Not now, but soon, she typed, knowing the battery could die at any moment. Where are you?

Somewhere safe. Are you close to Kenya?

200 km.

You must tell me when he is coming.

She frowned, not quite understanding. He's unpredictable.

It's the only way I can help you.

What do you mean?

But he didn't explain. You must make yourself ready.

For what?

Patience, Qosol. Tell me when he is coming.

Okay. Please wait.

Always.

Soon after she read his final text, her phone died. She looked up at the dark sky, wondering how he could help her and why he had asked about Kenya. She answered her own question: *He's in Kenya now. He's going to hire a vehicle and come get me the next time Najiib leaves the village.* The longer she pondered the notion, the more excited she became. She could escape in the night and meet him on the road to

Marere. By the time Najiib went looking for her, they would be across the border.

The flight of her musings ended as suddenly as it began. The border was no protection against Najiib. The Shabaab had spies in Kenya. If they claimed asylum in Dadaab or Nairobi, Najiib would find them. They could take shelter in Ethiopia, but getting there would require time and money, and they had no relatives there. The only certain way to escape Najiib was to flee the Horn of Africa.

Then she had a thought: *Najiib would never find us if he were dead.*

She shook her head in fright. She couldn't—*wouldn't*—consider it. His crimes were appalling, and too numerous to count, but his life was in Allah's hands. Once the idea struck her, however, she found it hard to banish. What if Ismail intended to do it? What if he meant to avenge Adan's death and rescue her at the same time? It would be almost poetic—that after years of living in the underworld and murdering with impunity, Najiib's lust would bring him to ruin.

She raised her eyes to the heavens and whispered a prayer. "Take me home to my brother. And bring us justice. Amen."

MEGAN

Megan sat with Kiley Frost, reviewing her notes for the depositions she was about to take. At her request, Barrington had arranged for her to use the NCIS conference room in Norfolk where Ismail had negotiated his deal with the government. After months of compiling evidence and interviewing witnesses from the Navy, the FBI, and the Parker family, Megan knew the timeline of the hijacking as exhaustively as a person could. She had also succeeded in reconstructing Ismail's past and clarifying his motivations. Yet the Holy Grail of the case—the truth about the shooting—still eluded her.

Only six people were privy to that information, and the four who were talking were telling lies—in her view, at least. Their story was too convenient. They had drawn a portrait of Ismail the zealot that she had thoroughly refuted. Today, she would examine the pirates under oath and judge their mannerisms along with their words. In her fifteen years as a trial lawyer, she had learned the body language of a liar—the shifting eyes and subtle hesitations, the gaps in an otherwise cohesive narrative that suggested facts were being shaded and memories suppressed. She couldn't tell any of this from a transcript. She needed to look the pirates in the eye and ask them questions that made them squirm.

She heard a knock on the door. Agent Matheson poked his head in. "Your client's here," he said. "Do you want to see him before you start?"

She nodded. "Bring him in and unshackle him, please." She turned to Kiley. "Will you give us a minute? I need to talk to him alone."

"Of course," the young associate said and slipped out of the room.

Matheson returned shortly with Ismail. He looked dapper in his charcoal suit and blue tie. She complimented him and he grinned. "You have a nice smile when you let people see it," she said. "Take a seat. I have good news."

He sat down and looked at her pensively. She had never seen him nervous before.

Megan leaned forward in her chair. "I heard from Bob. Yasmin responded to your message. They had an exchange. I think he did a pretty good job being you."

She pushed a printout across the table and watched as he read it, enjoying the way his eyes widened and began to glow. Then she explained the plan that the intelligence specialist—she was certain he was CIA—had outlined on the phone. Ismail gave her a look that bespoke his misgivings, but he had no choice. He had bought Yasmin a chance. To survive, she had to take it.

"Is there anything you want to tell me before I talk to your pirate friends?" Megan asked.

Ismail shook his head, implacable again.

She sighed. "The trial is two months away. The longer you wait to tell your story, the less likely people will believe it."

He angled his head. "That's a risk I have to take."

"You don't want to tell me about Mas?" she asked. As a favor, Barrington had sent her the recording of Quentin's conversation with Paul on the *Renaissance*. "I know the two of you argued."

She thought she saw a flash of irritation in Ismail's eyes, but it vanished before she could be sure. "It was an intense situation," he said ambiguously. "I had many conversations with my men."

She grimaced. "I'm getting tired of this game."

"You can leave if you want," he said equably. "I'm not paying you."

And throw you to the wolves? You obviously don't know me. Then it came to her: *I'm as much of an enigma to you as you are to me.* "I'm not going to quit. But you made me a promise."

He met her gaze. "It hasn't changed."

She stood up then, her decision never really in question. "All right. Let's do this."

When they entered the conference room, Megan greeted the Somali interpreter, a white-haired man named Sado,

Eldridge Jordan, Barrington's second, and Clifford Greene, an octogenarian solo practitioner who should have hung up his hat years ago. She sat down with Kiley and Ismail beside the court reporter and across from Greene and Sado. Jordan took a seat at the head of the table while Agent Matheson departed to get Greene's client—Dhuuban.

A minute later, the NCIS agent ushered the young Somali into the room and led him to the chair opposite Megan. She had seen Dhuuban only twice before—at his initial arraignment and his plea hearing—and always at a distance. She studied him as he slumped into his seat, his leg and ankle irons jangling like keys. He was a gangly kid with reed-thin limbs and eyes too large for his face. He stared at the table, saying nothing to his lawyer and refusing to look at Ismail.

After introducing herself, Megan worked through the preliminaries. "Dhuuban" was actually a nickname—a reference to his slender frame. His full name was Sahir Ahmed Shirma. He was a member of the Hawiye Habar Gidir Suleiman clan, and hailed from a village near Hobyo. His father owned a number of tea shops and had three wives and fifteen children. Dhuuban was the youngest of seven siblings born to his mother. He wasn't sure of his birthday, but he knew it was sometime during the *deyr* rains two years after the civil war began. By Megan's calculations, he was nineteen.

His father had earned enough to educate his children through the eighth grade. After that, he expected them to work. Dhuuban had done odd jobs before landing a position as a police officer in Hobyo. He stayed there until he didn't receive a paycheck—apparently, the regional government's budget was always in crisis. At that point, a friend had introduced him to Gedef, who was putting together a "coast guard" unit to drive foreign vessels out of Somali waters. Dhuuban had heard stories of million-dollar payoffs and joined Gedef's crew, bringing his own gun.

He had met Afyareh at the seaside camp where Gedef maintained his skiffs. The commander assigned Dhuuban to Afyareh's crew. After a few weeks, an Omani dhow appeared offshore, and they took two skiffs to meet it. Dhuuban didn't know how Gedef had obtained the dhow, but the Omanis never questioned Gedef's orders. They sailed for many days and nights into the ocean without sighting a ship. At last, when their food became scarce, they picked up the *Jade Dolphin* on radar. They tracked it overnight and mounted an attack at first light.

Dhuuban recounted the disastrous hijacking attempt with some animation—the explosion of Gedef's skiff, the search for survivors, recovering Mas, trying but failing to locate the Omani dhow, and making the decision to take refuge in the Seychelles. Megan pressed him for his personal feelings about Mas. He hesitated slightly, then said, "I was happy he survived. He was my friend."

Then came the *Renaissance*. Dhuuban described the capture of the sailboat in almost friendly terms, emphasizing that they never intended to harm the hostages. Their objective was to take the sailboat to Somalia, negotiate a ransom, and let the Parkers go. "Killing is bad for business," he said at least three times in the course of his narrative. "We wanted money, not blood."

Next, Megan led him through the stages of the naval intervention, eliciting his recollections about the *Gettysburg's* approach, the commencement of negotiations, the appearance of the *Truman* and *San Jacinto*, the first day of flight operations, and the offer of the secure radio. "After you saw the small boat on the water," she said, "did you have a discussion about what to do next?"

"*Ha*," Dhuuban mumbled, and Sado translated: "Yes."

"What was the nature of that discussion?"

"We thought it was a trap. We were afraid of the boat. We argued for a while, and then Afyareh told us he had a plan. He said he had permission to negotiate with the family."

An interesting choice of words, Megan thought. "Permission from whom?"

"From Gedef's relatives. They were the people with the money."

Megan glanced at Ismail. "Did Afyareh say which of Gedef's relatives gave him permission?"

"*Ha*," Dhuuban replied. "Gedef's father. He was in charge."

"What did you think about that?" Megan asked.

Dhuuban paused. "I believed Afyareh. He always told the truth."

Megan digested this. *Khadija said the same thing. But why did Dhuuban hesitate? Did his view of Ismail change?* "What did the others say about the idea?"

"Mas didn't believe him at first. He asked Afyareh for proof."

Megan raised an eyebrow. "What kind of proof?"

"He asked Afyareh to swear it on the name of Allah."

"Did he?"

"*Ha.* That was when Afyareh called the Captain's family."

"Tell me more about Mas," Megan said. "He was Gedef's cousin. Did he resent that Gedef had made Afyareh his lieutenant?"

Dhuuban shifted in his seat. "Afyareh spoke English. He had experience hijacking ships. That is why he was lieutenant. I don't know what Mas thought about it."

Power dynamics, Megan wrote on her pad. *Explore further.* Then she moved on, walking Dhuuban through the negotiations with the family, the haggling between Afyareh and Curtis, the deal they reached, and the delivery terms. "What did you think about the ransom amount?"

"We wanted two million," Dhuuban explained. "Afyareh said to give Curtis more time. But Mas thought it was a bad idea. He thought the Navy would do something if we waited. So did Liban."

"What did Afyareh say about that?"

"He changed his mind. Then he called Curtis."

Another clash, Megan thought. *But this time Mas prevailed. Is that a shift in influence?* She led him through the ransom drop and the counting of the cash and then focused on the breakdown with the Navy. "What happened when the helicopter took off?"

Dhuuban puckered his lips and started to suck on his teeth. "Afyareh didn't like the helicopter. He said the Navy was lying to us. He told them to put it away or he would kill the hostages."

"The Navy recalled the helicopter, didn't they?"

Dhuuban nodded.

"But you didn't let the hostages go?"

Without warning, Dhuuban gave her a broad smile. "We saw that the ship was too close."

Megan frowned. *What the hell does he have to smile about?* "Who saw that the ship was too close?"

"Afyareh. He got very angry about it. He started talking about how America has hurt Somalia. He said we needed to fight back. He told the Navy to move the ship or he would kill the hostages."

"What did the others say?" Megan persisted. "What did Mas say?"

Suddenly, Clifford Greene stirred from his slumber. "Objection to form."

Megan simplified the question: "What did Mas say about the ship?"

Dhuuban smiled brighter. "None of us liked it. But Afyareh was angriest. He started yelling at the Navy. He yelled at the negotiator. He said the Americans had betrayed us. They broke the deal."

I'm not buying this, Megan thought. *Mas demanded proof that Ismail had permission to negotiate with the family; he commandeered the decision about the ransom amount; but then he sat on the sidelines while Ismail ranted about America and the proximity of the ship? Dhuuban isn't telling me something.*

"What happened next?" she asked, leaving the question wide open.

"The Navy sent boats toward us," Dhuuban replied. "They turned on bright lights. That was when Afyareh lost his mind. He shot the Captain. Mas wrestled with him, but Afyareh won. Then he shot Timaha and told us to go to the boat."

The words knocked the wind out of Megan. She glanced at Ismail, hoping to see a flicker of feeling, but his face was sculpted out of granite. "I'm almost finished. Just a couple more questions. The gun that Afyareh used to shoot Timaha, was it the same gun he used on the Captain?"

Dhuuban's smile faltered. He sucked his teeth for a while. "I think it was the same gun."

Bingo, Megan thought. *The first crack in the façade.* "When all of this happened, you were close to the Somali coast, isn't that right?"

"Yes," Dhuuban said, smiling again.

"Were you near Hobyo or somewhere else?"

Dhuuban's eyes fell, then rebounded instantly. "We were close to Hobyo."

Megan stared him down. "No, you weren't. You were near Mogadishu."

"Objection," said Greene. "Is that a question?"

But Dhuuban ignored him. "Mogadishu?" he beamed. "Why would we go to Mogadishu?"

You're lying, Megan thought. *I see it now. But I don't know what's true and what's false.* "I'm finished with this witness," she said tersely. She stood up and looked at Kiley and Ismail. "Come with me."

She led them down the hall to the meeting room where they had done their preparations. After Kiley closed the door, Megan confronted Ismail. "This would be a whole lot easier if you would talk to me. I feel like I'm playing chess in the dark."

Ismail stared back at her. "The time isn't right."

She gave vent to her frustration. "Maybe you *are* crazy. He's lying under oath and you're letting him get away with it. This is your *life* on the line."

"He's a good boy," Ismail said with an affection that surprised her. "I don't blame him."

Megan shook her head, livid but unsure what to do about it. "Fine. The least you can do is help me understand his behavior. What was with all the teeth-sucking and smiley faces?"

Ismail spoke frankly. "When he was sucking his teeth, he was thinking about what you had just said. And when he was smiling, he was nervous."

Megan's mind raced with the implications. Dhuuban had started acting strangely when she asked him about the helicopter taking off, but his answers had come easily until she asked him the questions about Ismail's gun and the boat's location on the water. *He wasn't prepared for them,* she inferred. *They forced him to improvise. That's when I saw the lie.*

"Now I've told you something, haven't I?" Ismail said.

Her anger began to abate. "I suppose." She checked her

watch. It was ten thirty. "We're on schedule. Let's go talk to Osman."

It took Megan seven hours to complete the remaining depositions. By the time she dismissed Mas from the chair, she was exhausted but satisfied. The interviews had given her fresh insight into the minds and personalities of Ismail's accusers, and they had highlighted the point in their common narrative where fiction started to blend with fact—the launch of the Navy helicopter.

Osman was the least articulate and most immature in the bunch. During her questioning, he had alternated between periods of brooding silence and loud bursts of speech. Sondare was a sweet, shy teenager whose story had broken her heart. He hadn't wanted to go with the pirates; he had wanted to go to school. But his mother was too poor to feed his five brothers. He had stolen a gun from a friend and joined Gedef's crew at the last minute. Mas was more calculating than the others, and also more composed. He had answered her queries calmly, looking her in the eye. He was also the only one who didn't seem intimidated by Ismail, trading numerous glances with him during his deposition.

It was the smiles that gave away their charade. Sondare had turned into a beacon when he talked about the shooting. Osman had emerged from his passive-compulsive funk and smiled at her, too, though less eagerly. Even Mas had shown his teeth a couple of times, but only when she surprised him with the questions that had tripped up Dhuuban. Sondare and Osman guessed that Ismail used the same weapon to shoot Daniel and Quentin. But Mas professed his ignorance, claiming that his struggle with Ismail had obscured his view at the end. He also gave a cagey response to the question about the sailboat's location. "Afyareh was boss," he said. "I don't know where he took us."

Bullshit, Megan wrote on her pad.

When Mas left the room with his lawyer, Megan looked at Eldridge Jordan. "Can we talk?"

Jordan nodded. A thirtysomething African-American with an oval face and intense eyes, he was a graduate of Princeton and Virginia Law—the kind of upwardly mobile prosecutor who would one day be a judge. They took seats in the meeting room, and Megan got straight to the point.

"Eldridge, I respect you a lot. I respect Clyde. But the evidence isn't adding up. Their story is scripted. They follow the script until they hit a blank, then they start improvising. Daniel and Quentin were shot with different weapons. It doesn't make sense that Ismail was the only shooter."

Jordan tented his hands. "There was a scuffle. He lost control of his gun and picked up another one. If we had weapons, we could get fingerprints, but they're at the bottom of the ocean. All we have is testimony. And right now your client agrees with them. He's not denying he pulled the trigger."

"Did you notice how they started to smile when we talked about the shooting?" she asked. "That's what Somalis do when they get nervous."

Jordan's eyes darkened. "If your client has more to say, we're willing to listen. But right now, our theory is the only one supported by the evidence. The jury can decide if we're right or wrong."

Megan shook her head, trapped between a client who wouldn't talk and a system that placed his fate into the hands of twelve ordinary people with no legal training and no knowledge of Somalia other than the horror stories they saw in the news.

"I'll let you know if something changes," she said and headed toward the door.

YASMIN

When the rains of the *gu* began to fall, Yasmin's world transformed. The desert ground, once as dry as an elephant's hide, softened into loamy clay, giving birth to fields of grass and colorful flowers that seemed to exist for no other reason than beauty. The Juba swelled with the runoff and the languid current quickened into a lively rush, filling the air with water music.

She went about her duties with a spring in her step, going down to the river whenever she could. Sometimes she saw livestock in the distance—herds of goat and cattle and camels pasturing in the meadows. Other times she saw only trees and fields and sky and clouds, an uncluttered Eden that had appeared almost overnight, as if God himself had touched the earth and brought forth new life.

Jamaad kept her busy with chores. She cleaned the house, washed and mended clothing, prepared meals, drew water, and fed and watered the milk cow that Najiib had bought them before departing the last time. When she had a moment to herself, she thought about her conversation with Ismail. "Qosol," he had called her. It was the nickname Adan had given her when she was a little girl. She had loved to laugh. It was a part of herself she longed to recover. How glorious to be free again, to run with the wind and sing with the birds and delight in laughter for the pure enjoyment of it.

Every third night, she climbed the *higlo* tree and checked her phone for messages, but her inbox was always empty. She understood Ismail's silence, but it disappointed her. Before the attack they had been so close, sharing everything. *Soon,* she assured herself. *I will see him again soon.*

Then one afternoon when she was sweeping out the living room, she heard noise in the village. She felt the cold prick of apprehension. She had hoped to have some warning of Najiib's homecoming. She had asked Jamaad every day for news, but the woman had shooed her away, saying, "He'll come when he comes, child. That is how he protects himself."

Yasmin hurried to veil herself and went to the gate to wait for him. When the truck turned into the courtyard, she saw with relief that he had brought only two men this time. They would sleep in the yard, which would make it tricky to reach her phone. But if she was fortunate, the night would be dark and she would make no sound. She said a silent prayer for cloud cover and greeted her husband.

❇

That evening after her work was through, she went to her room and prepared herself to receive him, burning incense and anointing her skin with rose oil. He came to her like a wraith, moving from the shadows into the light. She looked into his eyes, hoping to see tenderness, but she saw only need. He took her without a word, satiating his lust, and then disappeared as quickly as he came.

She covered herself and lay back against the bed, trying to make sense of his silence. Was he angry because she had yet to conceive? Or was he troubled by something else? *Both*, she decided. *He's mad at me, and he's mad about the war. AMISOM is taking back towns left and right. Before long they'll recapture Kismayo and deprive the Shabaab of its primary source of income. Then Najiib will have nothing left but killing.*

Yasmin lay quietly, thinking he might return for a second act. But time passed and she didn't see him again. He had his own bedroom on the other side of the house. He probably planned to sleep there. She snuffed out the candles and turned off her lantern, plunging the room into darkness. Then she went to the window and pulled back the curtain, looking outside. She didn't see or hear his men. *Subhanallah!* she thought. *They're sleeping in the backyard in the shelter Najiib built for the cow.*

It was then that she heard a shuffle of feet. Adrenaline shot through her, but she made no sudden moves. She let the curtain fall back into place and hid her guilt.

"What are you doing?" Najiib asked, his face invisible to her.

She kept her voice steady despite her pounding heart. "I wanted to see the stars."

"What good are they?" he asked, taking her by the arm. "All that matters is here on the earth."

He dragged her to the bed and climbed on top of her, pressing his work-hardened hands into her. She felt a shock of fear. It wasn't lust guiding him this time. It was rage.

"Please," she begged softly. "You're hurting me."

But he didn't seem to care. He forced himself upon her, driving her into the mattress and taking his fill of her in a way that sent shards of pain through her body. She knew not to cry out or resist. Instead, she bit her lip until she tasted blood. She gave him what he wanted by the sheer force of her will, holding out for the moment when he would leave her alone.

At last, he rolled off of her and sat on the edge of the bed, staring at her silently. She wanted to cover herself, to hide her shame, but she knew it would only provoke him. He began to speak, and his tone cut her like a knife. There was no kindness in it, only malice.

"When I took you in, I promised to show you the righteous path. All I wanted in return was a son to teach the ways of *jihad*. You have failed me. You have become an impediment, just like your father was. He thought we should make peace with our enemies. He was a fool. The only way to make peace with a viper is to kill it. If I were less benevolent, I would divorce you. But you are good to Jamaad. I will keep you for her sake. But I will no longer tolerate your empty womb."

He stood up, pulled on his pants, and vanished into the darkness.

Yasmin didn't move, just stared at the ceiling, her heart paralyzed by disgrace. Eventually, she began to weep. The tears ran down her cheeks and moistened her pillow. She cried until the wave of anguish abated, and then she went to her bureau, putting on her black *abaya* and headscarf. She had no use for self-pity. What Najiib had done to her, he had done. Nothing could change it. But she wouldn't be his next casualty. She would survive until Ismail came. And then she would leave this life behind.

She stretched out on her bed and tried to rest, but her body was too sore for sleep. She lay half-awake, dreaming of the life she would make with her brother in Kenya. They would live in hiding for a while, using assumed names and trading on the favors of their relatives, until Najiib died or forgot about them. Then they would go into business together. They would borrow some money and start a restaurant. She was a talented cook, and he had a level head. They would make it work.

Somewhere in the midst of these musings she drifted off to sleep.

She woke again in the middle of the night. She opened her eyes and listened intently. The house and the yard were still. She moved to the doorway and looked down the hall toward the living room, breathing to steady herself. She couldn't see much in the gloom, just the dim outline of furniture. She waited a full minute, her senses on high alert. When she heard nothing, she walked to the front door on the balls of her feet, a shadow among shadows, her body wrapped in black.

She waited again at the door, looking and listening. The sky was mostly clear, but there was no moon. She slipped out of the house and crossed the yard to the *higlo* tree, hoisting herself onto a limb and traversing the wall with the agility of a leopard. She dropped to the ground with barely a sound and retrieved the phone. In the text window, she typed: He's here with two men. Don't know how long.

After sending it, she sat down among the roots of the tree, uncertain what to do. One minute passed, then two. She looked across the river into the dark heart of the desert. It was the middle of the night in Kenya. Why would Ismail be awake? She decided to wait fifteen minutes and then go back to bed. With Najiib in the house, it was all she could risk.

Suddenly, her phone vibrated in her hand. His message read: Good. Are you ready?

Her heart began to race. I am. What should I do?

Do you trust me, Qosol?

Of course.

His reply took her breath away. Then you must run. Go to Dadaab. Hooyo is alive. She is a nurse in the Dagahaley camp. Find her. She will know what to do.

In the moments that followed, time lost all meaning for Yasmin. She didn't notice when she started crying or understand why she stood up and went to the riverbank, dipping her fingers in the flowing current. She registered nothing beyond the raw delight and trepidation inspired by his words. *Hooyo is alive? Ismail found her? But Dadaab is so far. Why is he not coming for me?*

At last she concentrated long enough to write: Is there no other way?

No. You are strong, Qosol. You will make it.

She thought of the foodstuffs she had already secreted around the house. Walking to Dadaab was a desperate gamble, but it was possible if the rains held. Okay, she typed.

Don't wait. You must go tonight.

She narrowed her eyes, unsettled by his urgency. If she had another day, she could complete her preparations. Why not tomorrow?

Go now. There is no time to waste.

She looked up at the stars, trying to discern the time. She saw Scorpio hanging low in the sky to the southwest. That meant it was early morning. She wouldn't make it far before the sun rose, but Ismail had given her no other option. All right, she wrote.

There is something you must do first.

What?

You must hide your phone in his truck.

The request confused her. Why?

I will tell you when I see you. Make sure he can't find it. And delete the memory. Everything connecting it to you.

Okay, she agreed. Please pray for me.

I will, Qosol. Go now. Find Hooyo. See you soon.

Soon, she typed through her tears.

After the message was sent, she restored the factory set-tings on the phone and secreted it in her underwear. Then she turned away from the river and scaled the *higlo* tree again, blocking out all thought of the ordeal she would have to endure to make it out of Somalia alive.

It took Yasmin only twenty minutes to gather her belong-ings, but it felt like half a day in the liquid suspension of her fear. She moved through the house like a spirit, collect-ing everything in a laundry sack—dried goat meat, dates and nuts, a sturdy blanket, a tub of antibacterial ointment, a pouch of bandages, and two pairs of sandals. She gave thought to taking the Quran, but the book was heavy and she had memorized most of it. The words in her heart would guide her steps.

She was about to step out into the yard when she heard something near the gate. She stopped cold. The night was so dark that she couldn't see a shape, just a faint shadow, but she knew the sound in her ears—the crunch of rubber soles on dirt. She watched in terror as the shadow advanced along the wall, making its way toward the *higlo* tree. Her mind began churning out questions: *Is it one of Najiib's men? Did he see me? Why is he awake?*

The shadow reached the tree and disappeared beneath

the canopy. The sound, however, continued—crunch, crunch, pause, crunch. Yasmin waited anxiously, taking shallow breaths and peering into the branches. Finally, she saw the shadow again. It turned at the corner of the yard and followed the wall toward the back of the house. *He's inspecting the wall. I need to move quickly.*

Yasmin counted to three and then tiptoed toward the truck parked by the gate. She took out her phone and climbed softly onto the step. Thankfully, Najiib had left the window open. She reached into the cab and placed the unit beneath the passenger seat, giving it a shove with her fingers. She stepped down and went to the gate, grabbing an empty water jug and slinging it over her shoulder with the laundry bag. Then she made her way to the *higlo* tree.

The traverse took longer than usual with her load, but she didn't make a sound. After climbing down, she walked to the river and followed the bulrushes into the night. She looked at the stars to orient herself. She saw Draco in the north and Virgo in the west. It was fitting. She would flee the Dragon and trust the Maiden to guide her to Kenya.

She made her way along the Juba until she reached the beach she had seen from the eddy where she drew water. After years of studying the river, she knew where its banks were wide and its current calm. She doffed her clothes and put them in her sack, then waded out into the cool water, holding the sack on top of her head. She had considered a number of escape routes, but always she had returned to the same thought: *Najiib will expect me to follow the river, not ford it. He doesn't know that I can swim.*

She felt the water swirling around her legs, tugging at her as it flowed downstream. When she was waist-deep in the river, she pushed off and swam with her right arm even as she balanced the sack above her. The current swept her south toward the bend and Najiib's house. She thrust with her legs and pulled with her free arm, knifing through the water toward the far shore.

As soon as she felt mud between her toes, she walked into the reeds, dried off with her *abaya*, and then dressed again. She filled her jug with fresh water and set off into the desert at a steady gait. She reached a stand of trees just as the sky began to lighten. She searched the shadows carefully and watched the ground for snakes. Many creatures hunted in the trees. To some she was prey.

The sunrise happened suddenly, turning twilight into day and sending slanting light through the leaves. A few birds took flight when she passed beneath them, beating the air with their wings. Soon she emerged from the thicket and headed out across the desert again. In time, she stopped to take a drink of water. She looked back at the village, but she couldn't see it through the trees.

She was about to start walking again when she heard a faint sound in the sky, fading in and out. She looked up at the patches of blue and scudding clouds, searching for an explanation. The sound grew louder and more consistent. *That's not natural*, she thought. *That's a motor.* At first she guessed it was an airplane, but she saw no sign of one. Then she recalled a conversation she had had with her father and brother not long before the school attack.

They sound like an insect, Ismail had said. *The targets don't see them until it's too late.*

Do you think the Americans will use them here? she asked.

If they do, they'll invite a backlash, Adan replied. *The Shabaab will use them as a recruiting tool just like al-Qaeda has done in Afghanistan and Yemen. Remember Newton's third law. Every action has an equal and opposite reaction. It's as true in war as it is in science.*

Yasmin felt a stab of fear. *It's a drone.*

She scoured the sky for a reflection, anything that might give away its flight path, but she came up empty. She looked east toward the trees and the village—

It was then she saw the fireball.

It flared orange-red like the rising sun, then quickly turned black with smoke as the sound of an explosion rolled across the land. She watched in disbelief. *Najiib,* she thought. *The Americans came for him.* Then her shock turned into dread. *How many others are dead?* She had no idea what to think or do in that moment. She just stood there, unmoving, until the rumble died away and all was still again.

When at last her brain reengaged, she realized the uncanny timing of her escape. Only hours ago she had been asleep in her bed. Now her bedroom and the house around it were almost certainly gone. She recalled Ismail's words. *There is something you must do . . . You must hide your phone in his truck . . . Go tonight. There is no time to waste.*

Somehow the phone was linked to the drone strike.

Blood rushed to her head, and she fell to her knees in

horror. She thought of Jamaad and the families that lived beyond the walls. It was likely that dozens of villagers had been in the blast radius. She tried to stand up, but her legs were too wobbly to hold her. She crossed them instead, sitting on the dirt and struggling with the question that defied all explanation.

Why, Ismail? Why did you make me do it?

The longer she puzzled over it, the less sense it made. Her brother was a twenty-year-old Somali refugee in Kenya. How could he have been involved in an American drone strike? Yet the timing was too coincidental. She mulled over her last exchange with him. He had asked her to hide the phone in Najiib's truck. Why the truck? Why not the house? And why had he specified that she conceal it? Did he think Najiib would search for the phone? The answer came to her in a flash.

He knew Najiib would come looking for me.

This changed everything. If Najiib had been driving when the missile hit, he and his men might have been the only casualties. She held on to this theory like a lifeline. It had to be true. Ismail had asked her to trust him. Whatever he had gotten into, he would not have used her to murder innocent people. She buried her face in her hands and wept with relief. At long last, her captivity was over. Najiib would never kill or rape again. Adan's assassination was avenged. She was finally free.

She lifted herself to her feet and threw her sack and jug over her shoulder, looking into the brightness of the dawn.

The desert was alive with new grass and flowers. She had food for most of the journey, and water for a couple of days at least. The rains would sustain her. She had strong legs and a stronger heart. She would survive, *inshallah*.

With God's help, she would make it to Dadaab.

ISMAIL

The drone strike made headlines in the United States the day after it happened. When Ismail finished his exercises, he took the newspaper off the rack and sat down at a table in the common area. He had twenty-eight minutes to read before Longfellow took him back to his cell. He saw the words on the front page below the fold, and his heart did a backflip in his chest. US DRONE STRIKE IN SOMALIA KILLS AL-SHABAAB LEADER. He flew through the story as fast as his mind could process it.

> Sources within the militant group al-Shabaab say that a missile fired by an American drone killed a key leader in the group's intelligence unit, the Amniyat, outside a remote village in the Middle Juba province of Somalia on Friday. Hagi Abdulaziz, a commander in the Shabaab, said that the target of the attack, Mohamed Abdullah

al-Noor, was a close friend and advisor of the Shabaab emir, Ahmed Abdi Godane.

Known by many as "Azrael," the Angel of Death, al-Noor has long been accused by international authorities of orchestrating a brutal campaign of assassination, targeting moderates within the Somali government and business community who oppose the Shabaab's agenda. Abdulaziz reported that two other fighters were killed with al-Noor when a missile destroyed the truck they were driving in.

A US Defense Department spokesman confirmed the attack but offered no further details. Somalia's president called the killing a "serious blow" to the forces of extremism and instability that have dragged the nation's civil war into its third decade.

Al-Shabaab has been losing ground in Somalia ever since African Union troops drove it out of Mogadishu in 2011. In January, the group made its alliance with al-Qaeda official when Godane appeared in a video with Ayman al-Zawahiri, the leader of al-Qaeda. Though ousted from Mogadishu, the Shabaab remains in control of much of southern Somalia.

Ismail tossed the paper on the table and smiled grimly. He hated the drone war. Raining death from the skies was neither honorable nor infallible, and often led to collateral damage. But this time he made an exception. The strike had been righteous. The Amniyat had been decapitated, and Najiib had been judged. A verse from the Quran came to him: *And you will see the sinners on that day bound in fetters, their garments made of pitch and their faces covered with fire.* Najiib was in Allah's hands now.

Ismail stood up again and walked to the telephone mounted on the wall. He motioned to Longfellow. "I need to make a call."

"It's your time," the jailer replied.

He dialed Megan's mobile number. It was a weekend, but he didn't mind disturbing her.

"Ismail," she said. "I imagine you saw the story."

"Have you heard from Bob?" he asked. "Does he know where she is?"

"I just spoke to him. Yasmin escaped. They got a visual of her in the desert. They've made contact with your mother. The wheels are turning to get them green cards and authorize the reward. I've never seen the government move this quickly. They're clearly motivated."

Ismail leaned his head against the wall. "Now she just has to get there."

Megan took a reflective breath. "They're going to keep tabs on her."

More eyes in the sky, he thought. "I don't see why they can't just go out and get her."

"I know," Megan said. "I pushed Bob on it, but he wouldn't budge."

"Okay," he said resignedly. "Then we wait."

"Keep your chin up," she encouraged him. "She's made it this far."

"Yes, she has." He placed the phone back in its cradle. *Hooyo*, he thought. *She's coming to you. I've done what I promised to do.*

YASMIN

The vultures started to follow her after the third day. They flew high in the sky, making lazy circles in the air and occasionally descending to take a closer look. To a superstitious person, they might have been troubling, but Yasmin didn't believe in portents. The birds were just curious. She must have been a strange sight to them—a solitary figure robed in black trekking across the expanse, sometimes at night when the land was flat and denuded of foliage, sometimes during the day when she had to traverse a patch of forest. In a way, she welcomed the birds' company. It meant she wasn't alone.

She tried hard to walk a straight path just south of west, but there were times she had to detour to avoid attracting attention. Of the many dangers in the wilderness, it was the people that scared her most. Every time she came across a road, she hid behind a tree and watched it for half an hour before crossing it. Whenever she saw signs of human activity—ashes from a fire, recently chewed grass in a meadow, fresh hoofprints in the dirt—she concealed herself in the bush and listened carefully, waiting to see if anyone was nearby. The nomads were less of a concern. Most were kind, and the few who weren't she could outrun because they wouldn't leave their herds. The bandits, however, terrified her, as did the village people, for they were under the sway of the Shabaab.

During the day, she maintained a steady pace, brisk enough to cover ground but not enough to enervate her. The weather made no difference to her progress. She walked whether the sky was bright or wet with rain. But whenever a shower came, she took time to refresh her water supply, catching the raindrops in her hijab and funneling them into her jug. At night, she adopted a slower gait, walking carefully across the uneven terrain to minimize the risk of injury.

Every so often, she stopped to rest, curling up beneath a shade tree in the daytime or on a spot of open ground at night. It took her body a few days to adjust to her new sleep schedule, but after that she didn't notice the difference. She rationed her meals, eating a handful of dates and nuts in the morning and two strips of dried meat in the evening. She knew she was burning far more calories than she was taking in, but she didn't have to do it forever. Her mother was out there waiting for her.

As she walked, she allowed her mind to drift and spoke her thoughts out loud. She had never talked to herself, but she found the exercise cathartic, an antidote to the loneliness of the journey. When she grew tired of reminiscing and reflecting, she imagined herself conversing with her family.

She talked to her father about religion and duty, to her mother about poetry and love, to Ismail about science and music, and to Yusuf about the birds, bugs, and lizards she had seen.

On the sixth day, in a land of forest and low hills, she heard the sound of engines. She crouched down behind a *galool* tree and listened. As the seconds passed, the noise increased until the earth began to vibrate. She looked around, transfixed by dread. She had to be near a road, but the forest was too dense for her to make it out. She pulled her sack and jug closer, her nerves as taut as razor wire.

Then she saw it—a caravan of technicals about fifty meters away. The trucks were crammed with soldiers in green tunics brandishing AK-47s. Most had their heads uncovered, but a few were wearing black headscarves—the signature of the Shabaab. Two thoughts struck her at the same time: *This must be the road to Afmadow.* And: *They're just like the ones who came for Aabbe in the schoolyard.*

Suddenly, the trucks braked to a stop. Yasmin watched in horror as the soldiers jumped out, slung their rifles over their shoulders, and spread out into the trees, chatting amiably. *Of all the places to take a rest stop*, she thought, tightening herself into a ball. The shade around her was deep, thanks to the canopy of the tree and the halo of sun-drenched dirt around it, but she felt hopelessly exposed.

She closed her eyes, not wanting to see how close they were. She heard their footsteps on the earth, the bark of their male banter, the rustle of their belts when they unhooked them, and the splatter of their urine as they relieved themselves. *Allah, make me invisible*, she prayed. *Please don't let them see me.*

For a while they stood around making jokes and denouncing the apostates in the government and the infidels in the African Union. Then she heard a shout, and they began to move again, returning to their vehicles. She sat motionless until the trucks departed, waiting for the sounds of the forest—the birdsong and the quiet breeze—to swallow the last detestable remnants of the engines.

When she was alone again, she opened her sack and ate a few nuts and a date. Then she examined her feet for cuts. Her once-smooth skin was a patchwork of blisters, but they weren't an immediate concern. Only open wounds could invite an infection. Satisfied, she took a swig of water and stood up, ignoring the persistent ache in her joints and muscles. She had walked a great distance, but she was only halfway there. She heard Ismail's voice in her head: *Go now. There's no time to waste.*

"I'm going, Madaxa," she said quietly, touching the bark of the *galool* tree in gratitude. "I don't know where you are or what you have done, but I trust you."

Step by step, Yasmin turned the minutes into miles, boosting her pace as much as her weary body could sustain. It was fear as much as determination that drove her forward. Each day that passed increased her chances of being seen. In time, the trees thinned out and the hills flattened into a grassy plain, allowing her to walk in the moonlight as well as the day. Mornings were usually clear, but every afternoon clouds gathered overhead and poured out the blessing of fresh water. Occasionally, she came across a watering hole and gave it wide berth. Twice, she heard the gong of a camel bell, but she didn't see the animals or their herdsmen.

On the ninth day, just before sunset, she sat down beneath an acacia tree and leaned her head against the trunk, feeling exhaustion in every inch of her frame. She closed her eyes and concentrated on breathing, her mind blank. She didn't sense the presence until she heard a low growl like a tremor in the wind. She opened her eyes and was seized by terror.

A male lion stood ten feet away.

Her first instinct was to run, but she rejected it swiftly, certain that it would lead to her death. Instead, she sat perfectly still, watching the cat. She had heard stories of lions in the bush, but she had never seen one. She studied the beast and saw its bony shoulders and scrawny legs. It was hungry. It was then that she had a thought: *Stand up and talk to it. Tell it to leave you alone.* She didn't know where the idea came from, but it was better than nothing.

She stood up slowly and stared down the lion. "I know you haven't eaten in a while," she said in Somali, "but I am not good food. Do you see these arms and legs? I have no meat left on me."

The lion growled again, its mane shining like copper in the light of the setting sun.

Feeling desperate, she switched to English. "There is nothing here for you, just skin and bones. It is spring. There are other animals that will taste much better."

The cat lowered its head and pawed the ground, gazing at her through fearsome yellow eyes.

Another thought came to her: *Leave your sack and back away.* She stepped slowly to the side of the tree. "I'm going to leave now. You can have my food, but you can't have me."

She took one step backward, then another. At once, a gust of wind blew through her *abaya*, and it billowed outward like a sail. When the lion saw this, it looked at her strangely. She continued to back away, her heart throbbing in her chest. As soon as she left the shade of the tree, the lion moved toward her sack and put its nose into the opening. *That's right*, she thought. *Take all you want.*

With the beast momentarily distracted, she glanced over her shoulder and saw another acacia nearby. She threw her hands around the lowest limb and pulled herself up. The lion roared in anger, but by the time it reached the tree she was fifteen feet off the ground. She felt like she was moving through glue, so heightened were her senses, but she climbed onward, her arms and legs scorching from the strain. The cat leaned on the trunk and roared in frustration, but it made no attempt to follow her.

From her perch on the highest limb, Yasmin watched the sun sink toward the horizon, turning the clouds pink and casting long shadows across the grasslands. It took awhile for the lion to lose interest in her, but eventually it returned to her sack and dragged it into the bush.

She sat quietly, holding on to the trunk, until the sky was as dark as the land. The thought of leaving the tree terrified her, but she knew she couldn't stay there. She had four days of walking left before she would reach Dadaab. With her food gone, she had to hurry.

She dropped to the ground and collected her water jug, seeing no sign of the cat. It had taken her sack toward the northeast, which was fortunate. She saw the full moon rising in the east and turned in the opposite direction, toward Sirius, the brightest star in the heavens. She took off at a fast clip, spurred on by the residue of adrenaline and by her unwavering dedication to the goal.

Sometime in the early-morning hours, her energy ran out. She tried to sit down, but her legs were so weak that they collapsed beneath her. She fell in a heap, knocking the side of her head against a rock. She stared up at the sky for a long time, her thoughts wrapped in gauze. She saw the belt of the Milky Way twinkling above her and Scorpio stretched out behind the moon. She thought she heard a faint sound, like the crackle of radio static, but it faded out and she forgot about it.

Eventually, she turned on her side and looked west. The Maiden was there calling out to her, as she had from the banks of the Juba, but Yasmin didn't have the strength to take another step. Her journey would have to wait until daylight. She closed her eyes and fell into a dreamless sleep.

She awoke when her subconscious registered the sensation of something splashing on her face. It went on for half a minute before she opened her eyes and saw the rain. By the time she struggled into a sitting position, her *abaya* was drenched. The rain fell harder, turning the dirt into mud. She had such a hangover from sleep that she almost forgot to refill her water jug. After she washed it out and topped it off, the rain slackened and the clouds parted, revealing the sun. She was shocked to see it high in the western sky. She had slept for many hours.

After drinking deeply from the jug, she stood up with painstaking effort and looked into the distance. The land here was almost completely barren, its scrub trees low and stunted, like moles on skin. She imagined it in the dry season, baked by a merciless sun. It was why she had never tried to escape before. She took a hesitant step and felt pain radiate from her ankles and knees. *Three more days*, she thought. *I don't know if I can make it.* Her heart, however, rebelled against her weariness. She pictured her mother's face. *You will survive. Death is not an option.*

She used the sun to locate a landmark to the southwest—a plane tree. She fixed her eyes on it and began to walk. The first mile was excruciating, but the second mile wasn't so bad, and by the third mile she hit her stride again. She felt hunger gnawing at her insides, but she ignored the discomfort and concentrated on the tree. She passed it in an hour and replaced it with another landmark. She went on like this until sunset and then followed the stars until the moon reached its zenith. At last, she stretched out on the hard earth and slept until she woke again.

The next day, she found it much harder to get up. The

pain was like a cloud around her, suffocating her when she tried to move. She gritted her teeth and stood anyway, casting off the fetters of hunger and fatigue. She took a drink of water and shuffled forward, managing a decent gait. The hours passed by without account. She no longer had the energy to talk to herself. Her mind was like a balloon, floating from one sensory impression to another. Occasionally, she recited a verse from the Quran to boost her morale, but that was the extent of it.

She rested at midday and fell asleep until evening. When she woke again, she put the jug to her lips and drank thirstily. Then she realized something. The afternoon was gone and it hadn't rained. In fact, it had been a day and a half since the last shower. She swirled the jug and heard water sloshing in empty air. Food she could live without, but not liquid. She felt the despondency creeping in, like the vultures that continued to track her. *Allah*, she thought, *have you let me come this far only to die?*

On a whim, she decided to perform the *Maghrib* prayer. She had allowed her piety to lapse during the journey. Her prayers had become irregular, then optional. She picked up a handful of dirt and used it to cleanse her hands and face in accordance with the prescription. Then she spoke the *takbir* and proceeded through three repetitions of standing, kneeling, prostrating, and sitting. At the end, she spoke her petition. *Please take me home to my mother and my brother. They are all I have left.*

After this, she slept again.

The next time she opened her eyes, it was dawn. She

pulled her body upright, slaked her thirst with the last of her water, and started to walk. For most of the morning, her legs acquiesced to her will. But then she tripped on a rock and sprawled face-first across the ground. She struggled to her feet and stumbled on, but it wasn't long before she fell a second time. She sat in the shade of a bush and nursed her bruises, watching the bright sky and seeing no sign of clouds.

Get up! she commanded herself. *Go on!* And she did, for another hour, before she collapsed again and didn't have the strength to rise. The weight of exhaustion dragged her eyelids closed, and she slipped into a state somewhere between consciousness and sleep.

Eventually, she heard a sound in the background, a noise like a motor that cycled in and out. After that, an unknown amount of time passed. Then she heard another sound, like the crunching of gravel. A shadow passed over her, and she heard a shout. She was so far gone that she didn't feel terror, just the dull prod of concern. She felt herself being lifted and placed in a flatbed truck. There were faces all around, faces connected to bodies wearing military fatigues. *Al-Shabaab*, she thought. *It's over.*

The truck began to bump along, and more time passed. Someone put a canister to her lips and drizzled water onto them. She heard words being spoken in a fog. Nothing made sense. In time, the bumping stopped and hands grabbed her again, carrying her into shade. Shadows moved around her, touching her feet and arms. She opened her eyes to see what was happening to her and caught the blur of a red headscarf. *Who is it?* she thought, not understanding. Then she heard a woman whisper in her ear, "Yasmin. I'm here. It's going to be all right."

She opened her eyes wider and stared into the loveliest face she had ever seen. She mouthed the word once, twice, before she found her voice. "*Hooyo*," she said.

It was Khadija.

VI

THE RENAISSANCE

I held it truth, with him who sings
to one clear harp in divers tones,
that men may rise on stepping-stones
of their dead selves to higher things.
—ALFRED, LORD TENNYSON

PAUL

Paul parked beside the row of Tuscan pines and sat for a moment, staring at the house. He still didn't know what to think about Vanessa's invitation. She had called him a week ago out of the blue and asked if he would like to join her family for a spring cookout and sailing on the Chesapeake. He was so astonished by the offer that he hadn't answered right away.

For years, he had avoided cultivating personal relationships with the families of hostage victims. The emotional dynamics were tricky, the past was an ever-present backdrop, and he had obligations to the Bureau that sometimes conflicted with the family's wishes. With the Parkers, however, he had been swept into their orbit by circumstances out of his control, and he had forged a bond that he couldn't easily sever, even if he wanted to—which he didn't. He felt an unusual camaraderie with Quentin, along with the urge to protect him. And Vanessa was . . . She was . . . He didn't want to think about it.

"Is there an occasion?" he had asked at last.

"Nothing formal," she replied.

"Was it Quentin's idea?"

She took a breath. "He wants to remember what happened. He thinks hearing your voice might help." She went on quickly, "But that wasn't the only reason. He'd like to hear you play again."

"And you?" Paul asked. "How do you feel about it?"

Her voice softened. "I'd like to hear you play again, too."

For days, he had tried to purge his mind of those words. They didn't mean anything; they couldn't mean anything. She had a fond recollection of the song he had played and the way Quentin had responded, nothing more. But something inside of him didn't want to let go of her voice. Playing Chopin in her living room had been one of the most poignant experiences of his life.

At last, he left his car and walked to the door. She met him in the foyer clad in sandals, capris, and a navy-blue sweater with dots that looked like stars. Her hair was pulled back in a ponytail.

"Paul," she said with a smile. "Come in. Quentin and Ariadne are getting the boat ready. Can I get you anything to drink? Water, lemonade, coffee?"

"I'm fine, thanks," he said, following her into the living room and admiring the antique map of Rome on the wall. "I love the print. I didn't see it before."

She came up beside him. "Daniel had a fascination with maps." She fixed her green eyes on him. "I should warn you—Quentin hates using the motor. We'll be at the mercy of the wind."

He laughed, trying to ignore how fetching she looked. "It's good for me. According to my sister, I don't know how to relax."

Vanessa smiled warmly. "I know what you mean." She grabbed a sailing jacket off of one of the chairs and tossed it over her shoulder. "Come on. I want to introduce you to someone."

He trailed her out the back door and saw a man with silver hair tending the poolside grill.

"Ted," Vanessa said, "this is Paul Derrick. Ted is my stepfather and our chef du jour. He makes the best tenderloin on the East Coast."

"Somebody's got to cook the food," Ted said with a smile, looking Paul up and down. "Don't take this the wrong way, but you don't look like a G-man."

Paul smirked. "Nobody's ever said that to me before."

"Whoa, you have a sense of humor, too. I'm going to have to check your badge before I let you go out with my daughter." Ted grinned. "On the water, I mean."

Paul glanced at Vanessa and saw that she was blushing. *Shit. So I wasn't imagining things. All I have to do is get through the day. Then I can walk away graciously.*

"Bon voyage," Ted said, holding up a spatula. "Bring back a whetted appetite."

"Sorry about that," Vanessa said as she led Paul toward the river. "He has no filter."

"I like that," Paul replied. "I know where I stand."

He inhaled the fragrant air, scented by forest and sea, and drank in the day. The weather was magnificent—seventy-five degrees with spotless skies and just enough of a wind to fill the sails. He saw Ariadne in the cockpit of the *Relativity*, dressed in a long-sleeve shirt and cutoff jeans, and Quentin standing on the dock looking like a yachtsman in a windbreaker, shorts, and topsiders. As Paul watched, he handed Ariadne a cooler without losing his balance.

"He's really coming along," Paul said.

Vanessa laughed softly. "It's amazing what a girl can do."

Paul hesitated a moment, then asked the question that came to him. "I don't mean to pry, but has he talked about the future? Is he thinking about college?"

Vanessa nodded. "He's finishing the correspondence courses he was taking on the *Renaissance*. We'll send in college applications in the fall."

"He's going to take a gap year," Paul said.

"I think it will be good for him. Ariadne is going to take it with him. They'll work some and travel the rest. They want to go to college together."

Paul stopped on the sundeck. "They're really serious."

Vanessa shrugged. "I was skeptical at first, but not anymore. She's the best thing that ever happened to him. I don't know if it'll last. But right now it's a gift."

Paul looked into her eyes. "I like that perspective."

She smiled again. "I'm trying. You're not the only one who needs to learn how to relax."

✸

Thirty minutes later, they sailed out of the mouth of the Severn River and into the blue-gray embrace of the bay. Quentin stood at the helm, his hands on the wheel, and Ariadne scurried behind him making adjustments to lines and sheets. Paul sat with Vanessa in the shade of the dodger, sipping a Heineken. With alcohol in his system, he found it easier to loosen up.

So, apparently, did Vanessa. After they swapped anecdotes about life in DC, she gave him a truth-or-dare kind of stare and asked, "Were you ever married?"

"A long time ago," he said, watching the wind tousle her hair. "It was messy."

"Isn't it always? We're all a bit of a mess."

He tilted his head, refreshed by her candor. "I wouldn't know. I never tried again."

She gave him an inquisitive look. "Why not?"

"The Bureau keeps a tight leash. It's not fair to subject someone else to that." *At least that's the excuse I've always used,* he thought. *Kelly couldn't handle it, so neither could anyone else.*

Vanessa laughed. "That sounds miserable. Don't you get lonely?"

"I try not to focus on it," he replied, thinking, *Ted isn't the only one without a filter.*

She looked away and watched Quentin steer the boat in the direction of the Bay Bridge.

For some reason, her silence prompted him to explain himself. "It's like this. When you do what I do, the pace never relents. It's like a Ferrari stuck in top gear."

Her expression turned empathetic. "I understand. Many of my patients are refugees. There's always another family in need. I used to resent my limits. But I've learned to accept them. I'm only one person. If I don't take care of myself, I can't take care of anyone else."

He pondered her counsel, moved by the resemblance it bore to Megan's. But there was a difference—Megan had never taken her own advice.

"I'm sorry," Vanessa said, putting her bottle in the console between them. "I don't mean to preach." She gave him a playful look. "Let's go up to the bow."

He looked at her curiously. "I thought sailboats turned your stomach."

She showed him a patch behind her ear. "It's the newest remedy for motion sickness. I don't feel a thing anymore." She stepped onto the deck, using the dodger for support. "Come on."

Paul glanced briefly at Quentin, wondering what he was thinking. But the boy wasn't paying attention to them. He was lost in Ariadne's world. "Okay," he said and joined Vanessa in crab-walking to the bow. They took seats beneath the headsail as the *Relativity* pitched and rolled with the waves.

Vanessa raised her face toward the sun. "I love this bay. It's like heaven to me."

Paul looked across the water toward the bridge and back toward the Annapolis skyline. He was close enough to smell a hint of her perfume mixed in with the brine of the sea. He didn't know how to handle the way he was feeling. After his marriage imploded, he had boarded up his heart, giving himself only to people who knew they needed him—people at work and people in duress. But the void had never felt natural. He was made for companionship. He decided to take the plunge.

Be here now, he told himself. *Be here with her. Don't turn away the gift.*

After sailing under the bridge, they turned around and returned to the house, arriving just in time for Ted to serve up a banquet of tenderloin, yams, asparagus, and St. André cheese, along with an exceptional Virginia red called Octagon. They ate at a round table on the deck and enjoyed a freewheeling conversation guided mostly by Ted, who seemed enamored of his role as host.

The teenagers polished off their food with gusto and then took turns regaling them with stories from the South Pacific. Paul listened to them with fascination, wondering at moments where Quentin ended and Ariadne began. They traded jokes, interrupted each other with ease, and finished each other's sentences. *No wonder Vanessa likes her,* he thought. *She's adorable.*

"You must miss your family," Paul said after finishing his last bite of tenderloin.

Ariadne nodded, humor in her eyes. "My mum doesn't know what to do without me around. She's coming to visit in a couple of weeks."

"And we're going to go to Australia . . . after the trial

is over," Quentin added, his hesitation between words now barely a hiccup.

Paul regarded Vanessa. "You, too?"

She shook her head. "Just the two of them. I'd get in the way."

"Where do you want to go to college?" Paul asked Quentin.

"St. John's," the boy replied decisively. "I want to stay . . . in Annapolis."

Ariadne laughed. "He's going to spend four years sailing while I do all the studying."

"She wants to be . . . an occupational therapist," Quentin explained. "But we're going to sail around the world . . . before she goes to grad school."

Paul was astonished. He glanced at Vanessa and saw her apprehension, but she said nothing to dissuade them. "How long would that take?" he asked.

"If we follow the southern route around the great capes, we could do it in a year," Ariadne said.

They chatted for a while longer, savoring the wine and magical weather. When the sun fell behind the house, casting the deck into shadow, Quentin gave Paul a pointed look. "I don't mean to impose . . . but would you play for us again?"

Ariadne nudged him with her elbow. "He just finished eating."

Paul grinned. "It's all right. What do you want to hear?"

"Anything," Quentin said eagerly.

"That I can do," Paul replied, taking the last sip of his wine.

They retired to the living room, and Paul took a seat at the Bösendorfer while the others sat on the couch and chairs. He tried not to look at Vanessa, but he couldn't help it. She was watching him, her green eyes sparkling in the light. He stretched his hands over the keys and launched into a robust arrangement of Gershwin's *Rhapsody in Blue* that rattled the windows and made everyone laugh. After that, he improvised a bridge into Billy Joel's "Piano Man."

"You have to sing it," Ted said, clapping his hands. "It's one of my favorites."

Paul shook his head, but Vanessa urged him on. "Sing for us, Paul."

He raised his eyebrows in mock dismay, but he couldn't deny her, so he dug deep and gave it his best shot. He knew the lyrics, but he couldn't quite reach the high end of the register and had to deploy his falsetto. It didn't matter, though. In those minutes, he lost all sense of embarrassment. He gave voice to the music, and the music gave voice to the melody in his heart.

After he struck the final chord, he received their applause with a lopsided grin. Then he looked at Quentin and said, "That's enough for me. Now it's your turn."

The young man traded a glance with Vanessa. "Mom, will you join me?"

"Do you really want me to?" she asked, her reticence plain.

He nodded. "Let's play *Scheherazade*."

"All right," she acceded, and they stood together, moving to their instruments.

Paul watched, mesmerized, as Vanessa placed the violin beneath her chin and played the first haunting strains of the prelude. Then Quentin came in, and the notes erupted from the piano like sparks from a fire. They played the sonata side by side, her fingers dancing on the fingerboard and his on the keys, as the sun descended into the trees behind them. There was a synergy in their performance that spoke of something more elemental than music. *They're alive*, he mused, catching the same look of pleasure on the faces of mother and son. *And they are one.*

When they finished, Ted exclaimed, "Bravo! Bravo!"

Vanessa smiled sheepishly and put down her violin. "Thank you," she said for both of them.

Paul smiled along with her and took a picture of her face. The thought came to him: *No matter what happens, I don't want to forget this moment.*

Somehow he knew he never would.

VANESSA

The next morning, Vanessa took a long shower, allowing the steam to cleanse the cobwebs from her mind and clarify her feelings about the day before. What had started as a glimmer on the day Paul played Chopin's Nocturne No. 2 and redeemed Quentin's joy had grown into a flame she could no longer deny. It was true, she had experienced trauma and that the trauma made her vulnerable. But she had spent twenty years mastering her own psychology, and she was sharp enough to discern a trap. Paul Derrick didn't look like a trap. He looked like a good man who actually gave a damn.

She had agonized over the invitation for more than a week, wondering whether it was too soon. Daniel had been gone only six months. She talked it over with Aster, and her friend exposed the core of her fear—that Curtis and Yvonne would judge her for dishonoring their son.

"They love you," Aster had assured her. "They want you to be happy."

"I suppose," Vanessa had replied, not quite mollified.

"Daniel would say the same thing," Aster went on. "I'm sure of it."

Vanessa shrugged. She and Daniel had never talked about death. She didn't know why exactly, but she imagined that on a subconscious level they had considered divorce a more likely possibility.

It was then that Aster had offered her an olive branch from her own culture. "In Islam, a widow isn't permitted to mourn for more than four months and ten days. Death is the end only for the dead. The living must go on."

As the water suffused her skin with warmth, Vanessa wrestled with her doubt. She still didn't know what Daniel would say about Paul, but she took solace in the fact that if Aster were in her place, she wouldn't be afraid to befriend him. That's all it was, after all. She liked Paul. Something about him moved her. He was an engaging conversationalist, though he was guarded about his past. Even after a few inter-actions, she got the sense that his heart was as deep as the ocean. He was a gifted musician—not classically trained, but his instinct for the piano more than made up for that. And he loved Quentin. She saw the delight in his eyes when he looked at her son. It was that more than anything that endeared him to her. She had the intuition that Paul was a loyal soul, that once his heart formed a bond, he would be true to it for the rest of his life. It was a quality she found immensely attractive. She couldn't understand everything she was feeling, but she knew this much: she wanted to see him again.

After her shower, she dressed in a lacy white top and jeans and went to the kitchen to make breakfast. She saw Ted standing by the back door, watching the sunrise.

"I'm glad you had a nice time," he said, a glint in his eyes. "You could do much worse."

She felt the heat rising beneath her collar. "He's just a friend."

Ted gave her a knowing smile. "It's good to have friends."

"Are you packed?" Vanessa asked, starting the espresso machine.

"All ready to greet the TSA," he replied with a chuckle. "I'm going to miss this view."

"You'll have to come again then."

He searched her eyes. "You mean that."

She nodded. "It's been good to have you."

And it had, to her great surprise. When she picked him up at the airport, she had been prepared for an awkward visit. But he had fit right in, joining Quentin and Ariadne on the water, busying himself with house projects she didn't want to do, cooking whenever she relinquished the kitchen, and leaving the past in the past. By the middle of the week, she had realized that she was actually enjoying his company. Now that he was about to leave, she was sorry to see him go.

In time, Ariadne emerged from the guest suite and Quentin came downstairs dressed in running clothes. "Can we take Dad's car?" he asked. "We're going to . . . Greenbury Point."

Vanessa handed them plates of scrambled eggs. "That's

fine, so long as Ariadne drives. We'll be gone when you get back."

"I forgot," Quentin said, looking at Ted. "You're leaving today. Do you want us . . . to come with you to the airport?"

Ted shook his head. "I'll see you again soon."

After the young people scarfed down their food and wished Ted farewell, Vanessa grabbed her keys and purse out of the office nook and met her stepfather at the SUV. It took them ten minutes to reach the cemetery. They parked on the street and walked through the wrought-iron gate and across the meadow to Daniel's grave.

The headstone lay beneath an oak tree in a burial plot that Daniel's grandfather had reserved many years ago. Vanessa had chosen the inscription with help from Curtis and Yvonne: Daniel Everett Parker, Beloved Father and Husband, Man of the Sea and Faithful Son, In Sure and Certain Hope of the Resurrection, November 1, 1968 – November 14, 2011.

"I would have come to the funeral," Ted said, "but I didn't think you wanted me to."

"I'm sorry," Vanessa replied. "It wasn't right to keep you at a distance." She took a breath. "Do you ever think about forgiveness?"

Ted grunted. "I'm old. I have more than my share of regrets."

The breeze grazed her cheek like a feather. "Do you think it's possible?" she asked, thinking about Daniel's last letter and Father Minoli's charge in the confessional.

He gave her a wizened look. "It doesn't make the pain go

away. But there is a certain consolation in it." He asked the question she knew was coming. "Is this about your mother?"

She nodded slowly. "She left wounds in me that I don't think will ever heal. I might have been strong if she'd given me a single piece of solid ground to stand on."

Ted shook his head. "You're stronger than you think. You didn't start with much, but you've made a good life for yourself. You deserve it."

Vanessa struggled to keep the tears at bay. "Thank you," she whispered.

Ted knelt down and picked at a clump of grass. "There's something you don't know. I swore I'd never tell you, but she's gone now and I think it will help. There's a reason she always ran. I dragged it out of her one night when she was drunk and weepy and talking about divorcing me for the thousandth time. She never mentioned it again, but it made me understand." He studied Vanessa through mercurial eyes. "What do you know about your grandparents?"

"Nothing at all," Vanessa said. *I begged and pleaded, but she never budged.*

"They lived in a coal town in rural Virginia," he said. "Her father worked in the mines. He was a hard man and loved his liquor. Her mother died giving birth, and he never remarried. Trish had an older brother named Mick. Your grandfather used Mick like a punching bag. Sticks, brooms, belts—whatever he could find. He did it almost every day in a shed behind the house."

Ted winced. "At night when Mick was asleep, he came to your mother's bedroom and raped her. It started when she was eight and continued into high school. But she didn't run, not until he invited a couple of his buddies to try her out, too. It was just after the Miss Virginia contest. They were all drunk out of their minds. She ran away the next day."

Vanessa closed her eyes and listened to the birds chirping in the oak tree. She heard the cars passing on the street, the sound of people talking not far away, but she was somewhere else—in the hospital room in New York where her mother died. Trish was gaunt and frail, her body ravaged by the cancer and the chemotherapy that hadn't stopped it from spreading from her breast to her lymph nodes and bone marrow. She reached out and took Vanessa's hand.

"I've had a good ride," Trish said. "I'm ready to go."

"Please don't," Vanessa replied, squeezing her hand. "We need you."

"No, you don't. You don't need anybody but yourself."

Those were her mother's last words to her—neither a benediction nor an apology, just the same harsh counsel she had drummed into Vanessa all her life. Now, after years of incomprehension, Vanessa finally understood. *You told me what you told yourself. You taught me how to survive.*

Vanessa put a hand on Ted's shoulder. "Thank you for telling me," she said and then looked at Daniel's headstone. "Will you give me a minute? There's something I need to do."

"I'll meet you back at the car," he said and walked away.

Vanessa knelt before the headstone and traced the lines of Daniel's name. "That explains a lot, doesn't it?" she said in a quiet voice. "The way I was with you. Why I pushed you away even when I needed your support. I really did buy a ticket to Cape Town, you know. I wanted what you wanted—a second chance to make this work. But I didn't get it."

She looked up at the sky and watched a cloud float by. "I need to ask you something. We never talked about death. We should have, but we didn't, so I don't know your answer. I met someone. You know him. He tried to save your life. I like him a lot. I don't know where it's going, but I'd like to see. Can I have your blessing?"

She opened her heart and waited, ignoring the barbs from her rational brain about how foolish it was to imagine that he might respond. Seconds passed in silence, and then a turtledove landed on the grass in front of her, cooing softly and looking at her. Vanessa scanned the cemetery for a sign of its companion, but she didn't see it. The dove walked toward her and cooed again, then took off in a flutter of wings and landed on a bench. Suddenly, a second dove swooped down and came to rest on the bench. The birds sat there for a while, making pleasant sounds. Then they chased each other into the sky. Vanessa didn't know why, but she walked toward the bench. When she was ten feet away, she saw the words inscribed upon the stone and knew the answer to her question.

AND HE THAT SAT UPON THE THRONE SAID, "BEHOLD, I MAKE ALL THINGS NEW."

ISMAIL

In the heart of downtown Norfolk, on the banks of the Elizabeth River, there is a park with circular lawns and a brick promenade with benches facing the water. Ismail sat on one of these benches with Megan as two marshals hovered nearby to make sure he didn't run. He was wearing a polo shirt, jeans, and Adidas sneakers—all furnished by Megan for the occasion. His arms and legs were unbound. The afternoon sun was on his face. The sea air was in his lungs. It was as close to freedom as he would ever get again. But his chains didn't matter. His sister was free.

Megan had passed on the news of Yasmin's arrival in Dadaab as soon as she learned of it. He remembered the exact moment Longfellow had knocked on his cell door and told him he had a phone call. It was just before lunch, and he was in the midst of the final repetition of the *Dhuhr* prayer.

"It's your lawyer," the jailer had said. "If you want to talk, you need to come now."

Ismail had gone with him, of course, shuffling down the stairs and casting a glance at the inmate taking a shower in the open on the far side of the block. The ritual of public bathing was an indignity that still troubled him after six months in confinement. The jailers accommodated his religion in many ways, but when it came to security, they made no exceptions.

"Megan?" he said, picking up the phone. "What's going on?"

"She made it, Ismail," Megan replied without preamble. "She's with your mother now. She was in bad shape when they found her. They had to send the Kenyan military out to get her. But she crossed the border. That was enough for them to act."

More information had trickled in over the next two weeks—word that Yasmin had recovered from her dehydration; that UNHCR had flown her to Nairobi with Khadija to meet with officials at the US embassy; that the immigration paperwork had been processed and their travel arranged; that they had boarded a flight to Washington, DC; that Paul Derrick had greeted them on arrival and driven them to the Marriott hotel in Norfolk; and that Bob had pulled strings with the US attorney to allow him a one-hour meeting at a place of his choosing. Megan had suggested Town Point Park.

He heard the warble of her mobile phone. "It's Paul," she told him and then listened for a moment. "We're on a bench north of the theater . . . See you soon." She put the phone away and met Ismail's eyes. "They're in the cab."

Ismail allowed himself to smile. He looked toward Waterside Drive and waited pensively as taxi after taxi passed without stopping. Finally, one pulled to the curb. He tried to remain impassive, to restrain the storm of his emotions, but when his mother and sister stepped out of the vehicle, he was undone. He stood up without thought, his eyes moistening with the first tears he had shed since Yusuf died. *Waxay halkan!* he exulted. "They're here!"

They walked toward him slowly at first, their *abaya*s billowing in the wind. Suddenly, Yasmin lengthened her stride and Khadija followed suit. Ismail's feet moved instinctively. The marshals barked at him to stop, but he ignored them. When he saw his sister's face, then his mother's, the tears flowed with abandon. He ran toward them and embraced them with all his might. He heard himself babbling in Somali, speaking words that made no sense yet somehow made perfect sense to him.

When at last he calmed down, he led them back to the bench. He saw Paul and Megan standing nearby, giving them space. He sat down and they sat with him, Yasmin beside him and Khadija next to her. He looked into their eyes for long seconds without speaking. They were beautiful, so beautiful.

He touched Yasmin's cheek. "Is it really you?"

"Yes," she whispered.

"They told me you barely survived."

She smiled gently. "They came for me. And *Hooyo* was waiting."

Khadija gave him a look of deep distress. "I don't

understand, Ismail. I know what your lawyer told me. I know the accusations against you. But they bought us tickets. They gave us green cards. They told us they are going to give us money. What is happening?"

He took his mother's hand. "There are things I can't tell you. I need you to accept that. I gave them something they wanted, and they are repaying me by helping you."

"What have you done, Madaxa?" Yasmin asked anxiously. "They say you are a pirate. They say you shot people on a boat."

He felt the shame at the core of his soul. *It wasn't supposed to happen this way. It was supposed to be clean.* "I spilled innocent blood," he said. "It is right that I am being punished."

"But why?" Yasmin cried softly.

He wanted to say, *Everything I did, I did for you.* But he knew he couldn't. He would bear the burden alone. "It doesn't matter. All that matters is that you are here."

"It *does* matter, Ismail," Khadija rejoined. "Nothing matters more."

He looked at his hands, leveled by the censure in her eyes. "If I told you my reasons, it would bring you no solace. I ask only for your mercy."

Khadija's eyes remained troubled. "It is not I who must forgive. It is God."

Ismail nodded softly. "I have not given up hope." Suddenly, he shook off the guilt and focused on the present. "There are some things we must discuss. I do not want you to come to the trial. I have a good lawyer. Justice will be

served, *inshallah*. When it is over, I will ask the court to put
me in a prison close to you. You will be able to visit me. It
will be hard, but you will endure. Also, when you receive the
money from the government, please invest it wisely. Buy a
house near Uncle Farah. Send Yasmin to college. Get your
nursing license. Do not send it all back to Somalia. You will
need it."

Khadija gave him the grace of a smile. "You are just like
your father was, always giving orders."

"Will you do it?" he insisted.

"*Ha*," she replied. "I will do it."

He saw Megan pointing at her watch. "I need to go now,
but I will see you again soon."

"When?" Yasmin asked.

"I don't know. But I need you to trust me. Do you trust
me, Qosol?"

She squeezed his hand. "I trust you."

He stood and embraced them, then handed them over
to Paul and watched them walk away. They were creatures
from an alien world. They would no more understand
America than America would understand them. But they
would learn to make a life on these shores. They would find
friends and contribute to the community in keeping with
their duties and the goodness in their hearts. And perhaps
someday when Yasmin's children were grown, they would
follow in Adan's footsteps and return to Somalia to bring
their country back to life.

As soon as their cab pulled away, Ismail looked at Megan.
"I made you a promise. Now it is time to fulfill it. I will tell

you what happened on the sailboat."

"Thank God," she said, exhaling audibly.

He tilted his head. "Yes, but only when the work is done."

She put up her hands. "The trial starts in two weeks. I don't have time for any more favors."

"Do you want justice?" he asked, interrogating her with his eyes.

She sighed. "Of course."

"Then I need your help."

Megan

Norfolk, Virginia
June 1, 2012

From a legal perspective, it was madness, at once risible and absurd, but Megan knew she would do it exactly as Ismail had asked. He had won her over long ago, just as he had won over Paul. She listened to his story for three straight hours, pausing only to ask clarifying questions. He was candid with her, and his memory was astonishing in its detail. She tested his recollection by asking him to recount exchanges in the negotiations that she had memorized from the recordings. His error rate was impossibly low. He rehearsed sentences and paragraphs with near-verbatim accuracy.

She had thought it before, but his story proved it. He was a prodigy. His brain operated on a level of complexity that would make the average person's head spin. Like a game theorist, he saw every choice he made within a matrix of possible scenarios, all of which had probabilities and contingencies that, if realized, would influence the outcome. He populated the matrix with evaluative judgments of the people around him and updated it in real time so his decisions were always fresh, future-oriented, and nonreactive. In this way, he had kept the government guessing while he sailed the *Renaissance* toward Somalia and nearly escaped the barricade with $1.8 million in cash. It was also how he had managed to turn his capture and imprisonment into a path to liberation for Yasmin and Khadija.

But he wasn't infallible. He couldn't see the end from the beginning. When he made a mistake in his calculations, or when a person acted contrary to his own interest, his matrix collapsed like a tapestry unraveling from a single thread. As he told it, he had made two such mistakes—first, in trusting that Paul spoke for the government when he promised to let them go; and second, in believing that the money would satisfy his men, notwithstanding the fact that he had betrayed them.

He laid it all out in black and white—the choices made by all the parties that led to the moment of the shooting. And then he revealed the last piece of the puzzle—the reason he had concealed the truth until now and would not disclose it publicly until the trial. It was at this point that his tale turned from a tragedy into a doomsday prophecy. Megan understood the cold, hard logic of the sacrifice he had to make, but she couldn't bear the thought of watching him commit suicide.

She left the Chesapeake Correction Center in a daze and drove toward Washington, pushing her Jaguar far above the speed limit. She reached the Capital in record time and took the Beltway west toward Arlington. Her house was in the District, but she didn't want to go home tonight. Simon had moved out two months ago after trying, but failing, to adhere to the rule of strict monogamy. He was renting an apartment in Georgetown that gave him freedom to conduct his affairs without oversight. Megan had already spoken to a divorce attorney, and she expected him to sign the papers without a fight. He had always been fair in love and war. It was fidelity he had never managed to achieve.

Just before nine in the evening, Megan knocked on Paul's door. She had thought about calling ahead, but she didn't want to explain herself over the phone. She needed to talk about it in person.

He opened the door, dressed in his gym clothes, and stared at her in surprise. "What's going on? Is everything okay?"

"No," she replied. "I need some company." When he stepped aside, she walked into the living room and sat heavily on the couch. "Do you have any vodka?"

He shook his head. "Only bourbon and port."

She laughed dryly. "You're such a bachelor. What about wine?"

He held up a bottle of red. "I have a Montepulciano that won a bunch of awards."

"That'll do fine."

He poured two glasses and handed her one before sitting on a chair nearby. "Is it Simon?" he asked. "I know it's been hard."

"Not really," she said, grateful for the distraction. "I saw it coming. I wanted to make it work, but I can't do it anymore."

"I'm sorry, Meg. He's a fool to let you go." He took a sip

of his wine and gazed at her. "It's Ismail, isn't it? He told you something."

She nodded slowly. She had to be careful not to transgress the bounds of confidentiality. "You were right about him. He's not who anyone thinks he is."

"I know. I talked to his mother. She told me about his family."

Megan nodded. It was why she had asked him to chauffeur Khadija and Yasmin. "That's not what I mean. The backstory doesn't explain everything."

He narrowed his eyes. "You're talking about the shooting."

The emotions welled up in her again. "He's the brightest person I've ever met. He has so much potential. He could be the next president of Somalia." She felt a tear break loose. "I can't save him, Paul. The jury is never going to believe him. They're going to give him the death penalty."

She watched as her brother moved to the couch and pulled her into his embrace. His instinct was impeccable. For as long as she could remember, he had known exactly what she needed. She nestled her head against his chest, at home in his arms.

In time, he spoke. "There was a moment out on the water when I knew I'd lost control. I gave him the opening he needed, but I couldn't make him take it. The choice was his to make." Paul ran his fingers through her hair. "This is no different. He isn't yours to save."

Megan was silent for a long time, drifting in the ether of pain. She knew he was right, but the implications of what he said extended much further than the case. She remembered their dinner in Beaver Creek. She hadn't been in any condition to talk about the past, about Kyle. But now she felt differently. If she was going to survive the trial, she had to accept what she couldn't change.

"There was something you wanted to tell me in Colorado," she said. "What was it?"

He looked into her eyes. "You really want to do this?"

She braced herself. "I do."

He took her hand. "I wanted to say that what happened that day wasn't your fault. It wasn't my fault. It was Kyle's choice. We have to live with it, but we didn't make it happen."

In the moments that followed, she was there and she wasn't there. She saw Paul's face, but he was younger and clad in his football jersey. She saw him trying desperately to calm Kyle down. She saw his blue eyes darken at the sound of the gunshots. She saw him run to Kyle and lift him off the floor, tears coating his face and mixing with his brother's blood. And then she saw his expression change. She saw him turn toward her and tell her not to look, to leave the den and find a phone. She heard her mother shrieking hysterically. She didn't need a psychologist to tell her that the horror that had taken their father from them would claim their mother's sanity as well. She went with Paul because he was the only person in the world she could trust. She trusted him still.

"I need help letting it go," she said. "I want to, but I don't know how."

He spoke with clarity. "Come with me to Annandale. We'll do it together."

She winced, feeling profoundly vulnerable. "I can't right now. I need to focus on the trial."

He touched her cheek. "Take your time. When you're ready, let me know."

"Can I stay here tonight?" she asked.

"Stay as long as you want."

She looked at his piano and saw the lights of the city behind it. "Will you play me something?"

He nodded and moved to the bench, placing his fingers on the keys. After a moment's thought, he began to play. She recognized the piece immediately—an iconic collaboration between Bruce Hornsby and Don Henley that came out the year after Kyle died. It had been their anthem in the days of their mourning and afterward, as they struggled to believe in hope again.

It was called "The End of the Innocence."

PAUL

The courtroom was hushed when Paul entered. He walked briskly up the aisle, looking straight ahead and ignoring the packed gallery. He was the first witness of the day and the second of the trial—Gabriel Masters, the captain of the *Gettysburg*, had gone before him. Out of the corner of his eye, he saw Vanessa sitting next to Curtis and Yvonne. She was dressed in a demure white pantsuit, her hair pulled back in a French twist. He made no attempt to acknowledge her. What he had to say wasn't going to satisfy anyone in the prosecutorial camp—neither the government nor the Parker family. He had no idea how Vanessa would react to his testimony, or whether she would want to speak to him again.

He walked through the bar, nodding at Clyde Barrington, who was standing at the podium, and took his oath in front of the clerk.

"Do you solemnly swear that the testimony you are about to give is the truth, the whole truth, and nothing but the truth, so help you God?" the woman intoned.

"I do," he said and took the witness stand, glancing only briefly at the sixteen people in the jury box. He knew that to make an impression on them he was supposed to be friendly. But he didn't owe any favors to the government. He would tell the truth and let the jurors sort it out.

"Please state your name for the record," Barrington began, and Paul complied, focusing on the assistant US attorney and ignoring Ismail and Megan to his left and Vanessa in the back of the gallery.

Since the jury had already heard from Captain Masters, Barrington kept Paul's testimony simple and direct, establishing his credentials, elucidating the theory behind hostage negotiation, and leading him through the high points of his negotiation with Ismail—he called him "Ibrahim" for clarity—by admitting the audio recordings into evidence.

After playing the clip in which Paul and Ismail discussed the Quran, Barrington said, "Can you explain to the jury what your objective was in these early negotiations?"

"I wanted to get him talking, to open up a channel of communication and develop a rapport," Paul explained. "It's critical in a negotiation that both sides believe that they're dealing with the right person who can make binding decisions to end the standoff. I was trying to build his trust and get a sense of his trustworthiness."

Barrington moved from the podium to the floor in

front of the bench. "Did there come a time where Ibrahim broke off contact with you and reached out to the Parker family directly?"

"Yes," Paul said. "That was on the second day of the crisis. Ibrahim spoke with Vanessa Parker by satellite phone. He demanded five million dollars and set a deadline for the following Monday."

"Did this tactic surprise you?"

"It took all of us by surprise. Somali pirates don't usually negotiate a ransom until they reach land. When Ismail contacted the family, he was over five hundred miles from the coast. We had to decide if he was serious or if he was using it as a diversion to buy time."

"What was your opinion?"

Paul glanced at Ismail. "My instinct told me he meant what he said."

Barrington moved toward the jury box. "Did the government have authority to *stop* him from negotiating with the family?"

"No. It's not illegal to pay money to pirates, only to terrorist organizations. At the same time, we had control of the physical environment. Whatever the family agreed to do, it was our decision, ultimately, whether we let the pirates reach the coast."

"What was the government's position on that?" Barrington asked.

Against his better judgment, Paul glanced at Vanessa. He shouldn't have done it. When she met his eyes, he lost his train of thought. After a pause, he said, "Our orders were clear. We weren't allowed to let them make landfall."

"Even if the family paid them a ransom?"

Paul nodded. "That's right."

Barrington looked thoughtful. "What was the thinking behind that?"

Paul took a breath. "It is the policy of the United States to prevent hostage takers from profiting off the kidnapping of Americans. When we can stop it from happening, we do."

The prosecutor returned to the podium. "Did the family negotiate with the pirates?"

"Yes," Paul said. "Curtis Parker, Daniel's father, took the lead. They agreed on $1.85 million."

"What did you do while they were negotiating?"

Paul shifted in his seat. "My counterpart in Annapolis sent us recordings of the ransom calls. I followed them closely. I also had conversations with Captain Masters and the SEAL commander about the end game. The Navy's tactical options were limited while the *Renaissance* was moving. But we knew we would have an opening as soon as the sailboat reached the drop point."

"An opening to do what?"

"To contain them. That was the only way we could control the outcome."

Barrington held out his hands. "As you understood it, what was the Navy's end game?"

Paul glanced at Vanessa again. He saw the pain written in the lines of her face, in the stiffness of her jaw and the rigidity of her frame. He held her eyes just long enough to reflect her sorrow. "Our mission was to obtain the safe release of the hostages. But we were under orders to capture the pirates before they reached Somalia. To accomplish both objectives, we had to give Ibrahim and his crew the impression that we were going to let them get away with the money. Ibrahim gave us an opportunity. He asked for a boat from the *Gettysburg* to use as a getaway vehicle. We agreed, but we wired the engine to malfunction after a couple of miles. The Navy's plan was to let the pirates take the money in the sabotaged boat and capture them as soon as the engine died."

Over the next few minutes, Barrington led Paul through the ransom drop and the breakdown in negotiations—the mistrust engendered by the helicopter and the ship's proximity to the sailboat. The prosecutor steered him away from his disputes with Redman and limited his questions to what Ismail said and did. He played the recording of Ismail shouting, *"Back off or we will eat them like meat!"* twice for the benefit of the jurors.

"After he said that, did you talk to him again?" Barrington inquired.

Paul looked at Ismail. The young Somali was regarding him impassively. "No," he replied.

"Please describe for the jury what you observed over the next few minutes," Barrington said, injecting gravity into his voice.

Paul steeled his heart against the memories. "When the pirates refused to release the hostages, the SEAL commander executed a backup plan that involved surface and subsurface units. The idea was to disable the sailboat's propeller, hitch a tow cable to the keel, and surround the pirates with enough firepower to convince them that they couldn't renege on the deal. The SEAL boat team did exactly what it was supposed to do." He glanced at Vanessa and saw the tears in her eyes. "When they turned on their lights, that's when the shooting started."

"What exactly did you hear and see?" Barrington asked quietly.

"I heard three separate bursts of gunfire. I tried to call the *Renaissance* on the sat phone, but no one answered." He paused. "Then I saw the pirates emerge from the sailboat carrying their guns and a briefcase. They tried to flee in the Navy's small boat. Two SEAL boats went after them and the other one went to the *Renaissance*. The SEALs boarded the sailboat and entered the cabin. Then one of them came back out and yelled, 'Cas-evac. Hostages are down.'"

Barrington fixed his eyes on the jury. "Thank you, Agent Derrick. That's all I have."

After a brief recess, Paul took the stand again, this time answering questions from Kiley Frost. Megan had given him notice that her associate would cross-examine him to avoid the appearance of impropriety. She had also warned him that Kiley was brilliant and relentless. In a way, he was looking forward to the interrogation. It would give him the chance to speak his mind.

Kiley smiled at the jury and then focused on him. "Good morning, Agent Derrick."

"Morning," he said, folding his hands in his lap.

"You said that the Navy was under orders not to permit the pirates to reach the Somali coast. Where did those orders come from?"

Although Kiley's tone was light, Paul heard the barb below the surface. "I learned about them from the SEAL commander. I assume they came from somewhere above him."

"Were those orders ever confirmed by anyone with ultimate authority?"

Paul narrowed his eyes. Eldridge Jordan had briefed him on the national security constraints on his testimony. He couldn't disclose the names of anyone in the SEAL unit or anyone in the military or civilian hierarchy beyond the sailors on the *Gettysburg*. "They were confirmed by the White House in a teleconference," he answered and heard one of the jurors gasp.

Kiley nodded. "Earlier, you described for the jury the government's policy about paying ransoms to hostage takers. Do you agree with it?"

Clyde Barrington stood up quickly. "Objection to relevance, Your Honor."

"Sustained," Judge McKenzie replied. She looked at Kiley over her glasses. "Ms. Frost, the witness's *opinion* about the government's policy is immaterial to the charges at issue in this case."

"I understand, Your Honor," said the defense attorney. She tried another tack. "Leaving aside the policy, did you agree with the orders you received?"

"Objection," Barrington interrupted. "Relevance."

When the judge pondered this, Kiley jumped in. "Your Honor, the witness has already testified that he lied to the defendant about the government's intentions because of these orders. The jury has a right to know whether he was comfortable with the position the government put him in."

Barrington looked frustrated. "Your Honor, Ms. Frost is arguing her case."

At last, Judge McKenzie said, "I'm going to sustain the objection with respect to the question at hand. What the witness *felt* about the orders is outside the scope of direct examination. But the orders themselves were put at issue. If the question is phrased correctly, I'll allow it."

With this latitude, Kiley tried a third time. "Agent Derrick, as a negotiator, is it a common tactic for you to lie to a hostage taker about the government's intentions?"

Paul gave his answer to the jury: "In a barricade scenario where we have tactical units moving around, we prevaricate all the time about what the units are up to. We don't want the hostage takers to know our strategy if we have to mount a rescue mission. But when it comes to the terms of a bargain, I've never had to make a promise I didn't intend to keep. This was the first time."

"Did you ever question those orders?" Kiley asked.

Paul shook his head. "It would have accomplished nothing."

"Did you ever question any orders you received prior to the shooting?"

"Yes," Paul said, glancing at Vanessa. It was probably

wishful thinking, but he thought he saw her face soften.

"Let's set that aside for the moment," Kiley said. "We'll return to it later. You said your mission was to secure the safe release of the hostages, isn't that correct?"

"Yes. That was the preeminent objective."

Kiley crossed her arms over her chest. "Isn't it true that the orders you were under to prevent the pirates from reaching land were in direct conflict with that objective?"

"Objection," said Barrington. "She's asking for an opinion."

"Sustained," the judge intoned.

Kiley shrugged. "Have you ever heard of Paul and Rachel Chandler?"

Paul nodded, intuiting what she was trying to do. "They were British sailors hijacked by Somali pirates back in 2009. The pirates took them ashore and held them for over a year before their family paid a ransom and negotiated their release."

"Were you aware that a British warship was present when the pirates transferred the Chandlers from their sailboat to a cargo ship under their control?"

"Yes," Paul said, giving her the answer she wanted. "The warship didn't intervene. They were afraid that any action on their part would endanger the lives of the hostages."

Kiley smiled thinly. "During the course of the negotiations, did it ever occur to you that the Navy's aggressive approach might endanger Daniel and Quentin Parker?"

"It did," Paul admitted, once again looking at Vanessa.

Kiley gave him a hard look. "In fact, you had multiple

confrontations with the SEAL commander about this precise issue, isn't that correct?"

Paul chose his words cautiously. "We had some differences of opinion. It was a tense scene. I gave him my advice, and he made his decisions. But our goal was the same—to rescue the hostages."

"Of course," Kiley said dismissively. "But that didn't happen, did it?"

"No," Paul said softly.

"Isn't it true that the SEAL commander believed Ismail was being disingenuous in negotiating with the Parker family, and you disagreed with him?"

"He didn't trust Ismail's intentions," Paul replied. "I did."

"But Ismail *did* negotiate a ransom," Kiley said. "He *wasn't* just stalling for time."

Paul returned her stare. "I don't pretend to know what Ismail was thinking, but he did what he said he was going to do."

"So on this point you were right and the SEAL commander was wrong."

Paul put his response delicately. "I think the circumstances speak for themselves."

"Indeed." Kiley moved back to the podium. "You talked earlier about the two events that precipitated the breakdown in negotiations—the helicopter and the position of the *Gettysburg*. Ismail was right when he accused the Navy of moving the ship closer, wasn't he?"

"Yes," Paul admitted.

"Again, you disagreed with the SEAL commander, didn't you?"

"I advised him against it."

Kiley moved toward the jury box. "When Ismail accused the Navy of breaking its word, what advice did you give the SEAL commander?"

Paul remembered the fear that had gripped him in those moments, the sense that he had to convince Redman to make a concession to save Daniel and Quentin. "I advised him to move the ship in exchange for the release of Quentin Parker. He agreed to do it."

"Yes, we heard that on the recording," Kiley said. "But what advice did you give him after Ismail declined to release Quentin?"

Paul focused on Vanessa at the rear of the gallery. She was sitting primly, her eyes wide and lugubrious. She had asked him on numerous occasions to tell her what happened at the end, but he had been hamstrung by his professional obligations. When he spoke now, he spoke to her and felt the ache of her broken heart. "I advised him to move the ship. I felt the hostages were in imminent danger."

Kiley moderated her tone until it sounded almost gentle. "But he didn't move the ship, did he?"

"No, he did not."

Kiley smiled at Paul with her eyes. "Thank you. I have nothing further."

✦

When Paul left the stand, he was emotionally spent, as if he had just summited a mountain after a punishing climb. But he felt no sense of relief or accomplishment, only sadness. He looked into Megan's eyes and saw the apology in them, but she had done nothing wrong, only what he had asked her to do. He walked down the aisle, ignoring the gazes of the journalists who had stopped their scribbling to watch him go, and turning his head only once—to nod at Vanessa.

The hall outside the courtroom was empty, except for a middle-aged man in Navy blues. Paul was astonished. It was Gabriel Masters.

He offered his hand. "Paul, it's good to see you again."

"Likewise," Paul said. "Were you in there? I didn't notice you."

"I was discreet," Masters replied. "And you were preoccupied. I want to thank you for bypassing all the party-line bullshit. It took a weight off my shoulders."

You circumscribed your own testimony, Paul inferred. *You toed the line for Redman's sake.* "You're welcome," he said. "Are you still on the *Gettysburg*?"

Masters shook his head. "We finished our tour last month. I've been reassigned to the Pentagon. Joint Chiefs."

Paul grinned. "Congratulations. I hope you get a star out of it."

"There's another reason I came," Masters said. "I wanted to say, for the record, that you were right. I knew it when it was happening, but there wasn't a damn thing I could do. Frank's a good man. His heart was in the right place. But he should have listened to you."

Paul was deeply moved. He realized then that Masters had walked through the fire and emerged with the same scars. "We did what we could," he said. "It's a burden we have to bear."

Masters nodded with feeling, then handed Paul his card. "Give me a call sometime. We'll grab a beer and talk about something more enjoyable. Do you have kids?"

Paul shook his head.

Masters grinned, "There's always time."

Paul put the card in his pocket and watched the captain walk toward the elevator bank. He was completely unprepared for the soft voice he heard behind him. "Paul."

He turned around and saw Vanessa there, standing awkwardly like a schoolgirl meeting a boy in the hallway. She was beautiful, he admitted to himself—like the violin she played, fragile and exquisite. He smiled and saw her relax.

"Will you walk with me?" she asked. "It'll only take a minute."

"Of course," he said and followed her down a corridor to a window overlooking the city. The summer sky was pale blue and blanketed by haze.

She gazed into his eyes with an intimacy that concealed none of her emotions. "Whatever happened out there, I don't blame you for it. Neither does Quentin."

He felt the instinct to touch her face, but he restrained himself. "That's kind of you," he replied, embarrassed at the way his heart was pounding. "But it doesn't make things right."

"Nothing will," she said quietly. "All we can do is move on."

He thought about her words. She could have used the singular "you," but instead she used the plural "we." Was it intentional? He wanted it to be. But it was absurd. No one would understand it—well, Megan would, but no one else. People would judge him, accuse him of taking advantage of her when he had done nothing but try to protect her family. He thought of Daniel in the Conex box on the *Truman* and forced his desire aside. *I lost him*, he thought bitterly. *I won't tread on his grave.*

"I don't know if I can," he said at last, and saw the way his words wounded her.

She hugged herself. "I know it's crazy. It doesn't make any sense. But when I look at the Bösendorfer, I don't just see Quentin anymore. I see you."

His resolve began to waver. He looked into her eyes and remembered what she had said about Quentin and Ariadne. He didn't know where the road would lead, but right now her affection was a precious gift. "Okay," he said, giving in to the voice in his heart. "I'll try."

She grazed his hand with her fingers. "That's all I ask."

MEGAN

At nine in the morning on the sixth day of trial, Megan pushed aside the pigskin doors and entered Courtroom One. When she was trying a case, she always made a point to arrive an hour before anyone else. She loved to sit alone in the vaulted chamber, surrounded by portraits of justice past and present, and absorb the silence. A courtroom was a sacred space to her, like a mountaintop above the clouds. It gave her room to reflect and prepare for the day ahead.

She sat down at the defense table and surveyed the vacant bench. Ismail's trial had commenced as she expected, with a jury selection process that weeded out everyone who might have sympathy for either side. Judge McKenzie had given her wide latitude to strike jurors for cause—anyone who had served, or had family serving, in the armed forces; anyone who had been a victim of gun violence or knew someone who had been; anyone employed by the government. In a death penalty case, there were a host of constitutional trip wires. The judge wanted to avoid a biased jury at all cost.

Once the jury was empaneled, however, Megan had entered uncharted territory, following Ismail's instructions precisely as he had articulated them. She listened to Clyde Barrington's opening statement with dread. The story he told was so damning that she would have had difficulty countering it with her hands untied. In Ismail's straitjacket, however, she could only make bald assertions that sounded more like the sniping of the guilty than the protestations of the innocent. She told the jury that the government's case rested upon speculation and falsehood. There were two shooters, not one, and the other pirates were lying for reasons Ismail would make clear when he testified. But that was as far as she could go. When she sat down again, she caught a sideways glance from the judge that said, *What the hell was that?* Megan thought, *I know. This is crazy.*

She had taken some solace in cross-examining Captain Masters, eliciting two key admissions from him—that the Navy's confrontational approach had increased the risk that the pirates would retaliate, and that any number of available alternatives would have diminished that risk. But he balked when she invited him to cross swords with Captain Redman, labeling the SEAL commander's disputes with Paul "constructive discussions." Thankfully, Paul had set the record straight. With the help of Kiley Frost, he succeeded in sowing doubt in the minds of the jurors that the government was telling the whole story. That doubt and the far-fetched tale

Ismail would recount when he testified were all that stood between him and a death sentence.

Megan took out her legal pad. Today, Barrington planned to call two witnesses: Redman and Mas. She reviewed her outline and added notes here and there. A few minutes later, she heard the doors swing open behind her. She turned around and saw a Somali man in a blue-checked shirt take a seat in the corner of the gallery. Her heart lurched when she met his eyes. He had attended every minute of the trial, sitting alone and talking to no one. Ismail pointed him out during jury selection and explained his presence. She didn't believe him at first, but as time passed, she began to wonder.

What is your name? she wanted to ask. *Did Gedef's family really send you?* She shook her head. *If I have a hard time understanding the truth, how can I convince the jurors to believe it?*

Two hours later, Megan walked to the podium and stared into the face of Frank Redman. Out of the corner of her eye, she saw the twelve-foot black curtain that the Court had erected in front of the gallery to conceal his identity from the public. Only parties to the case, lawyers, and government officials with a top secret security clearance were allowed on this side of the barrier.

"Good morning, Captain," she said in a friendly voice.

"Good day, counselor," Redman replied.

Megan made a show of looking down at her notes, but her real intention was to let Redman squirm. It was a trick she used to tenderize adversarial witnesses. For over an hour, Barrington had tossed the SEAL commander softball questions, deferring to his judgment almost obsequiously. She knew Redman was accustomed to royal treatment. In the military, he was a demigod. But Megan wasn't impressed. To her he was just another man in uniform with an outsized ego and a penchant for violence. This was her turf. By the time she finished with him, he would know the meaning of humility.

Eventually, she looked up again. "Captain, you said that one of the first things you did when you arrived on the *Gettysburg* was to deploy your sniper unit around the ship, is that correct?"

"That's correct," Redman said.

"I suppose that's no different from what a SWAT team does? As soon as you get to the scene, you put the bad guy in your crosshairs."

Redman's eyes flashed in irritation. "It's quite a bit different, actually. My team isn't in the business of law enforcement. We're a special-operations unit with sea, air, and land capabilities."

Megan nodded. "Would it be fair to say that, as a military unit, your business is war?"

Redman bristled at her word choice. "Our business is saving American lives and prosecuting the enemies of the United States wherever they may be found."

Megan gave the jury a look of puzzlement. "When you

say 'prosecute,' you don't mean it like Mr. Barrington here. He prosecutes with paper. You use bullets."

Redman frowned. "I'm not interested in semantic games. I'm certain everyone here understands what my team does."

Megan smiled sardonically. "Captain, if bullets were only a matter of semantics, we would live in a very different world."

Clyde Barrington rose to his feet. "Objection."

"Sustained," said Judge McKenzie. "Please move on, Ms. Derrick."

Megan nodded. "As a *military* commander, you're not trained in the art of negotiation, are you?"

Redman grimaced. "Some of my SEALs have been cross-trained in negotiation. I've taken classes myself, and I've worked with negotiators before. There isn't much to it, really."

"About as much as putting a bad guy in your crosshairs, I suppose," Megan said.

On cue, Barrington voiced his objection, and Megan said, "I withdraw the question."

"Captain," she went on, "isn't it true that before your team deployed to the Indian Ocean, the White House asked the FBI to send a team of hostage negotiators to offer you advice in your quest to obtain the safe release of Daniel and Quentin Parker?"

Redman nodded. "That's correct."

Megan held out her hands in a gesture of reasonableness. "Are you aware that the lead negotiator deployed to the *Gettysburg*, Paul Derrick, has more experience in international kidnapping incidents than anyone in the US government?"

Redman began to fidget with his hands. "I wasn't aware of that. But, as you said, he was sent as an advisor. The White House put my team in charge of the incident."

Megan gave him a frank look. "So what you're saying is that you had no obligation to *accept* Paul Derrick's advice? He could offer it, but you were free to ignore it."

Redman took a breath, trying to contain his frustration. "Derrick was not part of my chain of command. I valued his opinion, but I didn't always agree with it."

Beautiful, Megan thought. *Keep it up.* "Let's talk about your orders for a minute. Who told you not to allow the pirates to take Daniel and Quentin Parker to Somalia?"

Redman shrugged. "I received my orders from my commander. Beyond that, I don't know."

"Did the order make sense to you?"

"Of course," said the SEAL commander testily. "If we had let the pirates take the Parkers to land, they would have achieved their objective. America isn't interested in letting hostage takers win, Ms. Derrick. Other countries might not care, but we do."

Megan raised her eyebrows. "So your goal was to prevent the pirates from winning?"

Redman shot her an angry look. "My mission was to secure the safe release of the hostages. I had to work within certain parameters. But the parameters were not the mission."

"Of course," Megan said breezily. "But this wasn't a military engagement, was it? The pirates weren't terrorists or enemy combatants."

Redman shifted impatiently in his seat. "They were

holding two American sailors at gunpoint. We treated them as enemy combatants. There's a long history of this, Ms. Derrick. In the old days, the Navy called pirates *hostis humani generis*—enemies of all mankind."

Touché, Megan thought. It was a fair point, but she pressed him anyway. "If they were enemy combatants, then why weren't you authorized to use deadly force against them?"

Redman hesitated, sensing the snare but not seeing any way around it. "Tactical action always entails risk. We didn't want to endanger the hostages."

Megan glanced at the jury and saw that they were riveted by the exchange. "Your orders were to negotiate with the pirates, correct?"

"Yes," Redman admitted.

Megan looked quizzical. "Let me get this straight. The government put an elite unit of Navy SEALs trained in the art of warfare in charge of a hostage negotiation, and gave the people trained in the art of negotiation only an advisory role. Can you explain that?"

"In a hostage event, tactical action is always a possibility," Redman said. "That's why we were in charge. But Paul Derrick handled the negotiation with my oversight."

Megan left the podium and moved toward the witness stand. "Let's talk about the negotiation. You didn't trust Ismail, did you? You thought he was acting in bad faith."

Redman leaned forward in his chair. "As a general rule, I don't trust anyone holding a gun to the head of innocent people."

"Exactly. In your mind, he was an enemy combatant, not a partner in resolving the standoff."

"Pardon my density," Redman said, "but I've never thought of a hostage taker as my partner in anything. Ismail was an obstacle to fulfilling my mission."

Megan tilted her head skeptically. "That makes it hard to negotiate, doesn't it? Unless you take the view that the other side has to make all the concessions."

The SEAL commander tried to hide his disgust. "Ms. Derrick, we offered Ismail ample opportunity to release the hostages and return to Somalia. He didn't want to deal with us."

"Paul Derrick disagreed with you on this point, didn't he?" Megan insisted. "He believed that Ismail was acting in good faith. That's why he suggested, over your objection, that the government allow Ismail to negotiate with the family."

Redman shrugged. "As I said, Agent Derrick and I didn't always agree. These scenarios are very fluid and evolve quickly. In this case, the people up the chain of command sided with him. But it didn't work out the way he wanted. Your client betrayed us in the end."

Megan stood perfectly still, weighing her options. If she asked the question her instinct told her to ask, it could blow up in her face. But if it worked, it could drive the thorn of doubt so deeply into the mind of the jury that they would look at Ismail with new eyes. She decided to go for broke.

"Isn't the truth exactly the opposite?" she asked quietly. "Isn't it you who betrayed him?"

Redman's eyes took on a furious light. "How dare you," he growled. "I've devoted my entire life to the cause of freedom. Your client is a brigand and a murderer. He promised us he would release the hostages when the money was delivered. The money came and he reneged. When we demanded that he honor his word, he shot the hostages in cold blood. Your accusation is not only wrong; it is a disgrace to the justice system you claim to serve."

Megan took a step closer to him. "But you moved the ship, Captain. You moved the ship without telling him when he was counting the money."

Redman's nose began to twitch. "The proximity of the ship wasn't relevant to the deal. Your client overreacted. He treated it as an excuse to ignore his obligations."

Megan didn't blink. "Isn't it true that Paul Derrick told you not to move the ship?"

The SEAL commander's twitch increased. "That was his advice, yes."

"The most experienced hostage negotiator in the United States government told you not to move the ship, and you ignored him, correct?"

Redman's eyes filled with loathing. "In my mind it was imperative to reinforce to the pirates that they weren't the ones in control."

Megan lowered her voice a notch. "But isn't it true that *you* weren't in control? They had the hostages, and you couldn't reach them."

At once, Redman lost his composure. "We *were* in control! We had jets and helicopters and snipers and small boats and a ten-thousand-ton warship. We gave them the chance to do the right thing. They chose to go down in flames."

This was the opening Megan had been waiting for. She went for the jugular. "Paul Derrick predicted it, didn't he? He told you the hostages were in danger, and you ignored him a second time."

For an instant, Redman looked like he was about to lash out again, but he managed to rein in his emotions. "Ms. Derrick, I don't care what you think of me. I would have given my life to save Daniel and Quentin Parker. We were four miles from the Somali coast and drifting toward Mogadishu. We were out of time. The pirates broke their word. I had to act."

It was a good response, better than Megan expected, but it wasn't enough to save him. "Yes, you did," she said. "You just made the wrong choice."

After lunch, Clyde Barrington called Mas to the stand. The bailiff brought the pirate into the courtroom through the back door and showed him where to sit. He was dressed in a mustard-yellow jumpsuit and rubber sandals, and his hair looked like it had just been cut. The scar on his right cheek was beige in contrast to the toffee-colored complexion of his skin. He smiled at the jury with his teeth, then looked around at the judge and the stenographer and the lawyers and the packed gallery before his eyes landed on Ismail. Megan saw the wordless exchange take place, the dare Mas

presented—*Talk all you want; who are they going to believe?*
She wanted to wring his neck.

For the next two hours, Barrington led Mas through the
story of the hijacking, the negotiation, the ransom drop, and
the shooting with the assistance of Sado, the white-haired
interpreter. As Megan had feared, the young Somali was a
powerful witness, and the jury hung on his every word, especially when he fingered Ismail, whom he called "Afyareh,"
as Daniel's killer. When the prosecutor finished his examination, Judge McKenzie called a fifteen-minute recess and
then assembled everyone again.

"Ms. Derrick," the judge said, "we'll go until you're
finished."

"Thank you, Your Honor," Megan said.

She stood up and went to the podium, feeling the tension in the courtroom. Hundreds of eyes were on her, waiting
to see how she would confront Ismail's accuser.

"Your father didn't name you Mas," she began. "That's
a nickname, isn't it?"

"*Ha*," he said, and Sado interpreted: "Yes."

"What does Mas mean in Somali?"

The pirate grinned and spoke a handful of words. "It
means 'snake,'" Sado said.

"Any particular kind of snake?"

"No."

Megan surveyed the jury. "Have you ever seen a spitting
cobra?"

Mas nodded. "It is red like desert rock."

Megan tilted her head. "Spitting cobras eject venom

from their fangs, don't they? They shoot for the eyes and they're remarkably accurate."

"Yes," Mas affirmed.

"If a person gets venom in his eyes, do you know what happens to him?"

Mas looked at her keenly. "He goes blind."

Megan smiled, speaking her next words to the jury. "A *mas* that inflicts blindness. How intriguing." When she saw Clyde Barrington about to object, she moved on quickly. "Gedef, the leader of your pirate crew, was your cousin, correct?"

"Yes," Mas replied. "His father and my father are brothers."

"You were close to Gedef before he died?"

The young Somali sat taller in his chair. "He trusted me."

"But he didn't put you in command of the second skiff, did he? He gave that job to Afyareh."

Mas glanced at Ismail, and the muscles in his jaw tightened. "Afyareh spoke good English, and he was talented with a gun. He was boss after Gedef."

"You resented Afyareh for that, didn't you? In fact, you still resent him for it?"

"No, no," Mas responded eagerly.

On her internal scoreboard, Megan notched another point. "Let's talk about your family. Isn't it true that Gedef's father was a senior officer in the Somali National Security Service under Siad Barre?"

"Yes," Mas confirmed. "He was close to Barre."

"The NSS was the Somali equivalent of the Russian KGB, am I right?"

"Yes," Mas said.

Megan left the podium and moved toward the witness stand. "I did some reading about the Barre regime. Isn't it true that the NSS kidnapped people from their homes in the middle of the night, detained them without trial, and tortured them until they confessed to spying on the government?"

When Mas heard the translation, his lips spread into a nervous smile. "I am sure my uncle didn't do those things. He is a good man."

Clearly, good *is a relative term*, Megan thought. "Gedef's father is still a prominent man in Somalia, isn't he?"

"He is a businessman," Mas replied. "He has interests in many things—mobile phone networks, *hawala* money transfer service, livestock, shipping."

Megan crossed her arms. "Isn't it true that he was also the primary source of funding for Gedef's piracy missions?"

Suddenly, Mas's smile expanded and his eyes shifted toward the corner of the gallery. *I'll be damned*, Megan thought, picturing the man in the blue-checked shirt. *Ismail was right*.

"I don't know where Gedef got his money," Mas said at last. "My uncle is not a criminal."

"What about *your* father?" Megan asked. "Isn't it true that he invested in piracy?"

"No, no," Mas replied, his smile swallowing his words.

"Isn't it true that many of your relatives invested money in Gedef's missions?"

Mas shook his head. "No, no, no."

Megan stepped closer. "You're afraid of them, aren't you? That's why you're lying to me."

"No, no," Mas responded, his eyes darting around. "I'm telling the truth."

Megan shook her head in mock wonderment. "You have reason to be afraid of them, don't you? They think you stole from them."

Mas looked at her in shock, the smile on his face set in concrete.

"In fact, your uncle isn't just a passive bystander," she continued. "He sent a representative from your clan to this very courtroom to see what you would say." She turned around and pointed at the seat where the man in the blue-checked shirt had been sitting. Her jaw dropped in astonishment.

The man was gone.

All at once, conversation broke out in the gallery. Judge McKenzie sat paralyzed for a moment, then struck her gavel twice and ordered everyone to be quiet. She glared at Megan and called a sidebar. Megan approached the bench with Barrington, who looked as unsettled as she had ever seen him.

"What is the meaning of this?" the judge demanded in a whisper.

"Your Honor," Megan said, "I have reason to believe that this witness is protecting some powerful people in Somalia, people who stand to lose a great deal if they are implicated in piracy. I have a right to impeach him. He's a criminal and a pathological liar."

"Are you aware of this?" the judge asked Barrington.

The prosecutor shook his head. "I'm as perplexed as you are, Your Honor."

"Did you notice the Somali man in the back corner?" Megan asked. "He isn't connected to my client, but he's been here every day of the trial. He was here this morning. Now he's gone."

The judge nodded. "He walked out just before you asked the question."

"I don't have proof," Megan said. "But I'm certain he's from Mas's clan."

"Those are very serious allegations," the judge said. "But for the moment they are ancillary to the case. I won't permit a sideshow. Please wrap this up soon." She turned to Barrington. "And, Clyde, I suggest you get someone to look into this. I don't like it."

"Yes, Your Honor," Megan and Barrington said almost simultaneously.

When everyone was situated again, Megan turned back to Mas. "Do you know the man who was sitting in the corner of the gallery until a few minutes ago?"

The pirate's plastic smile didn't slip. "What man?"

Megan traded a look with the judge. Then she moved on. "During the hijacking of the *Renaissance*, did you ever place a call to your uncle on the satellite phone?"

Mas looked at her strangely. "Why would I call him?"

"Did you ever tell Afyareh to call your uncle?"

Mas glanced at Ismail, then shook his head. "*Maya*. Afyareh was boss."

"You've said that before, but I don't believe you. The whole story you told the jury about the shooting is a lie, isn't it?"

"No, no," Mas said, turning his smile toward the jury. "I am telling the truth."

"Isn't it true that Afyareh didn't kill the Captain. You did."

Mas shook his head aggressively. "Afyareh did it. Afyareh was Shabaab."

"That's another lie, isn't it?" Megan spat back. "You're aware, are you not, that Afyareh was *kidnapped* by the Shabaab? They forced him to fight, but he escaped."

Mas kept shaking his head. "Afyareh did it. Afyareh shot the Captain."

Megan looked at the jurors and saw that they were with her. But they wanted something more—a smoking gun. It was the one thing she couldn't give them.

"What weapon did Afyareh use on the Captain?" she asked quietly.

The pirate shrugged. "I don't know."

"Was it the same weapon he used to shoot Quentin, whom you call 'Timaha'?"

Mas blinked. "I don't know."

Megan gave him a damning look. "If it turned out that the gun that shot the Captain was different from the gun that shot Timaha, how would you explain that?"

Mas didn't answer the question. "Afyareh did it," he said. "Afyareh was Shabaab."

Megan gave him a look of patent repugnance and then dismissed him with a wave. "I'm finished with this witness."

VANESSA

Vanessa found it strange that in twenty years of being married to a lawyer she had never been to a trial before. She didn't attend all of the proceedings, just the days Curtis suggested. She watched the witnesses come and go: Captain Masters, Paul Derrick, the SEAL captain, the pirate whose nickname was Mas, the SEAL petty officer who was the first to board the *Renaissance*, the helicopter pilot who airlifted Quentin to the *Truman*, Dr. Alvarez, who operated on him, Dr. Hancock, who pronounced Daniel dead, and Dr. Carl Attaway, a forensic scientist from the FBI's Firearms and Toolmarks Unit, who formed the conclusion that two guns had been used, not one. The rest of the parade—the pirates, sailors, investigators, technicians, and scientists—she didn't care about.

Sometimes the testimony set her blood boiling; sometimes it turned her heart to ice; other times it precipitated a hasty trip to the bathroom to conceal her tears. After the first few days, she found herself confused and emotionally adrift. Paul's testimony and Megan's withering cross-examinations of the SEAL captain and Mas had hopelessly muddied the clear river of her judgment. She heard Ismail's voice ringing in her head: *Back off or we will eat them like meat!* But now she knew the context—the clandestine approach of the *Gettysburg* while the pirates were counting the cash. She felt an indefinable rage toward the SEAL captain for acting preemptively and a deep sense of unease about Mas. What if what Megan alleged was true? Could the government have accused the wrong man?

The hardest part for her was listening to the doctors from the *Truman* describe Daniel's wounds. She couldn't bring herself to look at the postmortem photographs, but judging by the way Curtis stiffened and Yvonne began to cry, she knew they were gruesome. On the flip side, she felt an overwhelming sense of gratitude toward the Navy doctors for saving Quentin's life. What they had accomplished in pulling her son back from the brink was nothing short of a miracle. After Dr. Alvarez testified, she met him in the hallway and gave him a hug. "I can't tell you how thankful I am," she told him. "Because of you I still have hope."

After the first week of the trial, she spent more time in Maryland than she did in Virginia. When she wasn't seeing patients, she was home with Quentin and Ariadne. What had started as a tender friendship had blossomed into a full-fledged romance, with doe eyes and handholding and kisses stolen in private moments. Dr. Greenberg had warned her this would happen—that at some point Quentin would recover his sexual interest and become an ordinary adolescent again. Vanessa tried not to worry about what they did when they were alone, but she couldn't help it. So she monitored Quentin's studies and went sailing with them and kept herself visible in the hope that it would slow the advance of their affections. She expected Quentin to be annoyed, but most of the time he seemed to welcome her presence. It was as if his injuries had muted that part of his teenage brain that made him resent her.

What Quentin didn't like was being excluded from the trial. He had been looking forward to it for months, both because he wanted to see justice served and because he hoped it would close the last gaps in his memory. But Judge McKenzie forbade it after deciding he had the capacity to testify. While the judge accepted Dr. Greenberg's opinion that his recollection was accurate as far as it went, she felt that hearing the stories of others could materially alter his testimony. She granted only one exception: he could listen to Vanessa testify. Curtis tried to persuade Barrington to call Quentin first so he could attend the rest of the trial, but the prosecutor did the opposite, putting him last to make an impression on the jury. So Quentin stayed home until the middle of July, when his summons finally came.

On the morning of July 16, they arrived at the courthouse together, Vanessa on his right arm, Ariadne on his left, and Curtis and Yvonne bringing up the rear. They took the elevator to the third floor and made their way through the crowd of reporters, lawyers, and spectators to Courtroom One. For an uncomfortable moment, Vanessa thought that one of the journalists might ask Quentin for a comment, but none tried. They just followed him with their eyes and nodded as he passed.

She saw Paul Derrick across the hall talking to Agents Hewitt, Escobido, and Matheson. He returned her gaze and smiled slightly. She hadn't seen or spoken to him since the day he testified. She smiled back and felt a tickle of pleasure. *It's nice to see you again, too.*

At Quentin's request, they took seats in the front of the gallery. He was as tense as a coiled spring. She understood—she was nervous, too—but it was disconcerting to see him so unsettled. In the months since Ariadne arrived, he had acquired a remarkable self-assurance, taking every day as it came and giving little thought to the things he couldn't change. The solitary tremor in the oasis of his calm was the gap in his memory, but even that he had largely succeeded in setting aside, trusting that his brain would heal in time to tell the jury what he saw on the night his father died. Now, however, the trial was here and he had yet to remember. She felt his frustration as if it were her own.

At ten o'clock, Judge McKenzie appeared and took her seat on the bench. "Mr. Barrington," she began, "am I correct that you intend to wrap up your case in chief today?"

Barrington stood. "Yes, Your Honor. That's our hope."

"Wonderful," said the judge. "Let's get to it then."

Barrington turned around and met Vanessa's eyes. "I call Vanessa Parker."

Vanessa stood up and walked to the witness stand, taking quick stock of her appearance. The pins holding up her hair were still in place; she hadn't forgotten her lipstick or mascara; her dress wasn't riding too high on her thighs. When she completed the checklist, she felt little relief. She sat down on the witness stand and took a deep breath, ignoring everyone but Clyde Barrington.

The prosecutor wished her good morning and led her through the preliminaries: the general landscape of her marriage and family, the genesis of the circumnavigation—the dream, not the family crisis, which no one knew about—and a few touching memories from the nine months Daniel and Quentin had been at sea. Eventually, he got around to the hijacking.

"When did you first learn that the *Renaissance* had been pirated?" he asked.

"I got a call from my father-in-law, Curtis Parker," she replied. "He had received a distress message from my husband. Daniel sent it before the pirates took control."

Barrington nodded. "What did you do then?"

She recalled the terror and uncertainty of those moments. "I tried to stay calm. Curtis and Yvonne came over, and Curtis used his connections in the government to get information. The Navy moved quickly, but they were on the other side of the world. It took time."

"Will you describe for the jury what that time was like?"

She took a breath. "It was excruciating, but I had good support. The FBI assigned us a negotiator, Mary Patterson. She was amazing. And Curtis hired a private security firm to advise us. There wasn't much we could do. Then we got a call from one of the pirates. He identified himself as Ibrahim and demanded five million dollars."

Barrington tented his hands beneath his chin. "How did you respond?"

"We didn't know if the government would let us negotiate. But my father-in-law intervened, as did Paul Derrick. The government agreed to let us work out a deal with them."

"Was your family able to come to terms with Ibrahim?"

Vanessa looked at the jurors and saw their sympathy. Some of them were mothers like her. *I can do this*, she thought. "We did. Curtis negotiated the amount down to just under two million dollars. Then he and Yvonne cashed in their life savings. I flew to Kenya to make the delivery. I was with the security team on the plane when they dropped the package."

"When the drop happened, did you see anyone in the cockpit of the *Renaissance*?"

Vanessa fought back her tears. "I saw Daniel and Quentin with Ibrahim. I realize his name isn't Ibrahim; it's Ismail. I spoke to them briefly. They said they were okay. I told them . . ." Her voice cracked with emotion. "I told them I loved them and that I would see them soon."

"Is the pirate who called himself Ibrahim in this courtroom?" Barrington asked.

"Yes," she said, extending her finger toward Ismail. "He's over there."

"Let the record reflect the witness has identified the defendant," said Judge McKenzie.

Barrington went on, "Did you speak to Ibrahim at that time?"

Vanessa nodded. "I did. He told me to deliver what we

promised and he would do the same."

"Did you do that?"

"Yes," she said quietly. "I saw them take the package with my own eyes."

Barrington gave her a sorrowful look. "Did Ibrahim deliver what he promised?"

In an instant, she was there again, in the plane with Steyn and Flint, climbing into the sky as the sun set over Somalia. She remembered the call she made to Paul, the plea she had spoken, and the trust she had placed in Ibrahim. She closed her eyes, overcome by the memory of what came next.

"No," she finally said. "He didn't."

Barrington hesitated, then said, "I'm sorry to ask this, Mrs. Parker, but it's important to the case. Did you get the ransom money back?"

She nodded, recalling the blustery day in December when the FBI had returned the briefcases of cash. "We did, but it didn't matter. We wanted our family back."

The prosecutor surveyed the jury box. "Of course you did."

Over the next thirty minutes, Barrington led her through the aftermath—Daniel's funeral, the medical care Quentin received, and the challenges associated with his brain injury. The tears flowed freely as she recounted the day Quentin realized his father was dead. She told the jury how Daniel's postcards and letters had helped him out of the tunnel of despair. And then she told them about Ariadne— how she had become his polestar and inspired him to sail again. She met the girl's eyes and realized that she had never told her this. She saw that Ariadne was crying, too. *I need to be more open with them*, Vanessa thought. *I need to be more open with everyone.*

"Did there come a time when the government returned something to you from the sailboat, something that had been Daniel's?" Barrington asked.

"Yes," Vanessa said. "It was a chest his father gave him before they set sail."

Barrington took the box from Curtis and passed it along to her. "Is this the chest?"

"It is." She held it up for the jury to see. "It's from Zanzibar."

"Was there something in the chest?" Barrington asked gently.

"There was a letter," she said and opened the lid, pulling out the folded pages again. "It was unfinished. I would read it to you, but it's very personal. Daniel and I were going through some hard things when he left. He wrote this to say he was sorry."

Barrington waited a moment before asking, "Is there another letter you'd like to read instead?"

"There is," Vanessa replied. After Barrington retrieved it from Eldridge Jordan, she said, "This is the last letter Daniel sent before the hijacking. It gave me hope in my darkest hours."

She took a breath to center herself, and then she began to read. She pictured La Digue as Daniel had described it, the sun and sand and granite boulders that Quentin had climbed, the breeze and the sea and the freedom they offered from the hurried world. When she reached the part about

Quentin, she met his eyes and spoke the words to him for the first time.

."'The boy who once crawled like a caterpillar has become a butterfly. He is alive, Vanessa. I've never met anyone more alive than he is. He is beautiful and strong and intelligent and capable. He could sail the rest of the way on his own and I don't doubt he would make it home.

"'I give you more credit for this than I take myself. He sees the hearts of others like you do. He feels deep empathy for pain. There once was a day when I struggled to love him. Today, I look up to him. I wish I were more like he is. Maybe I will be someday. But even if I never make it, I am comforted that in this way, at least, I haven't failed. I haven't failed our son.

"'Where will he go? Only time will tell. But I believe that the stories he will pass on to his children will be greater than the story I'm telling you now. He's as close to bulletproof as a man can get in this life. Nothing can hold him back. He's learned to rise above his fears.'"

When Vanessa finished reading, she looked at the jury and saw that not a single eye was dry. She folded the letter and heard Barrington say, "Thank you, Mrs. Parker. I have nothing further."

She waited pensively while Megan Derrick rose to her feet, wondering what questions the defense lawyer could possibly ask, but Megan didn't approach the podium.

"Mrs. Parker," she said, "I'm so very sorry for your loss. I have no questions for you."

Judge McKenzie turned to Vanessa. "In that case, you

can step down."

Vanessa wanted only one thing at that moment—to embrace her son. She returned to the gallery, looking at no one but Quentin. He stood up and met her in the aisle, his face wet with tears. She wrapped her arms around him and hugged him tight.

"Your dad was right," she whispered. "You know that, don't you? Nothing can hold you back. Go up there and speak the truth. This isn't on you. It never was."

When Quentin took the witness stand, Vanessa's world shrank to the size of his face. He sat with his head erect, his shoulders square, and his hands in his lap, as if he were sitting for a portrait. She had never seen him behave so formally. Barrington went briefly to the podium to review his notes, and then he moved toward Quentin again, stopping a comfortable distance from the stand.

"Thanks so much for coming," the prosecutor began. "We're all very glad you're here."

Quentin nodded stiffly. "So am I."

"Will you please state your name for the record?"

"Quentin Everett Parker."

"How old are you?"

"Eighteen. I'll be nineteen in September."

Barrington made a few more background inquiries to set the stage, and then he moved on to the voyage. Vanessa listened closely, worried that the stress of the situation would cause Quentin's speech to lose its hard-won smoothness, but it didn't. His words came out strong and clear and almost completely free of hesitation.

He told the jury about the South Pacific, about meeting Ariadne in Rarotonga, about the Force 10 storm off New Zealand and the lightning strike in the Strait of Malacca, about crossing the Bay of Bengal and exploring the Maldives and Seychelles. For Vanessa, the experience of listening to him was overwhelming. She had never dreamed that the troubled teen who had drowned his angst in first-person shooter games, who had taken a wrap of cocaine from his best friend to give to a buddy at a football game—an exchange observed by campus security that nearly destroyed his life—would have the courage to face nature's wrath and then talk about it with such confidence. *Daniel, you were right*, she marveled. *The sea is what he needed. It brought him back to life.*

After Quentin told the jury about La Digue, Barrington asked him to describe the departure from Victoria and the prelude to the hijacking. It was a narrative Vanessa thought she knew, but she couldn't have been more wrong. She sat on the edge of her seat as Quentin described the piracy bulletin they had received and Daniel's desire to return to Mahé, escorted by the coast guard.

"What did you think about going back?" Barrington asked.

Quentin's bottom lip quivered. "I didn't want to. I told my dad I wouldn't go with him. I should have listened to him. None of this would have happened."

Vanessa felt tears well up in her again. It was then that she realized his trauma had another layer—the guilt he felt for putting his father in danger. She had the sudden urge to abandon decorum and take him into her arms. She wanted to carry the burden with him. It was too great a weight for anyone to bear alone. Suddenly, she felt her hand being squeezed. She looked at Ariadne and saw the truth in the girl's eyes. Quentin *had* shared the burden. He'd shared it with her.

Barrington next inquired about the night of the hijacking. Quentin answered his questions succinctly, showing little emotion. When the prosecutor asked him to describe the pirates' behavior, Quentin told the story of Afyareh and the frigatebirds. It was at this point that he looked at Ismail for the first time. It was just a glance, but it seemed to shake him and he looked away quickly.

As if sensing his disturbance, Barrington skipped over the ransom negotiations and moved straight to the drop. "What was it like to see your mother in the plane?" he asked.

Quentin met Vanessa's eyes. "I thought she was brave. She hates flying more than anything. I couldn't believe that she'd come all that way. Neither could my dad."

I'd do it again, Vanessa wanted to say, *because I love you more than anything.*

Barrington took a step toward the jury box. "Where were you and your father sitting when the pirates counted the money?"

Quentin blinked. "We were both in the dining booth."

"Who operated the cash machine?"

"Afyareh. He went through the first briefcase, but he didn't finish the second before the helicopter took off." Quentin narrowed his eyes. "That's when everything changed."

"What changed exactly?" Barrington probed.

Quentin looked down at the floor, concentrating. "Afyareh went to the radio. He told the Navy to put the helicopter back on the ship. The Navy didn't want to. Some boats had launched from shore. They wanted to check them out. Afyareh didn't like that. Neither did the others. They had an argument. We were scared. My dad told me if they started shooting to use the table as cover."

When Quentin took a moment to think, Vanessa realized that the courtroom was completely silent. Even the judge looked like she was holding her breath.

"Did they start shooting?" Barrington finally asked.

Quentin shook his head. "Not then." He paused. "I'm sorry. Some of this is hard."

"Take your time," said the prosecutor.

"After that, the shouting stopped," Quentin went on. "We thought it was over. But then Afyareh pointed his gun at my dad. He said, 'Make them listen, or you will die.'"

Vanessa frowned in confusion. She seemed to recall that when Quentin talked to Paul on the *Renaissance*, he had placed Ismail's threat just before the shooting, not while the helicopter was still in the air. For some reason the disparity seemed significant.

"What did your father do?" Barrington asked.

Quentin closed his eyes. "He called the Navy, and they agreed to bring back the helicopter. Afyareh wasn't happy with that. He wanted the helicopter inside the hangar. It took time for that to happen. I seem to remember . . . yes, there was another argument—Mas and Afyareh. They shouted at each other in Somali. Then Paul called back, and Afyareh accused him of moving the ship. He gave the Navy a deadline. I think it was five minutes."

Vanessa saw the surprise on Barrington's face. Quentin had never mentioned the argument before. "What happened in those five minutes?" the prosecutor asked, a trace of tension in his voice.

It took Quentin awhile to formulate his reply. "I think . . . there was another argument. Yeah, Mas was upset. Afyareh talked to him. Then . . ." Quentin shook his head. "I don't know what he said, but it made all of them go crazy." He thought some more. "I remember being scared. My dad was scared, too. Everything was spiraling out of control. That was when Paul called the last time."

Barrington traded an anxious glance with Eldridge Jordan. It was clear that the prosecutor had no idea where this was going. "Do you remember what happened after that conversation?"

Quentin closed his eyes again, focusing all his attention on remembering. "I think some time passed. Yes . . . they were watching the windows. Then there was more shouting. I don't . . . I don't remember who was doing it. Then . . . the lights came on. It looked like daylight again. I don't . . . I don't remember." Quentin grimaced. "I think . . . that's when—"

He opened his eyes and gave Barrington a look of distress. Vanessa's heart went out to him. He had crossed light-years of psychological distance in the past eight months, but still the final seconds before the shooting eluded him.

"It's okay if you don't remember," Barrington said.

"It's *not* okay," Quentin retorted. "The memories are there. I know they are."

It was then that he did something Vanessa never expected. He turned and stared at Ismail. She looked at the pirate and saw the gravity in his countenance, the recognition in his eyes. She sensed something passing between them, an acknowledgment of some kind. She faced Quentin again. His mouth was hanging open, and his pupils were dilated. *Where are you?* she thought. *Are you there again?*

Without warning, Quentin began to tremble. "I see it," he said. "I see the lights going on." He gripped the chair. "They were shocking . . . like the sun. We were terrified . . . I see a shape moving away from the window. He's aiming the gun. Oh God, he's shooting. I see the blood. It's everywhere." Quentin buried his head in his hands. "I couldn't stop him. Oh God, I couldn't stop him."

"Who couldn't you stop?" Barrington asked because he had no choice.

"It was Mas," Quentin blurted out.

Bedlam erupted in the courtroom. The judge tried to contain it, rapping her gavel and calling for order, but no one seemed to listen. Vanessa saw three things at once: Clyde Barrington rooted in place, Ismail hanging his head, and Quentin's lips moving, forming words she couldn't hear.

"He's saying something," she exclaimed, enraged at the mob for drowning out her son.

"Order! Order!" the judge shouted over the din. "Come to order or I will expel you all."

At last, the spectators quieted down, and Vanessa heard Quentin's voice. "There's more," he said, staring at the floor. "I remember . . . there was a fight between Afyareh and Mas. Everyone was yelling. Then . . . Afyareh picked up a gun. It happened so fast I couldn't . . . get under the table. He pointed it at me. Oh God, I see his face . . . I see him pulling the trigger."

When Quentin stopped speaking, no one in the courtroom made a sound. All eyes turned toward Ismail, who was sitting perfectly still, a trail of tears on his cheek. Vanessa felt as if her world had been turned upside down and shaken until she had lost all sense of direction. Mas had killed Daniel, but Ismail had shot Quentin. She felt the wrath again and held on to it for dear life.

Then Quentin spoke again, and her heart inverted a final time. "I remember his eyes . . . He was afraid . . . There was another gun . . . It was pointed at his head . . . He didn't want to do it."

A depthless silence descended on the courtroom. After a moment, the judge focused on Clyde Barrington and cleared her throat. The prosecutor looked shell-shocked. The only witness the jury would never disbelieve had just exonerated the man he was seeking to put to death.

"Who was pointing the gun at him?" Barrington finally asked, just above a whisper.

Quentin's eyes were full of pain. "Mas," he replied. "Mas made him do it."

Barrington winced. "You're absolutely certain of that?"

Quentin nodded. "I see it now."

The prosecutor took a ponderous breath. "I have nothing further."

As Vanessa watched, Megan stood and spoke to Quentin. "I'd like to say that what you did today was one of the bravest things I've ever seen. I have no questions. Only gratitude."

Quentin shrugged, looking embarrassed.

Judge McKenzie smiled at him. "Thank you for your testimony, young man. You may step down." She looked at Barrington. "Do you plan to put on any more evidence?"

Barrington shook his head slowly. "Your Honor, we've presented our case."

"I'll take up any motions after lunch," the judge said. "Then we'll hear from the defense."

Vanessa heard the gavel of the law clerk and the clamor that ensued, but she tuned all of it out. She met Quentin at the bar and wrapped him in her arms, telling him how well he did, how proud she was of him, how proud Daniel would be if he were here.

He hugged her back. "It's over, Mom," he said. "It's time to let it go."

ISMAIL

Ismail saw it all laid out before him, the entire record of wrong, and that is what he told the jury. He told them of the wrongs that had been done to him—Adan's assassination, the Shabaab kidnapping, the coercion that led him to take up arms against the government, Yasmin's long imprisonment, and Yusuf's terrible death. These were the axial events on which everything else had turned, the incitements that drove him to compound the evil in an attempt to restore what he had lost.

He gave the jury no excuses, only explanations. He told them of his escape from the Shabaab, his sojourn at Hawa Abdi's place, and the day he overheard young men from Hobyo talking about the money they could make hijacking ships. He told them about the scheme he had conceived to save Yasmin, about joining Gedef's crew, about taking the Malaysian cargo ship, and about the genesis of the mission to hijack a ship near the Seychelles. He traced the arc of wrong from the abortive attack on the *Jade Dolphin* to the decision they had made to take refuge on Mahé.

"It would have been better for the Captain and Timaha if we had died," he said to the jurors. "But it was not to be. I saw the sailboat in the night. I knew it wasn't mine. But I took it anyway. There was no going back. There never was."

He told them about the Navy next, the way the ships came, one after another, and penned him in, forcing him to take an unprecedented step that ultimately blew up in his face. He explained how ransoms are usually negotiated—by the pirate commander in concert with the investors once the ship is resting at anchor, not by the attackers at sea. And then he told them about his plan to take the boat to Mogadishu, to divide the spoils among his crew, and to take his share and find Yasmin.

He confessed to the jurors that he had deceived his men, that he had sworn an oath to Mas on the name of Allah, and that he had changed their course surreptitiously. He knew he was endangering them. He knew he was putting their families at risk. But he saw no way out of the dilemma. He couldn't return to Somalia with nothing. But neither could he negotiate with the Navy. He knew the story of the *Maersk Alabama*. He knew America would never let him take the hostages to land.

With help from Megan, he didn't belabor the obvious, skipping over the negotiations and moving to the night of the shooting. "My agreement with the Navy was simple," he said, glancing at Paul in the gallery. "After the drop, we would count the money, leave the hostages in the sailboat, and take the small boat to shore. Paul promised me the Navy wouldn't intervene."

"Did your men know you were near Mogadishu?" Megan asked.

Ismail shook his head. "I planned to tell them on the beach. They could take the money or not. It didn't matter to me. I would get them to the city. After that, they would be on their own."

Megan met his eyes. "Did you trust the Navy to honor its word?"

"I trusted Paul. But I was foolish. He wasn't in control."

"What happened when the helicopter took off?" Megan asked.

Ismail took a breath. "That was when everything began to unravel. My men were afraid. Mas accused me of betraying them. We had an argument."

"Tell us about that," Megan said.

Ismail looked at the floor and recalled the scene—the noise of the departing chopper, the terror in the eyes of his crew, his ineffectual conversation with Paul, and his dispute with Mas. The words came back to him as if they had been spoken yesterday.

Mas: You were a fool to trust them. They'll never
    let us go.
Ismail: I'll get them to ground the helicopter.
Mas: It doesn't matter. We're taking the hostages to
    the beach.
Ismail: That's not the deal!

Mas: Screw the deal! For all I know you're working
    with them.

Ismail: What are you talking about?

Mas: The skiff. How did it get loose? And your
    meeting with Paul. You looked like friends
    drinking Pepsi together.

Ismail: You're an imbecile. Why would I work with
    them? They want to put us in prison.

Mas: I don't care what you say! I'm not releasing the
    hostages until we're on the beach.

Ismail: If we break the deal, they'll never let us go. I'll
    get them to ground the helicopter. Then we go
    ashore. I checked the boat. The gas tank is full.

Liban: Listen to Afyareh. He got the Navy to ground
    their planes.

Guray: I agree. Afyareh can handle this.

Mas: You're all insane! They're not going to let us go!

Megan moved closer to him. "Did you convince the
Navy to ground the helicopter?"

Ismail nodded. "I did. But they took too long putting
it away."

"What do you mean?"

Ismail turned in his chair and told the jurors about the
beginning of the mutiny.

Mas: It's going to be dark soon. They can shoot us
    in the dark.

Ismail: Shut up, Mas!

Mas: What proof do you have that they're going to let us go? They want us to trust them, but they shot Garaad's men in the head. They're going to do that to us.

Ismail: You're crazy!

Mas: The ship is too close. Don't you see? It's closer than it was before. They're going to kill us all.

Osman: He's right. The ship is too close.

Guray: They moved the ship!

Mas: There's no way I'm releasing the hostages until the ship goes away.

Dhuuban: They're going to shoot us!

Ismail: There are seven of us. They don't have seven snipers.

Mas: He's making that up! He doesn't know what he's talking about!

Ismail: We break the deal and all bets are off.

Sondare: The ship is too close!

Osman: They need to move it back!

Ismail: They'll never do it.

Mas: They'll do it if we shoot someone.

Ismail: You're a lunatic!

Mas: Watch me.

Ismail: Stop! I'll get them to move the ship.

When he finished speaking, Megan waited a moment before asking, "When Paul called you and told you the helicopter was inside the ship, were you in command of your crew?"

"No," he replied. "The men were listening to Mas. I was afraid for the Captain and Quentin. I knew the Navy wouldn't move the ship. But I had to try. I gave them five minutes to comply."

"What happened then?" Megan inquired.

Ismail felt the noose around his neck. "That's when my men found out what I had done."

Mas: It isn't working! We need to call my uncle. He'll know what to do.

Ismail: We're not going to call anyone. We're sticking to the plan.

Mas: Call him! He could send us another ship!

Ismail: Why would he do that? He'd be putting himself at risk.

Mas: Call him or I'm going to shoot the Captain!

Ismail: I can't call him.

Mas: Why not?

Ismail: Gedef didn't have authority to negotiate with the family.

[Everyone shouting at once]

Mas: You betrayed us, you son of a whore!

Ismail: It was the only way! The Navy wasn't going to let us go! Look at this money! You can each have 250,000 dollars! Take it to Nairobi! Start a business! Do whatever you want!

Mas: You're trying to get us killed! My relatives will never let us go!

Ismail: Think, Mas! Use your brain for once! This is
    the chance of a lifetime!

Mas: You're a liar! I'm not listening anymore!

"What did the other pirates think of your proposal?"
Megan asked.

"All of them sided with Mas," Ismail replied, covering
for Liban, who had stayed loyal until the end. "They knew
the money belonged to Gedef's family."

Megan looked at him somberly. "When Paul offered to
move the ship in exchange for Quentin's release, how did
your men react?"

Ismail shook his head. "They had poison in their minds.
Everyone was yelling. It was madness."

"How did it end?" Megan inquired softly.

Ismail faced the jury, meeting their eyes one by one.
Their expressions were as diverse as human emotion—
disgust, contempt, grief, loathing, skepticism, horror,
sorrow, and pain. He knew then that he would accept their
decision without question, even if they voted to put him to
death. They were the instruments of God—the arbitrators
of his judgment.

"It happened just as Quentin told you," he replied. "I
pulled the trigger twice, aiming away from his head and
heart, and prayed he wouldn't die." He looked at Vanessa
and saw her anguish. "I wish every day I could change it.
But I can't. Everything that happened is my responsibility.
I am so sorry."

Megan waited awhile, allowing the jury to absorb his apology. Then she asked, "What became of your mother and sister?"

Ismail blinked once and blotted an eye with his sleeve. "Yasmin escaped from Somalia and found my mother. They're safe now. That is my only consolation."

Megan nodded. "I have nothing further."

When Clyde Barrington stood to cross-examine him, Ismail could see that the wind of conviction had left his sails. He looked worn and agitated, but he didn't give up without a fight.

"Daniel Parker died nine months ago," he began. "For nine months you have said *nothing* about Mas, *nothing* about a mutiny, *nothing* about losing control of your men and being forced to shoot Quentin Parker. What *possibly* compelled you to hold out until now?"

Ismail delivered his reply slowly. "I didn't want anyone else to get hurt."

"What are you talking about?" Barrington demanded.

For an instant, Ismail glanced away from the prosecutor and looked toward the corner of the courtroom. The man in the blue-checkered shirt hadn't returned, but another Somali had taken his place. He had a professorial face with oval glasses and a rotund frame.

"When the small boat died in the water, Mas shouted something to the Navy," Ismail said. "He accused me of being Shabaab. He also said something else, something in Somali. He ordered the men to say that I shot the hostages. He threatened their families."

Barrington's eyes widened. "How would he—?" At once, the prosecutor swiveled on his feet and glanced at the man in the back. "Mas was Gedef's cousin, correct?"

Ismail nodded. "His father is Gedef's father's younger brother."

"And Gedef's father was with the Somali security service under Siad Barre?"

"Yes," Ismail replied, gratified to see Barrington making the connections.

"What exactly are you saying?" the prosecutor asked.

Ismail fixed his eyes on the rotund man. "I'm saying that none of my men knew what I was doing when I turned the sailboat toward Mogadishu. None of them intended to steal money from Gedef's family. It was my plan, and only my plan. But Mas threatened to tell his uncle otherwise if the men didn't testify against me."

Again, whispers broke out in the gallery, and the judge silenced them with her gavel.

Barrington looked stricken. "Why didn't you tell us this before?"

Ismail held out his hands. "I had to let them go through with it. If I challenged them, their story would have fallen apart. Who knows what Mas would have done?"

Ismail watched the prosecutor carefully, sensing the struggle inside of him, the deep wound to his pride. He was a powerful man, but he had been played like a chess piece in a game he still didn't understand. Ismail remembered a line from Gaarriye. He offered it by way of explanation.

"There is a Somali poem called 'Aadmi.' In it the poet says that whatever things may look like, the meaning is always deeper. When I was a boy, my father told me to look for the deeper meaning in everything. What I have told you is the deeper meaning."

For a long moment, Barrington just stared at him. Then he turned around and walked away.

The next morning, Judge McKenzie dismissed the jury to deliberate. They returned a verdict in under an hour. Ismail watched the jurors file in and take their seats. A few of them glanced at him; most did not. The jury foreman—an older man with graying hair—handed an envelope to the bailiff who passed it up to the judge. The judge opened the envelope and read its contents.

"The verdict appears to be in order," she said. "Will the defendant please rise?"

Ismail stood up beside Megan and Kiley and the rest of their team, clasping his hands behind his back. He looked at the judge without fear. He had done everything he set out to do. Yasmin was safe with Khadija. He had made his confession and delivered his apology. The rest was in God's hands.

"Ismail Adan Ibrahim," the judge intoned, looking at the sheet in front of her, "on the charge of piracy under the law of nations, the jury finds you guilty. On the charge of conspiracy to commit hostage taking resulting in death, the jury finds you guilty. On the charge of hostage taking resulting in death, the jury finds you guilty. On the charge of conspiracy to commit kidnapping resulting in death, the jury finds you guilty. On the charge of kidnapping resulting in death . . ."

As the verdict was read, Ismail thought back to the day when it all began. He remembered the way the schoolyard looked in the morning light. He recalled the sound of the students' laughter in the hallways. He remembered the sadness that filled his father's eyes when the technicals pulled up to the gate and the men poured out with their guns. He recalled the way they dragged Adan into the yard and forced him to his knees. *You are an enemy of Islam!* they shouted. *You are guilty of spreading falsehoods and promoting immorality. Repent!* But his father didn't repent. Instead, he looked at his children and waited for the end to come. Ismail remembered the sound of gunfire, the *rat-tat-tat* of the AK-47s, as they cut Adan down. He recalled the way his father fell to the earth, his blood mixing with the yellow dirt. *If only they had left us alone*, he thought. *But they didn't leave us alone.*

Judge McKenzie's voice interrupted his reverie. "On the charge of using, carrying, brandishing, and discharging a firearm during a crime of violence resulting in death, the jury finds you guilty. On the charge of assault with a dangerous weapon on federal officers and employees, the jury finds you guilty."

Suddenly, the judge looked up, gazing at Ismail through her glasses. "On the charge of murder within the special maritime and territorial jurisdiction of the United States, the jury finds you *not guilty*."

Ismail closed his eyes and felt relief down deep in his bones. If the jurors had asked him to bear the condemnation of another, he would have done it. But they had seen the truth.

"On the charge of attempted murder within the special maritime and territorial jurisdiction of the United States," the judge went on, "the jury finds you *not guilty*."

And there it was—the judgment of man and God. Guilty and not guilty at the same time. He turned to Megan and accepted her embrace.

"If they didn't blame you for the shooting," she said, "they won't give you the death penalty."

He knew it was true, but it didn't matter as much as the knowledge that his father would have approved. "Thank you for believing in me," he replied. "I know it wasn't easy."

Megan smiled in a way that wove joy and sadness together. "I almost never get to say this. But today I will. The system worked. Justice was served."

YASMIN

For Yasmin, coming to America was a gloriously disorienting experience. She had lived most of her life in a world without regular plumbing and a reliable power grid and well-paved roads and supermarkets and high-speed Internet and air-conditioning. When she gained access to all of these things at once, she felt almost paralyzed by the possibilities. She had to retrain her mind to get water from the tap instead of the cistern or the river, to flip a wall switch to chase away the darkness instead of lighting a lantern, to walk to the store for milk instead of getting it from the cow or a neighbor with a herd of goats.

There were things she missed about Somalia—the frogs and the night birds and the sky full of stars. But they were a small sacrifice to make in comparison to the manifold blessings of living in Minneapolis—greeting her mother every morning, owning an apartment with nice furniture and rugs and a new television and computer, having Farah's family nearby, worshiping at a beautiful mosque, and receiving a generous monthly income that the State Department said would last for fifty years.

All of the goodness, however, couldn't banish Yasmin's sorrow over Ismail. She had come to the meeting in Norfolk certain that the charges against him were erroneous. Khadija had told her about Megan's visit to Dadaab and the story she had passed on about the shooting. But Yasmin had denied it fiercely, sure that the Americans had made a mistake. She knew her brother. He wasn't a criminal, let alone a killer. She had listened in shock as he confessed what he had done and the price he had to pay for his crimes. That evening at the Marriott, she spent two hours on a hotel computer reading about his case. What she learned broke her heart and left her with a question she had to answer: Why?

She hadn't rested until she found the truth. She talked to Farah, followed the news from the trial, and contacted Mahamoud in Mogadishu against her mother's wishes. No one admitted it to her directly, but she put the puzzle together and recognized her own face in the frame. The discovery horrified her and shackled her with guilt. Time had granted her no relief, only exacerbated her humiliation. The blood Ismail shed wasn't on his hands alone. He had done it for her.

For weeks she had agonized about what to do, praying ceaselessly for wisdom, and then an idea came to her. She discussed the matter with Khadija, and her mother agreed. She waited until the trial was over, until the jury had delivered its verdict and recommended a sentence—life without parole. Then she contacted Paul Derrick and explained her desire. He made the request and passed along Vanessa's number. She placed the call despite her trepidation, trusting the voice in her spirit.

When Vanessa answered, Yasmin introduced herself.

"Yes," Vanessa said, "Paul told me about you."

Yasmin took a breath and spoke what was on her heart. "I don't know if you will agree, but my mother and I would be honored to meet you. There are some things we would like to tell you."

Vanessa was quiet for a while, and Yasmin could only imagine what she was thinking. Then, mercifully, she opened the door. "Can you come to Annapolis? That would be easiest for us."

"Of course," Yasmin said. "We will come whenever you wish."

She heard Vanessa flipping pages. "How about Saturday, September 15?"

"That will be fine," Yasmin said and wrote down the address. "Thank you."

She bought their airline tickets from a travel agent at Farah's mall and flew with Khadija to Washington, DC, hiring a taxi to take them to Annapolis. The cabbie—an Armenian immigrant who spoke only broken English—let them out beside the row of Tuscan pines.

"This is address," he said, gesturing toward the mailbox.

"Are you sure?" Khadija asked, looking at the house in wonderment.

"Yes," the driver replied testily, pointing at his GPS unit.

The Cape Cod was a palace in Yasmin's eyes. There was nothing like it in all of Somalia.

She walked with her mother up the cobblestone drive and through the grape arbor to the porch, admiring the flower beds, the rich green lawn and verdant trees, and the sparkle of the river in the distance. She used the knocker to announce their arrival. She was dressed in a blousy sweater, blue jeans, sneakers, and a red and white headscarf. The infinite styles and immodesty of Western fashion had been her greatest challenge in transitioning to American life. While Khadija was content to wear the *abaya* and hijab, Yasmin had made an attempt to blend in without compromising her dignity.

In time, she heard the lock retract. Then the door opened and she saw Vanessa for the first time. She was lovely, with red-brown hair and the greenest eyes Yasmin had ever seen. Yasmin laughed out loud when a dog with golden fur approached her with its eyes wide and its tongue out.

"That's Skipper," Vanessa said kindly.

Yasmin knelt down and patted the dog's head. "He's beautiful."

Vanessa held out her arm in invitation. "Please, come in."

Yasmin followed her mother into the foyer, looking around in awe. The rooms were filled with handsome furniture, elegant mirrors and artwork, and expansive Oriental rugs. Vanessa led them across the living room and out the back door to the deck.

"Please make yourselves comfortable," she said, gesturing

to a round table by the pool. "I made a pot of tea. It isn't as sweet as *shah*, but I think you'll like it."

"You know Somali tea?" Khadija inquired in surprise.

Vanessa gave her a tentative smile. "I did some reading on the Internet. I realized how little I know about your country."

When Vanessa left to get the tea, Yasmin sat down beside her mother and looked toward the river. She watched a sailboat float by, its mainsail luffing in the breeze. There was so much she wanted to express, but words seemed inadequate to the task. Nothing could restore what Vanessa had lost.

A minute later, Vanessa appeared with a tray and handed them steaming mugs. "It's rooibos from South Africa. There's sugar and cream as well."

"*Mahabsenid*," Khadija said. "Thank you."

Yasmin waited for her mother to fix her tea and then stirred three cubes of sugar into her cup, along with a large dose of cream. She took a sip and her eyes lit up. "It's delicious!"

"I'm glad," Vanessa said, taking a sip from her own cup.

After an awkward silence, Khadija spoke up. "Thank you so much for your hospitality. It was Yasmin's idea to meet with you. Sometimes God grants wisdom to the young." She took a pensive breath. "I do not know what Ismail said at the trial, but I know what it is like to lose a husband. Not a day passes when I don't think of Adan. I would do anything to bring him back. As a mother, I feel responsible for what Ismail did to your family. Yasmin, too, feels responsible.

What he took from you, we can't give back. There is nothing we can do for you except to ask your forgiveness and to offer you, if you will permit it, a glimpse of the boy we knew before the war stole him from us."

Vanessa turned away, and Yasmin saw the pain shining in her eyes. It was awhile before she looked back at them. "Please," she said. "I'd like to hear your story."

So Khadija told her about her firstborn son. She told her of the child who at the age of three had looked at the stars and asked where they came from, the boy who memorized the Quran in Arabic and English, the teenager who mastered the art of rhetoric, occasionally besting his father in debates, the young man who was loyal to a fault, utterly devoted to his family. Finally, Khadija told her about the charge she had given Ismail before Adan was murdered, the charge to protect Yasmin and Yusuf at all cost. Her hands began to shake as she spoke of the lengths he went to honor her request, to shield Yusuf from the carnage of the war and to find Yasmin after she disappeared.

"I never imagined . . . ," she said, choking up. "I never imagined what would happen. I am so sorry for all you have suffered. We are sorry."

By now, Yasmin's face was wet with tears. She thought back to the day in Lanta Buro when Najiib had taken her out of the lineup and piled her into the Land Cruiser for the trip to Jamaad's house. She remembered the scene she had glimpsed out the window—Ismail with a gun in his hands, a boy kneeling before him in the dirt, like Adan in the schoolyard. She had seen the gun jump, seen the boy crumple to the ground, seen her brother turn away and take Yusuf into his arms. She had known then that they would never be the same. Death had begotten death. All that remained was to survive.

Vanessa wiped her own eyes. "Will you walk with me? There is someone I'd like you to meet."

Yasmin stood with Khadija and followed Vanessa down the path to the river. She saw a young man in surf shorts and a black T-shirt and a blond-haired girl about his age in cutoff jeans and a white top polishing the deck of a sailboat. They scrambled to their feet and hopped over to the dock.

Vanessa introduced them. "This is Quentin. And this is Ariadne, his girlfriend. They were just getting the boat ready to take out on the bay."

"Hello," Quentin said, extending his hand in greeting.

"Pardon me," Khadija said in embarrassment. "It is against my religion."

Yasmin glanced at her mother and then disregarded decorum. "I will do it," she said, reaching out and shaking his hand. "It is a pleasure to meet you, Quentin."

As Yasmin watched, Vanessa's lips spread into a smile. It was an expression of warmth, an expression of welcome, an expression of absolution.

"Have you ever been sailing?" she asked them, gesturing toward the sailboat. "It's going to be a lovely sunset."

MEGAN

Megan found her brother sitting on a bench at Lafayette Square not far from the equestrian statue of Andrew Jackson. The White House stood in the background, a flag fluttering over it on a tall pole. It was a blustery Friday afternoon in mid-autumn, the sky as blue as the canvas of Van Gogh's *Starry Night* and the trees in the park festooned with color. A gusty wind was blowing, sending leaves cartwheeling across the grass, but the temperature was still pleasant, the dry air carrying a hint of Indian summer.

"Nice place you've got here," Paul said with a grin, closing the book he was reading. "It's a shame they keep you chained to a desk."

Megan smiled back. The park was a five-minute walk from Mason & Wagner and her favorite respite in DC. "I come here almost every day," she retorted. "Just not for long."

He stood and gave her a hug. "Are you ready?"

She nodded. "As ready as I'll ever be."

They took a leaf-strewn path out of the park and walked up Connecticut Avenue to the parking garage just past the Army and Navy Club, where Paul had left his car. He gave the attendant his ticket and took the keys when the man returned with his Audi. He climbed into the driver's seat and Megan slipped in beside him, feeling the growl of the engine as he accelerated into traffic.

"You should do consulting work," she ribbed him. "Then you could buy a real sports car."

He laughed and threw the Audi into a quick turn. "She's not a Jaguar, but I like her just fine.

"How's Ismail?" he asked, taking New York Avenue toward the E Street Expressway. "I wanted to make it to the sentencing, but I had a conference in San Diego."

"He got what we expected," Megan replied. "Twenty life sentences, eighteen consecutive. They're never going to let him out. But I asked them to transfer him to a facility near the Twin Cities. The judge was sympathetic. She told him that in all her years on the bench, she'd never seen a case like his. She made quite a speech, actually. She told him he had a choice. He could wither in prison, or he could find a way to transcend the walls and leave the world a better place. He was moved. We all were. The judge is going to reconsider Mas's plea bargain. But I don't know if Barrington has the stomach for another capital trial. I told him it might be better to let it rest."

Paul took the on-ramp to I-66 West. "I bet your partners

are glad it's over."

Megan chuckled. "I have to tell you, when they heard about the State Department reward, they started salivating. They couldn't believe we weren't going to get a piece of it. They're relieved to have me billing full-time again."

He glanced at her as they rounded the curve and took the Theodore Roosevelt Memorial Bridge across the Potomac. "Do you really charge your clients eight hundred dollars an hour? Who can afford that?"

"You'd be surprised. We have to turn them away." She looked out at the river and smiled to herself. "How are Quentin and Vanessa?"

"They're good," he replied with affection. "I've gone sailing with them the last couple of weekends. Vanessa says he still isn't quite the same. There are moments when he forgets a word or loses his balance. But they're rare. He's a great kid and a hell of a mariner."

"And Vanessa?" she persisted. "How is she?"

He laughed under his breath. "We're having fun. That's all it is right now. We talk. We play music. We spend time on the water. But she seems to be enjoying it."

"I'm so happy for you," Megan said with feeling.

"I was worried about Quentin," Paul confessed. "I thought he'd resent me. But I've never gotten that sense from him. He really seems to like having me around."

Megan nodded. "You're a bridge for him. He doesn't have to explain himself." She grinned. "I'm sure the piano has helped, too."

"The piano makes everything better," her brother said.

Megan watched the neighborhoods of Arlington and Falls Church fly by and braced herself for what they were about to do. She couldn't deny it any longer. Paul was right. She had spent the last two and a half decades living in the black shadow of a single day. She blamed herself for Kyle's death, for the choice he made, for not stopping him, even though she had tried with all her might. It was her father—the man whose name she hadn't spoken since his funeral—who had turned her brother into a time bomb. She still hated him for it, hated the ground he walked on, hated the fact that her birth certificate bore his name and his genes lived on in her. In fact, if she were brutally honest, he was the reason she had never had children. She wanted to rid the earth of him.

They merged onto the Capital Beltway and drove south, eventually taking the Little River Turnpike toward Annandale. When they reached the town center, they turned down an intersecting road and entered their old neighborhood—an arterial network of brick ranch houses set on pancake-flat patches of grass. Paul slowed down and turned onto their street, pulling to the curb.

Megan shuddered when she saw the split-level house—half redbrick, half dingy white clapboard with a faux chimney and a peeling roof. The trees in the yard were bigger than she remembered, but everything else was the same. The memories came back to her in a flood, but she resisted them. She wasn't here to relive the horror. She was here to release it.

"How do I do this?" she asked softly.

"I don't know," Paul replied. "But whatever it is, I'm with you."

She closed her eyes and cleansed her mind, breathing steadily and searching for a silver bullet. Then it came to her. She needed to say her father's name. She clenched her jaw and took Paul's hand, tears springing to her eyes. The hatred overcame her. *You bastard! You thought you were God's gift to the world, but you were the devil in disguise. You drove a beautiful boy to kill himself, and you sent our mother to an early grave. All for what? Because you couldn't stand the thought that Kyle might be gay.*

"John Derrick," she said in a voice as hard as marble, "you stole my brother from me. You poisoned my mother's soul. You robbed me of my childhood. I will not let you steal my future. On this day I bury you. All that you were is dead to me now."

Paul squeezed her hand. "I'd like to say it with you. Do you mind?"

Megan shook her head. They repeated her words together, their voices uniting in a chorus of valediction, sealed by their blood and singularity of purpose. But she knew it wasn't enough. She had to let Kyle go, too. She took a breath and told Paul, feeling the emotions pressing against the dam in her heart. All at once, she opened the sluice gate and let them out, the pain and the shame, the confusion and the grief, and, finally, the love she still tended like a votive flame for him.

"I miss you, Kyle," she whispered. "I miss the way you sang for me, the way you looked for the good in everything.

The world didn't deserve you. Sing with the angels now, and help me let you go."

When she had nothing more to say, she looked at Paul and he touched her cheek, wiping a tear from her eye. "I love you, Meg," he said. "I always will."

"I love you, too," she replied. "You're the best thing in my life."

He pulled away from the curb and accelerated up the lane, leaving the house and the memories behind. She did not look back.

ISMAIL

Just after lunch, Longfellow delivered the stack of paper Ismail had requested, along with a ballpoint pen. He had only two more days before he was scheduled to board a bus bound for a medium-security correctional institution in Wisconsin, where he would spend the rest of his natural life. According to the jailer, it was the kind of place where he would be able to visit the library, play basketball in the gymnasium, attend worship services, take walks in the yard, and meet his mother and sister whenever they could make the three-hour trip from Minneapolis. It was the best Judge McKenzie had been able to do for him, and he was thankful. But the move was still two days away. Right now he had only one thing on his mind—writing a letter to Mahamoud.

The idea had come to him in the night, like the old dream of Yasmin. It had so excited him that he hadn't been able to sleep again. It was a stretch, but it was possible now that the Shabaab was on the run and security was better in

Mogadishu. He sat down on his rack, placed the pages on top of the book of Islamic poetry he had checked out of the library, and began to write.

Dear Uncle Mahamoud,

I know you are aware of my situation. My lawyer said she spoke to you and passed along the good news about my mother and sister. I am sorry we were not able to meet as we planned. It would have been a joy to see you again. I have a simple request to make of you today, though I know it will be a challenge for you to fulfill. I ask it not only for myself but also for my father and for the future of our country.

When we last met, you told me that our school closed after the attack. You said there wasn't money to pay the staff, and that everyone was afraid. From what I have read in the newspapers, things are different now. I ask that you take the money I gave you and hire the teachers again. I ask that you use your resources to reopen the school and to educate a new generation of students in the manner my father envisioned—to honor Allah, to value truth, to love their neighbors, and to work for the good of Somalia. I will never leave the place where I am going. But that thought does not trouble me as much as the thought that my father's legacy will have no one to sustain it. Please, Mahamoud, take the influence that God has given you and use it for good.

As for me, I plan to take up writing and

demonstrate to our brothers and sisters that the pen is
more powerful than the gun. I have only one aspira-
tion for the years I have left, the aspiration of Rumi,
written in his epitaph: When I am dead, seek not my
tomb in the earth, but find it in the hearts of men.

    Go well, my uncle, and thank you for your
kindness.

    —Ismail

He folded the letter in half, wrote Mahamoud's address on the back, and went to the door, knocking on it twice. Before long, Longfellow appeared and took it from him.

"Mogadishu, eh?" the jailer grunted, reading Ismail's scrawling handwriting. "That's going to cost you a pretty penny for the stamps. It's a good thing you have a generous lawyer. What does it say, if you don't mind me asking?"

"It's to my uncle," Ismail told him, seeing no reason to dissemble. "My father founded a school that closed down when he died. I'm asking my uncle to reopen it."

Longfellow stared at him in disbelief. "You're one odd bird, Ismail, or Afyareh—whatever the hell you go by." He winked. "But I'm going to miss you when you're gone."

Ismail smiled at the jailer as the door swung closed. Then he moved to the center of his cell, faced east toward Mecca, closed his eyes, and began to pray.

PAUL

The place was called Breezes, and the name suited it well. The trade winds blew in off the Indian Ocean as they had for millennia, rustling the leaves in the palm groves that lined the beach, stirring the surface of the water inside the barrier reef, and sculpting the sand along the seashore like an unseen hand. The island air was scented with spice and flowers. Never had Paul seen so many colors of bougainvillea, so many varieties of tropical trees, all growing together in a garden as virginal as Eden. Zanzibar had a peculiar effect on him. It made him want to wax poetic even though he had no talent for it.

He still couldn't believe he was here, on this day, with these people—with Vanessa and Quentin and Ariadne, to memorialize Daniel and to say good-bye a final time. He couldn't believe how much the past year had changed him, how after decades of shutting people out—everyone but Megan—he had stumbled upon people who wanted in, who actually seemed to understand him and who didn't ask for more than he could give. He couldn't believe the way Vanessa had come to look at him since the trial ended, the way she held his hand, the way she laughed at his jokes, the way her music transported him, and the passion she had shown when at last she invited him into her bed. She wasn't quite his. She never would be. But somehow it didn't feel wrong to enjoy her, perhaps even love her. Was it possible? Had he really fallen in love with her?

They were sitting together on the sloping beach as the sun set behind them, sending shafts of ruby light through the palm forest and casting long shadows across the tourmaline water. In the distance, Paul could see waves crashing on the reef. Quentin and Ariadne were snorkeling about a hundred yards out in the lagoon. They were creatures of the sea. They never seemed to tire of swimming and kayaking and cavorting in the shallows.

"Sometimes I wonder if they were twins in another life," Vanessa said, glancing at him through her sunglasses. She was wearing a sheer white cover-up over her turquoise bathing suit, her pale legs slightly pink from the sun. "Were you and Megan like that?"

He looked back at her, fingering a shell he had found in the sand. "We were. But we never got to travel like this. My dad believed that work was life."

"It's easy to see things that way," she said. "It takes effort to learn how to relax. But we're doing pretty well, don't you think?"

"This is paradise," he replied. "The real test comes when

we go home."

She pushed her sunglasses onto her head. "What is home to you, Paul? Your apartment in Arlington?"

He took a slow breath. "I don't know. I've never lived anywhere for more than a few years."

"That's sad," she said softly, placing her hand on his. "We'll have to do something about that."

It was conversations like this that convinced Paul he wasn't totally crazy, that this wasn't just some post-traumatic rebound for her, that she really, legitimately, genuinely cared for him. But thought of a common future raised a host of questions he couldn't yet answer. The Bureau was a demanding master. He loved his job—well, he loved negotiating; he loved teaching; he loved doing deals. The thrill of bouncing from one crisis to the next, never sinking his roots in anywhere, had grown old. He couldn't do it forever; he knew that. Perhaps now was the time to start planning an exit. He could do consulting work. There were universities where he could teach. Life didn't have to get boring. But predictable didn't sound so bad anymore, especially if Annapolis was nearby.

When the sun disappeared behind the island and the light began to fade from the sky, Quentin and Ariadne emerged from the water and dried themselves with their towels.

"You look like prunes." Vanessa laughed. "I thought you were going to sleep out there."

"We saw these amazing yellow fish by the reef," Quentin said, putting on his flip-flops and T-shirt and grabbing his snorkeling gear. "And fire coral, too."

"I took some awesome pictures," Ariadne said, holding up a waterproof camera.

Vanessa smiled. "I hope you're hungry. We're eating at the Sultan's Table tonight."

Quentin laughed. "Do we get to wear turbans? I'd love to see Paul in one."

Paul began to laugh, marveling at the young man standing before him. A year ago, he was a hostage on a sailboat, hours away from sustaining injuries that would nearly take his life. Now he was back on his feet, moving on and making jokes. *Kids*, Paul mused affectionately. *If only we had their resilience*. He turned toward Vanessa and saw her subtle grin, her uncomplicated grace. The thought struck him: *Perhaps we can recover it. Perhaps, like Quentin, we can remember.*

Vanessa

The next morning, one year to the day after Daniel died, Vanessa woke early, dressed quietly so as not to wake anyone in the bungalow, and slipped out into the stillness of the garden, clutching a waterproof pouch she had packed the night before. She meandered down the path to the beach and crossed the sand to the cabana where resort guests could rent watercraft and schedule dive sessions. A young Zanzibari man, Ali, met her with a sea kayak.

"*Jambo*, Ms. Parker," he said with a smile. "It is ready for you."

Ali dragged the kayak into the surf and helped her climb aboard, securing the pouch in the netting behind her and handing her the double-bladed paddle.

"Bon voyage!" he said, pushing her off.

She paddled vigorously into the brilliant dawn, toward the reef and the rising sun. She was alone on the water as far as her eyes could see. Her skin tingled in air as humid and still as the breath of a sleeping child. She was wearing her bathing suit beneath cotton shorts and an airy linen shirt, her feet clad in sandals. She expected to get wet.

When she reached the reef, she pulled the kayak across the coral and jumped onto the seat again, paddling hard to escape the breakers. The water beyond the waves was as transparent as glass, the sea floor like an ivory shadow beneath her. She paddled toward the horizon, keeping no track of time. After a while, she turned around and looked back toward the island, unnerved at the distance she had covered. All she could see of the land was a thin stretch of muted brown and green above the cobalt sea. *It's far enough*, she thought, breathing to steady her racing heart.

She opened the waterproof pouch and took out the glass bottle. She dried her hands on her shirt and twisted off the cork, gently removing the rolled pages. She knew the letters by heart. The first was the one Daniel had never finished, the one in which he had asked a question that had haunted her ever since: *Is it possible to forgive?* She had wrestled with the question more than she had ever wrestled with anything in her life, because, in a way, it summed up her entire life. It was the pivot point Archimedes had speculated about, the lever that could move the world.

But taking hold of the lever and giving it a pull was far more difficult than thinking about it. Once she did it, there was no going back, no room for recrimination or regret. She had asked the question in a thousand different ways as Quentin recovered and the trial progressed and the stream of her fondness for Paul deepened into a river. Even after she learned the truth about Ismail, she hadn't been able to answer it, not until she met Khadija and Yasmin and realized that their pain was no different from her own, though their history and culture and religion were beyond her understanding. When she saw Yasmin shake Quentin's hand, when her son and Ismail's sister smiled at each other, she knew the time had come. There was only one way forward—to leave her wrath behind.

She read Daniel's letter one last time in the light of the Zanzibari sun, and then she turned over the pages and read her answer.

Dearest D,

Is it possible to disentangle the knot of wrong? I've tried so hard to do it, pulling the strands one by one, thinking that I've identified the wrongdoer. But I've only succeeded in making the knot tighter. I've fumbled and fretted, assigning blame for the wounds I bear in my soul, but it's only driven me deeper into despair.

The truth is that everyone is to blame, and no one. When I've tried to force one person to shoulder the weight of guilt—my mother or Ted for my childhood, or you or me for the way our marriage fell apart, or Ismail or Mas or the SEAL captain for the shooting—it has only exacerbated the wrong.

The knot cannot be undone. The strands are bound together for all of time. There is only one way to overcome it and that is to cast it over the side and let the sea of forgiveness wash it away.

Today, I'm letting go of the past. I'm moving on. I'm going to love again. I'm going to watch your beautiful son grow up and get married and have children of his own. I'm going to support him when he sails around the world with Ariadne, and this time I have no doubt that he will make it.

Farewell, my husband. Thank you for the good times we spent together and for the glimpse of redemption you gave me in the end. I'll see you again one day, I think, though I know not where or how. And when I do I will have nothing left to say, except: "All is well."

—V

She rolled up the pages again and slid them back into the bottle, twisting the cork until it was tight. When she was satisfied with the seal, she lifted the bottle and threw it as far as she could out to sea. She watched it spiral through the air and land with a splash, bobbing to the surface again. She smiled and picked up her paddle, turning about and pointing the kayak toward land—toward Quentin and Ariadne and Paul. She put the blades into the water and pulled until her arms began to burn from the strain. It was a good burn, the burn of desire. She had not a minute to waste.

It was time to live again.

AUTHOR'S NOTE

On February 18, 2011, a band of Somali pirates hijacked the US-flagged sailing vessel *Quest* in the Indian Ocean, taking four Americans hostage. The US government responded to the crisis with overwhelming force, deploying three Navy ships, a crack team of SEALs, and an FBI negotiator to bring the sailors home. For four days, the pirates sailed the *Quest* toward Somalia while the Navy tried to negotiate a resolution. Finally, sixty miles from the coast, the USS *Sterett*, a Navy destroyer, attempted a "shouldering" maneuver, hoping to change the sailboat's course and buy additional time. As the *Sterett* closed in, three pirates opened fire on the hostages, killing all of them.

I watched the media coverage of the tragedy with a heavy heart and a curious eye, wondering how the government's extraordinary intervention could have gone so terribly wrong. After the incident faded from the headlines, my literary agent suggested I write a novel about lawlessness in the Horn of Africa. I was working on *The Garden of Burning Sand* at the time and set the concept aside. When my publishers asked for a third book, I dusted it off and dived in.

Before I go on, I should be clear: *The Tears of Dark Water* is not a fictionalized retelling of the *Quest* incident. I took great care to ensure that neither my characters nor the events in the story paralleled real life, beyond the fixed stars of ethnicity, US government policy, and the tactics and procedures of various government agencies, military and civilian. Daniel Parker died only on the page. The deaths of Scott and Jean Adam, Bob Riggle, and Phyllis Macay were all too real. As much as I devoted myself to the research, this novel is a product of my imagination.

The attentive reader will no doubt surmise that *The Tears of Dark Water* is not really "about" Somali piracy. It is about the multidimensional fallout of Somalia's disintegration over the past two decades. Piracy offered me a narrative framework to explore not only how a hijacking and hostage crisis could end in tragedy but also how the breakdown of social order on land could inspire young Somalis to take to the ocean. In contrast to the buccaneers of Blackbeard's day, most Somali pirates are motivated as much by desperation as they are by greed, perhaps more so. As Sarandac, the leader of the *Quest* pirates, told the Navy during the negotiations (the recording of which I heard at his trial): "The situation in Somalia is bad. It is better for us to die than to return [empty-handed]."

At the same time, hostage taking for ransom is an evil that cannot be justified by appealing to the misfortunes of its perpetrators. Some accounts of Somali piracy have construed the pirates as victims rather than criminals, muddying the moral waters and creating undue sympathy for their plight. It requires a fine balance to humanize a wrongdoer without compromising one's judgment about the wrong. Yet that is the balance I attempted to strike in the story. As much as Najiib and the Shabaab deserved the blame for what happened, Ismail made no attempt to excuse the hijacking on account of their crimes. He took the punishment himself, recognizing that in the realm of criminal activity, as in all human society, a multiplication of wrongs can never make the world right.

As for Somalia itself, I found it to be a truly fascinating place, far more than I imagined when I began my research. Straddling the cultural and spiritual border between Africa and Arabia, it is a land of extremes, where waterless deserts give way to fertile farmland and tropical seacoasts, and where the warrior spirit so evident in the Somali character is tempered by a national passion for poetry. Having visited the country and befriended Somalis from all walks of life, both in Mogadishu and in the diaspora, I echo the great British journalist Richard Dowden, who called them "people times ten." Somalis are *sui generis*, unique in many ways, and I consider it a privilege to have immersed myself in their culture, their faith, and their history, both tragic and inspiring.

Although I am not an expert in these matters, it is my view that the future of Somalia is as bright as the young Somalis I met who believe that with the right combination of education, entrepreneurism, ingenuity, and outside support their country will rise again. It is already happening despite the ongoing campaign of senseless violence by the Shabaab. For the first time in twenty years, Somalia has a democratically elected government. Numerous countries, including Britain and Turkey, have embassies in Mogadishu. High-speed Internet has made its debut. Educated Somalis who could live in the diaspora are risking their lives to invest in their country—people like Dr. Deqo Mohammed, daughter of Dr. Hawa Abdi, the Nobel Peace Prize nominee and founder of Hawa Abdi Village (www.dhaf.org), and Omar Nor, a journalist in Mogadishu, both of whom I had the privilege to spend time with. Shop by shop, street by street, neighborhood by neighborhood, the Somali people are rebuilding. It is my hope and prayer that one day Mogadishu will again deserve to be called the "Jewel of the Indian Ocean."

What a joy it would be to see it.

Corban Addison
March 2015

ACKNOWLEDGMENTS

Before I wrote *The Tears of Dark Water*, I went on a research odyssey unlike anything I have attempted before. Along with immersing myself in the relevant literature, I conducted many interviews with officials in the US government, got to know a former hostage negotiator from the FBI, learned how to sail on the Chesapeake Bay, toured the FBI Academy, the Norfolk federal courthouse, and the Chesapeake Correctional Center, went to the trial of the *Quest* pirates, and spent time with Somali friends in Minneapolis. After that, I flew to the Horn of Africa and sailed in the Seychelles, interviewed officials in Bahrain, landed on the USS *Truman* in the Arabian Sea, spent a night aboard the carrier and two nights aboard the USS *Gettysburg*, traveled to Nairobi, Mogadishu, and the Dadaab refugee area, and then wrapped it all up with a trip to Zanzibar.

Like I said, an odyssey.

I have countless people to thank for opening doors and opening my eyes during this process. If I enumerated their kindnesses, I would make this rather long book even longer. As such, their names will have to suffice. But before I get to them, I want to express my profoundest gratitude to the most important person in my life—my wife, Marcy—whose infinite patience, tolerance, and generosity of spirit remain indispensable to my work. I am honored to be your husband and to walk this fascinating, harrowing, and sometimes exhausting road with you.

In the United States, I wish to thank John Schmidt at the Elliott School of International Affairs; Christopher Voss at the Black Swan Group; Farley Mesko at the Center for Advanced Defense Studies; Captain Alexander Martin, USMC (retired); the Honorable B. Waugh Crigler (retired); Imam Muhammed Musri at the Islamic Society of Central Florida (www.iscf.org); Mohammed Idris at the American Relief Agency for the Horn of Africa (www.araha.org); Derek Berry, Cathy Ellis, Carrie Koenig, and Dr. William Garmoe at the MedStar National Rehabilitation Hospital; Sheriff Jim O'Sullivan and Sergeant Dave Rosado at the Chesapeake County Sheriff's Office; Captain Mike McEwan; Dr. Gregory Gelburd; Tim and Rhonda Feist; Jason Scully; Claude Berube; Admiral Terry McKnight (retired); Vijai Rahaman; and Scott McClelland.

In the US government, I wish to thank Donna Hopkins, Marc Porter, Erik Rye, and Pamela Fierst at the State Department; Wayne Raabe, Krishna Patel, and John Fitzgerald at the Justice Department; Beth Lefebvre, Royce Curtin, Willie Session, and Stephen Laycock at the FBI; Mark Garhart and James Blitzer at NCIS; Col. Anne Edgecomb and Cheryl Irwin at the Office of the Secretary of Defense; Lt. Callie Ferrari at the Navy Office of Information East; and Bobby

Mathieson, US Marshal for the Eastern District of Virginia.

In the Somali diaspora, I wish to thank Ahmed Mohamed Ahmed, Ismail Ali Ismail, Jaylani Hussein, Ahmed Saleh Dhoodi, Munira Khalif, Muna Khalif, Yassin Mohamed, Imam Abdisalam Adam, Seynab Sharmarke Mohamed, Mohamed Hassan, and Said Salah.

In the Seychelles, I wish to thank Declan Barber at the Regional Anti-Piracy Intelligence Coordination Center, and Noel Mooney at the Seychelles Piracy Prosecution and Intelligence Cell.

In Bahrain, I wish to thank Cmdr. Jason Salata, Lt. Jessica McNulty, and Lt. Marissa Myatt at US Navy Central Command; Captain Robert Slaven of the Royal Australian Navy; and Lt. Cmdr. Andrew Mills, Lt. Cmdr. James Gleave, and Lt. Cmdr. Iain Beaton of the Royal Navy.

On the USS *Truman*, I wish to thank Captain Robert Roth, Captain Pat Hannifin, Admiral Kevin Sweeney, Lt. Cmdr. John Fage, Ensign Frederick Middlebrooks, Cmdr. William Mann, Lt. Cmdr. Camilo Santiago, Lt. Tamera Larsen, Master-at-Arms Petty Officer 1st Class Thomas Staton, Lt. Cmdr. Christopher Williams, Cmdr. Scott Curtis, and Cmdr. Jason Darish.

On the USS *Gettysburg*, I wish to thank Captain Brad Cooper, Lt. Cmdr. Nathan Sherry, Ensign Kiley Provenzano, Lt. JG Michael Burris, and Lt. JG Caitlin Parks.

In Mogadishu, I wish to thank Fatuma Noor at the AU/UN Information Support Team; the AMISOM soldiers who escorted me safely to Hawa Abdi Village; Dr. Deqo Aden Mohamed and her team at the Dr. Hawa Abdi Foundation;

Sean Mendis and the team at SKA Mogadishu; and Omar Nor with the Shabelle Media Network.

In Nairobi, I wish to thank Jay Bahadur; Larry and Mary Warren; Anna Mayumi Kerber; Hassan Abdi Ahmed; Dr. Elena Velilla and Heather Pagano at Médecins Sans Frontières; Matthew Espenshade at the Office of the Legal Attaché, Embassy Nairobi; and Peter Njue.

In Dadaab, I wish to thank Mans Nyberg, Duke Mwancha, Eric Groonis, Loutfi Beldjelti, and Venanzio Njuki at UNHCR; Halima Noor; Batula Ali Isaack; Hassan Abdirahman Hassan; Fatuma Abdikarim Kasim; Abshiro Muktar Ismail; Awes Mohamed Gulled; Gerald Ghates; and the Somali/Kenyan security team who escorted me to the Dagahaley camp.

Finally, I wish to thank my fabulous agents, Dan Raines and Danny Baror, for your tireless advocacy and encouragement; my editors, Jane Wood at Quercus Books and Daisy Hutton and Lorissa Sengara at HarperCollins, for your capacious enthusiasm and eagle eyes; and my publishers in every territory for caring so much about the story and getting it into the hands of readers. As an author, I trade in words. Without the passionate assistance of everyone in my publishing universe, my words would never reach the world.

Heartfelt thanks to all of you for believing in me.

DISCUSSION QUESTIONS

1. At the beginning of the story, Ismail and his
   crew appear to have a fairly straightforward
   reason for hijacking the *Renaissance*: old-
   fashioned greed and opportunism. As the story
   progresses, however, we see that the knot of
   wrong is far more complex. We learn about
   the tragedy of Ismail's life, the horrors he
   suffered at the hands of al-Shabaab, and his
   extraordinary commitment to reunite with
   Yasmin. We also learn of the desperation that
   compelled his confederates to join him at sea.
   In your mind, who bears ultimate responsibility for Daniel Parker's death and Quentin's
   injuries? Is it enough to say that the pirates are

responsible, or do others share the blame?

2. Some have said that love born in the crucible of extreme circumstances is doomed to failure. At the outset of the story, Daniel hopes that his voyage around the world will offer him a chance to salvage his marriage. Vanessa, however, is not so sanguine. Given the burdens of their shared history, do you think Daniel was naïve in thinking the trip might have that effect? Had the hijacking not happened and Daniel had returned home to the realities of ordinary life, do you think he and Vanessa would have stayed together?

3. After the hijacking, Vanessa learns that the US government will not allow substantial concessions in negotiating with pirates. While she understands the government's desire to avoid ransom payments, she is more concerned about the safety of her family than about deterring future hostage taking. What do you think about the government's stance? How should a nation balance the social cost of hostage taking against the personal cost of discouraging a hostage's family from negotiating a ransom (or banning them outright when the kidnappers are terrorists)? What do you think about Julius Caesar's approach, which Paul Derrick advocates—pay the ransom to save the hostage's life, then bring the kidnappers to justice?

4. On the bridge of the *Gettysburg*, Paul Derrick reconnects with the tragedy of his brother's suicide and his father's murder in a profoundly personal way. Do you think this sense of déjà vu clouds or clarifies his

judgment about Ismail's intentions?

5. After the SEALs of DEVGRU rescue the kidnapped aid workers in Somalia, Paul Derrick draws a conclusion about the efficacy of Special Forces units in hostage rescue operations: even the most highly trained troops require proper conditions for a successful mission. Recent news stories about unsuccessful SEAL raids in Somalia and Yemen—one of which led to the deaths of two hostages—underscore this point. In light of the dangers associated with hostage rescue operations, do you think Western governments are justified in relying so heavily on the military to resolve hostage crises?

6. Beneath the surface of the story is the clash—both practical and theological—between moderate and radical Islam. Ismail and his family are devout Muslims, but they believe the violent creed of al-Shabaab is a fundamental perversion of their faith. Najiib, on the other hand, is confident of his own devotion, yet he believes that Adan, Ismail's father, is an apostate worthy of death. Radical groups like al-Shabaab have proliferated in recent years. In your mind, what is the responsibility of the broader Muslim community in countering those who advocate and perpetrate violence in the name of Islam? How can people of goodwill outside the Muslim community aid their Muslim neighbors in challenging violent interpretations of their faith?

7. At the heart of Ismail's story is the age-old conflict between morality and necessity. Ismail knows that hostage taking for ransom is reprehensible. He knows the

Quran and remembers his father's teachings about perdition. Yet his father is dead—murdered by the men he opposed with education and reason—and Ismail is adrift in a world of lawlessness and violence. In this context, he concludes that the only way left for him to save his sister is the way of the gun. What do you think about his reasoning? How does necessity shape a person's moral conclusions? In your mind, is it ever justified for a person to engage in criminal activity that endangers innocent life in order to save the life of another?

8. Soon after Yasmin escapes from Najiib's clutches, she witnesses an American drone strike against Najiib's village. In the aftermath of the explosion, she is overcome by emotion—horror, grief, fear, and guilt—as she wrestles with the unintended consequences of her actions. Eventually, after consoling herself that Ismail would not have involved her in the murder of innocent people, she feels great relief, knowing that Najiib's reign of terror has come to an end. Ismail, too, feels relief and vindication when he learns of Najiib's death, despite his misgivings about drone warfare. What do you think about the American drone program? Is drone warfare justified if only terrorists are killed? How does your thinking change when you take into account the inevitability of collateral damage?

9. At the end of Ismail's story, he is convicted of piracy under the law of nations, among other crimes, and he is sentenced to life in prison without the possibility of

parole. Are you satisfied with this outcome? Do you feel it is too lenient or too harsh? What do you think about the request Ismail makes of his uncle, Mahamoud— to use the ransom money he obtained from prior hijackings to reopen his father's school in Mogadishu? Knowing what you do about Mahamoud, do you think he will honor Ismail's request?

10. The Somali nation is at the center of the story—the twenty-year civil war, the refugee crisis, piracy and terrorism, the use of child soldiers in the conflict, the forced marriage of young girls to Shabaab commanders, and the African Union's protracted struggle to drive al-Shabaab out of power. How has your impression of Somalia changed in reading the story? For those of us outside the Somali community, what can we do to assist Somalis like Dr. Hawa Abdi—whose real-life humanitarian camp is highlighted in the story—in rebuilding their nation?

11. In the final chapter of the story, Vanessa wrestles with one of the greatest questions in the human experience: Is forgiveness possible in the face of irremediably wrong? What do you think about her answer to this question? If you were in her position, having suffered as she suffered, how would you answer this question?